2017

2017

A Novel of Political Intrigue

E. A. Stillwell

Printed in the United States of America.

ISBN   Paperback   978-1-947995-46-8
              Hardback   978-1-947995-47-5
              eBook   978-1-947995-48-2

Greenberry Publishing LLC
20 Atlantic Cir #104 Pittsburg,
CA 94565

www.greenberrypublishing.com

Also by E. A. Stillwell

Deceptions
Odyssey of the Heart
From Olympus

CONTENTS

Part 2
2017

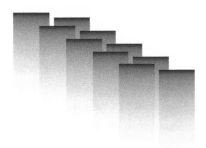

PROLOGUE

Paul Thoros Estate
South Hampton, New York
Tuesday, November 4, 2008

The five men who had gathered in their host's TV room were not close friends but business associates bound by a belief system they thought was the future of the world. Though each had always contributed heavily to progressive causes, until a few years previously, they had met only a few times a year to debate the future of the world, exchange ideas, and analyze international affairs.

Each was rich beyond comprehension—rich enough to buy a country or two if he wished. Each had inherited tremendous wealth and had multiplied his inheritance exponentially. They all despised the capitalist economic development model that had been in use in the country since its birth though it had been the system by which they had acquired their wealth.

They were also arrogant men with huge egos and feelings of intellectual superiority. They considered themselves infallible. Not once had any of them felt he had made a mistake. They found it impossible to imagine they could be blinded by feelings of infallibility and consequently miscalculate and be destroyed by their own conceit.

They believed that almost everything they had been taught about democracy, or what posed as democracy at the time, had been wrong. As far as they were concerned, democracy had never worked and never could. There was only one superior form of governance—the philosophy of Thomas Hobbs, a seventeenth-century philosopher who believed all individuals must yield their rights to a sovereign authority for the sake of their own good and protection.

As the men watched the election results on the ultra-slim six-monitor display panels that were tuned to CNN, CBS, ABC, NBC, C-SPAN, and Fox, they did not converse. Each seemed to know what the others were thinking. They periodically rose and made their way to a well-stocked bar to get adult beverages and return to their suede-leather seats to continue viewing.

Once in a while, depending upon which talking head was speaking, their host would switch the screens to a single seventy-two-inch panel. The talking heads were gleefully speaking about their projections, which were that Hal Garson, the former vice president, was gaining an insurmountable lead in the Electoral College. But as the polls across the country were closing, those same talking heads began to worry because the presidential race was beginning to tighten.

As midnight approached, all the talking heads except those on Fox were in sheer panic. An upset was in the making. As the projected results on the West Coast were announced, the unthinkable happened. The cowboy from Texas had come out of nowhere like the cavalry riding to the rescue and upset the odds-on favorite exactly as they had planned.

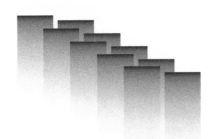

PART 1
2010 to 2014

CHAPTER 1

Thai Roma Restaurant
237 Pennsylvania Avenue SE
Washington, DC
Friday, April 23, 2010

Dr. Bradford Jenkins had no way of knowing that the book tour he was about to embark on would lead to a series of events that would affect the lives of 350 million people.

Jenkins, a professor of Middle Eastern studies at Princeton University, had previously written three scholarly books about the Middle East. After his third book had been published, his friends Miriam and Paul Bernstein had suggested he write a novel. As Miriam had said, he had had a number of experiences that could be the genesis of a good story. At first, he had sloughed off their suggestions, but ultimately, he had succumbed and had written *The Sword of Retribution*.

Because the settings for his book took place in the nation's capital and the Middle East, Jenkins had suggested his book tour start with two particular Barnes & Noble bookstores in the Washington, DC, area, and his publisher had agreed. What Jenkins had not told his agent or publisher when he had suggested Barnes & Noble stores at Tysons Corner in Fairfax, Virginia, and Pentagon City in Arlington County, Virginia, was that he had an ulterior motive. That was why he was sitting at a table in the Thai Roma Restaurant on Pennsylvania Avenue with his friend Jack Wharton.

Jenkins, who had known Wharton for several years, could have been Gregory Peck's brother. He had inherited his facial features from his white Anglo-Saxon Protestant father and his full head of black hair from his Lebanese Christian mother. He had met Wharton twelve years earlier when they were first-class seatmates on a flight to Israel and Wharton was escorting a group of twenty on a tour of the Holy Land. Upon their arrival in Tel Aviv, he had helped Wharton solve a problem at Ben Gurion Airport and subsequently ended up assisting Wharton on his tour.

Through the years, their friendship had grown, and though Jenkins and Wharton saw each other only three or four times a year, they constantly kept in touch via e-mail. Jenkins was also a contributor to Wharton's political newsletter *The Wharton Report*, a once-a-week Internet subscription service.

The Wharton Report was not Wharton's main source of income. To use Wharton's own words, the newsletter was more of a passion. The tours, or treks, as he called them, that Wharton led three or four times a year had allowed him to earn the money he needed to live in the shadow of the nation's capital. Anytime the treks included anything Hebrew or Arabic and Jenkins's schedule permitted, Jenkins had assisted his friend.

Jenkins had driven to Trenton from his home in Princeton and took the 9:08 train to Washington, which was scheduled to arrive at Union Station at eleven thirty. After his arrival, he quickly made his way through the concourse and hailed a taxi that took him to their usual watering hole before he would head to the Wharton residence in McLean, Virginia.

Their usual watering hole was a small, rather nondescript restaurant almost in the shadow of the Capitol Building with tables covered by red-and-white-checkered tablecloths and an overabundance of pictures of Rome, Venice, and the Amalfi coast hanging on cream-colored plaster walls. But the price was right and the food excellent.

"So you ended up prostrating yourself at the altar after all," said Wharton, referring to the novel Jenkins had written after their drinks were served. "I guess someone didn't like the idea of a book about a small organization running around assassinating the recruiters and trainers of terrorists. Obviously, in our era of political correctness, Arabs are a protected species."

"It really wasn't that bad," said Jenkins. "It was easier making the revisions than standing on principle. The way the book was originally structured made it relatively easy to make changes."

"Whatever. Here's to success for number four," said Wharton as he raised his glass.

"I guess I'll find the answer to that one as the tour unfolds."

"I'm surprised they let you start your book tour here like you wanted and not in the Big Apple. Isn't that a bit unusual?"

"According to my agent, the wizards of smart thought my suggestion was a good one, so they're going to save the Boston–New York corridor for last. As far as I'm concerned, regardless of where and how I started, it will still be a grueling experience traveling around the country. As it is, my only time-outs on this tour will be my one here in Washington and another in San Francisco, where I plan to visit another friend."

"It's too bad tomorrow's book signing couldn't be a two-day affair," Wharton said. "I think Barnes & Noble at Tysons Corner in the morning and then another in the afternoon at Pentagon City and then climbing on an airplane is a bit much. Anyway, before we get down to business, how are Miriam and Paul? I know it's been a year since Susan and I were up to Princeton visiting with you all, but it seems like yesterday."

"They still remember your visit," said Jenkins with a chuckle.

"I hope they weren't too put off by my irreverent sense of humor and climbing on my soapbox."

"I don't think they minded," said Jenkins. "It was probably one of the few times they got to speak with a real conservative other than me. And for your information, Paul still gets quite a chuckle when he thinks about your asking those students in Starbucks what they meant about fair shares, living wages, and economic justice."

"I couldn't help myself," said Wharton laughing. "I find university communities quite challenging. Princeton is really a beautiful place, and I think spring break was a good time to reconnoiter your liberal enclave without having to worry about getting mugged. Most of the young skulls full of mush were boozing it up on a beach somewhere."

"One does what one has to do," replied Jenkins, referring to his book tour with a sigh as he raised his glass for another sip of his wine. He could see that his friend was beginning to get on his soapbox and thought their conversation should be steered toward the real reason for their get-together. "How about bringing me up to date with the happenings in your life? Particularly the Indiana Jones adventure you wanted to discuss with me."

Wharton was sometimes referred to as Indiana Jones by his friends because of the many treks he led. In spite of his mustache, he did resemble

Harrison Ford because he liked to wear the same type of hat that was used in the Indiana Jones films.

"Where are you planning on heading to this time?"

"Somalia," Wharton said.

"Isn't that a rather dangerous place these days?"

Wharton chuckled. "Brad, no matter where you go these days, you'll either be shot at, taxed to death, or overregulated."

"I won't argue that one, but what the hell is in Somalia of all places?"

"It's a place that has suddenly popped up in one of the intelligence reports I've been reading. As I usually do, I'll take a small group to a very unusual place where tourists would never think of going and then charge confiscatory prices that will allow Susan and me to live in the manner to which we've become accustomed."

"You sound like one of those greedy capitalists our liberal friends keep railing about," said Jenkins with a chuckle.

"You know how it is, Brad. Think of the taxes I'll have to pay on my obscene profits. Someone has to think of that forty-seven percent and rising who feel no obligation to work for a living."

Jenkins chuckled. "What kind of group will we be babysitting this time?"

"Geologists. I'm not supposed to know they're geologists, but after reading the intelligence reports Nate gave me, it wasn't difficult to put two and two together."

"Geologists? I wonder what's so geologically interesting in that part of the world."

"Having learned the Chinese are interested in that part of the world and taking into consideration how close it is to Saudi Arabia, I'd guess it's probably the black stuff, you know, that stuff you drill for. And there's probably a lot more going on than we'll ever know about, but let's forget about all that. The people we'll be shepherding around will be our cover for something we've been discussing ad nauseam. While these people are looking for black gold, you and I will look for acceptable transmitter sights for an alternative to Al Jazeera."

"Forgive me if I have a look of disbelief on my face, but I thought we'd have Al Jazeera in America before anyone but us wrapped his or her arms around that."

"As I told you during last year's spring break, someone must have read one of your books, you know, the one in which you mentioned an alternative to Al Jazeera. There's been talk of an increase in foreign aid to finance your idea of a public-private entity. The pinstripe set at Foggy Bottom doesn't want it, but Nate likes the idea and thinks there's a good chance of getting it out of committee. That's why we're going to try to get up to Berbera and Bossaso."

Jenkins nodded his approval of good news for a change and drifted away in thought. He had been to Somalia many years earlier in a different life, and there hadn't been much improvement since. What passed then for Somalia was only a region comprising six territories ostensibly ruled by Mogadishu, but the gangster who ran the city was able to do that only with the help of several thousand African Union soldiers.

It was nice to know an idea he had promulgated was being considered, and he was particularly pleased to know that Nate Grishom, the Speaker of the House, liked the idea. He would in a few months be accompanying Jack on another trek because Arabic was an unofficial national language in Somalia because of its centuries-old ties with the Arab world.

What the place really needs is freedom from the Islamic nut jobs running the place, not more money to bribe them to be nice. Wouldn't it be nice if President Branch gave this part of the world some real thought? If he did, we might become free of the pirate menace.

Jenkins came out of his reverie. "The last time I was in Somalia, I was busy dodging bullets. Let's hope the next venture of Wharton Expeditions is successful and we don't get shot at. Been there, done that."

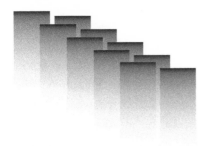

CHAPTER 2
Love Nest East
Washington, DC
Friday, May 7, 2010

Love Nest East was a code name for a one-bedroom apartment on the ground floor of a two-story town house four blocks from the Capitol Building. The building had been purchased in early 2009 along with a small apartment building in the Pacific Heights section of San Francisco that contained Love Nest West by a private investment group that was really a two-man partnership. The reason for the purchases was the belief that "entry by landlord" was preferable to breaking and entering while conducting electronic political espionage of Congresswoman Barbara Pellegrino and Rob Lowen, her lover, who was also her chief of staff.

Barbara Pellegrino was an attractive, slim, trim, fifty-year-old, short-haired brunette with a youthful face because of the Retin-A she always used. She also tried to eat properly and exercise often, though Lowen always said her exercising really was the romping they did together. Pellegrino had a voracious sexual appetite. She wished she didn't like it so much, but she did, particularly with Rob, a dark-haired charmer who she thought could sell bikinis to Eskimos.

That afternoon, after their venture into sexual fulfillment, Pellegrino thought about the path she and Lowen had taken and would continue to travel. They had been lovers during their years at Cal Berkeley, but after graduation, they had gone their separate ways, and the years had passed. Then ten years later, they had reconnected via one of those reunion websites and began keeping in touch via e-mail, bringing each other up to date with the happenings of their lives.

Then the inevitable happened. Lowen had to go to Seattle on business and United had no direct flights from JFK to Seattle. En route, he would have to make stopovers at either Dulles, LAX, or San Francisco. The suggestion that he travel through San Francisco and they have lunch had been impossible to resist. The lunch together at the Top of the Mark, however, never materialized. During their second martini in the cocktail lounge, as they sat side by side, Lowen had placed his hand on her thigh. They were soon on their way to his room on the twelfth floor, which he had previously booked in anticipation.

Sex that afternoon had been a three-hour affair of appetite satisfaction and the beginning of an affair involving work and pleasure. Their first afternoon together had led to another on his way back to New York. Then, as the frequency of Lowen's business trips increased, their afternoons together evolved into the occasional night together.

While she had always been politically active to some degree, it was only after Lowen had come back into her life that Pellegrino really immersed herself in the political arena. He had encouraged her to seek the seat of Congressman Feldstein when he suddenly announced his retirement.

Rob Lowen was a swarthy man with dark-brown, shoulder-length hair with a sleek finish who looked like a man whose life revolved around catching the next wave. After rolling from between Barbara Pellegrino's legs, he lay on his back for a few moments to catch his breath. He was tired, but it wasn't just because of his sexcapades with Babbs. He was tired because he had been finding it more and more difficult to deal with and please two women.

It had all started more than twenty years earlier. Way back when Lowen had been just another high-paid analyst at Goldman Sachs, he had been invited to lunch by Charles Atherton, a tall, slender, partially bald man with a fiendish smile.

"I gather you and Barbara Pellegrino were lovers once," said Atherton after they had each taken a sip of their martinis.

Lowen had been blindsided by the statement and for a brief moment was speechless.

"Mr. Atherton, I've known only two Barbaras in my life, and neither was Pellegrino."

"Oh, I'm sorry," said Atherton feigning an apology. "Pellegrino is her married name. Her maiden name was Canady."

Again, Lowen had been shocked. *How did Atherton know about him and Babbs, and why has the subject of her come up?*

"That was ten years ago," Lowen replied after regaining his composure. "In another life. Might I ask why you find something in this other life of particular interest?"

Atherton smiled. "Because my associates and I would like to make you an offer you can't refuse."

An offer that couldn't be refused was a common phrase that was always bandied about, yet its usage was usually effective in getting one's attention, and it had gotten his.

Lowen had often wondered what might have happened if he had turned down the offer that day, but he hadn't because he had become intrigued and had started to feel a twinge of lust at the thought of once again being with an old lover. Particularly Babbs.

It took a few weeks for the reunion process to develop, a process that was aided and abetted by Atherton's associates. Then there were the pseudo flights to Seattle on business with the necessary changing of planes in San Francisco, which also included lunches with Babbs and trips to his hotel room, where they indulged themselves in sexual pleasure. Then there was the pseudo transfer to a pseudo job in San Francisco, which quickly evolved into his helping her begin her political career.

Babbs had a tremendous sexual appetite, but as the years passed, Lowen had found it more and more difficult to please two women. After all, his wife was far from being cool and indifferent. Every Monday, Wednesday, and Friday afternoon, Lowen and Babbs would adjourn from work and go to their love nests, where they would spend the rest of the working day in bed. They would also spend other times together whenever they could, times like when Pellegrino's husband and his wife were simultaneously out of town or when Babbs had to travel alone somewhere.

But things will probably change big-time when Babbs became president, thought Lowen as he caught his breath. While their sexual relationship would likely continue to some extent, it would not be as easy as it had been. Once Pellegrino became president, they would no longer be able to just duck out of the office when Babbs or he got the urge.

Going for a romp had so far always been simple, particularly in San Francisco. There, they would take separate taxis to some store or other place of business and then another taxi to the apartment in Pacific Heights. Even though she would probably never be recognized in the big city, Babbs would always do something to alter her appearance.

It was almost as easy in Washington. They would just leave the office and take the underground tram from the Rayburn Building to the Capitol, then the underground walkways to the Library of Congress and then the Annex. After leaving the Annex, there was only about a block and a half walk to their apartment, but by the time they had emerged aboveground, they had partially disguised themselves because in that city, it seemed everybody recognized everybody else.

Things would obviously be a lot different in the White House because there would be too many eyes and ears. Even if he had to take a shit somewhere, it would probably be logged into some journal.

Lowen knew other presidents had pushed their luck. The Oval Office. A closet somewhere. Even the White House swimming pool on occasion. He doubted they would be reckless because they were always conscious of their surroundings. Maybe their times would be reduced to whenever she had to travel and could do so without her husband. If handled the right way, those could be occasions for overnight stays somewhere in adjoining bedrooms. Then he would not give a shit what the Secret Service might be thinking.

After catching his breath, Lowen sat up and reached for the bottle of wine on his nightstand wondering why he was having all these stupid fucking thoughts as he did. After all, there was still a hell of a lot of thinking and planning to do during the next four years. But then, who the hell ever knew what could happen tomorrow?

"There's still a half bottle left," Lowen said to Pellegrino as he refilled his glass, unaware what he was saying was being recorded.

"All right," said Pellegrino as she sat up.

"You know, we'll have to figure out how to keep doing this once we get you into the White House."

"I think we still have a lot of time to go before we have to address that problem. We have more to worry about at the moment than sex."

"Babbs, when I'm with an oversexed woman like you, it's hard to think of anything else."

"Has anyone ever told you what a bastard you are?"

"Yes, you. Every time I tell you you're oversexed."

This is a game we always play, thought Lowen as he finished his wine. He knew she secretly liked him saying she was oversexed. As far as he was concerned, she really was an oversexed woman particularly for her age, and he could play her body like a violin.

"I think it's time we put our clothes back on," said Pellegrino as she finished her wine. "I've got a party to attend tonight, and I don't want to go looking as if I just got out of bed."

"One more time," said Lowen as he caressed that magic spot between her legs.

"You really are a bastard," she said as she began to respond to his touch and slid back down on the bed.

"And you love it," responded Lowen as he entered the Promised Land.

for her to have children like her son and his wife, but it hadn't come to pass. At age forty-one, Candy would never present her parents with any grandchildren, and there was also a very strong possibility of Candy never marrying. Middleton had once asked Harry if he or Kym had ever had a talk with Candy, and Harry had looked at him as if he had just been asked to commit suicide.

But that was all water over the proverbial dam. The problem now was how to play cupid. Some judicious planning would be required, and it would be necessary to get the wives in on the action. He wanted to call Harry and tell him all about Dr. Bradford Jenkins, but it was only four in the morning in Washington. Even though Harry was an early riser, he didn't get up that early.

Middleton had become intrigued during dinner when Dr. Bradford Jenkins, a dinner guest and friend of his son and daughter-in-law, had said there was a jihadist plot to destroy American society from within that had started back in the Carter days, a plot that was actually a series of well-financed schemes by the Saudis and the Iranians. He had been so intrigued at the time that when everyone was saying good night, he had asked Dr. Jenkins if he would join him for a nightcap.

"Dr. Jenkins," Middleton had said as he raised his glass of brandy with a here's-to-you smile, "I found your earlier comments about the Islamists financing the cultural decay of our country just as the Russians did through the Castro regime in the sixties very intriguing to say the least. You made no bones about this being a purposeful act of war."

"Mr. Middleton," said Jenkins, "not only is this being done; it is being done without most of the country even realizing it. Most people, and that includes those on both sides of the political spectrum, don't have a clue. Our side of the aisle has been blaming our moral decay on things like Hollywood, rap music, quality of education, court decisions, and liberalism in general without realizing that it has all been well organized and paid for. To begin to understand, one would have to believe in conspiracies, but most people don't except for vast, right-wing ones."

"How can you be so sure?"

"Mr. Middleton, I grew up in the Middle East. I speak several dialects of Arabic and understand all the nuances. I have friends in that part of the world. I have been in mosques in at least eight countries and several in this country. I know the call to jihad when I hear it. Good friends of mine and I have been researching this for some time for a publication that will be titled *The Enemy Within*. I could go on and on, but I don't wish to bore you and wear out my welcome."

"Dr. Jenkins," said Middleton, "I can assure you that anything you say I will not find boring. Please continue. In fact, I insist."

"To understand what's happening," Jenkins said, "we need to rid ourselves of some things that have been preached and unfortunately accepted as common wisdom, things such as Islam being a peaceful religion and all Muslims not being jihadists. First, Islam is not a religion. It is a total way of life that rejects every aspect of Western law and culture.

"Second, while it's undoubtedly true that all Muslims are not jihadists, those who believe in jihad are in power. The others are irrelevant. Once these tenets are accepted, we have to understand the history of the modern left. Rousseau's *Discourse on the Origin and Basis of Inequality among Men*, in which he condemned the institution of private property, is perhaps the origin of the left's present-day attitudes.

"Around the middle 1800s, French liberals started gravitating toward his philosophy, and many of their liberal philosophies made their way to our hemisphere in the 1870s. At the time, these intellectuals were called progressives. Thanks to Woodrow Wilson and Franklin Delano Roosevelt, many of their cherished beliefs were incorporated into our social fabric. In the 1960s, the left evolved into what I will call the new left, and with the help of Russian-sourced money via Cuba, it romanticized the revolutionaries of the Third World such as Mao Zedong, Ho Chi Minh, Fidel Castro, and Daniel Ortega. In the seventies, during the Carter administration, the Islamists saw an opportunity because of the failures of so many of our educators and leaders.

"The enemy of my enemy is my friend. While it may seem strange that Shia Islam, Sunni Islam, liberals, progressives, and the left are working together, I can assure you a lot of money has changed hands. Unless something is done to recognize the threat in the near future, I think you know who the ultimate victors will be."

After they had drained their second glass of brandy, Jenkins had called it a night and left him with an overactive mind.

As the veil of sleep started to descend, Middleton rose from his chair, switched off the light, and began to make his way to his bedroom.

It's probably best I didn't call Harry after all. It would probably be better for me to have a talk with Marianne first. She'd probably then have a talk with Kym. They've been friends and confidants ever since those days way back when they were secretaries at the embassy in Saigon. Once the girls get their act together, Kym could have a conversation with Harry. Maybe then, Harry can enlist the help of the president with regards to Bradford Jenkins.

CHAPTER 4

Harry Reason's Condominium
Watergate West
2700 Virginia Avenue NW
Washington, DC
Wednesday, May 12, 2010

Secretary of Defense Harry Reason was not one to waste time. The sixty-nine-year-old former army captain and Vietnam veteran was also the cofounder of Globaltronix International, one of the largest electronics and telecommunications companies in the world. Though he still had the jet-black hair of his younger days, it was streaked with gray; with his naturally tan skin, he could easily pass as a Mexican if he were sitting in a café in Mexico.

As his limo was making its way from the Pentagon to the Watergate, he was in a particularly good mood. He was feeling very satisfied with how things had progressed since he had inherited a military that had become a combination of the Salvation Army, the Red Cross, and the children's school lunch program during the reign of Billy Bob Clayton. Once George Branch had been elected, Reason had swung into action looking for the type of people who thought like him. His first selection had been Colonel Ralph S. Peterson, US Army, retired.

Three years prior to the presidential election, he had read some articles written by Peterson and had been impressed. Then he saw Peterson on TV and was even more impressed. By Election Day, he knew the man with dark-brown, curly hair and roundish face that exuded a boyish charm would become his right-hand man. Together, they would transform a politically correct, meals-on-wheels military into a cutting-edge fighting force capable of battling the wars of the future.

Because he had sensed that Peterson was not the type of man who suffered fools easily, when he had finally met the man, he had gotten down to business. He vividly remembered how the colonel had been astounded when he made him an offer that had been more a pronouncement. It took at least fifteen seconds before Peterson responded.

"Colonel," Reason had said with a slight smile, "I think you and I are kindred spirits. We want the same things when it comes to our military. You'll be my right-hand man."

"You make it sound like a given, Mr. Reason," said Colonel Peterson. "I don't remember any offer being given or there being any agreement. Suppose I have prior commitments, or suppose we can't come to a monetary agreement?"

But Reason had been prepared in case Peterson decided to take a rain check or reject the offer outright. "Colonel, you have two choices. You can be an overpaid consultant and become my right-hand man and we can start our relationship immediately, or we can wait until after the inauguration in January and I'll have President Branch have you recalled to active duty at a tremendous pay cut."

Though Peterson did not officially come aboard until after the president was sworn in, they had begun their relationship that afternoon. From that afternoon until the president was sworn into office, they would get together three times a week for two or more hours of brainstorming. Reason would drive the seven miles from his home at the Watergate to an area of obscure, strip-mall shopping centers with their share of fast-food places, real estate offices, and gas stations on North Old Dominion Drive in Arlington County, Virginia, just before the Fairfax County line. There, he and Peterson would have breakfast in an obscure restaurant where they would sit in a secluded booth in the back and discuss the future of the US military. Reason had chosen a surreptitious method because during the previous year, Colonel Peterson had been a guest on several TV programs and was a readily recognizable figure. Reason had felt prudence was called for.

As the holiday season neared, it became obvious that they would have a staffing problem. There were thousands of files to review for just the senior officer corps, a task that would require several people for an unknown amount of time, but additional bodies meant a dilution in the quality of analysis and a weakening of the secrecy he was hoping to achieve.

"What we need," Reason said to Peterson one morning, "are several of you."

Enter Douglas Northridge, a retired marine intelligence officer who was living near Jacksonville, Florida, and an acquaintance of Peterson. Northridge was in his early fifties, and his dark-brown hair was parted in a soft style perched above probing eyes. In spite of his affable manner, there was no doubt he was still a marine. Peterson had assured Reason that Northridge thought as they did, so as they had entered the new year, the brainstorming sessions had included Northridge.

The inaugural day had been less than a month away when they decided to double the research and analysis team by the inclusion of their wives. Peterson and Northridge had each written a few books and had had many op-ed pieces published; their wives had served as their research assistants.

Four people to perform a mountain of work that was ongoing was a horrendous task, but at least by keeping it all in the family, so to speak, Reason was able to play his cards close to the vest and achieve a modicum of secrecy. So far, in a city where it would be easier to resurrect the dead than to keep a secret, Reason had been able to escape the armchair generals, those in and out of uniform who seemed to work overtime venting their opinions in the op-ed pages with pontification, speculation, and accusation.

"Honey, I'm home," called out Reason as he stepped into the foyer of his fourteenth-floor condo.

"Did you have a nice day?" asked his Vietnamese wife, Kym, as she greeted him with a hug and a kiss.

"It's always a nice day in that five-sided building," responded Reason with a chuckle, "particularly if it ends with something tall, cold, and adult. How about yourself?"

"I've had a very interesting day," replied his wife with a mischievous lilt to her voice. "Why don't you hang up your jacket and make yourself comfortable. I'll make us something to drink."

"So what's with the books?" asked Reason a short time later after taking a sip of scotch and soda and noticing four books on the coffee table. "Looks like you're planning on doing some serious reading."

"They're actually for both of us dear. Marianne called this morning. After she called, I went into Georgetown and got these at a Barnes & Noble."

"Hmm," said Reason as he picked up two books to study their jackets. "Marianne calls and then you go book shopping, but none of these looks like the kind of things either of you would read. Might I ask what the connection is?"

"Marianne and Mike think they've found the ideal man for Candy."

It was a good thing Reason was holding the books instead of his scotch and soda because he dropped one of the books.

"When did this happen?" he tried to ask matter-of-factly.

"Two days ago. His name is Bradford Jenkins. He was a houseguest of Marianne and Mike. He's a friend of Ken's on a book tour. He's the author of those books."

"Bradford Jenkins?"

"Yes, he's a professor of Middle Eastern studies at Princeton."

"If he's a professor at Princeton, that's enemy territory, which means he's probably a liberal, so we can stop right now. He wouldn't even get halfway to first with Candy."

"On the contrary. According to Marianne and Mike, he's extremely conservative."

CHAPTER 5
The White House
1600 Pennsylvania Avenue NW
Washington, DC
Wednesday, May 26, 2010

To the media, George Branch, the man from the Lone Star state, was the affable cowboy who had come from someplace where they rode horses and had things called ranches—as if Austin and the State of Texas never existed—to defeat former vice president Harold Garson in one of the greatest upsets of the modern era. Of course, implied in their sarcasm was that the president came from an unsophisticated part of the country and was in over his head.

Branch, however, was as far from being an unrefined, dim-witted cowboy as a sly old fox was. The former air force colonel, who went into early retirement after someone drove a truck across a runway as he was making a dead-stick landing, had become a very successful businessman in San Antonio. One of the secrets to his success was the fact he had always surrounded himself with very competent people who would tell it like it was.

With a presidency almost a year and a half old, Branch had been pleased with his successes to date. In spite of an all-out media assault, which included a lot of ranting and raving about how any tax cuts needed to be paid for by many reputed experts, he had succeeded in lowering taxes from the high rates of the Billy Bob Clayton administration.

While the fact that the economy was beginning its transformation was heartening, he was more pleased with the transformations that would never become a topic of public discourse if everything continued as planned.

Secretary of Defense Harry Reason and his close group of associates was succeeding in transforming the military into a twenty-first-century fighting force. Though Branch had doubted it could be achieved, Candy Reason, his national security adviser, had succeeded in seeking a rapprochement with the government of India with the Israelis' help.

After reading Ambassador Pickering's report the second time, the president gazed through the window toward the South Lawn. It had been after the Monday cabinet meeting the previous week that Harry Reason had told him that he, Mike, and their wives thought they had found the ideal man for Candy and would like his help at playing matchmaker.

At first, Branch had wondered how he could possibly help in that regard, but then realizing that Mike and Harry had obviously concocted some sort of scheme, he had asked the obvious questions.

"Israel," Harry had said. "Something involving Israel here in Washington. Candy's spent the best part of last year working with the Israelis in connection with your rapprochement plans for India. Bradford Jenkins grew up in that part of the world. He's an expert on the Middle East."

Branch hadn't made any promises to Reason at the time other than to review the books and particulars given him, but later, when he read Jenkins's CV and discovered he held a doctorate from Cambridge University in England, he became curious. *Perhaps the Brits know something we don't,* he had thought. So he had asked Ambassador Pickering to make appropriate inquiries at the British Foreign Office.

Branch didn't expect much to come of his request, but after reading the report from Pickering, he was truly astonished. According to British intelligence, Bradford Jenkins—while doing a doctorate at Cambridge— had been a good friend of Raj Kumar, who was just one step from becoming the prime minister of India. Dr. Reason had said he would become the next prime minister of India and that she would bet it would be sooner than later.

Never let a good coincidence go to waste, Branch thought. Even if the matchmaking didn't work out, he thought as he reached for one of the phones and pressed a button, he had his own plans for Dr. Bradford Jenkins.

"Sarah," Branch said, "would you please place a call to the Israeli prime minister?"

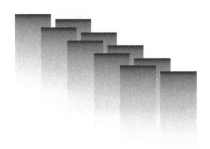

CHAPTER 6
Embassy of Israel
Washington, DC
Saturday, July 24, 2010

After stepping from the limousine, Bradford Jenkins stood on the pavement and watched it head toward Connecticut Avenue. After the limo disappeared down Van Ness Street, he walked along International Drive to the Israeli embassy with thoughts of his luncheon with Jack Wharton the previous day.

To his surprise, the luncheon at the Thai Roma had included David Hawkins and Nate Grishom. Jenkins had met Hawkins, who could almost pass as a double for Robert Redford, and Grishom, a fifty-year-old of medium height with a cherubic face and a full head of gray hair, earlier that month before he and Jack Wharton left on their trek to Somalia.

Jenkins had driven from Princeton to the Wharton home in McLean, Virginia, the day before the Independence Day holiday. On July 4, they had spent the day picnicking on Jack's boat on the Potomac with Hawkins, the number-one political columnist for the *Washington Times*, and his wife and the Speaker of the House, Nathan Grishom, and his wife. It had been a very pleasurable day that had ended with them all watching fireworks from Jack's boat.

The next day, Jenkins and Wharton had left Dulles on a flight to Dubai, where, after a thirteen-hour flight, they had changed planes and flown to Nairobi to catch a special charter flight to Mogadishu, where they began their quest looking for acceptable transmitter sites for an alternative to Al Jazeera.

"Brad," said Jack Wharton after everyone had ordered drinks, "you must have drunk the water on your last visit. You've already made more trips to Washington this year than you did last year."

"I can't pass up another award, Jack. It will look good on my CV and help me sell more books so I can become wealthy like you."

"Don't you wish."

"I'm glad you had a smile on your face when you said that," said Jenkins with a chuckle. "Before we get sidetracked about the *Friends of Israel*, what's the scoop regarding our last Indiana Jones adventure? It's been a few weeks and you haven't mentioned diddly-squat."

"I think I can answer that one better than Jack," said Grishom with his usual boyish smile.

"Oh?" responded Wharton and Jenkins in unison.

"Jack never said anything," said Grishom, "because he was waiting for word from me, and I couldn't give him a heads-up until I knew something myself. It was only this morning that I got some feedback, and it was typical of the crap that usually happens."

"What the fuck happened?" asked Wharton.

"Unfortunately, you can kiss your idea of a public-private partnership as an alternative to Al Jazeera good-bye," answered Grishom.

"What the hell happened, Nate?" asked Hawkins as Jenkins and Wharton sat in stunned silence.

"For starters, VOA got involved."

"You mean as an alternative to Al Jazeera?" asked Wharton practically screeching. "You gotta be kidding!"

"I wish I were, my friend, because by the time the politically correct Arab component of the Voice of America gets unreeled …"

Jenkins shook his head in disgust.

"I understand your frustration," said Grishom. "But this is what happens when State gets the opportunity to dip its oar into things. Your only ghost of a chance now is to know someone in high places, and I don't think anyone at this table has a personal relationship with the president."

"Perhaps not," said a disappointed Wharton. "But perhaps we can get close."

A perplexed Grishom and Hawkins stared at Wharton. Jenkins, seeing the smile on his friend's face, connected the dots and attempted to change the direction of their conversation. "Have you found out anything more about the *Friends of Israel* than we already knew?"

"Not much more than what we each found out via the net," answered Wharton. He turned to Hawkins and Grishom. "You know who won the award last year, don't you?"

"Yeah," answered Hawkins. "The president's national security adviser. Beautiful woman. At least she sure seemed beautiful on TV when she gave that speech at the convention a couple years ago. Right now, she's probably the most eligible bachelorette in town."

"If she's there, this might be a golden opportunity for us. And for Brad."

"If you think I'll approach her about an alternative to Al Jazeera," said Jenkins firmly, "you're whistling Dixie. I'll just be one of the many faces that come and go in her life."

"You can never tell," said Grishom with a chuckle; he had also started connecting the dots. "At a lot of these functions, the previous recipient introduces the current one."

"Don't hold your breath."

"While I'd like to wish Brad here a successful romantic encounter," said Hawkins, "I'm not going to hold my breath. Candy Reason may be the most eligible woman in town, but depending on your perspective, she has also been referred to as the Ice Queen or the Dragon Lady."

"Dragon Lady?" exclaimed Jenkins. "How did she ever get that name?"

"A journalist at the *Post* gave it to her," said Grishom. "Seems there was a comic strip in the early part of the last century called *Terry and the Pirates*. The setting was in the Far East. One of the characters, a Chinese woman, was called the Dragon Lady. Candy Reason's mother is Vietnamese."

Jenkins nodded.

"Another journalist at the *Post* called her the Ice Queen," said Hawkins. "Probably because there doesn't seem to be a man in her life."

"For what it's worth," said Jenkins, "we can forget the president's national security adviser. Even if I do get a chance to say hello, I'll probably never see her again."

By the time Jenkins got to the embassy, his thoughts of the previous day's luncheon had been replaced by other concerns. Because he was to receive an award, he would have to give an acceptance speech, and he had never felt comfortable speaking in public.

Two security men greeted him, and one politely asked his name. With his name checked off the guest list, the second security man opened the door for him. "Have a pleasant evening, Dr. Jenkins."

Jenkins introduced himself to those in the receiving line followed by Ambassador and Mrs. Aaron. "Good evening, Dr. Jenkins," said Ambassador Aaron as he shook Jenkins's hand. "It is indeed a pleasure to welcome you here this evening, particularly as you are a true friend of Israel."

Jenkins barely had time to tell the ambassador how honored he felt before he found himself being escorted by the ambassador into the world of the cocktail party where he was introduced to several guests, most of whom he did not know, and others whom he had only read about or had seen on TV and had thought he would never meet.

As Jenkins and the ambassador were speaking to a ranking official in the Branch administration, he caught sight of Dr. Candice Reason and was amazed. Though she had been discussed facetiously the previous day, he had seen her only on TV a couple of times, the main time being when she had given a speech at the president's nominating convention. He remembered her then as being a beautiful woman. She was wearing a long, royal-blue, sleeveless dress; one side of her long, black hair was pinned back and exposed a dangling earring giving greater emphasis to one side of her face. She looked even more beautiful than he had remembered.

Ambassador Aaron, noting Jenkins's surprised reaction and then its cause, quickly made his apologies to the couple they were speaking with and deftly guided them toward the president's national security adviser. When they reached Dr. Reason and the couple she was speaking with, Ambassador Aaron said, "Excuse me, may I?" with a look that tactfully told the people speaking with Candy Reason that he wished to speak with her. The couple excused themselves.

"Dr. Reason," said Ambassador Aaron, "I'd like to introduce you to Dr. Bradford Jenkins, our honored guest. Dr. Jenkins, Dr. Candice Reason, who will present you this evening."

Jenkins was transfixed. He started to raise his hand only to discover that Candy Reason's outstretched arm and hand had beaten him to it.

"Good evening, Dr. Jenkins," she said. "It's indeed a pleasure to meet you though I feel we've met before."

"Good evening, Dr. Reason. It's indeed a pleasure meeting you. Might I say that you are even more beautiful in person than on television?"

She chuckled. "Do you say that to all the women you meet for the first time?"

"Only the intelligent ones." He smiled.

After the introductions, Ambassador Aaron, Dr. Reason, and Dr. Jenkins became engaged in mundane conversation until the ambassador excused himself. A veil of silence then engulfed Reason and Jenkins, who looked at each other momentarily not knowing what to say.

"Might I ask why you feel we've met before?" asked Jenkins while thinking about how she had rewarded his compliments with smiles that had sent mixed messages. She had appreciated the flattery but had given an implicit warning that it would get him nowhere.

"I read your CV," she answered with a chuckle.

"Hmm. I feel somewhat at a disadvantage. You seem to know all about me yet I know nothing about you."

Her smile was enigmatic. "I've also read your books."

"It's nice to know someone has," he responded faking surprise.

"Actually, I've found them very insightful, but I do have some questions particularly about your third book. That is if you don't mind?"

"Oh oh," he said with a chuckle. "I don't have my crib sheet with me, but I'll do my best."

"In your third book, you mention all the things that need to be done in the Middle East, yet not once do you mention how to achieve them. I found that strange. You must have some idea or opinion."

"I have many ideas and some pretty strong opinions, but I'm afraid that if I had put them in print, the book wouldn't have been published, or if it was …" He stopped to gather his thoughts and saw that more questions were forming in her mind. "Let's just say that treating cancer requires radical surgery. It's not something one can cure with a Band-Aid."

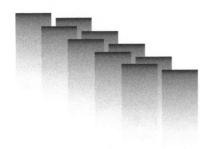

CHAPTER 7

The White House
1600 Pennsylvania Avenue NW
Washington, DC
Wednesday, July 28, 2010

"Candy," said President George Branch after she had entered the Oval Office and was standing in front of his desk, "I have four books here that Brenda suggested I read. I have. I suggest you do the same. Other than to say I'd like to meet the author, I'll refrain from further comment until I hear from you. One is a novel and quite a good one, but it's the other three I'd like you to read."

"I've read them, and I've met the author," Candy said after noticing the titles and author. "He received the *Friends of Israel* award Saturday evening. As the recipient of last year's award, I introduced him before his speech."

The president feigned surprise. "If you've already met Dr. Jenkins, I guess there will be no need for me to wait until you get back to me."

"I was quite impressed with his books and his CV. He appears to be more than your typical college professor. He was born in Lebanon and grew up in the Middle East, which is, as you know, a part of the world many people think they know all about when actually they know very little."

"I'd like to meet this man," the president said. "I was going to put any thoughts of inviting him to the White House on the back burner, but after noticing he had a doctorate from Cambridge, I asked Ambassador Pickering to make a few discreet inquiries. Seems Dr. Jenkins is a friend of Raj Kumar."

"Oh my God!" exclaimed a flabbergasted Candy Reason. It had taken her six trips to New Delhi with stops in Israel going and coming, but she had succeeded in seeking the rapprochement with the Indian government the president had hoped for, particularly with the Chinese Dragon flapping its tail and throwing its weight around. While she had enjoyed working with Prime Minister Sudhir Srivastava and his advisers, there was one adviser in particular she had enjoyed working with—Raj Kumar. She was willing to bet he would become the next prime minister of India.

"Small world, isn't it?" said the president with a chuckle.

"Small world indeed."

"This bit of knowledge, by the way, is strictly between us. I have a feeling Jenkins will become very useful in our conduct of foreign policy."

CHAPTER 8
On the Tourist Trail
Washington, DC
Friday, August 6, 2010

I'd like to be able to say shazam and make everything right, but it would take more than a magician to deal with that part of the world, Jenkins thought as he left the White House grounds after his meeting with President Branch. *I'd also like to call Jack and tell him all about the meeting, but he's off on another one of his treks.*

With five hours to go before his dinner engagement with Dr. Candy Reason and no one to talk to, Jenkins decided to become a tourist to while away the time. After leaving the White House, he was escorted down West Executive Avenue until he reached State Place, NW, where he then made a right turn at the guard booth and headed toward Seventeenth Street NW and the exit from the White House grounds.

Amazing how things can change.

Eight days earlier, Candy Reason had called him and said the president had read his books and had expressed a desire to meet him. She had invited him to the White House the next week. At the time, Jenkins had facetiously told Reason that he could rearrange his schedule but that it would be conditional on their having dinner together.

President Branch had a very affable personality, and Jenkins could tell by the president's eyes and the caliber of his questions that he was no dumbbell. The president was also a very direct person. After thanking him for coming, he told him that after reading his books he knew he needed to meet him.

During their meeting, the president had also told Jenkins that his books mentioned what needed to be done in the Middle East but had said nothing about how to do it. Facetiously, Jenkins said he would have to be God to do what needed to be done there. The president asked him what he would do if he were God, and he had told him.

"Mr. President," said Jenkins. "I believe in fighting fire with fire. I believe one of the reasons the Muslims are doing what they are doing is not just because it's Islam's nature. It's because they believe we're weak. The jihadists are hyenas. If strength is shown, they may test you, but if you show force, they'll leave you alone. Actually, Islam is a weak, predatory way of life that respects only force because there is no love in what poses as a religion. If one stops to think about Christianity, you will find kindness, compassion, respect, and love, all characteristics that are mocked by the Islamists.

"I'd create a three-part entity consisting of a financial component, a surgical component, and a communication component. The financial component would set up international business accounts that would be required to operate. It would also consist of a small team of hackers whose job would be to relieve the jihadists of as much of their operating funds as possible. It takes money, a lot of money, to fight a global war, which is what they're doing. It's time we hit them in the pocketbook.

"The surgical component would consist of twenty-five three-man teams as a surgical strike force that would kill those who teach terrorists how to become terrorists. You know that saying about giving a man a fish and feeding him for a day or teaching him to fish and feeding him for a lifetime. Well, the corollary is instead of just killing individual terrorists, we kill those who teach terrorism to the hundreds or thousands of wannabe terrorists.

"The communication component would be a real alternative to Al Jazeera, not a watered-down, politically correct one like VOA, which would take it to the jihadists. They mock our religion and values because we are compassionate, kind, and respectful. It's time to start making fun of their religion and their way of life. I don't think they can take ridicule or criticism."

"Why couldn't what you suggest be accomplished by one of our government agencies?"

"Mr. President, if you were to even think about doing what I have suggested, you would probably read about it in the *Washington Post* or the *New York Times* the next morning."

Their meeting led to a two-hour lunch in the presidential quarters.

After walking south on Seventeenth Street, Jenkins crossed Constitution Avenue and made his way to the National World War II Memorial, where he took some pictures. He then made his way to the FDR Memorial on the west side of the Tidal Basin. After spending some time there, he headed to the Korean War Memorial and the Lincoln Memorial. At the Lincoln Memorial, he looked at the reflecting pool and the Washington Monument in the distance as he sat on one of the steps and meditated for a while.

After a long period of meditation, he consulted his guide map for the best route to take to the Watergate. Because of the vast spaghetti network of roads between him and the Watergate, he decided to walk to the Vietnam Veterans Memorial and then north on Twenty-Third Street NW to Virginia Avenue and then to the Watergate. As Jenkins approached his hotel, his thoughts drifted to Candy Reason again.

"You spent the night with her!" Jack Wharton had exclaimed the day after Jenkins had received his award at the Israeli embassy. Jenkins had been having lunch with Wharton and his wife, Susan, at their home at the time. Of course it hadn't been anything like Wharton had been thinking. Jenkins had spent the night only talking with Dr. Reason first at the embassy and then at her apartment.

She had been very friendly and seemed genuinely interested in his books. Her questions had been the prelude to an intensive question-and-answer conversation that consumed them before dinner, and they had become oblivious to the other guests in the room. After being served a second glass of champagne, they made their way to the fringe of the crowd and then to the patio. An hour passed before everyone was called to dinner.

When they moved to their assigned seats, Jenkins had been surprised to discover he was to be seated next to Candy Reason. He held out the chair for her and thought the night was one of his luckier evenings.

When dinner was finished, several speakers made their way to the lectern and gave brief speeches regarding the *Friends of Israel* Society. They were followed by Ambassador Aaron, who introduced Reason and spoke of her credentials, which were impressive.

Dr. Reason had a bachelor's degree from Texas A&M, a master's from the University of Texas, and a doctorate from Stanford. She was fluent in Spanish and French and had been studying Arabic until her appointment as national security adviser.

After the speeches were over, Jenkins had been surprised when it was suggested by the ambassador that inasmuch as he and Dr. Reason would be returning to the Watergate, perhaps they could share a limousine. Neither of them had a problem with the suggestion.

While Jenkins had facetiously told Wharton that he and Candy Reason had spent the night together, he had never told him they had shared a limousine back to the Watergate. Nor had he told him about her inviting him in for a nightcap.

After escorting her to her condominium, they had sat on her balcony and talked as they had before dinner. Jenkins sensed a certain feeling in the air, an undercurrent he couldn't explain. That was when he decided not to wear out his welcome. They had slowly walked to her foyer and stood by the door. Their good-night kiss seemed to linger just a tad too long. Then he shook her hand and said, "Good night. Perhaps we can do this again."

"That would be lovely," she said.

Jenkins made his way to his hotel room while wondering if he would ever see her again. He realized he was fantasizing and reading too much into something that had been only a short interlude in his life. Yet he wondered what might have happened if he had put his arms around her when he kissed her good night.

It was 6:10 p.m. as Jenkins entered the commercial part of the Watergate. He was not due at Candy's place until seven, enough time to purchase a bottle of wine and flowers and have a good shower.

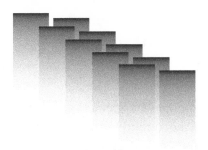

CHAPTER 9

Final Approach
Ben Gurion International Airport
Tel Aviv, Israel
Friday, August 13, 2010

It was approaching 4:15 p.m. local time as a very tired Brad Jenkins stared out the window of the 767 as it began its descent. In spite of flying first class, the seven-hour time difference had finally caught up with him and he was ready to crash, but he still had to go through passport control, collect his luggage, and be a perfect guest before his body could feel the comfort of a mattress. *I hope I haven't bitten off more than I can chew*, Jenkins thought as he remembered the past few days.

Ever since the meeting Candy Reason and Brad Jenkins had had with the president, life for Jenkins had been on a fast track. He had not expected such a meeting because when he awoke the Saturday morning after their dinner date, he was still in a daze. While he had dreams of spending the night with Candy as he walked along the corridor to her condo the night before, Jenkins had not really expected their evening to unfold as it had.

Jenkins arrived at Candy's apartment and was surprised to learn that instead of going out to dinner, she had decided because she had become a celebrity and wanted a modicum of privacy that they would dine at her place.

Fueled by two martinis, hypnotized by the single candle between them as they ate her Chicken Hawaiian, drank the bottle of Chardonnay he had brought, and listened to romantic music in the background, they had walked to her bedroom, made love, and fallen asleep.

In the morning, they had just finished making love. Jenkins was on his back with romantic visions dancing through his mind as he ran his fingers through Candy's hair as she lay with her head against his chest, when suddenly she interrupted his thoughts.

"Can you see what time it is?"

"It's six thirty," said Jenkins after straining to get a look at the clock.

"Oh my God!" exclaimed Candy as she abruptly sat up and then jumped out of bed. "We have an eight o'clock with the president!"

"What? You can't be serious."

"I forgot to tell you last night. Now here I am romping around like some teenager and we're running out of time. President Branch wants you to play God!"

During their two-hour meeting, the president had expressed interest in the development of a secret way of targeting Islamic terrorists particularly if it could be done without any media knowledge and below the antenna of any foreign intelligence radar.

"Dr. Jenkins," the president said, "I've always tried to think outside the box. That's why your ideas have appealed to me. If I can get the Israeli prime minister to buy into your ideas, do you have the wherewithal to create a nongovernmental entity as you suggested?"

Sensing that the president was a man of action, Jenkins had said that because it was August and school wouldn't start until after Labor Day, there was no reason he couldn't start the preliminary work. He already had four people in mind he believed he could count on and who were like family. The only other personnel necessities were a few computer-savvy people and the ingredients for the surgical component.

"Suppose I could get the Israeli prime minister to meet with you sometime next week. Would that be too early for you?" the president asked.

After doing some quick mental calculations, Jenkins said Friday of the next week would be the earliest practical date considering all the logistics, but the day after was the Israeli Sabbath, so any meeting would probably occur on the following Sunday.

The meeting had concluded with the president telling them he would arrange for a meeting with the prime minister and make arrangements for someone from the embassy in Tel Aviv to meet him at the airport.

When they returned to her apartment, Candy noticed the mess from their dinner the evening before and began to clean up. Jenkins instinctively pitched in and began to carry things to the kitchen. When their paths crossed in the process, Jenkins put his arms around her. As he held her tightly, he felt her tears moistening his shirt. Instinctively, Candy knew he knew she was silently crying and drew her head back and asked, "What have you done to me?"

"The same thing you've done to me," Jenkins said as he gave her an affectionate kiss. "I think we're going to be together for a while."

"You were supposed to be returning to Trenton today."

"Yes I was, but it looks like we have some work to do."

"Yes," said Candy with a sigh and a nod. "Why don't you go back to your hotel, check out, and come back here with your luggage?"

Saturday evolved into a day-long discussion about the framework of their task. They had given their undertaking a name: Project Abraham, Abe for short.

The first major problem to be addressed had been Jenkins's flight arrangements to Israel and back. It had been his primary concern when he had gone to his hotel to check out and while returning to Candy's apartment. In the past, Jenkins had always taken a commuter flight from Princeton to Newark and then flights to Paris and then Tel Aviv or straight to Tel Aviv. But the fact that they had already spent a night together and were no doubt about to spend a second, Jenkins had started wondering about leaving from Dulles.

With Candy's concurrence, Jenkins took the train to Trenton Sunday afternoon instead of Saturday as originally planned. After arriving in Trenton, he got his van from the public parking garage and drove home to Princeton. From Sunday until Tuesday morning, he packed and attended to various personal chores usually required before setting off on a long journey.

On Tuesday morning, Jenkins drove back to Washington. Before he had left Sunday, Candy had given him her pass card that allowed him entry to her Watergate parking garage and space. After another intimate candlelight dinner replete with cocktails and wine, they had bedded down for another night of discovery and revelation.

Then the ordeal had begun. Immediately after having a Wednesday lunch with Candy, Jenkins took a taxi to Dulles for his 4:15 p.m. Air France flight to Paris. In Paris, he changed planes and continued on another Air France flight and was about to land in Tel Aviv.

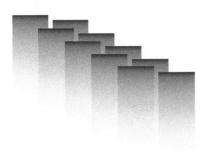

CHAPTER 10
Evans Residence
Foster City, California
Tuesday, August 17, 2010

Larry Evans, a man in his late sixties, loved to get up early. Tall and slender, weighing only ten or so pounds more than he had during his army days many moons ago, Evans once was the quintessential boy next door. In later life, he had graying hair with only streaks left of his natural hair coloring.

Each morning, he would make coffee, sit on his deck overlooking the waterway that ran into San Francisco Bay, and meditate. After his first cup, he would usually get another cup before going to his study to check his e-mails.

This morning, perhaps due to the foggy early-morning air or because he had always been a hands-on problem solver and was now in bored retirement, his thoughts drifted into deeper retrospection than usual. They ranged from the days years ago when he had first met Michael Middleton until the present era when Middleton had asked him if he would like to play detective.

Evans couldn't remember why Major Middleton had been with them on that trek to Laos because Captain Harry Reason had been the commander of Charlie Company. At the time, Evans and his friend, Royce Bartlett, had been the platoon leaders of a specially handpicked group of radio reconnaissance specialists and linguists.

The men of Charlie Company had made their way to Laos in March of '75 and had set up their special listening posts only to learn that the tides of war had taken a dramatic turn for the South Vietnamese. With the fall of Saigon in April, they had found themselves trapped behind enemy lines with the only way to safety being through Thailand.

It was because Sergeant Rikker had had to take a crap in the jungles of Thailand that they discovered the gold in an Air America plane that had crashed many years earlier. At first, everyone felt rich, but not for long, because Major Middleton made them realize they would never have a snowball's chance in hell of being able to keep any of it unless everyone was willing to gamble.

Based on nothing but trust and hope, they had successfully hidden the gold and retrieved it two years later. With the help of the major's father, an investment banker from San Francisco, they had successfully laundered the gold and used the proceeds to create a well-financed company that later made them additional fortunes via currency speculation in the Thai baht and the Malaysian ringgit.

Their company, Globaltronix, began in Bangkok under the name of Global Investments and later moved to Singapore. Then when the men of Global Investments and their wives had lived in South East Asia long enough to safely take advantage of American tax law, they had all moved back to the States. The company relocated to Silicon Valley and became part of the high-tech revolution.

Global Investments became Globaltronix, but everyone wanted a name that implied something larger in scope, so the word *international* was added, and an in-house joke was born because at the time, the only thing international about Globaltronix had been the wives, only a third of whom were Americans. The rest had been Eurasians, Thais, Chinese, Australians, and Europeans who had been living in Southeast Asia at the time of the company's founding.

Two years earlier, Mike Middleton had been advised by one of Globaltronix's founders, Tyler Morton, that Tyler's son, Josh, who had become chief of staff to California senator Dianne Feldon, had inadvertently said something about Barbara Pellegrino having an affair. "It was just a passing comment that Josh inadvertently made to his father," Middleton said to Evans and Royce Bartlett that morning two years ago. "But Tyler, knowing that Pellegrino one day could become the Speaker of the House, thought it was worth advising me."

"Well well," said Bartlett flippantly. He was similar in appearance except for an angular face and mustache. "I guess she likes to get laid. That doesn't surprise me. Hell, she's a liberal. With them, fucking around is a badge of honor. Anyway, what's all this got to do with Larry and me?"

"I thought the two of you might like to play detective," answered Middleton after he stopped laughing. "I know the two of you are getting bored playing golf every day, so I thought you might like to sink your teeth into something interesting. If we can confirm that she is in fact getting it on the side, we can possibly take things to another level. I thought of you guys rather than hiring an agency for obvious reasons. But if you all don't feel up to it or don't think you're experienced enough, I'll go to plan two."

"I guess we can run with the ball for a while," said Evans. "Might be an interesting change of scene. What say you, Royce?"

"I guess we can handle it. We've read a lot of books and seen a lot of movies."

That meeting concluded with Middleton giving Bartlett the finger.

It took a couple of months to confirm that Pellegrino was in fact having an affair with her chief of staff, Rob Lowen. It took time because Pellegrino was a clever bitch. She used disguises—sunglasses, wigs, the whole nine yards. She'd take a taxi from her office or home to some store or place of business, and when she came out to take a taxi to that little apartment building in Pacific Heights, she looked like a different woman.

Then a little over two months after the bugging of what they called Love Nest West, Evans and Bartlett discovered there was another love nest. So the two of them headed for the nation's capital, where once again they played detective while their wives played tourists by going to the Smithsonian, wandering through Georgetown, and visiting art galleries.

When Evans and Bartlett arrived in Washington, they knew Pellegrino's office was in the Rayburn House Office Building. They discovered there was no way they could stake out that office building because there was no parking anywhere nearby and the sidewalks were not conducive to standing around and waiting; the police kept good watch over the comings and goings. To compound things, they had learned that the House and Senate office buildings were connected to the Capitol Building via an underground railway and there was also a tunnel that went from the Capitol Building to the Library of Congress and another one on to the

Library Annex. This gave Pellegrino and Lowen at least seven buildings from which to exit and disappear.

Evans and Bartlett had also learned, before leaving California, that Rob Lowen had a house in the Spring Valley section of the city. After several days of staking out Lowen's place, they discovered that each morning, Lowen would drive to an apartment building in the Wesley Heights section of the city to pick up Pellegrino and they would drive to work together. But one morning, Pellegrino and Lowen made a two-hour stop at a town house on the 100 Block of Fourth Street SE, four blocks from the Capitol, before continuing to the Rayburn Building.

While Evans and Bartlett waited in their respective cars keeping an eye on the town house, they saw a For Sale sign in the window of the town house directly across the street from the one Pellegrino and Lowen had entered. After Pellegrino and Lowen left their town house and continued to work, Evans and Bartlett got out of their cars and walked to the town house with the For Sale sign. After a few moments of thought and discussion, Evans dialed the number on the sign. A half hour later, a heavyset, balding man by the name of Boyd appeared on the scene.

According to Boyd, the seller had been a staffer with the previous administration and had plans of converting each floor of the town house to apartments. Had Boyd not wondered if Evans or Bartlett were interested in doing anything like that, Evans might not have said with a chuckle, "I've been known to dabble a bit." That led to Boyd wondering if they might be interested in something that already had apartments and if they were, the one across the street at 118 was just going on the market. It had been difficult for Evans and Bartlett to conceal their surprise and enthusiasm, but somehow they had managed, and thirty minutes later, they were on another walk-through across the street.

It wasn't every day Evans wrote $50,000 checks and did business with a Realtor using a kitchen counter as a desk. The two contracts of sale—one for the house at 117 and one for the house at 118—were prepared, and after a call to Wells Fargo in San Francisco, Dale Boyd had accepted the personal checks and had agreed to a cash sale settlement date of April 23.

Evans might not have been so readily agreeable to purchase the two town houses so quickly, but after the walk-through, the one at 118, particularly the ground-floor apartment, which ostensibly a Mr. Lowen had leased for his daughter who often traveled from her home in California to Washington on business, he was convinced he was making the right decision. As Mike had once said, entry by the landlord was better than breaking and entering.

After his second cup of coffee, Evans went to work. He booted up his desktop and laptop computers and let his fingers do the walking. In moments, a very sophisticated program began chugging away; he wondered what he would find that morning. It was a state-of-the-art eavesdropping system they had put into use; six bugs in each love nest sent voice-activated signals to digital recorders that at programmed intervals downloaded their audio files to a computer that uploaded them to a Globaltronix satellite. Evans's computer downloaded the audio files and converted them to text files. The text and audio files were time and date stamped and filed under the code name Sparkling Water.

Evans read the text files while also hoping whatever appeared was nice and juicy or answers to one of his theories. So far, he had learned that Pellegrino had presidential aspirations and Paul Thoros, a.k.a. Zorba the Greek, was the primary financial backer. He had also learned that Charles Atherton, a business associate of Thoros though only remotely, was on the boards of several leftist foundations. Atherton also had a sister married to that asshole mayor of New York City, and his father-in-law was the governor of Connecticut.

Evans read the transcript again. *What the hell are Atherton and Lowen up to? And Lowen and Pellegrino?*

> "Nice pad you have here, Rob. Must really help you enjoy your work. Ever think about bringing some of that stuff floating around the Capitol Building here for some R&R?"

> "God no. I'd have to be out of my fucking mind. Christ, if I did that and Babbs found out, it would ruin everything."

> "Yeah. You're probably right. Too much to lose, particularly as we're getting close. Say, have you got anything to drink around here other than wine?"

"I think we have some gin and some vermouth. Might even have some tonic. Once in a while, we have a G & T or a martini. Depends on the time of day."

"Why don't you fire up your laptop? I'll make us a couple of martinis, then we can enjoy ourselves while going over the material I brought with me."

***

"All right. You with me now? Copy this and then hide it someplace secure. You have such a place?"

"Yeah. Here, see this?"

"That's neat. Did you make that?"

"No. I found it by accident."

"All right, let's get back to work. First, these associations. It's imperative you use them exactly as I'm explaining or nothing will happen, all right? Everything will happen automatically for all the different groups, factions, and organizations."

***

"Where you going?"

"To open another bottle of wine. All this between-the-sheets exercise makes me thirsty."

"Has anyone ever told you you're a bastard?"

"Yes, you do every time I engage in some sexual innuendo."

"Here, let me have your glass. If you're a good girl, I'll let you have some."

"I'm always a good girl. You know that. Now, quit sidetracking me and tell me more about last night. Do you think it will work?"

"I think so. Everything should work automatically. We have all our people in place. They don't need to be told what to do. They know how to use the machinery. They think that by having all the senior positions under their control, they'll be able to control things. But that's all right. That's the beauty of it. These people will just take it upon themselves to pass the info, and our organizations will know how to run with it."

"Imagine your nemesis having to deal with the crap the media will be publishing. We get *Progress for the Future* in Atlanta passing carefully packaged material to the blogosphere, and soon, it will pass into the mainstream, and voilà."

Seven months earlier, the use of associations had been just a theory. The theory had become a reality. Three names had arisen through the fog of pillow talk fueled by wine and overconfidence. That morning, Evans would have been happy just knowing about *Progress for the Future*, but he had also learned of two other liberal associations: the *Center for American Progress* and the *Center for Responsible Progress*. It was time for a meeting with Mike.

CHAPTER 11
Thirty-Two Thousand Feet
Air France 1621
Thursday, August 19, 2010

It had been a very successful yet grueling trip, although Jenkins, sipping champagne and munching on snacks, thought he could have done without the long layover in Paris. After eight days, he was eagerly looking forward to seeing Candy again. He thought about that afternoon between when he had left President Branch and had arrived at her apartment, but his eager thoughts were tempered by the realization that it would be nine in the evening when he arrived at her apartment. In spite of what he was looking forward to, he wondered if he would have the energy to perform.

The morning after Jenkins's arrival in Tel Aviv, his friend, Paul Bernstein, drove him to the US embassy, where he met with an assistant consul Harold Walker. After he had introduced himself, Walker had given him an envelope that had been sent by diplomatic courier on Tuesday.

Dr. Paul Bernstein, Jenkins's first recruit for Project Abraham, was a man in his early fifties who had grown up on a kibbutz in northern Israel. Bernstein possessed the typical Semitic facial features and black hair, but his graying sideburns and glasses gave him a distinguished look.

Like all Israelis, he started his adult life by serving in the Israeli Defense Force, but his military career had come to an early and abrupt end when he was severely wounded in one of the IDF's incursions into enemy territory. During his convalescence, he met and married a young American exchange student from New York. After his marriage to Miriam Cooperman, Bernstein immigrated to the United States on a student visa, and because Miriam's family had connections, he had attended Princeton, where her brother was a student. Ultimately, Bernstein obtained doctorates in economics and international business development and became a tenured professor.

While Bernstein was climbing the academic ladder, Miriam, a beautiful woman also in her early fifties with short, well-coiffed black hair who could easily have been on a fashion magazine cover, had started a career in the literary world. An uncle was a partner in the company that published her first books; it had published fourteen Robert Ludlum–type novels under the pseudonym of David Conway.

Before he had left Washington, one of Jenkins's major concerns had been getting his friends Michele and Marshall Golden to arrive in Tel Aviv no later than Saturday. A directive sent to Colonel Golden's commander in Afghanistan by the secretary of defense directed the colonel to go to the US embassy in Tel Aviv and be there no later than Friday; that had solved the problem concerning Golden. But at the time, Jenkins had no idea where Michele was.

That was why one of the first things he did the Saturday before he left Washington was telephone Michele to learn whether she was in Paris or at their apartment in Newburg, New York, a place they called home while their sons were attending West Point. When Jenkins called Michele's cell, a very surprised Michele told him she was visiting her parents in Paris. She was even more surprised when he had told her that arrangements were underway for her husband to be at the American embassy no later than Friday and that he wanted her to fly to Tel Aviv and arrive no later than the same day.

Everyone had each managed to get to Tel Aviv on Friday, and they had been safely checked into their hotel before the Sabbath began at sunset. While Miriam and Paul Bernstein commenced observing the Sabbath, Jenkins, Michele, and Colonel Golden had dinner in the hotel dining room.

Saturday until sunset had been a day of R&R and catching up with old friends Jenkins hadn't seen for a while. At sunset, he and the Goldens had gone to the Bernstein condominium for a lavish dinner that only a good Jewish woman like Miriam could prepare.

Sunday, Paul Bernstein drove everyone to Jerusalem, where they checked into the King David Hotel. They planned for the meeting with the Israeli prime minister the rest of the day.

On Monday, Jenkins, Bernstein, and Golden had met with Prime Minister Sharon and his NSA general Ari Ben Gul. Then on Tuesday, they all left for Tel Aviv. Jenkins felt everything had gone far better than he had guessed it would. It was time for the last two recruits.

After his meeting with Sharon and Ben Gul, Jenkins e-mailed Jack Wharton about having dinner the coming Saturday evening. He had some friends he wanted Jack to meet; it would be a combination of business and pleasure. He wanted dinner at a restaurant where the rich and famous could dine without being recognized.

After Wharton's response in the affirmative, Jenkins sent Ken Middleton an e-mail asking him if he was tired of the humdrum of the corporate world and if so, he had something exciting in mind. He and Nancy could take one of Globaltronix's Gulfstreams to Washington. He told him that he would find the excitement he was looking for and that he and Nancy would have dinner with him and his girlfriend.

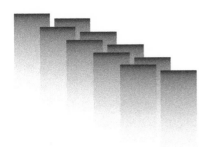

CHAPTER 12

Candice Reason's Condominium
Watergate South
700 New Hampshire Avenue NW
Washington, DC
Friday, August 20, 2010

Candy Reason usually woke up early. Slowly and carefully, she slipped out of bed while Brad Jenkins was sleeping, slipped into her robe, and made her way to the kitchen.

She retrieved a coffee mug from a cabinet and poured some half-and-half into it. She put it under the spout of the one-cup coffeemaker and pressed the start button. After her cup was filled, she took it to the small table in the breakfast area, sat, and reflected on her brief relationship with Jenkins and how she had felt while he had been away.

She had always been in control of her emotions. Maybe that was why that idiot at the *Washington Post* had sarcastically called her the Dragon Lady. But ever since the night she had met Brad, she had been fighting a losing battle with her emotions, particularly during the past eight days.

After Jenkins had left for Israel, Candy had started to feel like a caged animal, and she didn't know what to do with herself. While his e-mails helped, they couldn't replace the man to whom she had given her body.

Candy had looked forward to Jenkins's return and had envisioned a romantic evening, but with his arrival at Dulles at a quarter to seven in the evening, she knew her hopes and desires would be compromised because he probably would have been stuffed with food and drink on his flights. So instead of the candlelit dinner she had dreamed of, they would celebrate Jenkins's return with cocktails and snacks.

He called her after his taxi left Interstate 66 and was making its way to the Watergate complex. She had turned on the CD player filling her apartment with romantic music.

"Might I join you?" Jenkins asked as he walked into the kitchen.

"Good morning, sleepyhead. Did you have a good night? You had to be exhausted after all that time in the air and an almost five-hour layover."

"Nothing that a good cup of black coffee wouldn't cure."

"Have a seat. I'll have one for you in a minute. Can I get you something to eat?"

"No, just coffee." He noticed her nervousness. "Is something the matter?"

"No," she said as she made his coffee.

"Really?" he questioned again as she placed his mug of coffee in front of him.

"Oh, Brad, if you must know, I was thinking how I felt while you were gone. I feel like all I've done lately has been waiting for you."

Instead of saying anything, Jenkins rose from his seat and took Candy in his arms.

"Damn you, Brad Jenkins," she said as tears formed in her eyes, "for making me feel how much I missed you while you were gone. I haven't been in control of my emotions since the night we met."

"In that case," he said as he gave her a kiss, "I think there is only one thing to do."

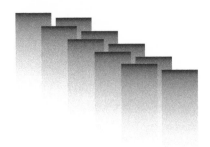

CHAPTER 13

Middleton Family Condominium
Watergate West
2700 Virginia Avenue NW
Washington, DC
Saturday, August 21, 2010

"We'll have to pay Candy a visit," said Ken Middleton to his slim, trim, blonde wife, Nancy, as he looked at his watch. "She lives in this complex somewhere. Perhaps you could give her or Uncle Harry a call tomorrow."

In response to an e-mail from Jenkins, Middleton, a blond version of Cary Grant, and Nancy had arrived at the family condo early the evening before and were looking forward to dinner with Jenkins and his girlfriend.

"No way we could come here and not visit. I'll give her a call tomorrow," Nancy said.

"There's the doorbell," Middleton said. "I'll get it."

"Hello, Ken," Jenkins said to Middleton, who was surprised to see Candy Reason with him.

"Candy!" Middleton said.

"Ken!" exclaimed an equally surprised Candy. "What are you doing here?"

"You know each other?" Brad was astonished.

"Ken and I have known each other since we were tiny tots," she said after giving Middleton a hug and a kiss.

"Nancy," said Middleton over his shoulder, "you're not going to believe this."

"Oh my God!" Nancy exclaimed. She threw her arms around Candy and gave her a big hug. "Candy, it's so good to see you again! I was going to call you tomorrow."

"I guess you won't have to make that telephone call tomorrow after all," said Ken to Nancy. Then to a perplexed Jenkins, he said, "We were going to call Candy tomorrow. There was no way we could come to town and not see her. She's always been family." He turned to Candy. "Brad and I were rangers together. He's the one who saved my life."

"Oh, my God, really?"

"What can I get you to drink?" Ken asked once everyone was seated.

"Just some white wine for us," replied Jenkins. "We have to be at the Indiana Jones residence in McLean at seven."

"Indiana Jones?"

"My friend Jack Wharton's place. I don't remember your meeting him, but I may have mentioned him from time to time."

"Is he your trekking buddy?"

"You nailed it."

"Candy," said Nancy as they all raised their glasses in a toast, "we had no idea you were dating anyone let alone Brad."

"If you are and it's serious," added Ken, "you couldn't have picked a better person."

"Brad and I have known each other for less than a month," replied Candy, trying to slough off what Ken had said, but then she hesitated. "But I do think I've kind of gotten used to having him around."

"I think what she's trying to say," said Brad, "is that she misses the hell out of me when I'm not around."

"Then you're a very lucky man," said Ken, "because I've not known Candy to miss anyone."

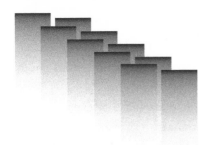

CHAPTER 14

Wharton Residence
McLean, Virginia
Saturday, August 21, 2010

At six forty-five, Susan Wharton stood in front of the full-length mirror for a final inspection. *Not bad for an old bird*, she thought. But she was hardly an old bird; she was an attractive, slim forty-two-year-old of medium height with blonde hair she always wore in a classic bob.

Her review of her appearance was because she and Jack were going to dinner this evening with Brad Jenkins and some of his friends he had wanted her and Jack to meet. She wanted to make a good first impression. She was wearing a basic black, sleeveless cocktail dress, low-heeled black pumps, gold hoop earrings, a red, soft, crinkle texture wrap, and a black clutch with a gold clasp.

"Are you ready for the big event, hon?" asked Jack, who was wearing a dark-blue blazer, gray trousers, and light-blue shirt with a tie.

"I wonder who Brad's friends are," said Susan as she stepped away from the mirror.

"Whoever they are, they must be important for Brad wanting to go somewhere where the rich and famous won't be recognized."

"Surprise, surprise," said Jenkins to Jack Wharton twenty minutes later when Wharton answered the front door. "Sorry we're a little late. I'd like to introduce my friends Ken, Nancy, and Candy."

Wharton was speechless when he saw Candy Reason.

"Jack," said Jenkins, "put your eyeballs back in your head and close your mouth."

"If you wanted to surprise the hell out of me, Brad, you've succeeded. No wonder you inquired about a place where the rich and famous could go and not be recognized."

It was because of the way the evening had started that everyone had not gone out to dinner. After introducing Jenkins's guests to Susan, who had been as equally flabbergasted as he had been, there had been a silent communication between Wharton and his wife that an impromptu meal at home would be far more enjoyable than going to a restaurant.

The evening turned out to be one of the most surprising of Jack Wharton's life—one surprise after another. It had been an evening of business and pleasure, but it had been hard to discern where one ended and the other began. Everyone realized they were more than friends; they were family. They had gathered in the kitchen and conversed, drank, and prepared salads while steaks were grilling and potatoes were baking.

It had all started when Brad Jenkins had purposely masterminded the get-together because Wharton had teased Jenkins about Candy Reason being the Ice Queen or the Dragon Lady. That was why Jenkins had not mentioned the names of the friends he was bringing to dinner

Jenkins had told the story of how he and Candy had met at the Friends of Israel banquet and how President Branch had requested a meeting. He told them about how that meeting had led him and Candy to start the creation of a nongovernmental project called Abraham.

By the time Jenkins had finished, Wharton knew he would be part of Abraham. He and Susan had known Jenkins for years and had also known Paul and Miriam Bernstein. In the years past, he had learned of Brad's friends Nancy and Ken Middleton and Michele and Marshall Golden. Only Candy was the newcomer to the group, but after watching her and Brad the whole evening, Wharton had agreed with Ken Middleton that the two of them would be together for the long haul.

"Christ," said Wharton later in the evening after everyone had finally said good night and their guests had left, "can you believe what happened tonight? I guess Candy Reason will no longer be the most eligible bachelorette in Washington."

"Wouldn't the secrecy of Abraham become compromised if word ever got out that she is engaged or married to a Princeton professor?" Susan asked.

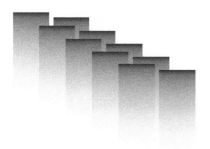

CHAPTER 15
Prairie View Ranch
Kendall County, Texas
Monday, September 6, 2010

It was the first time that Mike Middleton had been to the president's ranch since he, Harry Reason, and Alberto Garcia had met with the president three days after the 2008 election when they had gotten together to discuss strategy for the new Branch administration. He was accompanied by Larry Evans. As on the previous occasion, everyone was sitting on the terrace adjoining the president's study enjoying cold beers and engaging in some chitchat before getting down to business.

President George Branch, a man in his late fifties with an affable personality—which was why the media usually referred to him as the affable cowboy—was not a man to waste time. He drained his beer and said to Middleton, "I gather you've had some success with your eavesdropping operations."

"George," said Middleton, "what we have might not be as much as we had hoped for, but I think that's about to change."

"You've really found something substantive?" asked Al Garcia, the president's chief of staff. "I mean other than this Zorba the Greek bankrolling her if she decides to run for president?"

"I think so," Middleton said while looking at the president. "Something I think should at least be investigated."

"What do you have?" the president asked, knowing whatever Middleton had uncovered in his eavesdropping operation had to be serious or he and Evans would not have wanted to make a special trip to Texas.

"George," replied Middleton, "before I let Larry here explain his theory, let me give you a little background. One problem with reading transcripts of conversations is context. There are other problems also. Someone named Charles had been a visitor to the Capitol Hill love nest on several occasions and kept referring to a man by the name of Paul. It was only by accident we learned Charles's last name was Atherton and Paul's last name was Thoros."

It has only been thirteen days ago, thought Larry Evans as Middleton was speaking to the president. He was midway through his second cup of morning coffee when the lightbulb in his head suddenly switched on. Something had been bothering him for several weeks, something he couldn't put his finger on. It came to him suddenly due to a thought about the daughter of one of his friends and former business associates and her doctoral thesis. He'd have to call Taffy's father on that one later. Meanwhile, there was a year and a half of transcripts to study.

After firing up his computer, he went to the Pellegrino file and one by one studied every document for all the appropriate words and highlighted them.

As he searched, bit by bit, words such as *associations* and *associated* were highlighted along with those of *Charles, Paul, Babbs*, and *Rob*. He worked all day except for quick meals and to call Ben Sorenson, Taffy's father, to get the title of her thesis. He learned it had been published, and he downloaded it from Amazon onto his iPad. By the time Evans called it quits for the day, he knew he had only scratched the surface and it would take the rest of the week to complete his task. A week later, he drove to Boulder Creek to meet with Mike Middleton.

The meeting had resulted in the meeting with the president. As Middleton continued his attempt to explain the context, Al Garcia, who was getting a bit impatient, started to say something, but the president raised his hand. "Let Mike finish."

A few moments later, it was up to Evans to present his theory. "Mr. President, I've gone through a year and a half of transcripts. Individually, they're meaningless, but if they're read collectively, a picture emerges. All the mentions of when she becomes president and all the times the words *association* and *associations* were mentioned were—"

"Associations?" Garcia blurted out. "You mean like in trade associations?"

"Or nonprofits," said Middleton.

"Mike," said President Branch, "you're starting to lose me."

"George," said Middleton, "the point Larry is trying to make is that words mean something only in a context. We were too busy looking at individual trees in the forest and not the whole forest. That's why things slipped past us. Then one day, Larry remembered Ben Sorenson's daughter Taffy."

"Who the hell is Ben Sorenson?" Al Garcia asked. "And what the hell does some daughter have to do with whatever?"

"Actually, everything Al," said Middleton, trying not to lose his temper. "One morning, Larry remembered a book this woman had published for her doctoral thesis, so he went over the transcripts again. Then he called me and asked if he could drive down to Boulder Creek. Said that he wanted to run something by me. After listening to him and going over everything, I agreed that his thesis was right on."

"And what exactly is this thesis?" the president asked.

"Mr. President," interjected Evans, "the book is titled *Foundations of Deceit*. It is about the corrupt interlocking relationships involving many of the nonprofits extending into the government. There were too many occasions when Lowen and this Charles had conversations regarding the usage of associations and how they were the key to what they were trying to achieve. I believe that Pellegrino and Lowen, with the help of Charles Atherton and Paul Thoros—Zorba the Greek—are deeply involved in something like this and that it extends into the government and has something to do with Pellegrino's presidential ambitions and the destruction of your presidency."

"George," said Middleton to a momentary dumbfounded president, "you have to remember that Pellegrino and Lowen are ideologues. Particularly Pellegrino. Everything she does is in a political context, which is why it would be a good idea to have Justice do a little investigating."

"I think you've made some good points," the president said as he put his hands in a prayer position and closed his eyes. Several moments passed before he said, "I can't do it, Mike."

"If you think we're on the mark, why not?"

"The operative word is *can't*, Mike. If I turn something like this as you suggest over to Justice, I'll probably end up reading about it in the *Post* the next day. Wasn't it you who told me once that it would be easier to resurrect the dead than keep a secret in Washington?"

"No, that was me," said Harry Reason speaking for the first time.

"Right," said the president smiling as he looked at Harry. "I stand corrected. Mike, I see where both of you are coming from, but I think it's too chancy to involve any government agency. I think it would be better to keep this in-house so to speak. You apparently know this woman who's already done some research in this area. Perhaps you could get her to do what you suggest. If you can do that, I think we can find a way to quietly give you any required assistance."

CHAPTER 16

**La Maison Verte
59 Abdulhameed Badees Street
Shmeisani, Amman, Jordan
Sunday, September 26, 2010**

The color of the "Goldens" hair did not match their last names. Because Colonel Marshall Golden's mother had been Lebanese and Michele Golden was French, they had black hair. Size wise, Michele Golden bordered somewhere between petite and medium. Her hair was short, and she loved to wear loop earrings that emphasized her round face. Colonel Golden was a six-foot, no-nonsense former army ranger with an angular face and deep, probing eyes.

"It's certainly been a very interesting five days," said Michele as she and her husband touched their wineglasses. "I never dreamed that Amman was so Westernized and so liberal. And I certainly didn't expect to be taken to such a lovely and elegant restaurant as this. The ambiance is so exquisite, so romantic."

"I told you when I called you that Jordan had changed," the colonel said. "Every place I've gone on this fact-finding trip and everything I've seen has been so different from what I remember twenty-five years ago. Perhaps there's hope for the Arabland yet, but I won't hold my breath. There are still too many crazies out there. They may not be hijacking airplanes anymore, but the Western world is still in their crosshairs."

Because he had not been in Jordan for almost twenty-five years, Golden knew that he had changed and so had the country. That was why he had decided to come to Jordan on a fact-finding trip. He needed to get comfortable with the lay of the land. Read the newspapers. Listen to radio and television. Sit in the cafés and just look and listen. Though he knew the old culture and he spoke the language, he was culturally rusty and needed time to readjust and absorb so everything once again would become second nature and allow for mental adjustments as required.

Golden knew there was a lot of work to do if he was going to create the surgical strike force as envisioned by Brad Jenkins. Twenty-five teams of three members each would be difficult enough to recruit particularly when all the team members had to be fluent in Arabic and be able to pass themselves off as Arabic. If that weren't difficult enough, Brad Jenkins's idea of a mixture of Israelis, Lebanese Christian Arabs, and Americans with military experience would be even more difficult.

That's why with Jordan one of only two countries in the Arab world that allowed airline travel to and from Israel, Golden had flown from Tel Aviv to the Queen Alia International Airport in Amman. He checked into the Amman Marriott in the western part of the city and had taken a taxi to El Balad, the old heart of the city where he began his cultural reawakening.

For two and a half days, Golden walked the city, read newspapers while sipping coffee in the many coffeehouses, and talked to the locals. He spent two more days as a guest at the home of Tariq Azziz, a university professor and acquaintance.

On the sixth day, Golden had left with his driver, Abdul, the son of Tariq, on a ten-day tour of the western part of the country, visiting villages and small cities from Irbid in the north to Aqaba in the south. On the sixteenth day, they had left Aqaba and drove north to the Wadi Araba South Border where by prior arrangement he met up with his wife.

During the last five days in Jordan, Golden and his wife had been typical tourists. They spent two nights at the Marriott Petra Hotel in Wadi Musa and two days touring the ancient, rock-carved Nabataean city of Petra before continuing to Amman. There, they browsed the shops, ate at the cafés, and visited archaeological sites such as the Roman theater, Nymphaeum, and Temple of Heracles.

"I'm glad you've enjoyed your first visit to Arabland since way back when," Golden told his wife, "particularly inasmuch as this visit is much more pleasurable than the last one."

With the exception of Lebanon, the only Arab country Michele Golden had been to before this current trip to Jordan had been Iraq, and that had not been on her itinerary. Golden and Jenkins had been on thirty days' leave at the time and were traveling Air France first class from Paris to Beirut to visit their families. Though their seat assignments were supposed to be together, somehow, they had ended up with aisle seats across from each other, and his seatmate had turned out to be a beautiful young woman. As their flight had progressed, it hadn't taken him long to discover that the young woman came from a wealthy Parisian family and was a student at the Sorbonne. He also learned that she was antiestablishment, antiwar, and anti-American. Fortunately for him at the time, she had thought he was French because he spoke the language fluently and was not in uniform.

They had been two-thirds of the way into their journey when the plane was hijacked and diverted to a desert area in northern Iraq. The first mistake the hijackers—three young men, kids really—made was to have made the passengers get off the plane and surrender their passports. As they left the plane, Golden had grabbed Michele's hand and told her to stay with him. It had been a command, not a request, and she had not objected.

The hijackers' second mistake had been the failure to take into consideration what could be done in the darkness of the night particularly by Special Forces soldiers who had been trained to kill. By dawn, there were three dead hijackers and Golden and Jenkins had asked the Air France pilot if it was possible to start the engines so everyone could get the hell away from wherever they were.

In Beirut, Golden and Jenkins became celebrities for a few days, and Michele's uncle had invited them to dinner as a thank-you for taking care of his niece. That dinner led to Golden and Michele spending much time together until they had to leave Beirut. Fortunately for them, absence made their hearts grow fonder, and before the year was over, they had married.

"Oui," responded Michele with a sigh as she briefly remembered that time that had been her wake-up call in life. "It is indeed more pleasurable."

So much had changed through the years. As her husband had said about Amman, Michele too had changed. After their marriage, in spite of her former antiwar and anti-American views, she had become the wife of a US Army officer and had become a very conservative woman with two sons attending West Point.

"Will you be coming back soon?" she asked.

"Not for a while and only briefly if I do. It'll take some time for the recruiting. If all goes well, I probably won't be back until at least next spring."

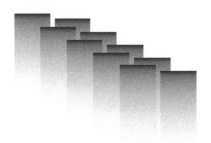

CHAPTER 17
Seats 3A and 3B
United Flight 217
Sunday, October 3, 2010

"I wouldn't let it bother you, dear," said Marianne Middleton to her husband as they sat in the first-class section of the 757 waiting for their flight to leave Washington Dulles. "You've allowed Su Ki and Ben to have a nice visit with Taffy. We've had a lovely Sunday in Atlanta, and we've had a nice time visiting with Kym and Harry in Washington again. You've found office space where you wanted, and you've persuaded two talented young women to make a major relocation in their lives. I think you also did the right thing by bowing out and leaving them to it. After all, they aren't little girls. They're more than qualified to continue on their own."

Mike Middleton finished his champagne, closed his eyes, and rested his head against his headrest. There was no point in further discussion with Marianne particularly when he knew she was right. There were other things on his mind.

There had been no doubt that Taffy and her friend Carol were capable young women particularly with a very efficient and capable Sarah Nunnelly, a thirty-eight-year-old executive assistant in Globaltronix's Washington office, who was closer to their age, to assist them, and Harry and company were available if necessary. What really concerned him were the half-truths involved in the creation of Association Research and the recruitment of Taffy and Carol.

It had been a long and unexpected road to Atlanta. On the company jet from San Antonio, after Larry Evans and he had met with the president, to the Watsonville airport not far from his Boulder Creek home, he had thought long and hard about what the president had suggested. By the time he and Larry had arrived at the Watsonville airport, he knew the trail would have to start at Ben Sorenson's home in Tiburon.

Middleton's original thought had been for Larry Evans, who was closer to Ben Sorenson than he was, to find out where Taffy was living and how to contact her. Unfortunately, that call had resulted in them learning that after graduating Cal Berkeley, Taffy had moved to Marietta, Georgia, with her engineer husband. They had divorced three years later, and she was still in the Atlanta area.

Taffy Lafayette might have been a divorced woman, but she hadn't wasted any time. Law school, membership in the Georgia Bar, and a master's and a doctorate from Georgia Tech were enough to make any parent proud, and her parents had been very proud. Their only disappointment had been her refusal to return to California, where they felt she belonged.

Middleton hadn't seen Taffy Lafayette, née Sorenson, since she was in her late teens. When he met her after so many years, he carefully studied her. The tall, slender teenager who had once shown only a hint of a beauty yet to develop had become an extremely beautiful woman with many of her Eurasian mother's fine features. He wondered how this gorgeous woman had managed to graduate from the notorious bastion of liberal orthodoxy, Cal Berkeley, and remain a conservative. Perhaps, he thought, her superior intellect had saved her.

When he had learned that Taffy lived in the trendy Atlanta suburb of Buckhead, it was suggested that her father made a call to get her to travel to California so he could meet her and make her an offer, but she had refused. She would not return to California until Christmas to visit her family.

Middleton had no choice but to travel to Atlanta. So he and Marianne, Larry Evans and his wife, Sylvia, and Taffy's father and mother had flown to Atlanta's Hartsfield-Jackson Airport on a Friday. The plan was to combine business and pleasure; Ben and Su Ki Sorenson had spent the weekend visiting their daughter. Middleton, Evans, and their wives, who were the guests of John York, the owner of the San Francisco Forty-Niners, attended Sunday's Falcons–Forty-Niners football game. On Saturday, everyone had met for lunch and then discreetly left Middleton and Taffy alone to discuss business.

"Dad tells me you'd like to make me an offer I can't refuse," said Taffy.

"These days, every offer is one that can't be refused," Middleton said, "but I want to make one I hope you'll accept."

Taffy nodded in a way that said, "Try me." Middleton's attention was drawn to how her jet- black hair was in a bun and how she had parked her sunglasses on top of her head.

"Before I make my sales pitch, may I ask how you came to write *Foundations of Deceit*? Whatever led you to do such research?"

"After my divorce, I worked for a law firm here in Buckhead that had a client who brought suit against a foundation. The client contended that the board of directors had violated the original foundation charter established by his grandfather. I was intimately involved in the case. I found the work fascinating and the conduct of the board disgusting. You probably know the rest of the story."

"Do you remember Harry Reason?"

"Vaguely."

"His daughter Candy?"

"Again vaguely."

"That's not too surprising. Harry and family moved to Houston fifteen-sixteen years ago when we opened a new production facility."

Taffy was displaying a bit of impatience. "Mr. Middleton—"

"Please call me Mike or Uncle Mike. I realize I'm an old man, but when I hear someone call me Mr. Middleton, it makes me feel older."

"Uncle Mike it will be then," said Taffy, regaining composure. "I'd feel I was disrespectful if I just called you Mike."

"Thank you," Middleton said with a big smile. "I asked if you knew Harry Reason because he is now President Branch's secretary of defense, and his daughter, Candy, is the president's national security adviser."

"Oh my God! I never connected the dots when you asked if I knew them."

"No problem," said Middleton. "I was asked by the president to become the secretary of Homeland Security, but I told the president I could be of more help outside his administration, which brings us to why we're meeting. Most anyone on the left coast of any means or position thinks I'm a Democrat. Consequently, I become privy to all sorts of information, the latest being exactly what you've researched and written about."

CHAPTER 18

Thai Roma Restaurant
237 Pennsylvania Avenue SE
Washington, DC
Friday, November 5, 2010

Jack Wharton's usual watering hole was particularly busy during lunch this afternoon as he and David Hawkins sipped wine while waiting for their meals.

"I still find it unbelievable that Nate lost the election," said Wharton.

"I'm still grappling with what happened myself," responded Hawkins. "Nate Grishom was only the second Speaker of the House to ever be voted out of office."

"How the hell could he go from six points ahead two days before the election and then lose by six? It doesn't compute."

"It may not, but there won't be a recount because the margin of victory assures there will be no automatic recount, and with the secretary of state and supervisor of elections being Democrats, he'll need to file a lawsuit, and even then, his chances will range from slim to zero."

"It still doesn't pass the smell test," Wharton said. "I'd bet the farm that he lost because of election fraud."

"My friend, I'm inclined to agree with you, but that won't help Nate, and it sure as hell isn't going to help the president. We have to face the possibility that there really was no fraud involved and what actually did him in was all the negative media coverage he was getting. It may have all been a pack of lies, but what you call the low-information voter buys into that crap. The exit polling also indicated that he lost the independents."

"Dave, if I hear any more about the goddamned independents, I'll scream. The same goes for all those other dumb bastards who vote. You know whom I mean. Those nincompoops who don't have a clue. If I had my way, I'd raise the voting age to twenty-five, and everyone would have to have a voter card with a picture on it as well as an address and precinct number. And to get that, they would have to prove they were citizens and then take a test. Something like a 250-question multiple-choice test that covers history, geography, civics, and finance.

"We live in an age when life is running at warp speed. If the great unwashed out there choose to live in ignorance, they deserve to get the government they get whether they like it or not. We need voters with skin in the game or else we'll end up going down the tubes like other societies before us."

David Hawkins laughed. "Jack, it'll never happen. It'll never get close. For anything even remotely close, we'd need a dictatorship, and of course with a dictatorship, we wouldn't need voters. Even intelligent ones."

CHAPTER 19

Sheraton Maui Resort and Spa
Lahaina, Maui, Hawaii
Saturday, November 27, 2010

The night was the last evening of the celebration for Globaltronix's fourteenth year. In attendance were the founders and their immediate families and select friends. As on previous occasions, the event was being held on one of the hotel's private patios. The hotel had erected a podium on a dance floor for the master of ceremonies. Behind the dance floor, a band waited to play when the speaker had finished. On two sides of the guests were buffet tables laden with a royal feast. Five bars were strategically located around the patio.

"Folks," said Jack Wharton to his nine tablemates, "the party's over, and tomorrow, we'll head back to the real world. It's been a pretty successful and enjoyable two weeks. Las Vegas for a wedding and then on to Hawaii for the honeymoon. And we even found some time to get some business done. So with this last drop of my last adult beverage before retiring, I once again congratulate Candy and Brad on deciding to make their relationship permanent. Would our chief conspirator please say a few parting words?"

"Well," said Brad, "if you think I'm going to give a speech—"

"That's more than a few," interjected Ken Middleton, and everyone laughed.

"Ken," said Jenkins, "I think you and Jack have been drinking the same water."

"You mean rum," Colonel Golden said. "Those mai tais were pretty strong."

"Okay you clowns," said Jenkins with a chuckle, "let me be serious for a minute before we call it a night. First, Candy and I appreciate your good wishes. Second, yes, as Jack said, we managed to get some work done. Though we're only three months old and we're still a work in progress, I feel good about things. I think the coming year will see us off and running.

"In the beginning, when I was asked if I had the wherewithal to create our little organization, I immediately said yes because I believed all of you could be recruited, and none of you let me down. Thank you all, and sleep tight."

"I don't know about you folks," said Middleton mostly to Harry Reason, Larry Evans, and Royce Bartlett, who were at another table with their wives, "but my twitching nose says the kids are up to something."

"Kids are always up to something," said Marianne Middleton dismissively. "Just like their fathers."

That got a laugh from the other wives.

Dismissing his wife's comment, Mike Middleton continued. "And I'm also surprised that the two people here at this table who once said they were great detectives because they read a lot of books and saw a lot of movies have similar suspicions. Too bad they haven't been able to find out what the kids are up to."

"We can always go into early retirement, Mike," said Royce Bartlett humorously. "Right, Larry?"

"I'll drink to that," Evans said with a chuckle.

"Interesting," Middleton said. "Brad suddenly does special consulting work for the president, work he won't discuss with Harry; and he and Candy didn't want anybody to know about their marriage except close family and friends."

"You and Harry schemed to get Candy and Brad together," said Marianne Middleton with a shake of her head and a roll of her eyes. "Now you're wondering what they're scheming. That's the pot calling the kettle black."

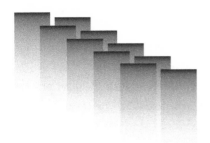

CHAPTER 20
Association Research
600 New Hampshire Avenue NW
Washington, DC
Wednesday, December 15, 2010

"Taffy," said Carol Gardner, a slender, five-seven, strawberry blonde to her friend and coworker at the adjoining workstation in the small office they shared, "I got another of those sites."

"You mean with all those squiggly characters?" asked Taffy Lafayette, who had been preoccupied with thoughts about the busy past two months that had helped them erase Georgia from their minds.

From the moment that afternoon when Mr. Middleton, or Uncle Mike, as he had suggested he be called, had made his offer, their lives had been on a fast track. After hearing Uncle Mike's story about how one of the wealthiest men in the world was attempting to use nonprofit foundations to further the presidential aspirations of Barbara Pellegrino, Taffy had become very interested in his offer. However, instead of immediately accepting it, she had told Uncle Mike she preferred to think about things overnight.

After discussing the offer with her friend Carol Gardner instead of her parents, which she was sure had been Uncle Mike's assumption, she had phoned him the next morning before everyone left for the Falcons–Forty-Niners game.

The hassle of moving from one city to another to start new lives had been expected. What had not been expected had been a dinner invitation to the White House earlier that month. They had assumed correctly that the invitation had been the result of their new relationship with the secretary of defense, Uncle Harry, and his daughter, Candy.

If ever there had been a need for Sarah Nunnely to help shop for proper evening attire, which neither Taffy nor Carol had had for several years, in a new city, it was then. Sarah had kicked into overdrive and had taken them on three different shopping expeditions.

On the evening of the big event, two young, nervous women had been escorted by young army officers in their dress blues and had met the president. Fortunately, his affable manner enabled them to relax, and for the short time they had spoken with him, he had conveyed his knowledge of what they were about to do and his appreciation without actually saying so.

"Yes," answered Carol.

"Let me take a look," said Taffy.

A few moments passed while Taffy looked at Carol's computer screen.

"What do we do?" asked Carol. "It's just like the last ones. I don't have a clue what I'm looking at. I'll probably have to totally get out of Google like I did the last time."

"Do you know how you got there?"

"No. It was like with the others. I was following links, and then this happened."

"Links from what?"

'I was surfing one of the Florida universities. Florida Atlantic. Then one thing led to another."

"Copy everything you can, Carol. That is, if you can. You were able to do that with the others, weren't you?"

"For the most part."

"All right. Whatever you have I'll copy to my laptop, and it can go with me when I leave for San Francisco Friday. I'll drive to Foster City to visit with Mr. Evans. Maybe he'll know what this is all about."

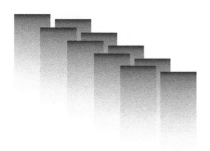

CHAPTER 21
Middleton Estate
Big Basin Way
Boulder Creek, California
Tuesday, January 4, 2011

After hanging up the phone, Michael Middleton swiveled his chair and gazed out his study window with a feeling of relief because his son had agreed to his request without asking a lot of questions.

During her return to Tiburon to spend Christmas with her parents, Taffy had driven down to Foster City to meet with Larry Evans and show him what she and her friend had run across. She had asked him what they should do about it. After reviewing the screen shots she had brought with her, Evans had thought the graphics for the websites were Arabic and had passed the ball to him.

After speaking with Evans, Middleton had at first been tempted to dismiss Taffy's discovery, but after some serious thought, the fact that Taffy and her friend had somehow accidentally entered some Arabic websites was something that could not cavalierly be dismissed. Obviously, the situation needed to be analyzed so an appropriate course of action could be initiated, but to do that, someone who knew Arabic would be needed, and there was only one person he could think of who could speak and read Arabic and be controllable if he wanted to keep Association Research secret. He had telephoned his son, Ken, who could speak and read Arabic, and asked him if he could stop by the Association Research office when he returned to Washington.

Middleton felt it would be better to keep things in the family rather than involve a stranger. While he wished Ken's help, he also wished to divulge as little as possible, so he had simply said that he had become privy to some information and as a result had hired Ben Sorenson's daughter to do some political research regarding nonprofit associations.

Though Middleton had been worried about having to go into greater detail, he fortunately did not have to mention anything about bugging Pellegrino and her lover.

CHAPTER 22

Evans Residence
Foster City, California
Wednesday, January 12, 2011

I wonder what the hell we have this morning, Larry Evans thought as he noted the "Avon Calling" message appearing on his desktop screen. *Congress has just gotten back in session. I guess they had a crimp put in their style over the holidays and couldn't wait.*

Quickly as usual, Evans let his fingers do the walking across the keyboard and sat back while the computer chugged away translating the audio file to a text file.

"I think a little champagne to celebrate is in order."

"You know what champagne does to me."

"I know what I hope it will do to you."

"Have I ever told you that you're—"

"Hold the thought while I fill your glass. There, now a toast to the one who wasn't there."

Pause

"And will never be again."

"You know, Babbs, the beauty of it all is that nobody has a clue."

Laughter

"Not a friggin' clue. They all think the media did him in."

"Who do you think they'll choose now as Speaker?"

"Who gives a shit? There's no one in line who can help. And next year it'll be too late."

Pause

"Ready for more?"

"I think so."

"Good. You know, I think you have too many clothes on."

Because Evans wasn't interested in listening to the bed springs squeak, he rose from his seat and headed for the kitchen to make himself another cup of coffee. His presence wasn't needed for the computer to translate the audio to text. As he stood by the one-cup coffee maker watching the coffee fill his cup, he couldn't help wondering what the connection was between Pellegrino, Lowen, and the loss of an election by Congressman Nathan Grishom.

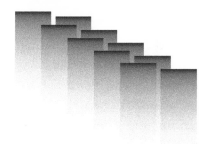

CHAPTER 23
The Amman Souk
El Balad, Amman, Jordan
Thursday, January 13, 2011

To most Jordanians, the downtown, or El Balad, was considered a commercial area where they wouldn't go unless necessary. But to most foreigners and some Jordanians, it was a place to walk, meet people and experience local food, cafés, shopping, music, and books in a traditional way, which is why Colonel Golden had scheduled the meeting there and not in the Swéfiéh area in the western part of the city, which would have been more convenient for him.

Golden wished he had worn a heavier jacket as he meandered through the souk this fifty-degree winter morning, but he had forgotten that Amman was one of the coldest of any major cities in the Mideast. *I should be thankful it's only drizzling. It could be snowing in the western part of town,* he thought as he pretended to look at the various goods on display in the shops.

As Golden neared the café where the meeting was to be held, he glanced at his watch and noticed he would be fashionably late, which was exactly what he had programmed himself to do. He was not about to throw caution to the wind. Professor Faros Rashid of the Applied Science University in the Shafa Badran suburb was to have suffered a fatal heart attack, and the colonel wanted a full team report before authorizing plan number two.

As Golden passed the café, he saw Mario and Joseph seated and involved in an animated discussion he hoped was only a charade. He assumed that because Ahmad wasn't with them, he was busy with the car somewhere.

Mario, Joseph, and Ahmad were actually three retired soldiers who had served their country for twenty-five years. Joseph, whose real name was Joseph Golan, had spent his time with the Israeli Defense Force and had learned Arabic naturally growing up in Israel, where Arabic was the second language. Mario Barrera, a Mexican-American, and Ahmad Rashid, a Christian Arab from Michigan, had spent their careers in the US Army. Ahmad had spent half his army career teaching Arabic at the Defense Language Institute in Monterrey, California, before ending his career in Special Forces. Mario, who also spent a good part of his career in Special Forces, had learned Arabic at the Defense Language Institute and had at one time been Ahmad's student.

After passing the café, Golden continued for a few more shops ostensibly viewing their wares before making his way back to the café.

"Good morning," said Golden in Arabic as he took a seat. "I hope you've had an interesting morning."

"I don't know about interesting," said Mario Barrera, "but it was certainly surprising."

"What happened?"

"The Jordanians beat us to him," said Joseph Golan solemnly.

"The Jordanians?" exclaimed Golden. "What the hell happened?"

"We started to go in," said Barrera, "but Joseph said he sensed something was wrong and thought we should wait. Damned good thing we did or we might not be here now."

Golden glanced at Joseph.

"I can sense them a kilometer away," said Joseph, answering the unasked question. "Just one of those things. What do we do now?"

Golden glanced at his watch and then at Mario and Joseph. Then after a momentary thought, he said, "Plan two."

"The journalist," said Joseph more as an affirmation than a question.

"Right," said Golden. "I have to go. You know the drill."

Ari was correct, thought Colonel Golden. *He did say ever since 1967, Jordan had changed, but it was probably the bombing of the three hotels here in Amman in November 2005 that was the icing on the cake. Al-Zarqawi from Zarqa, less than thirty kilometers from here, has obviously made our job a lot easier.*

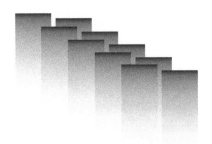

CHAPTER 24

Thai Roma Restaurant
237 Pennsylvania Avenue SE
Washington, DC
Friday, January 14, 2011

Because he had traveled to Tel Aviv in October, November, and December of the previous year, Jack Wharton hadn't seen Nate Grishom since before the election or his friend David Hawkins since the Friday after the election debacle. In Wharton's mind, Grishom was probably one of the greatest political thinkers of the century and was one of his favorite political friends because he knew Nate was one of the few honest ones.

When Grishom had first entered the political area, he had made a tactical decision to keep him on the straight and narrow. From the beginning, to keep him from succumbing to the charms of the many women on the Hill who would willingly open their legs as well as other temptations, his wife, Gerri, or Gigi as she was commonly known on the Hill, had become his chief of staff.

"We should do this more often," said Grishom, "particularly now that I have the time and don't have to keep looking over my shoulder."

"I'll drink to that," said Hawkins as he took a sip of his Cabernet.

"And I'll second the motion," responded Wharton.

"Nate, what will you do now that you're officially ex–Speaker of the House?" asked Hawkins.

"He's going to live on that generous pension they voted for themselves," answered Wharton with a chuckle.

Grishom smiled his usual boyish smile and sipped his martini. "Jack, my friend, now that I'm without portfolio, I'll join you on that soapbox of yours and say a few things that might surprise you. Mind you, you might need a second drink by the time I'm finished, or even a third."

"Then perhaps we should order first," said Hawkins. "I'm hungry."

"Now where was I?" asked Grishom after their orders were taken. "Oh, I was going to join Jack on his soapbox, but I think I'll beg off or we might be here all day. So instead, I'll just say I'm in complete agreement with all of Jack's rants and stipulate that our Congress is as corrupt as the Roman senate during the last days of the Republic. Unless the Tooth Fairy flies over Capitol Hill and waves her magic wand, nothing will ever change."

"Wow!" exclaimed Wharton. "Why haven't you said this before?"

Grishom chuckled. "Because we have a mutual friend who always walked around with a notebook or tape recorder. But also, I didn't think I needed to. I think you've always read between the lines."

"Nate, you haven't answered my question," Hawkins said.

"What am I going to do? Nothing, at least for a while. It's time to sip the wine and smell the flowers. That's why Gerri and I will take one of those round-the-world cruises and just relax and enjoy ourselves. No more having to think about which battles to fight. That's why I never got anywhere near congressional pension and benefit reform, which I knew three-quarters of the house would vote against. Remember, forgetting those on the other side of the aisle, there's only a handful of members on our side who are truly grassroots conservatives."

"Will you run again in 2012?" asked Hawkins.

"Dave," said Grishom, "for the record, I'll keep my options open."

"And off the record?"

"I doubt it very much because I think we'll lose the House next election."

"You're joking of course," responded an astonished Hawkins. "Granted, we lost seats in the last two elections, but—"

"I wish I were joking, my friend, but in the recesses of my mind, something isn't computing. Admittedly, it's just a feeling, but I had the same feeling before the last election."

"I think you lost that one because of voter fraud," said Wharton.

"Once again I agree with you."

"Then why didn't you challenge the results?" Hawkins asked. "How did you find out?"

"We had some people working on things. We took exit polling data and our internal polling data and ran the numbers. Going from six points up to six down was impossible. Of course, proving it in court was another story."

"Christ," said Wharton. "If we lose the House, that means the wicked witch of the west will probably become Speaker. It was bad enough losing you, but with her in the Speaker's chair, we could lose the country."

"Amen," said Hawkins.

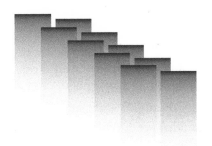

CHAPTER 25

Association Research
600 New Hampshire Avenue NW
Washington, DC
Monday, January 17, 2011

Taffy said just knock and she'd let me in, Ken Middleton thought as he knocked on the Association Research office door. Rather than making a cold call, Middleton had telephoned Taffy Lafayette and introduced himself. He had said that his father had probably already notified her about his dropping by to see if he could be of assistance.

"Hi. I'm Taffy," said the beautiful woman with jet-black hair and fine facial features after responding to his knock. "Mr. Middleton, I presume."

"In the flesh," said Middleton as he extended his hand. "I gather from Dad and my father-in-law that you've been experiencing a few problems."

"Father-in-law?"

"Yes. Larry Evans is my wife's father."

"Oh," said Taffy apologetically. "I'm afraid I didn't know about any family relationships."

"No problem. If you can show me what you've found, I'll take a quick peek. I'll probably be out of here before you know it."

"I'm afraid I wasn't the one who found the sites," said Taffy. "My associate Carol did. I'll let her show you what happened. Come into our computer haven and I'll introduce you."

"All right," said Middleton as he pulled up a chair alongside Carol Gardner. "Take me through the drill."

"I was following some linkage," said Carol as she tapped on her keyboard, "from Florida Atlantic University, and suddenly I got a different-looking page. I was unable to get out of the site or whatever."

"According to the screen shots Taffy brought with her during Christmas, it was an Arabic site, and you couldn't get out probably because you couldn't read the text. Why don't you show me what you did?"

"All right," said Carol once she had the university home page. "Here goes."

Slowly, with Middleton carefully watching, Carol retraced the steps that had taken her to the strange site. When the site in question appeared, Middleton studied it and asked Carol to slide her chair over so he could get a better read and be able to use her mouse. For several minutes, he read and scrolled from one screen to another. "Do you have something I can write on?"

"Is something wrong?" Carol asked.

The answer was no, but the tone of voice was not very convincing.

"Show me the next site."

Carol went through the drill. "This one is from a small university in Louisiana."

It was approaching eleven thirty when Middleton, after viewing the third site, leaned back in his chair and pondered the matter. Then, he made a call. "Damn," he said when his call went to voice mail.

"Have we done anything wrong?" asked Taffy, who had been observing with interest.

"No," answered Middleton, "you haven't done anything wrong, but something is just not computing." He checked his watch. "I told my wife I'd probably not be here long, and she's probably wondering what happened. I'm going back to my place for some lunch, but I'd like to return with my laptop. I could sit in your reception area or conference room and continue following all the links I came across and let Carol get on with her work."

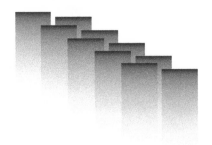

CHAPTER 26

Terrace Restaurant
610 New Hampshire Avenue NW
Washington, DC
Monday, January 17, 2011

"This is a lovely change of plans," said Nancy Middleton as she scooted into the booth. "I was expecting you home instead of an invitation for lunch. Your morning seems to have run longer than anticipated. You obviously either ran into some problem or were dazzled by two females. Were they good looking?"

"They were indeed two very good-looking women," said Middleton with a chuckle. "I was dazzled also, but not by them. Seems Taffy Lafayette and her friend Carol Gardner somehow managed to enter the backdoors of three and still counting Arabic websites I think are involved in fundraising for terrorist activities."

"You're joking."

"I wish I were. I tried to call Brad about it, but my calls kept going to his voice mail."

"So that's why you asked me to bring your laptop when you called?"

"Yeah. After lunch, I'll go back to their office. I'd like to network my laptop with their computers and hope I can do some surfing."

"Somehow, I don't think you mean surfing for anything Arabic."

"No," said Ken with an air of resignation. "I think this terror thing the women have run into is only part of the picture, particularly with Dad having said that Taffy and her friend were doing some political research for him. I let it go then. Now, I can't help but wonder."

"And I guess if your father is involved in political research, so is mine."

"And Uncle Harry no doubt."

"Be very careful. These two young women just might be a lot smarter than you think."

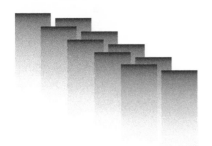

CHAPTER 27
Association Research
600 New Hampshire Avenue NW
Washington, DC
Monday, January 17, 2011

"Taffy," Middleton said after returning from lunch, "would you mind joining me in the conference room? I want to set up my laptop to run on your network. I hope you don't mind."

A hesitant and torn Taffy stood silently for a moment wondering what she should do. Uncle Mike had been concerned about secrecy, but Ken was his son.

Middleton, thinking that Taffy was worried that she or Carol had done something wrong, felt compelled to tell her that they had stumbled through the backdoor of terrorist websites.

"You and Carol have done nothing wrong, but there are some things that concern me. Actually, several. I think you and Carol have inadvertently entered three Islamic jihad websites. I'm not familiar with these three sites, which is why I tried to call a colleague this morning, but when I followed one of the links, I was led to one called the Holy Land Society, which I'm familiar with."

"Who or what is the Holy Land Society?" asked Taffy.

"It was involved in the largest terrorism-financing prosecution since the beginning of our war on terrorism. Last November, at least half a dozen members of this organization were convicted of funneling money to terrorist organizations in the Middle East. Many more people probably should have been prosecuted but weren't for reasons about which I can only speculate."

"Oh my God!"

"If you'll allow me into your network, I'll sit here quietly without interfering with you or Carol and follow all the available links in connection with these sites."

"Shouldn't that be a job for the FBI?"

"They may well be working on it already, but then again, they may not. I'd like to go as far as I can go and then pass whatever I learn to a colleague far more versed in this than I am."

"You won't be doing anything illegal, will you? I told your father in the very beginning that I wouldn't do anything illegal."

"Nothing illegal, I promise."

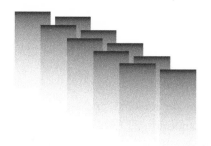

CHAPTER 28

Middleton Family Condominium
Watergate West
2700 Virginia Avenue NW
Washington, DC
Monday, January 17, 2011

It was supposed to be a quiet evening get-together. As Nancy Middleton had said, because Candy probably had had a tough day saving the country while she pined for Brad, any discussion of Taffy, Carol, and Ken's day at Association Research could wait until Brad returned.

However, somewhere during the second round of cocktails, Candy Reason had asked if Ken Middleton had spoken to Brad. She said she had tried calling him several times but each attempt had gone into voice mail.

"Do you know Taffy Lafayette?" asked Ken Middleton.

"Goodness, yes," responded Candy. "We've had dinner together several times, that is, she and her friend Carol. We all even went to a dinner at the White House together."

Nancy and Ken looked at each other in disbelief.

"But that was before I met Brad," Candy said. "I suppose I should invite them again. It's been so long. Why do you ask?"

Ken told Candy the story of the day. "And that's it, at least on the surface. Knowing our respective parents, I think there's a little bit more to the story."

Candy nodded. "Yes. Behind the obvious is usually the rest of the story."

"Particularly when it comes to politics," Nancy said. "If one's involved, so are the others."

"I'm surprised you were able to network with their computers," said Candy.

"She was reluctant to let me do that at first. That's when I had to tell her about my discoveries in more detail. But she relented, and I continued my searching while doing the occasional snooping. I didn't come across any smoking gun, but a few tidbits that in conjunction with what Dad had said when he asked for my help told me there was more to the story."

"What do we do now?"

"Nothing at the moment," Ken said. "Let's wait until Brad gets back, but even then, I don't think there's anything we can do."

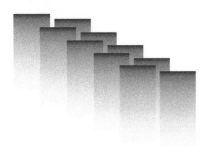

CHAPTER 29

Abbe Research Associates
4 Yehezkel Kaufmann
Tel Aviv, Israel
Tuesday, January 18, 2011

Brad Jenkins was upset with himself this morning because of his stupidity the previous day, and that stupidity had been the reason he'd had a restless night and had gotten into the office very early.

The previous day, he had walked around without realizing he did not have a working cell phone because he had foolishly let the battery run down. He had also left his iPad in his hotel room when he and Paul Bernstein went to Jerusalem to meet with General Ari Ben Gul.

En route to the office this morning, Jenkins had stopped at the small shop next door to Abbe Research for a salt bagel with cream cheese and a large cappuccino. At his office, he fired up his iPad to see what he had missed the day before while he ate his breakfast. Two e-mails were from his wife; one read that she had tried to call him, but her call had gone into voice mail. The other advised him she was going to dinner with Nancy and Ken Middleton. Relieved that her messages were not life-threatening, he then opened the message he had received from Ken. He had just finished reading it and the attachments when Mykro Lehner entered the office.

"Good morning, Dr. Jenkins," said Mykro. "I didn't expect to see anyone here this early."

"Couldn't sleep. Do you always come to work so early?"

"Usually. There isn't much for me to do except work."

If he had a good woman in his life, he wouldn't come in so early, thought Jenkins. But he thought Mykro was lucky to have a life here instead of behind bars. When he had made the request of the president for a couple of the nation's top hackers, he had gotten Mykro and David Perlinger, two Caltech students who needed only to complete their dissertations to get doctorates. They had been sentenced to five years in jail for hacking into the Federal Reserve and other government institutions.

Soon after Mykro and David appeared on the scene, General Gul had given them Sharon, another computer genius, whom he thought was still part of Israeli intelligence. Sharon had arrived on the scene the previous October. She and David had become an item, and in December, they had wed.

"Myk, I'll forward you an e-mail I received from Mr. Middleton along with several attachments. I think everything is self-explanatory. I'd appreciate it if you all would do some investigating."

CHAPTER 30

Candice Reason's Condominium
Watergate South
700 New Hampshire Avenue NW
Washington, DC
Saturday, January 22, 2011

The evening's combination of business and socializing would have included the Whartons, but they were unable to come to dinner this evening because of a prior commitment. Within moments of relaxing to enjoy their before-dinner drinks and nibble on the hors d'oeuvres, Ken told Brad about his father's request and his experiences at Association Research.

"I think there's more to their involvement than meets the eye."

"Ken," said a perplexed Jenkins, "what are you talking about?"

"You don't really know our fathers," said Candy.

"Then perhaps a little education might be in order."

"Brad," said Ken, "my father and Candy's father are clones when it comes to politics. Nancy's father and another man by the name of Royce Bartlett are their enablers. In their old company back in Vietnam, which you heard them refer to during Thanksgiving week as Charlie Communications, Larry and Royce were the two platoon leaders. Granted, all Dad said when he asked for my help was that he had become privy to some information and as a result had hired the daughter of one of his friends and associates to do some political research regarding nonprofit associations.

"At the time, I let it go because I didn't think it was a big deal, but I should have seen the first red flag when he used the words *political research*. Then after following the links to the Arabic sites, I got curious and started thinking. That's why I returned to Taffy's office with my laptop and got her permission to log onto her network. Though I didn't learn a hell of a lot, I discovered enough smoke and started looking for the fire."

"I guess the two of you are in concurrence," said a surprised Jenkins addressing his wife and Nancy Middleton and noticing their facial expressions.

"I'm afraid so," said Candy sighing.

"Well," said Jenkins dismissively, "there's nothing we can do about it at the moment, so let me tell you some of what's been learned since Ken's e-mail. When I got the e-mail, I immediately put Mykro, Sharon, and David to work on it. Mykro says he'll have a detailed report as soon as possible, but there was so much to follow that I could get only some preliminary readings before I left. There were many threads to follow, as you well know, Ken, and according to the folks, every step led to more steps, but the highlights are as follows. First, I'm glad you did, as you said to Taffy, not do anything illegal and attempt to probe further in connection with the Holy Land Society. The last thing we need to do is open a Pandora's box at home even with the president's blessing.

"One thread led to a series of mosques in England. The one in London is particularly interesting. The cleric there is known to praise public beheadings and has preached that Islam's enemies are permitted to be decapitated. Apparently, there's been talk of expelling him for his extremist views and his alleged links to Al Qaeda, but so far, it's only been talk."

"Maybe Colonel Golden's surgeons should expand the scope of their operations," said Ken with a chuckle.

"That might be biting off a bit more than we can chew in more ways than one," replied Jenkins. "But who knows what the future might bring in this upside-down world we're living in."

"I'll drink to that," Ken said.

"Another thread led down several paths," Brad said. "This one raised Paul's antenna. It had to do with the penetration of Western financial markets and strategic industries. The reason it got Paul's attention is because it ties in with what he and I had been researching before I met Candy."

Candy, perplexed, gave Brad an inquiring look.

"Paul and I were doing research on a book we were going to title *The Enemy Within*," said Jenkins in answer to the unspoken question. "It was to be about the jihadist plot to destroy American society from within, which started in the seventies."

"Are you serious?" asked Candy. "You never said anything."

"I apologize for that, sweetie, but our time together has been on a fast track since we met."

Candy smiled and nodded.

"Ken, remember when I was on my book tour and we were all at your father's?"

"God, now I remember," Ken said. "You said the Saudis and the Iranians were financing the cultural decay of our country just as the Russians did through the Castro regime in the sixties. You made no bones about this being a purposeful act of war."

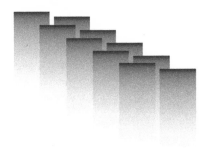

CHAPTER 31
Association Research
600 New Hampshire Avenue NW
Washington, DC
Monday, January 24, 2011

"Taffy," Ken Middleton said, "I'd like you to meet a colleague, Dr. Bradford Jenkins. Brad, Taffy Lafayette."

"Good morning, Taffy," said Jenkins. "I've been hearing some interesting things about you and your associate."

"Goodness," said Taffy, flashing a devilish smile. "I hope they were only good things."

"Brad is the colleague I wanted to speak with when I was here last week," Middleton said.

"I spent a day with a dead phone," said Jenkins. "I forgot to keep the battery charged, and I left my iPad in my hotel room when another colleague of mine and I went to Jerusalem."

"Jerusalem!" exclaimed Taffy.

"Yes. I had some business to attend to last week. Had I been here in the States when Mr. Middleton tried to get in touch, I might have been able to answer some of his questions."

"He still hasn't been able to answer them," added Middleton.

"When I received Mr. Middleton's e-mail," Jenkins said, "I passed the information to another colleague, and apparently, things are more complicated than we thought because I haven't yet received a report. So this visit this morning is just a social visit for all practical purposes. I hope you're not too disappointed."

"To be honest, Dr. Jenkins, when Mr. Middleton telephoned this morning, I naturally thought the colleague he was bringing would have some information to satisfy my curiosity. But I do understand."

"Thank you," said Jenkins. "Now for the real reason I'm here this morning. I gather you know my wife."

"Wife?" asked a perplexed Taffy.

"Dr. Reason. Candy Reason."

"Oh my God! Of course I know her! But I haven't seen her for some time."

"I think I'm probably the reason why you haven't heard from her for several months," said Jenkins with a chuckle.

"Dr. Reason and Dr. Jenkins just met last August," Middleton said.

"I think I understand," said Taffy with a laugh.

"To make amends," continued Jenkins, "if you and your friend Carol are free this coming Saturday, Candy and I would like to invite the two of you to dinner. Say sevenish?"

CHAPTER 32
Four Seasons Hotel
2800 Pennsylvania Avenue NW
Washington, DC
Sunday, January 30, 2011

The Sunday brunch at the Bourbon Steak restaurant seemed to have started early as the two couples sat in a booth and reflected on the previous evening. It had been a very well-orchestrated evening that had let Taffy and Carol know Brad and Ken were doing some consulting for the president though they hadn't said too much about that.

"I must confess," said Nancy, "I was quite impressed. When I think of all the Globaltronix activities I went to growing up, I was surprised I'd never met Taffy before."

Ken chuckled. "You're thirteen years older. That would be a pretty good reason, wouldn't it?" His question was followed by a playful elbow to the ribs.

"Changing the subject," Candy said, "what's the next step in this little drama of ours?"

"How about we sublet some of their office space?" Ken asked. "They don't use even half of it, just that one room."

"I think you're just looking for a way to keep tabs on them," said Nancy. "You're still looking for that smoking gun."

"I know you're suspicious of your fathers," said Brad, "but they do have another office, a conference room, and a reception area that's not being used."

"Wouldn't subletting, if it were possible, be a little dicey?" Candy asked. "Remember, Abraham is supposed to be a secret."

"They could become part of Abe," Ken said facetiously. "Join Sharon, David, and Mykro."

"I think you just want access to that database they developed," Brad said.

"That would be helpful."

"Right." Nancy's tone of voice said she wasn't buying any of it.

"Let's put any thoughts of the girls getting involved with Abe on the back burner," Brad said. "We have enough on our plate as it is without having problems with Uncle Mike. Besides, even if we wanted them, there would probably be a problem luring them away."

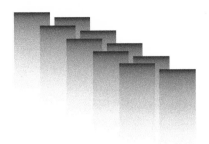

CHAPTER 33

Association Research
600 New Hampshire Avenue NW
Washington, DC
Wednesday, February 2, 2011

Taffy Lafayette was floored. "Unbelievable," she said after reading the report from Mykro Lehner that had been delivered to the Israeli embassy by diplomatic courier for Brad Jenkins to pick up. "How did you get this information?" she asked. "Are you sure whoever got this information didn't do something illegal? I told Uncle Mike that I wouldn't be party to any illegal activities."

"Taffy," Brad said, "if anything illegal was done, it wasn't done in this country, so there's nothing to worry about. If my colleague did resort to some extraneous efforts, I can assure you he will be well protected and his efforts will never be made known anywhere."

"What will you do with this? What do I tell your father, Ken? He'll ask how I got this info."

"While I think Ken's father is entitled to some sort of explanation," Jenkins said, "I'd prefer to wait until I can show this to the president."

"We debated whether to show this to you," said Ken, "but we finally decided you and Carol should know you've been victimized. Why don't you ask her to come on in so we can show her."

"Have you ever received any official looking e-mail?" Ken asked Carol once she had taken a seat at the conference room table. "Say, something that looked like it might have been from your bank yet just before you clicked on the button you were supposed to click, you became suspicious?"

Carol looked at Taffy and back at Middleton. "Yes, I suppose so."

"It was a variation of that theme you fell prey to and why I had trouble putting the pieces together."

"I'm afraid you're confusing me, Mr. Middleton," Carol said.

"The sites you had logged onto were fraudulent sites," Brad said. "They weren't the real university sites. They were imitations. The only difference between the real sites and the fake sites were periods between some words."

"Don't blame yourself," Ken said as he noticed Carol was distraught. "I fell for it too."

"Before we leave," Brad said, "I want to reiterate that you've done nothing wrong, nor will there be any fallout from this. I'll have Candy make arrangements for me to meet with President Branch. With all this information, I have no choice."

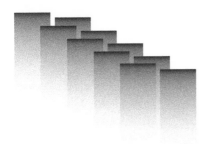

CHAPTER 34

The White House
1600 Pennsylvania Avenue NW
Washington, DC
Saturday, February 5, 2011

President Branch did his best thinking the first half hour after he had started his day in the Oval Office and that half hour while enjoying a brandy before retiring for the night as he was doing.

Until this morning, he hadn't seen or spoken to Dr. Jenkins since that Saturday morning the previous year when he had asked the man if he was willing to play God. As per the plan, Candy Reason had been the go-between for him and Jenkins. Jenkins's little organization had remained secret, but now, its work in the shadows of the war on terror ran the risk of being exposed.

"Thank you, Mr. President, for agreeing to this meeting," Brad Jenkins said. "I realize Abraham is supposed to be a secret nongovernmental organization, but under the circumstances, I felt compelled to request this meeting."

"I understand," said the president. "The information in the report Dr. Reason gave me yesterday is way beyond the scope of Abraham, or Abe, as I gather you call it. The problem is how I handle the situation. We have this very expensive agency called the CIA, and not once has its director even hinted about anything in this report. We also have another very expensive agency called the FBI, and they seem to have been equally deficient. Yet your small group with only a fraction of these agencies' resources comes up with something like this in record time."

"Perhaps they already have the same information but for some reason haven't shared it."

"That makes it even worse, Dr. Jenkins. I'm supposed to get a security briefing every Monday, and I've yet to be advised of any linkage between Islamists and nonprofit organizations as well as the fraudulent solicitation of funds being used to construct mosques and subvert American businesses. Also, this five-step World Underground Movement Plan of the Muslim Brotherhood really made for some chilly reading. I find it incredible that our very expensive intelligence services haven't seen fit to brief me on that one assuming they knew about it in the first place."

Amazing. Two young women Mike Middleton hired with my blessing think they're accessing a university website and inadvertently enter a backdoor to terror, the president thought. *Perhaps I should have said no to Mike back in September last year, but I didn't. Now I'll have to confront the CIA and the FBI directors, and they'll want to know how I obtained the information. And the Brits will also have to be notified because some of what Jenkins's people found pertains to them. And of course they too will ask questions, and the problem with questions is that one always leads to another.*

As he drained his brandy, President Branch realized there was only one thing to do: confront the issue head-on. He would speak with Harry Reason Monday morning after the cabinet meeting.

CHAPTER 35

Middleton Estate
Big Basin Way
Boulder Creek, California
Friday, February 12, 2011

The scene in Mike Middleton's study was not very pleasant.

"I'm not mad, Harry," he said vehemently. "I'm pissed, royally pissed. We spend all the fucking time and money on this Association Research business and now George wants to punt."

"Mike, he doesn't want to punt," Harry Reason said. "With an election year coming up, he wants to get ahead of the curve. He's nervous in the service and doesn't want to get caught with his pants down. You know there's only a handful of people in Washington he really trusts."

"Harry, that's BS and you know it. Everything he's told you is BS to justify a decision he'd already made. You know, I knew the kids were up to something. I could tell the way my nose itched that evening last November during our Thanksgiving week. We've worked our asses off to find the right man for your daughter, and the next thing we know, they're running some kind of terror consultancy and George wants to give them the farm."

"Mike, calm down. All we know is that George wanted Brad to do some consulting work regarding the Middle East and Brad put together a small group of his friends to do so. The kids still don't know anything about l'affaire Pellegrino. The government personnel information I was getting from Al Garcia and passing to Larry and his passing it to Taffy will continue with the exception that Brad will now be the recipient instead of Larry. Other than that, nothing really changes except the location. The girls can still conduct their research like they're doing now, but they'll just be doing it offshore."

"What do you mean offshore?"

"George thought Israel would be a good place to start."

CHAPTER 36

Association Research
600 New Hampshire Avenue NW
Washington, DC
Monday, February 14, 2011

"All we have to do now is convince two young women to move to Israel," Jenkins said to Ken Middleton and Jack Wharton, who were at the conference room table.

With Taffy's acquiescence, they had been using the Association Research conference room as a meeting place since the morning of February 2, when she and Carol had learned how they had been deceived by a fraudulent website. This morning, they had been in the conference room since eight thirty, a half hour earlier than usual. For the past hour, they had been discussing how to handle Taffy and Carol. Of paramount concern at the moment was not divulging too much about Abe.

"I guess it's time to call the women in," said Middleton. "Let's all cross our fingers."

"Taffy," said Jenkins after she and Carol had sat, "the wheels of progress sometimes spin slowly, but the president has received the report and has given it careful study and consequently has made some suggestions. Because of the terror aspect and with election time on the horizon, the president has decided he would prefer the two of you work with us, not Ken's father."

"I don't understand," said Taffy. "We're not doing anything wrong. We have nothing to do with this terror business, and 2012 is ten months from now. I don't see how there could be any conflict between what Carol and I are doing and next year's election."

"If I might interject," said Wharton, "there's long been a saying in this town about it being easier to resurrect the dead than to keep a secret. That's why we must assume all the walls and ceilings around you have eyes and ears."

"I think the president is concerned rightly or wrongly that he might wake up one morning and read about what you're doing," Middleton said.

"But we haven't told anyone about what we're doing!" exclaimed Taffy.

"If you've paid any fees to access any information at any time in your work," said Jenkins, "you've left a trail, particularly if you used a credit card."

"Oh my God," Carol said.

"But we still haven't done anything wrong," Taffy said. "As I told your father, Ken, I would not break any laws, and we haven't."

"I'm sure you haven't, Taffy," said Wharton, "but that's not the way it works in this town, particularly for people on our side of the fence. The media always have a narrative, and their reporting is always from that perspective. Because the public is woefully ignorant, no matter how scrupulous you may have been to not do anything illegal, if even a hint of your activities is discovered, I can assure you that the media will distort it in their zeal to injure the president."

"I think we're going off on a tangent," Middleton said. "While everything Jack has said may be true, the bottom line is the president has made a request everyone's obligated to honor. Other than that, nothing's changed."

"So from now on, I guess we just have different supervisors," said Taffy. "Same family, different faces. It's not as though we're changing employers."

"I'm afraid there will be some other changes," said Jenkins. "For security reasons, the president has suggested that you be offshore."

"Offshore?" Carol asked.

"Offshore where?" Taffy asked.

"Tel Aviv," said Jenkins.

"Tel Aviv!" exclaimed Taffy.

"Israel?" asked Carol.

"I'd like you to work with certain people," said Jenkins.

"The people who got the information in that report?"

"Yes."

"I told you I don't want to do anything illegal."

"Taffy, once you're at our office in Tel Aviv, you can continue to do exactly as you've been doing here, and I can assure you you'll have nothing to worry about even if you accidentally do something wrong. If that should ever happen, I can assure you that there would be unimaginable forces available to protect you."

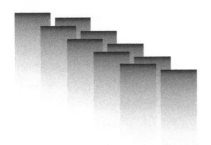

CHAPTER 37

Market Café
Nahalat Binyamin 6
Tel Aviv, Israel
Friday, April 8, 2011

"I just love the arts and crafts here, Taff," said Carol. "It's fun looking around all the stalls. I can't believe we ended up in such a nice city."

Carol and Taffy were enjoying a late lunch at a small café on the pedestrian walkway that was always jam-packed with street stalls on Tuesdays and Fridays and where just about everything imaginable was for sale.

"This is such an enjoyable way to spend a Friday afternoon," Carol said.

"I can't believe we ended up in Israel," Taffy said. "Even after almost two months, I'm still having trouble wrapping myself around what we've done. I feel like I'm living in a James Bond movie. I'm also having a problem grappling with the work week starting on Sunday and ending on Thursday."

Carol laughed in agreement.

When Jenkins had suggested they think things over, Taffy and Carol had immediately wondered how they could just up and leave for another country and start all over again, but Jenkins and his associates had ready answers.

There were no telephones to worry about because they each had smartphones that would allow them to be reached anywhere in the world; they never used the landlines installed for their apartments, and the landline at the office was there only for the DSL. The problem with mail was as easily taken care of. All they needed to do was file a change of address with the new address being the office address of Association Research. Any important mail could be brought to Tel Aviv the same way Jenkins had sent things—via diplomatic courier.

Their rent and utility bills would be paid as they always had via the Internet. So all in all, what had seemed like insurmountable problems had been figments of their imaginations. All they needed to do was pack, lock their doors, and leave. The Associated Research office was now being used by Jenkins and his associates.

Almost three weeks later, Taffy and Carol were flying first class with Dr. Jenkins and Mr. Middleton from Washington Dulles on a late Saturday afternoon flight to Paris, where they changed planes for Tel Aviv.

Upon their arrival at Ben Gurion Airport, they were met by Dr. Paul Bernstein and his wife, Miriam, and were taken to the InterContinental David Tel Aviv. Because it had been four fifteen in the afternoon Israeli time when they had arrived but nine-fifteen in the morning according to their body clocks, Dr. Bernstein and his wife had suggested they get a bite to eat after checking in and go to bed to catch up with themselves.

Monday morning, the day after their arrival, instead of being greeted by Dr. and Mrs. Bernstein, Taffy and Carol were greeted by Mykro Lehner. He was a tall, slender man with dark hair and boyish features who wore dark-framed glasses. He was the quintessential boy next door who became their chaperone and tour guide for the next several days.

Upon their arrival at the office of Abbe Research Associates, Taffy and Carol had been introduced to David and Sharon Perlinger. After being introduced and shown around the office, Dr. Jenkins had suggested that Mykro, David, and Sharon take a few days and show them around Tel Aviv and Israel itself.

The rest of Monday had been a walking sightseeing adventure in Tel Aviv that to Taffy's and Carol's surprise was quite a modern city with streets teeming with lively sidewalk cafés, elegant restaurants, shops, and simple kiosks.

The following day, everyone had driven north along the Mediterranean to Haifa, stopping en route at the old Roman city of Caesarea. After spending a night in Haifa, they made their way to Nazareth, Tiberius, and

Jerusalem, where they spent Thursday night before returning to Tel Aviv late Friday afternoon before the Sabbath commenced.

"Yes," Carol said, "now that you mention it, there has been a James Bond atmosphere. Almost every time except when anyone speaks to us, a language other than English is spoken. I would still like to know what everyone does."

"I think Mykro is a hacker," said Taffy with a chuckle. "I asked him once what kind of work he was doing, and all he said was doing research similar to what we're doing. I asked him if Sharon and David were doing the same thing, and he smiled and said David was but Sharon was a spy."

"A spy?"

"Yes. He said she's a sabra with Israeli intelligence."

"A sabra? What's that?"

"A native-born Israeli. She's first-generation Israeli because her parents came from Romania. Apparently, she grew up on a kibbutz in northern Israel."

"She may not be a spy, but she is extremely attractive. I can see why David fell for her in a heartbeat. I wonder where the two of them will ultimately live."

"So do I," said Taffy. "I remember him saying that Israel can be a difficult place to live because it's surrounded by enemies and that's why military service is compulsory for men and women. After she finished high school, she served two years in the army."

"I guess we were lucky. I can't begin to imagine spending two years in the army."

"Right. I think we've had other things to worry about in our lives."

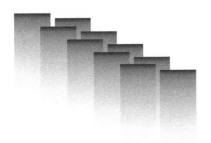

CHAPTER 38

Hertsel Street
Tel Aviv, Israel
Monday, May 9, 2011

Stan Portman did not realize that his life would change forever today. He knew only that Israel was the last place in the world he thought he would ever find himself, but thanks to his publisher, Mel Cohen, he would be here for the next three weeks.

"Why Israel?" he had asked when the suggestion was made.

"Stanley," said his publisher, "I think they're doing something right over there. The Israeli government made a decision several years ago to invest in its people, and today, it's paying off."

Mel's enthusiasm didn't surprise Portman because Mel was Jewish and recently had friends who had just returned from a visit to the country.

"It made a calculated choice to make science and innovation the cornerstone of its economy," Mel said. "The country has no natural resources yet it's spawned several world-class, high-tech companies."

"Is suicide bombing considered a high-tech business?"

"You and your irreverent sense of humor."

"Just thought I'd ask. How about rocket launching?"

"All right, this is not an audition for the comedy hour. You'll probably be spending most of your time in Tel Aviv, and that's probably safer than Baltimore."

"Oh, that really makes me feel comfortable."

"Look, Stanley, the country is brimming with opportunity. Not too many newsletter writers are writing about Israeli companies, so you'll have a golden opportunity."

"How long do you think I'll need to become a target of opportunity?"

"A couple of weeks probably, but I'd plan on being there three. Since you'll be in the Holy Land, it might be a good idea to do some sightseeing. Maybe you'll get a little religion."

"Maybe I'll become a good target too."

"Go," said Cohen shaking his head while trying to hide a smile. "Do not pass go and do not collect two hundred dollars."

After being dismissed, Portman had stood at attention, saluted, and said good-bye while wondering how he could avoid becoming a target of opportunity.

He spent the next several days at his computer checking out a host of Israeli high-tech and medical diagnostics companies. To his amazement, he had discovered that after the United States, Israel had the greatest number of companies listed on the stock exchanges.

After his business research, as per Mel's suggestion, Portman checked out Israel's Weizmann Institute of Science and had been impressed with the way scientists and others were recruited based on their talents and interest in innovation.

Last, he researched what he personally would need to know in an unknown land while he played the part of a tourist disguised as a financial analyst who had been sent to Israel to analyze six Israeli tech companies. To his surprise, though Israel had once been a British mandate, they nonetheless drove left-hand-drive cars on the right side of the road as in the States, so driving would be no problem. When he checked out the food situation, he discovered he wouldn't go hungry but he would have to forgo bacon and sausage at breakfast. He would also have to forgo coffee the way he liked it, but at least he could drink cappuccino, so all was not lost.

Two weeks after the conclusion of his research, Portman took a late Saturday afternoon commuter flight to Newark, and after a three-and-a-half hour layover, he boarded United Flight 90 for Tel Aviv. Ten hours and thirty-five minutes later, he arrived at Ben Gurion Airport at 4:20 p.m. Sunday, the next day.

After passport control, baggage claim, and customs, it was after six in the evening local time though his old body clock was telling him it was eleven in the morning, close enough to lunch time back home and dinner time where he was. So after he checked in, he went to the dining room.

After two glasses of wine and what turned out to be a snack, he called it a night.

Surprisingly, this morning, even though he woke up earlier than he would have liked, he felt bright-eyed and bushy tailed after taking a shower and getting ready for his appointment. However, his appointment at Brant Pharmaceuticals on 4 Yehezkel Kaufmann, which was not too far away, was not until ten o'clock, which meant he had almost four hours to kill.

He decided that after being stuffed with food on his flight and then venturing to the dining room the night before, the thought of facing a large buffet—an extravagant buffet as the hotel literature called it—wasn't appealing. He wanted to wander around.

After making sure he had his iPad and other important things in his attaché case, he dusted off his attitude, checked himself in the mirror to make sure there was no bull's-eye on his back, said a silent prayer that all suicide bombers were sleeping that morning, and left his room.

He made his way across the street that fed into a roundabout to his left as he exited the hotel and began walking up Ha Carmel Street. *Mel said that Israel had an aggressive workforce, and it sure looks like all Israelis have two cars and are driving them aggressively to work.*

Portman passed a large park across the street; a big, red Coca-Cola truck being unloaded; a series of small shops, one of which had a sign in English above its door that read Change; and a bookstore. To the left of the bookstore was another shop with two roll-down shutter doors decorated with graffiti. *I guess someone wanted me to feel at home.*

The street soon turned into close-quarter combat. Stall after stall with large awnings to protect the wares from the sun were selling everything imaginable. Portman thought that everyone must have gotten up early this morning to shop.

After escaping from the human sardine can, Portman came to Allenby Street. He turned right and saw his first café. *Ahh, a chair. I can watch the world go by while I have a cappuccino.*

"You're an American, aren't you?" said the waiter in perfect English with a New York accent after Portman ordered his cappuccino.

"Is it still there?" he asked the waiter.

"Is what still there?"

"The label on my back that says made in the USA."

"I don't see any label," said the waiter as he cast a surreptitious look and then realized the bit of morning humor. "You're funny."

"No, I'm from Baltimore."

"I used to live in New York. My brother still does. You know, the Big Apple."

"And even bigger taxes."

After two cappuccinos, a large pastry, and a blintz, it was time to march on. Portman continued down Allenby Street for a way and made a right turn on a street he had assumed, because of his map, would take him back to the area of his hotel. He quickly ran into a problem.

Maps are wonderful tools, thought Portman as he walked along in frustration because the street signs were in Hebrew only. *People always have a way of changing the damn ground conditions.*

One road was closed because of construction and another due to road work. That led to turn after turn, and Portman soon realized he was lost. Frustrated, he glanced at his watch and realized that he would need to take a taxi, but as usual, taxis, like waiters and waitresses, were never available when you wanted them. He saw a woman standing on the corner waiting for the traffic light. She had long, light, sandy-colored hair he thought was quite in contrast to his brief Israeli experience because all the women he had seen so far had had black hair.

"Excuse me, miss …"

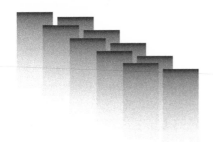

CHAPTER 39

Market Café
Nahalat Binyamin 6
Tel Aviv, Israel
Saturday, May 28, 2011

Taffy Lafayette had had no plans to fall in love with the boy next door who wore dark-framed glasses, but as the days passed without Carol in her social life because of a young man from Baltimore she had met, Taffy had found herself spending more and more time with him, and the inevitable happened.

Mykro, like her, had also grown up in California, and that became the foundation of their relationship. Like his friend David, who had also went to Caltech, he was a genius who seemed to absorb knowledge like a sponge.

The day had been idyllic. She and Mykro spent the latter part of the morning and the early afternoon on the beach, which was less crowded than usual because of the Sabbath. After a late lunch at a small café near the beach, they returned to Mykro's condo to shower and dress for an afternoon of meandering around the city enjoying the parks and any shops that were open. As the day of the Sabbath was drawing to a close, they found a place for dinner.

"It's been such a nice day," said Taffy. "So peaceful, so enjoyable."

"Remember what I told you," said Mykro jokingly.

"Yes," replied Taffy.

Mykro had said that peacefulness in this part of the world could be deceiving. This Saturday evening, the streets were still quiet, but the quietness wouldn't last. As darkness fell, Tel Aviv would become a city of raucous nightlife.

"Will there ever be peace in this part of the world?" asked Taffy after a moment's reflection.

"I doubt it," answered Mykro. "There's been talk about the so-called peace process for as long as I can remember, but peace will never be accomplished in this part of the world unless Islam is either defeated or it accepts the actual Arabic word for the kind of peace we want."

"I'm not sure I know what you mean, Myk."

"There are three Arabic words that translate as 'peace' in English: *salaam, hudna,* and *suhl,* but *suhl* must be used in any agreement. It's the only Arabic word that can be used that would be legally binding for the Arabs even if other parties to the agreement aren't. I doubt this will ever happen because from day one, there has been Arab resistance to the use of the word. *Salaam* has been the word usually insisted on, but the use of that word would give the Arabs a way to renege because there can be no *salaam*, peace, between Muslims and infidels unless the infidels submit to the rule of the Muslims."

"How do you know all this, Myk? What you've said sounds perfectly dreadful."

"Dr. Jenkins grew up in this part of the world. I've read his books."

"Why isn't what you've just said mentioned in the media back home? I've never read or heard anything about there being three different Arabic words for peace."

"Probably because the liberal media and the politicians have bought into the propaganda of the Palestinians, Arabs, and Islamists. They also probably don't have the first clue about the language. The popular conception is that the Palestinians want their own country, but I have a problem with that because there are no Palestinians. The word *Palestinians* is a modern invention. Before 1967, Gaza was owned by Egypt, and the West Bank was owned by Jordan. Something else that's ignored by our liberal media is how Jews and Christians here live, work, and play together amicably usually without serious incident."

"I hope that amicable relationship continues as long as we're here."

"I don't think you have anything to worry about, Taff. Tel Aviv is probably the safest city in the country. The only rocket attacks the city has experienced have been via TV."

"I hope so," said Taffy just before the lights went out.

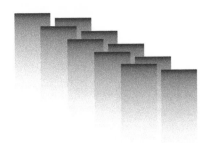

CHAPTER 40
Carol Gardner's Apartment
Gruzenberg 8
Tel Aviv, Israel
Saturday, May 28, 2011

As Carol lay in the embrace of Stan Portman, she was the happiest woman in the world, but the day had started with her being in the depths of despair. She had fallen in love with a man again, a young man her age with an irreverent sense of humor that masked an immeasurable financial intelligence, and once again, the man in her life was about to leave her. Though Stan said he would write and they would see each other again, she knew better. Three-week stands were little better than one-night stands.

It was 9:00 a.m. when Carol and Stan made their way to the lobby of Carol's apartment building to await the taxi that would take him to the airport for his eleven forty-five flight. When the taxi came, they kissed good-bye. Stan got in the cab saying once again that he would keep in touch.

After Stan's good-bye, Carol stood on the sidewalk and watched until the taxi disappeared from sight. Instead of returning to an empty apartment, she decided to walk. It was the only remedy she knew on this Sabbath day to remove the sickness she felt inside.

It was mid-afternoon when Carol finally got a grip on her emotions and decided to return to her apartment. For almost five hours, she had walked and walked wondering if she had been a fool or what would happen if she were to return to Washington. But as quickly as she thought of returning to Washington, she dismissed the thought because she feared the worst: rejection.

Carol lay once again in the arms of the young man who three weeks earlier had asked her for directions. Because he was going to the same commercial complex where her office was, she had suggested he walk with her.

That day of their meeting, Carol had waited for him after work like a nineteen-year-old going on a first date. By one of the strangest coincidences in life, that night when Stan appeared, he had asked if the little café where she waited for him was all right or would she like something nicer. Carol said that it was sufficient, and thus began their romantic interlude.

As usually happens when boy meets girl, particularly thousands of miles away from home, they told each other all about themselves over a span of two bottles of wine and several hours.

Stan lived in Baltimore and was a financial analyst who published a monthly newsletter. He had come to Israel because his publisher had suggested he check out Israeli high-tech companies.

Interesting, Carol had thought at the time. Nearby cities just an hour apart by car and even less by train. They also each originally came from Florida—he from Delray Beach and she from Gainesville, where her father was a professor of economics at the University of Florida. They had both attended the University of Florida. Stan had been a bit embarrassed when he learned that Carol's father had been one of his professors.

"I don't think you would want to bring me home to meet your father."

"Why? You seem like a very nice person to me."

"I don't think he appreciated my irreverent sense of humor."

It had long since been dark when they rose to leave the café. Stan insisted on getting a cab and seeing her safely to her apartment.

The original thinking was that Stan would see her safely to her apartment and then go to his hotel. Instead, she invited him in, and he accepted, and from then on, they had been almost inseparable. Carol had spent three weeks with Stan. From that first night, she had given her body, and then it had come to an end.

Carol hadn't wanted to go home this afternoon. She almost changed her mind as she rounded the corner and started down the street to her apartment. And that's when she saw Portman sitting on one of his suitcases, his sandy brown hair mussed as usual.

"Stan? What are you doing here? Did you miss your plane?"

"I guess you could say that." He rose and walked to her. "I couldn't go," he said as he took her in his arms. "I just couldn't leave you."

Instead of going out to eat at the Market Café on Nahalat Binyamin as they had often done, she made dinner, and they stayed home for an intimate evening.

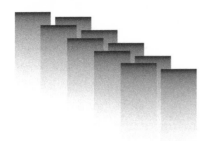

CHAPTER 41

Abbe Research Associates
4 Yehezkel Kaufmann
Tel Aviv, Israel
Sunday, May 29, 2011

Taffy knew she had changed. Of course, a life-threatening experience would be enough to change anyone. Mykro wanted her to stay home that morning and rest, and he was willing to stay with her, but she refused. They walked from his apartment to the office, stopping first at the little café next to the office to purchase some bagels and cream cheese. At the office, he made American-style coffee, which they were unable to purchase at any café in Israel.

As Taffy booted up her computer, she had a momentary thought regarding the work that Sharon, David, and Mykro were doing and realized that within little more than twelve hours, she had mentally crossed over a line but didn't care.

The previous day had been so nice that she felt she could have walked forever, but as Mykro had said, looks could be deceiving especially in Israel. After a few bites of her bagel, she realized she didn't have much of an appetite. She stared at her screen as the voices of yesterday reappeared one by one.

"Taffy, are you all right?" asked one voice. "Taffy, speak to me, please."

Then she heard the other voices and the sirens. Slowly, the picture emerged in her mind as the voices grew in number.

"Is something wrong?" said Carol, suddenly appearing at her side.

"No, nothing's wrong. I'm just having a silly spell."

"Taffy," said Sharon, who also suddenly appeared. "David just told me about the bombing by the Market Café. He said that you were both lucky but that you got a nasty bump on the head."

"Bombing?" said Carol in disbelief. "Market Café?"

"I'm okay," replied Taffy. "I think Mykro tripped when he tried to push me down after someone shouted a warning. My head hit the pavement. My head's a little sore, but I'm okay."

"Taff," said Sharon, "I was ten years old when a rocket hit our house and killed everyone but me. We may survive and go on with our lives, but we're never okay afterward."

"Taffy," said Carol, "I'm so sorry. I didn't know. Stan and I almost went there last night."

"Stan!" exclaimed Sharon and Taffy almost in unison.

"I thought he was leaving for the states yesterday," said Taffy.

"He got only as far as the airport," said Carol. "He said he couldn't leave me."

Taffy looked at Carol and saw tears trickling down her cheeks, but they were tears of thanks for having found the man in her life and for whoever had been looking over their shoulders the previous evening. Then she noticed tears trickling down Sharon's cheeks and instinctively realized the woman with long, black hair who was always quiet and reserved had bottled up much inside through all the years.

Then, her own eyes filled with tears.

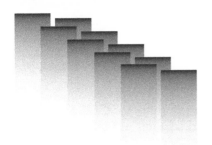

CHAPTER 42
Thai Roma Restaurant
237 Pennsylvania Avenue SE
Washington, DC
Friday, October 14, 2011

"I'm surprised Nate isn't here," said Jack Wharton as he raised his glass of wine to take a sip.

"I didn't invite him," replied Dave Hawkins. "You're the one I wanted to talk to today, and I guess I can consider myself lucky with all the traveling you've been doing. The trekking business must really be profitable these days."

"As I always say, I am in need of the money to maintain Susan's and my decadent lifestyle. What's the occasion?"

"I wanted to show you this," said Hawkins as he removed a folded piece of paper from his sports coat pocket. "It came in over the AP wire. I thought you'd find it interesting."

"If it isn't, will you buy me lunch?"

"Just read it. I don't think I have anything to worry about."

(AP) 12 Wednesday, 2011

Unknown Radio & Television Broadcasts Offensive to Islam.

According to the *Egyptian Ahram Daily*, clerics at Al-Azar University issued a fatwa against a radio and television station broadcasting from an unknown location. The fatwa affirms that any offensive operations against these stations are a legitimate part of a defensive jihad.

"Wow," exclaimed Wharton.

"I can tell by the smile on your face, Jack, that you find it amusing that someone somewhere has stolen your thunder."

No one has stolen my thunder, thought Wharton. It was the alternative to Al-Jazeera Brad Jenkins had envisioned, though not quite as he had envisioned. And that secret location had been the very location in Berbera that Jenkins and he had looked at as a location for a voice of Arabia transmitter the previous year.

"Whoever is responsible for this is obviously successful and having an impact if some dumb clerics have issued a fatwa," Wharton said. "It serves the Arabs right to be ridiculed once in a while and have what poses as a religion made fun of. The bastards can rant and rave all they want, but I'm glad that someone somewhere has taken it to them."

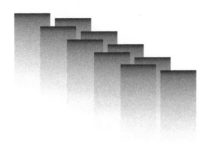

CHAPTER 43
Abbe Research Associates
4 Yehezkel Kaufmann
Tel Aviv, Israel
Sunday, October 30, 2011

According to the *Jerusalem Post*, a leading member of the Muslim Brotherhood in Egypt told the Arabic-Iranian news network Al-Alam on Monday that the Egyptian people should prepare for war against Israel.

Muhammad Alfarsi reportedly told Al-Alam that the Suez Canal should be closed immediately and that the flow of gas from Egypt to Israel should cease in order to bring about the downfall of the Mubarak regime.

Let's hope that doesn't happen, thought Colonel Golden after reading the article. *At least not for a while.*

Mubarak and his supporters had tried to hold on, but the escalating violence on Cairo's streets as police thugs clashed with protesters was just the beginning of a civil war. Unfortunately, the chaos had led to the overthrow of the Mubarak government. The Muslim Brotherhood had gained control of the country, and Colonel Golden's surgeons had lost their opportunity to work in Gaza because Egypt was to have been the entry to the Gaza Strip.

Egypt's problems were not the only ones created by the shifting sands of the Middle East. Jenkins's original plan of sanctioning the teachers and recruiters of terrorists had looked good on paper a year earlier, but with storm clouds on the horizon all over the Middle East, the surgical strike force plan of operation would have to be modified.

The original game plan had been to start operations in Jordan and the West Bank, then move counterclockwise geographically into Syria and Lebanon. If things progressed satisfactorily, operations could commence in Gaza, but circumstances were changing faster than the desert winds.

Jordan had been the first selected country for his surgeons because, being the most liberal country in the Levant, it was considered the easiest in which to conduct the initial operations. However, as General Ari Ben Gul had said, Jordan had changed very much since the 1967 war.

It wasn't widely known, and it was certainly something never mentioned in the Western media, but the Jordanians and the Israelis had quietly been doing a thriving business with each other for several years, and the applecart of trade was not going to be upset by the jihadists. Because of that, Jordan lacked a sufficient number of targets of opportunity for all his teams, and consequently, there had been only moderate success. Too many times, the Jordanian security forces had removed a target of opportunity before his surgeons could carry out their mission. Considering everything, he didn't think Jordan had been worth the effort.

In accordance with the original plan, Colonel Golden had sent five teams to the West Bank to commence operations, but that still left him with twenty teams of three. If he had sent everyone to the West Bank, they probably would have been tripping over each other and all hell might have broken loose. Thus, the question Golden had to answer was how to utilize these twenty teams, and the answers were elusive.

Syria, which was to become the next area of operations, was also in the early stages of a civil war, and the Syrians were more interested in killing each other than in recruiting jihadists, so that effectively removed Syria from the game plan.

Prevented from being able to follow the original script and wanting to keep his forces intact, Golden had moved five more teams into Lebanon, but due to the chaos in Syria, Lebanon had become a very chaotic place to operate. Because of the commentary from various team members, Golden had sent the remaining fifteen teams on reconnaissance missions to Britain, France, and Spain with instructions to just observe and report.

"Where we should be operating," one of the SAS members of his teams had said, "is back in the bloody homeland." A Frenchman who had been a former legionnaire had said the same thing about France. Even the American team members were wishing they could go home and clean house. "Let the fuckin' Arabs over here kill themselves," one member said. "We'd be more useful going back home and putting the brakes on building all those fuckin' mosques."

The thought was intriguing and could work because the people he would be sending would be entering the country legally and doing nothing more than attending church. But he had to talk to Brad Jenkins before sending anyone back.

CHAPTER 44
Double R Bar Ranch
Kendall County, Texas
Friday, November 25, 2011

It was one of those mornings when Brad Jenkins woke early and couldn't get back to sleep. To keep from waking Candy, he slipped out of bed and into his robe and quietly left the bedroom.

After making himself a cup of coffee, he made his way to the terrace that overlooked the valley. In spite of the time of year, it was an unusually warm Texas morning conducive to reflection.

Jenkins had much to be thankful for this Thanksgiving week as he sat at the patio table meditating in the darkness slowly giving way to the gray morning light that was a prelude to sunrise. Perhaps it was because Thanksgiving was usually the prelude to the Christmas holiday season that his first thoughts were about the Christmas season of 1993 when his first wife, sister, mother, and father had been killed by Arab terrorists at Charles de Gaulle Airport in Paris. The family had spent Christmas week in Paris. Jenkins and his wife were about to fly back to the States, and his sister, mother, and father were about to return to Beirut. Jenkins had been spared only because he had insisted on dropping off the family and luggage at the terminal before returning the rental car rather than humping luggage on and off a shuttle bus to the terminal.

It took years for Jenkins to get over the tragedy of losing his family. He had met and married a woman who had changed his life, and in the process, he had gotten involved in an adventure of international intrigue similar to what Miriam Bernstein usually wrote about in her novels.

Would Project Abraham have ever come into existence, wondered Jenkins, *if I hadn't facetiously told President Branch that I would have to be God to do some of the things I'd recommended?* But he had opened his mouth, and the president had asked him to play God, and Abraham had been born.

Abe had come a long way in fifteen months, far faster than he had envisioned, but like any start-up business or operation, it had also experienced growing pains and some problems. On the plus side, Paul Bernstein had done a masterful job at the financial end, and with the addition of Mykro, David, and Sharon, Abe had become a profitable enterprise because they had stolen so much money from the jihadists. Also on the plus side, Jack Wharton, Ken Middleton, and Miriam Bernstein had created a successful alternative to Al Jazeera though the final product had developed into something far different from what he had envisioned.

On the minus side of the ledger, Colonel Golden's surgeons were having only moderate success due to uncontrollable events in the Middle East. As he had said, it would be a shame to disband this part of Abraham, so the next day, Jenkins would have another meeting with the president to discuss alternatives.

The addition of Taffy, Carol, and indirectly Stan Porter had also been a cause for concern. Jenkins could understand why the president had wanted to incorporate Association Research into Abe, which had grown by two people when Taffy and Carol were folded into his operation, but the appearance of Portman on the scene had posed some problems because he had been a real outsider.

However, Miriam Bernstein, working with Sharon, had efficiently taken care of everything. Mykro, who had been reluctant to ask Taffy to marry him because he was Jewish and she wasn't, had relented, and they had married. Carol had also married Stan Portman, and they were living in Carol's apartment on Twenty-Fifth Street NW in Washington and were now using the office space she and Taffy had shared.

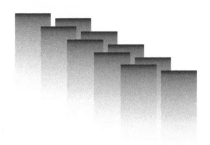

CHAPTER 45
Evans Residence
Foster City, California
Sunday, January 8, 2012

The thermometer read fifty-two degrees, and it was drizzling, weather not conducive to sitting on the deck and meditating, which was why Larry Evans decided to enjoy his first cup of morning coffee in the comfort of his sunroom.

Something had been bothering Evans about the Pellegrino-Lowen eavesdropping operation for some time, but that was only when he stopped thinking the operation was a waste of time. There were several times he had wanted to discuss what was on his mind with Mike Middleton, but ever since Mike was told to let Taffy and her friend work under Brad Jenkins's supervision, he had seemed to lose interest. Evans couldn't blame Middleton because he himself had thought about chucking the whole operation at times because so far they had gotten precious little to show for their efforts. Yet in spite of such thoughts, something kept nagging him, something similar to the way he had felt back when he discovered the bit about nonprofit associations that had led to Ben Sorenson's daughter becoming involved.

It came to him as he was finishing his cup of coffee. *Shit! Why the hell didn't I think of that before? We just combine all the damned files into one and do a word or phrase search.* He headed to his study and began the time-consuming process of merging all the transcript files into one.

CHAPTER 46

Middleton Estate
Big Basin Way
Boulder Creek, California
Tuesday, February 7, 2012

It was a warm, springlike afternoon as Michael Middleton and Larry Evans enjoyed a quiet lunch while their wives were off shopping.

"And that's what I believe, Michael," Evans said after a long explanation of his latest theory. "I think all those nights have been working sessions, not bullshit sessions. There may have been a lot of bullshitting going on while they worked, but I think they've been doing computer work."

"Why after all this time are you so damned concerned whether they're using a computer in their love nest?"

"Little things, Mike, little things."

"You know, Larry, I sometimes think you're getting paranoid in your old age."

"Look. We've been bugging the shit out of them for three years, Mike, and while we've learned a few things, I don't think we know half in spite of all the pillow talk. When they speak to each other, they know what they're talking about. We don't until much later if we're lucky. For instance, he might ask, 'Do you have it?' but we don't know what 'it' is.

"Back in the beginning, this Atherton person said to Lowen, 'Hide this.' We never learned what it was. The same evening, Lowen said he hid it 'here,' but we still don't have a clue where 'here' is. It's the fucking little things, Mike, that bothers me. Then it became words."

"Words?"

"Yeah. Words usually mean something. So what I did was combine all the files into a single file and then did a word search."

"And you entered the word computer and got a hit."

"Smartass. If only it could be that easy. It took me several hours just to merge all the files. Then, Royce and I developed a list of search words. I kept a small notebook with me during the time we were working so whenever I thought of a word I could write it down."

"Tell me, Larry, why the hell would someone from New York or Connecticut come down to Washington two, three, even four times a month to a small apartment at night to sit at a computer with someone? Whatever Atherton is doing, he could do up north in the comfort of his own home or office and then transmit whatever to Lowen to do whatever. It just doesn't make sense."

"Perhaps they're trying to be extra careful, Mike. Perhaps whatever they're up to is so secret they're not taking any chances."

"Sounds like you're looking for another trip to Washington."

"I think it's the only way, Mike. If we'd had a camera, all this wouldn't be necessary."

"If we had a camera, it would have been spotted ages ago."

Middleton leaned back in his chair and put his hands in the prayer position. He put his fingers to his mouth with his thumbs under his chin and thought for a few moments. "Something tells me I'm going to regret this. If you and Royce are hell-bent on going to Washington, go ahead. Just remember rule number one when you go. Particularly since this is an election year."

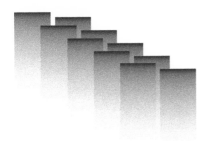

CHAPTER 47

Market Inn
200 E. Street SW
Washington, DC
Monday, April 2, 2012

"Man, it's been like work today," Royce Bartlett said after a sip of his martini. "I feel like we've been all over the damned landscape."

"Yeah," said Larry Evans as he drifted off in thought.

It was one of those momentary things one could never explain. Larry and Royce had done many things together through the years. Back in their RR Unit days, they had been often referred to as the brothers because they looked so much alike. They still were, though their angular faces were weathered from age and their receding hairlines were streaked with gray. The most distinguishing feature of either of them was the mustache adorning Bartlett's face.

"It's certainly been that," continued Evans.

"A shame we couldn't have made things easier for ourselves and pulled some stunt like that changing insurance company scheme we used a while back. It could have made our work easier."

"Yeah," replied Evans, remembering the ruse they had pulled on a previous occasion. Because the building where the love nest was located, was considered a commercial property for insurance purposes, they had notified the tenant that they were changing the insurance company and an inspection by an underwriter's representative was required.

"But we wouldn't have been able to scour the place like we did today. Besides, when we pulled that stunt, we had Lowen make a visit to look over our shoulder."

"Well, Mike should be proud of us for the way we handled things today," said Bartlett. "He wanted us to be super cautious, and I think we were that in spades."

Yes, we were super cautious, thought Evans. When Mike had told him to remember rule number one, it meant under no circumstances to screw up because it was an election year. So Evans had decided the best time to search the Washington love nest would be a time when they were sure nothing bad would happen or interfere with their efforts, and that time probably would be when they knew where Pellegrino and Lowen would be and when. Thus, the decision was made to enter the apartment when Pellegrino and Lowen were on a plane to San Francisco.

The previous Friday had been the last day Congress had been in session before the Easter recess. Evans and Bartlett had assumed that Pellegrino and Lowen would be traveling either later that day from National or the first thing Saturday morning, but instead, Pellegrino and Lowen had spent the weekend together at her place and had left today from Dulles. Unfortunately, the bugging of Love Nest East had not picked up any details, and they were forced into a weekend stakeout of Pellegrino's building.

Finally, this morning, they followed Pellegrino's taxi to Dulles. While Evans drove their car around, Bartlett went into the terminal and watched Pellegrino and Lowen get the VIP treatment for checking in and going through security.

Satisfied that all systems were a go, Evans and Bartlett headed back to town. After renting a small panel truck from a place on South Capitol Street, Evans drove their rental car back to the love nest and Bartlett drove the panel truck, which had two magnetic signs attached to the doors that read Watts of Power Electric with two fictitious phone numbers.

A short time after Evans had gotten to the love nest and had turned off the power to the building, Bartlett appeared and got out of the truck wearing a work belt filled with tools.

"Shit," said Bartlett within moments of their entering the apartment. "You see what I see?"

"Christ," said Evans as he noticed the first of two security cameras. "They weren't here when we changed the bugs last year."

"Damned good thing we're always super cautious."

"This means they probably have them installed in Pacific Heights too."

After the discovery of the cameras, they quickly and methodically, searched the love nest with a fine-toothed comb.

"Shit," said Bartlett after they had scoured everything. "No fucking computer."

While there had been no computer, they did find a modem on a bookshelf above a desk and some cables and flash drives in a desk drawer.

"Maybe he has it with him," said Evans. "How else would you explain the modem and cables along with the flash drives?"

"The modem could just be for the Internet cameras."

"You don't need flash drives and cables for the cameras, so he has to have the computer with him or it's at his home."

"All right," said Bartlett, "I won't argue. Why don't you fire up your laptop and see if anything is on the flash drives while I copy all the modem and camera info."

And that had been that. When Evans and Bartlett were finished, the truck was returned to the rental place, and they went to a new restaurant where they were commiserating. They may not have found a computer or anything to prove one had ever been used in the apartment, but they still had struck some gold. The Internet cameras they discovered were the latest models that Globaltronix sold to the public. With the information they had obtained and some information from Harry's son, Don, who ran the Globaltronix security division in Houston, they thought they might be able to have visual surveillance after all, if they were lucky.

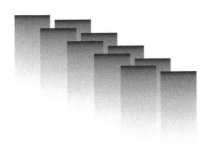

CHAPTER 48

Evans Residence
Foster City, California
Monday, June 18, 2012

It sure as hell took long enough, Evans thought as he checked his computer. *Now that we can see you, you son of a bitch, you can run but you can't hide.* It had been a hard row to hoe from the time Evans and Bartlett had searched Love Nest East until that morning when Evans was finally able to log onto camera number one there.

Usually, the IP network cameras Globaltronix sold, particularly the NLS1494IP, had the MAC ID numbers and the DDNS HTTP camera addresses somewhere on the cameras, but Lowen or whoever had installed the cameras had removed the information. The same was true regarding the default usernames and passwords. All Evans and Bartlett had been able to obtain from the label on the cameras was the make and model number. That meant everything had to be done the hard way.

Saying he was involved in a national security situation, Harry Reason had contacted his son, Don, and requested a customer search to see if anyone by the name of Lowen had purchased an NLS1494IP security camera in the past year. Of course, that presented a problem because the company was geared to track by order number instead of names and addresses.

Ultimately, it was learned that an R. W. Lowen, from Washington, DC, had purchased four cameras that had been shipped to 5187 Yuma Street NW, and the order number had been 10407260. With the order number, name, and address of the purchaser verified, the properties of each camera needed to be ascertained, and that resulted in more hurdles to jump because the cameras had been manufactured at Globaltronix's plant in Malaysia. Three weeks had passed from the initial customer search request until Evans had received the Internet addresses for each camera as well as the default passwords and user IDs, but they were still not out of the woods.

After receipt of the camera information, Evans's major concern had been whether Lowen or someone else had changed all the defaults. Unfortunately, only some of Evans's prayers had been answered. While the user default names had not been changed, the passwords had. It had been just too much to hope that Lowen would operate the cameras without changing something.

As time passed, Evans and Bartlett tried every conceivable password to no avail. Finally, they had gone back over the transcripts, desperately hoping to find something, and luck was with them. It had been in plain sight all the time.

Neither of them thought Lowen was that computer savvy. Someone had to have helped him set up the cameras. One of the times Charles Atherton had been with Lowen, there had been a woman present. This woman had also been present at the Pacific Heights location on occasion. After going back through the transcripts and carefully analyzing the dialog, they had finally hit pay dirt. Voilà. Babbs One and Babbs Two were the passwords. Evans then knew which cameras were in Love Nest West and which were in Love Nest East.

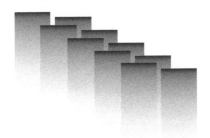

CHAPTER 49
Thirty-Two Thousand Feet Somewhere over the Atlantic
Globaltronix Gulfstream G550
1245 hrs, Monday, September 10, 2012

Well, thought Brad Jenkins as the G550 was climbing to its final cruising altitude of thirty-eight thousand feet, *if Carol and Stan Portman didn't know all about Abe before, they sure as hell will now. I'm damned glad that Jack and Stan became close.*

It had been one hell of a past few days since he and Candy had had dinner with her parents the previous Thursday evening during which the plan had been sprung.

"Tell me," Harry Reason had asked as Brad Jenkins and Candy Reason were enjoying cocktails, "are there any other people who know about your marriage besides those who attended your wedding?"

Candy and Brad looked at each other in surprise because it was the first time since they had married almost two years earlier that the subject of the secrecy of their marriage had come up.

"Actually, there are two others," replied Candy. "Why do you ask?"

That was when her father explained that President Branch had begun a serious slide in the polls and said that if something wasn't done immediately, the election could well be lost.

After glancing at each other again, Candy and Brad smiled as they remembered a conversation with Nancy and Ken Middleton early the previous year when it had been explained to him how politically devious their fathers were.

"And I bet you and Uncle Mike have figured out a solution to the problem," Candy said facetiously.

"Actually we have," replied her father. "But for it to work, it'll require your help and for the media to continue acting true to form."

"Then I think perhaps a little explanation is in order," Jenkins said with trepidation.

"I hate to bring both of you into this," said Harry after telling them about a plan that had been discussed by him, Mike Middleton, Al Garcia, and the president during the Labor Day weekend at the president's Prairie View ranch. "But it was the only way we could think of to regain the initiative that could assure George getting reelected."

Jenkins and Candy didn't like what was suggested, but they realized Abraham could be in danger if the president didn't win in November, so reluctantly, plans were made that required a lot of work in a very short time.

Harry Reason had assured them that Candy's brother and his wife would suddenly be off on a prolonged business trip to one of the Globaltronix factories in Malaysia where he would be joining up with Ken Middleton's brother-in-law and his wife. That would remove the possibility of four family members accidentally taking issue with something they knew not to be true.

That had left Brad and Candy to cover most of the other bases. Nancy and Ken Middleton and Susan and Jack Wharton were quickly brought up to speed, leaving, with the exception of Carol and Stan Portman, only the folks in Tel Aviv to be advised. How to handle Carol and Stan had been the $64,000 question, but Wharton said he would handle things, and he had been successful.

"I suggest the two of you leave town," Candy's father said. "If you stay around, what you might find yourselves in for will be brutal. The media will be absolutely relentless."

And Harry Reason was correct; Jenkins's and Candy's voice mail boxes had filled up quickly that morning after the news had broken.

Early that morning, Nancy and Ken Middleton had driven Jenkins's van out of the Watergate parking garage and headed for Princeton, New Jersey, with some media types following. After parking the van at Jenkins's condominium in Princeton, they had taken a taxi to the Princeton airport, boarded a waiting Globaltronix G550, and had flown to Dulles.

In the meantime, Jack Wharton drove to the "Portmans" apartment, collected them, and then drove to the Watergate. After Wharton had received the appropriate call from Middleton, he drove everyone to the general aviation section at Dulles, where after going through the necessary paperwork, they were off to Tel Aviv.

CHAPTER 50

Thai Roma Restaurant
237 Pennsylvania Avenue SE
Washington, DC
Tuesday, September 11, 2012

Jack Wharton knew it would be a difficult lunch. He had been wondering how to handle things ever since Dave Hawkins had called him this morning.

"Look at these," said Hawkins as he handed Wharton three newspapers with headlines impossible to miss: "The Dragon Lady & the Professor"; "Love Nest at the Watergate"; "National Security Adviser Has Lover."

"I've already read them, Dave."

"Did you know your friend was shacking up with Candy Reason?"

What the hell do I say? thought Wharton. "Dave, please don't go there."

"Don't go there? What the hell do you mean? Your Princeton buddy shacking up with the president's national security adviser, and all I ask is if you knew, and you say, 'Don't go there'?"

"Dave, stop for a moment and consider the source. That damned *National Gossip Journal* broke the story, the same rag that publishes stories about having sex with Martians. I wonder how much they paid someone to dream up a story."

"*National Gossip Journal.*" Hawkins was sneering. "That's a good one. You know fuckin' A, pardon my French, that it was the *National Insider*, and so what the you-know-what if they do publish crap. The story has been verified by other sources."

Shit, thought Wharton. *Why the hell didn't Susan and I leave town as Brad had suggested?* "Who the hell verified the story?"

"Everybody," answered Hawkins. "The *Post*, the *New York Times*, everyone. They've all talked to the maid. There were also others who saw them coming and going."

"Amazing, isn't it," said Wharton, "how the media can get out the old microscope and find things if they want. You know damned well if they were Democrats, there wouldn't be a peep."

"Jack, you still haven't answered my question. On second thought, maybe you have."

Wharton knew his friendship with Hawkins would depend on the next thing he would say. So, he chose his words carefully. "Dave, we've been friends a long time. I've never attempted to use you or lead you astray. And I'm not attempting to lead you astray now, but I'm going to ask you a big favor. Please trust me when I say don't go there. Don't go there for your own sake and for the sake of your employer."

"You did know, didn't you?"

"Yes, I knew."

"What do I get for backing off?"

"A head start."

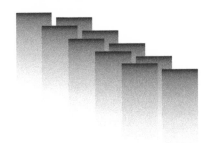

CHAPTER 51

Starbucks
700 Fourteenth Street NW
Washington, DC
Monday, October 1, 2012

"All right, what's up?" asked David Hawkins immediately after getting a latte and sitting down. "What's so damned important that you wanted to meet me here now? I've got to be at the National Press Club before ten."

"I wanted to give you something, and if you'll quit looking at your damned watch and read it, I think the last place you'll want to be is at the Press Club."

"Jack, what possibly could be so important that would make me want to miss the press conference?"

"Dave, when we had lunch last month, I suggested that you keep your powder dry regarding Brad Jenkins and Candy Reason."

"Yeah, I remember, and I also remember asking you what I would get, and you just said a head start. In about fifty minutes, there'll be a big press conference during which they'll probably admit their affair. So much for a head start."

"Here," said Wharton after retrieving a large brown envelope from his attaché case. "I think you'll find this is more than a head start."

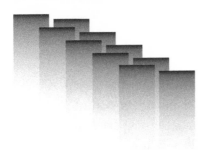

CHAPTER 52

Ken Middleton Condominium
Watergate West
2700 Virginia Avenue NW
Washington, DC
Monday, October 1, 2012

It was almost ten in the morning as the two couples stared at the wide-screen TV patiently waiting for the drama to unfold.

"It's too bad Brad and Candy aren't here," said Nancy Middleton.

"I hope they're watching the coverage on TV over there," Susan Wharton said.

"If it's covered," said Nancy.

"Hopefully after this morning, Kerrigan's poll numbers will plummet," said Ken Middleton as he switched to Fox.

"I think they'll sink like a rock," said Jack Wharton.

"It couldn't happen to a nicer liberal. By the way, how did your reporter friend act this morning when you gave him the material?"

"His eyes popped out. He couldn't get out the door and get a cab fast enough."

"How about the article you wrote for him? Do you think he'll accept it?"

"I gave him a flash drive with the hard copy, so there might be a few changes depending on column length and word count," said Jack Wharton with a chuckle as he remembered how stunned David Hawkins had been as he scanned the article.

The Corruption of the Media

Today was payback time for a media that has always professed to be fair and balanced but is, in reality, a campaign committee for Democrats running for public office and a propaganda arm for liberal causes.

"Wait a minute," Middleton yelled, his tone of voice indicating everyone should be quiet. "Fox has just gone to a split screen."

The words Breaking News flashed on the left screen while the right screen focused on the press conference at the National Press Club remained silent.

"I think it's going to happen just as we hoped," said a gleeful Jack Wharton.

"Fox News has just learned that—" said Bill Hemmer.

CHAPTER 53

National Press Club
529 Fourteenth Street NW
Washington, DC
Monday, October 1, 2012

For almost thirty minutes, Sheldon Kellogg Esq. stood at the podium studying the audience. However, instead of seeing people, he was seeing only dollar signs. *The sharks smell blood in the water. Too bad they'll all be disappointed.*

It was standing room only in the auditorium. As 10:00 a.m. approached, everyone was anxiously anticipating an announcement that Candy Reason has or would soon submit her resignation. At exactly ten, the lights intermittently dimmed and brightened signaling the press conference was ready to begin.

"Good morning. My name is Sheldon Kellogg, senior partner in the firm of Kellogg, Kellogg, and Anderson. I have scheduled this press conference to advise all of you that our firm represents Dr. Candice Reason and Dr. Bradford Jenkins. I'm sure you are all here in anticipation of an announcement of importance, so I'll be brief, and as soon as my associates pass out some material, I'll make the announcement."

As Kellogg's associates passed out large, brown envelopes, Kellogg was salivating because it wasn't often someone could successfully entertain a lawsuit against the media, but this would be one of those times, and his firm would make a small fortune and so would the charities to which his clients had planned on donating their shares of any settlement.

"I see we have enough material handed out," Kellogg said as gasps of surprise began to emanate from the audience as the documents were read.

"I'll continue. Ladies and gentlemen, I'm sure you are all well versed in the laws pertaining to libel, slander, and defamation of character. While I'm sure some of you will argue that Dr. Candice Reason is a public figure, it is my firm's contention that she is simply another government employee working in the Executive Office Building and as such is entitled to the same protections of any other nonpublic figure. Also, it's indisputable that Dr. Bradford Jenkins is not nor ever has been a public figure.

"As some of you can now see, one of the documents you have is a representation of a typical bill of complaint that will be filed in various courts of law around the country. To be more specific, Drs. Candice Reason and Bradford Jenkins are suing anyone who has written and or published the false and capricious lies about them. That includes individual media types, their employers, the major broadcast networks, the Kerrigan campaign, the Democratic National Committee, and certain members of Congress who will not be able this time to declare congressional immunity.

"You'll also find in your packages a copy of a marriage license issued by Clark County, Nevada, dated November seventeenth, 2010, a copy of the marriage certificate, and an affidavit from the minister who performed the ceremony.

"It does seem, ladies and gentlemen," said Kellogg confidently, "that Drs. Reason and Jenkins, who have been husband and wife for just a bit less than two years, have not been engaging in an illicit relationship as most of you have suggested. Their marriage has been a matter of public record and has been there for all to see with minimal effort, yet most of you here and the organizations you work for, instead of doing due diligence, have worked overtime libeling and slandering my clients.

"Many of us have known it for a long time, but today, you are part of a new low in what is supposed to be called journalism. This concludes our press conference. Thank you all for attending and good day. I will see you all in court."

CHAPTER 54

Thai Roma Restaurant
237 Pennsylvania Avenue SE
Washington, DC
Tuesday, October 2, 2012

"All right, I'm all ears," said an impatient David Hawkins as soon as their drinks were served. "You said there was a rest of the story, so I'm assuming you want to set the record straight."

"You don't sound grateful for my saving your ass," said Jack Wharton with a quiet laugh as he tapped his fingers on the tablecloth. "After what I gave you to write yesterday, you'll probably be nominated for a Pulitzer."

"It doesn't work that way, my friend, particularly with people like us on the other side of the fence," said Hawkins dismissively. "Tell me the rest of the story."

"Okey-dokey," said Wharton. "Some of what I'm about to tell you will be off the record, and you'll have to talk to our star players before you use the information. Brad Jenkins wrote three books about the Middle East. I'm assuming that's why the *Friends of Israel* Society chose to give him that award back in July 2010. That's where he met Candy Reason.

"Nothing might have come of it that evening except that the president had read Dr. Jenkins's books and had entertained thoughts of meeting the author. Again, nothing might have gone any further than that, but after reading Brad's CV in one of the books, the president noticed he had gotten a doctorate at Cambridge University in England. He asked our ambassador to the UK to make some inquiries of the Brits, and that led to the icing on the cake."

"Jack, you're losing me. So what if Jenkins got a doctorate at Cambridge? Are you telling me that the Brits keep a file on all foreign students?"

"That's what apparently happened, except it was the file of someone else that caught the president's eye. A man by the name of Raj Kumar."

"Who the hell is Raj Kumar?"

"I'm coming to that, Jack, but we have to go back a bit, all the way back to the first year of Branch's administration. Seems that when Branch became president, the Chinese Dragon was flapping its tail, and he felt it might be a good time to attempt seeking a rapprochement with India. That became Candy's job. For a year, she shuttled between Washington and Delhi and actually was successful."

"Come on, get to the point."

"Hold on," said Wharton, who was enjoying the conversation. "I'm getting there."

"I sure hope so," said Hawkins as he rolled his eyes.

"One of the Indians Candy dealt with was this Raj Kumar. Candy believed Kumar would probably become the next prime minister of India sooner rather than later. And da da lup, da da lup, da da lup, a little Rush Limbaugh music," said Wharton after a momentary pause trying to taunt Hawkins, "it seems Brad Jenkins and Raj Kumar were friends at Cambridge and still remain friends. Are you now starting to figure things out, my friend?"

"So this Kumar was the icing on the cake?"

"You got it. When the president learned of the relationship, he wanted to keep Brad close because he had some ideas for the future that involved India. That's why he engaged Brad as a special consultant on the Middle East. I guess you can pretty much figure out the rest of the story."

CHAPTER 55
Presidential Suite, Marriott River Walk Hotel
San Antonio, Texas
Wednesday, November 7, 2012

It was one thirty in the morning. The mood in the room was euphoric because President George Branch had just won a landslide victory.

"Congratulations, George," said a very pleased Harry Reason as he raised a glass of brandy in a toast. "That was a landslide."

"I second that," added Alberto Garcia. "That was a great victory speech you gave, George."

"Thank you, Harry, Al," said President Branch. "And particular thanks to Candy and Brad. Because of them, Kerrigan never knew what hit him." The president looked at Candy and Brad. "If I live to be a hundred, I'd never be able to say thank you enough times for what you've endured. I was going to wait until the end of the year before making some announcements, but after considering how you two helped make this victory possible, I'll give you a heads up on two of them.

"One of the announcements will be that Secretary of State Gene Powers will be submitting his resignation effective the end of the year. Another announcement will be that Dr. Candice Reason will be nominated to replace him."

"Oh my God!" Candy Reason gasped. "I had no idea."

"When Powers leaves, you'll be given a recess appointment effective January first, which should tide things over until your Senate ratification. And to succeed Candy, I couldn't think of a better choice for NSA than her husband, Brad."

If Candy was surprised, Jenkins was flabbergasted. Seeing the look on Brad's face, the president said, "I hope Abe is mature enough now that your full-time help won't be required."

"Thank you, Mr. President," was all Jenkins could think to say.

Harry and his wife, Kym, surreptitiously looked at each other and smiled. The second of the four steps to Candy becoming the first female president of the United States had been taken. Only becoming vice president during George's last two years followed by the nomination to represent the party remained.

CHAPTER 56

Coffee Shop, Pro Center
Kaanapali North Course
Sheraton Maui Resort and Spa
Lahaina, Maui, Hawaii
Tuesday, November 20, 2012

It was a beautiful, blue-sky morning with the temperature in the mid-seventies as the four men finished breakfast before sallying forth on the golf course.

"Michael," said Larry Evans, "we're going to need some help accessing those flash drives we copied in August."

"What do you mean you need help?" asked a surprised Mike Middleton.

"Mike," Evans said, "we farted around with those damned flash drives for several weeks now but no dice. We either cut our losses or get some help."

"I thought you and Royce were computer experts."

"Perhaps we've finally risen to the level of our incompetence," said Evans.

"Or got tired of keeping up with the new technology," said Harry Reason facetiously.

"Humor is not becoming of you this morning, Harry," said a somewhat irritated Royce Bartlett. "If the dog won't hunt, you either get another dog or you stop hunting."

"So what do you suggest?" asked Middleton. "Do you have someone in mind, or are you just crying in your coffee this morning?"

"I thought we might ask Ben Sorenson's son-in-law," answered Evans. "I gather he's a computer genius. At least that's what Taffy has said. He's also young enough to be with all the new technology inasmuch as he went to Caltech."

"Christ's sakes. I hope you haven't told him anything," Middleton said.

"I've spoken to him only in passing. You know, things like how happy I was Taffy had remarried. That's how I learned about her husband."

"I don't know, Larry," said Middleton. "Right now, there are only six people not including any wives aware of our little project. I'm reluctant to expand the circle."

"Suppose he could get Taffy's husband to help without divulging anything?" asked Reason.

"If you believe that," Middleton said, "I have a bridge to sell you. We don't have a clue what's on those drives, so even if he could be recruited without divulging anything, he'd end up finding out."

"Mike," said an exasperated Evans, "Royce and I have babysat this project from the get-go always looking for the smoking gun. As far as I'm concerned, this is the end of the road. We either get help or we're washing our hands."

"Speaking of the devil," said Harry Reason as he noticed Brad Jenkins, Jack Wharton, Colonel Golden, and Ken Middleton enter the coffee shop.

"Good morning," said Mike Middleton as he and Harry Reason approached the table where Jenkins, Wharton, Golden, and Ken Middleton were seated.

"Good morning," said everyone seated almost in unison.

"Dr. Wharton," Middleton continued, "Colonel Golden, would you mind taking our place and playing with Larry and Royce this morning? Something has come up. We need to talk to Ken and Brad."

Wharton and Golden looked at each other and shrugged.

"No problem," said Wharton.

"Thank you," Middleton said. "We appreciate it. Harry and I will take your places and play with Ken and Brad. We'll be behind you shortly."

"What's come up?" asked Ken Middleton. "Or shouldn't I ask?"

"We need a favor," answered Mike Middleton.

"That sounds like a euphemism for help."

"All right, we'd like your help."

"Somehow, I don't think it has anything to do with Arabic. We've been there done that."

"No, nothing Arabic," said Mike Middleton with a laugh.

"What's come up then that you're in need of our help?"

"I gather Taffy's husband is a computer genius. At least that's what her father told Larry."

"That's not an answer, Dad, that's a statement. What's Taffy's husband being a computer genius have to do with your needing help?"

"For Christ's sakes, Mike," Reason said, "stop dancing or we'll never get to play."

"I'll second the motion," said Jenkins, speaking for the first time.

"We have some encrypted flash drives we'd like to access," said Middleton. "Larry and Royce have been trying for several weeks without success."

Jenkins and Ken Middleton glanced at each other and smiled.

"All right," said Ken. "What the hell have the two of you and Larry and Royce been up to? If you want our help, I want the truth, the whole truth, and nothing but the truth particularly as you now know all about Abe. Candy and Brad wanted to keep their marriage secret because they didn't want Abe compromised, but then, you come along and want them to help dig Branch's chestnuts from the fire."

"Ken's right," said Reason. "The kids are on our side of the fence, so I think dance time is over and it's time to get on with things."

"Okay," said Middleton resignedly. "Back when Branch first ran for office, I received a tip that Barbara Pellegrino and her chief of staff were having an affair."

Jenkins and Middleton glanced at each other in disbelief.

"That's when Larry and Royce started playing detective, and one thing led to another."

"And that's the whole story," said Mike Middleton a half hour later. "Back during the August recess, Larry and Mike went to Washington and entered the love nest while Pellegrino and Lowen were en route to San Francisco. They made copies of three flash drives and have been trying to get into them ever since. With Taffy and her husband working for you, I'm in essence asking your permission to use one of your employees."

"As Harry said," said Jenkins, "we're on the same side of the fence, so I'll refrain from any comment regarding your activities. I suggest Larry and Mykro get together and discuss things."

"Is there any way we can keep this to ourselves?"

"No. Myk and Taffy work as a team, and before this is all over with, it's quite possible Sharon and David will also need to get involved."

"Who the devil are Sharon and David, and why would it be necessary for them to be involved?"

"They're part of the team. David and Myk went to Caltech together. Sharon's an Israeli and David's wife. The four work as a team because decryption often requires lots of detective work."

Middleton closed his eyes and shook his head as his worst fears were being realized.

"Look," said Jenkins, "when we all leave here, Taffy and Myk will be heading for Los Angeles to spend a week with his family. They're planning on heading to Washington to spend some time with their friends Carol, whom I believe you know, and her husband, Stan. I'll speak to Myk and have him speak to Larry. They can make the arrangements for a rendezvous in Washington."

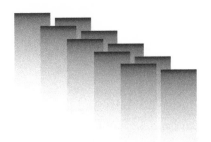

CHAPTER 57
Sheraton Maui Resort and Spa
Lahaina, Maui, Hawaii
Saturday, November 24, 2012

Tonight was the last evening of Globaltronix's celebration of its fifteenth biennial year for its founders, their families, and selected friends. It had always been a joyful and relaxing occasion for Mike Middleton, and it had been that way until four days previously.

Ever since Middleton had asked for Mykro Lehner's help, he had had noticeable misgivings. Marianne, his wife, had been the first to notice and had asked what was wrong. As most husbands would have, Mike had said, "Nothing." But his moodiness had continued the rest of the week and had finally become a topic of discussion this evening.

"Do you know what your problem is?" Larry Evans asked after Marianne had told her husband to enjoy himself.

"If he does, I'd like to know," said Marianne. "I have to live with him."

"He feels he's lost control. It's that simple."

"Are you now attempting a new career in psychoanalysis since you rose to your level of incompetence playing detective?" Middleton asked.

"Mike!" said Marianne. "That was unfair."

"That's all right, Marianne," Evans said with a chuckle. "I'll consider the source. What say you, Royce?"

"Actually," Royce replied, "I quite agree, but I'll leave it at that and just sit here and listen to the lieutenant take it to the major. This is one time rank has no privileges."

"I'm glad you're all enjoying your bit of humor at my expense," said Mike.

"Look, Mike," said Larry, "so you had to ask the kids for help. That's not the end of the world."

"That's what this is all about?" Marianne asked.

"That's the size of it," Larry said. "First, he lost Taffy and her friend to Brad and Ken last year, and then a few days ago, he had to ask them for help, and they wanted some information before they would commit. He had a lot of storytelling to do."

"Says Mister Perfect," interjected Mike after sipping his drink.

"Men," said Marianne, shaking her head.

"Little boys are more like it," said Joan Bartlett.

The four women at the table laughed.

CHAPTER 58
Association Research
600 New Hampshire Avenue NW
Washington, DC
Thursday, December 20, 2012

As December began, the Association Research office became a sardine can. Carol and Stan Portman still worked together in the office where Carol and Taffy had worked. Brad Jenkins, Ken Middleton, and Jack Wharton squeezed themselves into the second office. Taffy and Mykro Lehner, Sharon and David Perlinger, and Larry Evans had set up shop in the conference room.

The breakthrough that everyone hoped for—access to the three flash drives—came just before lunch. Unfortunately, success was tempered.

"The good news," said Mykro to Jenkins, Middleton, and Wharton, "is that we've accessed the drives. The bad news is we can't go any further."

"Why not?" asked Jenkins.

"They're not data drives, Dr. Jenkins. Each drive is a program drive, and as soon as we load the program, we get a password request."

"Shit," said Jenkins. "Ken, I'm glad as hell your father isn't here. He'd be fit to be tied."

"I think it would be a bit worse than that," responded Middleton with a chuckle.

"So we're back to square one," said Jenkins to Mykro.

"That's about the size of it, Dr. Jenkins."

"Anyone have any suggestions?" asked Jenkins.

"How about drowning our sorrows with an adult beverage or two?" Wharton asked.

Jenkins looked at his watch. "Myk, you, Taff, Sharon, and David must be tired. Why don't you get some lunch with Carol and Stan. We'll take Larry. We'll get together later."

Jenkins was glad to receive the news that Myk and company had accessed the flash drives though it had taken almost two weeks, but he also felt sorry for him and Taffy because their reason for coming to Washington was to visit Carol and Stan. Within a few days after their arrival, they were joined by Sharon and David, who flew in from Tel Aviv, and the detective work had begun.

Jenkins would have preferred that Taffy and Mykro take the drives to Israel and attempt the decrypting in the Abbe Research Associates office there. But Myk wanted Larry Evans working with him because Evans had quarterbacked the eavesdropping of Barbara Pellegrino, and there was a possibility of his being helpful, particularly if it would require analysis of the video camera footage.

Larry Evans, however, because it was too far into the holiday season, was willing to go only to Washington with his wife and be a guest of his daughter and son-in-law. Consequently, Taffy, Mykro, Sharon, and David had set up shop in the conference room and began what became a long period of frustration.

The first workday, with everyone watching with interest, Mykro ran a program that he had called Flash One, a special program that came to Project Abraham via Sharon and General Ben Gul courtesy of Israeli intelligence. While the program did not allow access to the drives, it did ultimately determine how many characters needed to be contended with.

It took a while that first morning, but the Flash One program was able to determine that the drives were random word protected—two words separated by a space. One word had six characters and the other had five. That's when the going got tough; they needed a program that could sort through every possibility.

With an alphabet of twenty-six letters, ten numeric characters, plus all the other printable characters pertaining to punctuation, etc., and each character being eight bits in length, they were looking at days if not weeks to decrypt the drives. The NSA could probably have decrypted the drives in a matter of hours or even minutes, but Jenkins's team didn't have that kind of power at their fingertips, so there was no choice but to go with the flow and hope for the best.

In the meantime, while the computers were cranking away, a frame-by-frame analysis of the Love Nest videos was conducted. Unfortunately, that process was like watching paint dry because video operated at fifty frames per second.

At one thirty, everyone crowded into the conference room and Mykro immediately got down to business. "It was Taff's machine that cracked the initial passwording," he said. "We discovered that each drive had a separate password, but we got lucky. Pays to guess sometimes. The drive we first accessed, the password was wealth2 and power2. We then guessed that there would be a number one and a number three for the remaining two, and voilà."

"So you were able to access all three drives?" Jenkins asked. "But then you were asked for another password?"

"Correct," answered Mykro.

"Did you guess again?"

"We tried every variation of the passwords we discovered. Actually, we weren't asked for a password per se. When the program on the drives loaded, we got a command prompt, but then we needed to give an instruction, obviously a command for another program that's probably also on Mr. Lowen's computer."

"Great!" Jenkins was disgusted. "You believe the programs on the flash drives are already loaded on his computer?"

"Yes, sir," Mykro said.

"And they have to access a program he may already have on his computer?"

"Yes, sir."

"A program we conveniently don't have."

"Yes, sir."

"And no one here has any further suggestions."

No one said anything.

"Larry, do you think this is worth pursuing, or should we all fold our tents and cut our losses?" Jenkins asked.

"Brad, from the time I began to think they were up to something computer-wise, I thought there was something important they were up to or were hiding. We got so damned much money and effort in this whole f—, whoops I forgot, damned affair. So I'm not ready to quit."

"What do you think, Myk?" Jenkins asked.

"I'm inclined to agree with Mr. Evans, but I don't know what should be the next step."

"All right," said Jenkins. "Back when you all started your code-breaking, you mentioned something about playing detective, correct?"

"That was about examining the video frames," Evans said.

"And you didn't come up with anything."

"Nothing usable."

"Actually, we do have something usable," Jenkins said with a smile. "We have names. Whether they'll lead us to victory remains to be seen, but we have names."

"What names?" Taffy asked.

"For starters, we have Rob Lowen's and his wife's. We also have Pellegrino's and her husband's. And there's this Charles Atherton, and how about his wife. There's that woman who assisted in the security camera setup. I don't remember her name, but you have the info, don't you, Larry?"

"It won't be hard to find."

"And all these people can lead to others. Do you see where I'm going, Myk?"

Mykro smiled. "I think I do understand."

"Good. The holiday season is upon us. Hanukkah has already started. I'm sorry for that, Sharon, and you too, David. I suggest you all proceed with your holiday plans. When you're back in Tel Aviv, get to work and do whatever you need to do, and while doing that, pray."

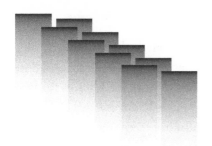

CHAPTER 59

Lehner Apartment
11 Balfour
Tel Aviv, Israel
Friday, January 4, 2013

It was an unusually warm January morning when Taffy and Mykro were sitting on their condo's balcony and drinking coffee. With the background noise of traffic punctuating their first day of the weekend, their thoughts periodically drifted to how their lives had changed since the Globaltronix week of Thanksgiving. That was when Dr. Jenkins had told them their cryptographic services would be needed when they got to Washington. They had visited Mykro's parents in Southern California and had gone to Washington to visit Carol and Stan Portman. That was where and when their game plan had begun to change.

Sharon and David had also arrived in Washington at Dr. Jenkins's request, and instead of a few days visiting Carol and Stan before going to Tel Aviv, they had spent two weeks attempting to decrypt and access three flash drives. They had not planned on going to Florida for the holidays, nor had Sharon and David. In fact, Sharon and David had not planned on even being in the United States, but as one thing led to another, they all ended up in Florida as guests of Carol and Stan.

The fact that six people instead of four were then involved probably had begun when Dr. Jenkins had suggested they start a no-holds-barred investigation of several people. They no longer had to wonder how much Carol and Stan knew about Abe, so they were able to freely discuss things in hopes that somehow they would be able to connect the dots.

When the comment about Paul Thoros was made that evening during dinner with Carol and Stan at their apartment, they had been surprised to learn that Stan had an acquaintance who used to work for Thoros. Rodger Jameson was apparently an audacious person. He had come out of college and had approached Thoros, and Thoros must have seen something he had liked because in record-breaking time, Jameson was running a hedge fund that became one of the most successful funds ever on Wall Street. Jameson was so rich that he had retired before he was thirty-five.

The knowledge that Stan knew Jameson had led to some in-depth discussions about Thoros. Stan Portman zeroed in on the theory that the command prompt instruction had to be an instruction to the drive letter on Lowen's computer, which was not necessarily the letters they had assigned to the drives, to instruct another program, and that program would be the access to the cloud that Stan had thought was being used.

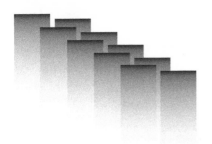

CHAPTER 60

Abbe Research Associates
4 Yehezkel Kaufmann
Tel Aviv, Israel
Saturday, January 26, 2013

It was the Sabbath. While Mykro was Jewish, he didn't make a habit of practicing the rituals of Judaism. Instead, he and Taffy would usually spend the day sightseeing in the city and letting things happen. Today, however, had been the exception because they knew they had stumbled on something the day before, so they had gone to the office and continued their research.

As the days had passed, the team had been successful in hacking into the computers of the people Dr. Jenkins had suggested. The only one who seemed not to use e-mail was Paul Thoros. He lived in the shadows. They had learned that any publicity about him was solely a purposeful distraction. He even seemed to like being called Zorba the Greek because it was a distraction.

Taffy had once said that once something is in the digital universe, it's there forever and can be accessed anywhere, anyhow, anytime.

When Dr. Jenkins suggested they start an in-depth investigation of Pellegrino, Lowen, Atherton, and their spouses, he had meant for them to do anything that needed to be done legally or illegally, which was why he had suggested they return to Tel Aviv, where they would be afforded the utmost protection.

The first step in their investigations had been the acquisition of one of Lowen's e-mail addresses. Larry Evans had simply asked Harry Reason if an e-mail address had been given when Lowen had used a credit card when he had purchased the Internet security cameras. Reason had called his son, and Don had given him the e-mail address and the credit card information.

Dr. Wharton had also swung into action; he had met with Nathan Grishom, the former Speaker of the House, and Grishom had provided him with a supply of e-mail addresses for all House and Senate members.

Then, as Dr. Jenkins had phased into his new role as the president's national security adviser, he had solicited help from the president, who had seen to it that he received an additional supply to add to those already on file at the NSA.

Within the first two weeks of the new year, they had had a plethora of e-mail addresses, an embarrassment of riches that was helpful but that also required analysis.

As they sifted and analyzed, they knew it would only be a matter of time because somewhere there would be a weak link that would lead to another weak link and so on. They crafted a few e-mails that would bypass spam filters and sent them to the various addresses they had selected. All it took was for the given message to be opened and the spybot that had been secretly embedded in the e-mails would invade the respective computers and go to work.

Mykro had been correct in his original assessment of the computer Lowen had been using. It had indeed had its hard drive encrypted, but Lowen had made one simple mistake; he had used that computer one time to send something to his wife's computer, and that was all it had taken. As far as Mykro was concerned, he owned that machine and shortly knew every program on it. With that knowledge, a secret keystroke program had been installed and the data collection had begun.

The programs on the three flash drives had indeed been loaded on Lowen's laptop, but they had been loaded as hidden programs. Mykro thought that a bit odd, but he assumed it had been another security measure. However, as soon as he went into DOS and changed the command prompt to another drive letter, he was successful; all he had to do was command the program to load another program called View Port, an off-the-shelf application, and he was in the cloud. That's when everything had come to a screeching halt; the cloud was password protected.

"Shit!" was Mykro's response when he discovered he could go no further.

"What's wrong?" Taffy asked.

He explained the situation, and as their workday was almost over, they knocked off and went out to dinner, hoping the next day would be better.

Sharon and David had joined them for dinner, and after an hour of venting their frustration, they turned their conversation to the more-mundane aspects of their lives. It had been an innocent remembrance by Taffy of how and why Association Research in Washington had been formed in conjunction with how Dr. Jenkins had once said something about words meaning something that had jogged David's memory.

When they had been reviewing the text translations of the Pellegrino-Lowen audio files in December as part of their attempt to access the flash drives, Atherton had told Lowen to hide them somewhere secure. He had also mentioned the word *associations* and had instructed Lowen to use them exactly as he had explained or nothing would happen.

"Well, Taff," said Mykro after he and Taffy had booted up their computers, "we're about to find out if David's theory of word associations for the passphrase is correct."

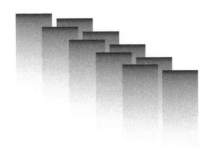

CHAPTER 61

Bottom Line Restaurant
1716 Eye Street NW
Washington, DC
Monday, February 4, 2013

"This isn't a bad place, Brad," said Jack Wharton as he surveyed the crowded restaurant. "Do you lunch here every day?"

"No," Jenkins said. "I think I've been here only once before. I'm still scouting out the restaurant scene within striking distance of the Executive Office Building. What's so important that you wanted to have lunch together?"

Wharton handed Jenkins an envelope. "This came this morning via the pouch. It's from Ken. I thought you'd find it very interesting."

"Inasmuch as it's already been opened, I'll read it later. Just give me the gist."

"Myk and company have gotten into the cloud."

"The cloud?"

"Yeah. Apparently, everything's stored in the cloud, not on Lowen's computer. Anyway, there's good news and bad."

"Shit. What else is new these days?"

"It's not really that bad, the bad news I mean. Accessing the cloud is the good news. The bad is that there's a lot of information there. Myk says there must be close to two terabytes."

"Two terabytes? My God, you could store all the—"

"Yeah, I know, but we have to find a way to deal with it. That's what the letter's about. Myk says it could take several days to download all the info with their computers, and he feels that would be risky. That's why he wanted to run a couple of options by you. The last thing we want is for someone else to attempt accessing the information while we're downloading."

Jenkins sighed. "Now that we've managed to come this far, it would be a shame to screw things up because of a simple downloading problem."

"It's more complicated than that, Brad. Seems we actually have two problems or at least potential problems: the upload speed of their server and the download capability at our end. If they have a server with a superfast upload speed, the problem might be at our end, but Myk feels anything at our end can be handled easily. But he doubts their server has a really high-speed connection, so the time required will depend on their server's upload speed."

"You said that Myk thought it could take several days to download all the info from the cloud. Was he more specific?"

"Wait a minute. Let me look at the letter," said Wharton. He picked it up and read it. "Ah, here it is. He says in all probability it would take about four days."

"Ouch. No wonder he's concerned."

"That's why the options."

"And they are?"

"One possibility was to hack into their server and install some automatic backup software that would tell their server to upload whenever it was not being used. The total transfer time would be four-plus days, but he thinks it could be done without detection."

"What's the second possibility?"

"He thinks that anyone constructing a two-terabyte database would absolutely want to have it backed up off-site, so they'd probably have a second secure server and have a backup program that transferred the data whenever something changed. So all that would be necessary to copy the database would be to hack the server and change the destination address of the backup program for about five days."

"Is that it?"

"No. The last option would be to get General Gul's assistance."

"The Israelis are on our side of the fence, but we don't have a clue what's stored in the cloud, so I don't feel comfortable with that option. Let's forget about that one."

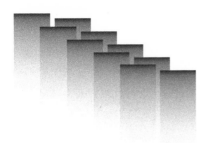

CHAPTER 62

Association Research
600 New Hampshire Avenue NW
Washington, DC
Tuesday, February 19, 2013

Brad Jenkins looked around the conference room. *The production is about to start now that all the pieces are together and the gang's all here.*

Taffy, Mykro, Sharon, and David had left Tel Aviv on the morning of the Jewish Sabbath and had arrived at Dulles on Sunday afternoon. After spending the next morning shopping, they had returned to the Watergate, and after lunch, had begun the installation of the equipment purchased and had gotten ready for some serious file viewing the next day.

The single LG 27" LED IPS wall-mounted monitor used in December had three additional monitors of the same specification hanging alongside, each with NetGear wireless adapters connected to them with HDMI cables. On the credenza behind Mykro, Taffy, David, and Sharon were two wireless printers: a Canon Image Class MF880dw multifunction laser printer and an Epson Stylus R3000 color printer.

Mykro and Taffy Lehner and David and Sharon Perlinger were at the conference table with Ken Middleton, Larry Evans, Mike Middleton, Stan Portman, Jack Wharton, and Brad Jenkins.

"Though it's taken a while," said Mykro, "getting to this point was rather easy. It was like fishing. We spent most of our time waiting and reading. We simply took all the e-mail addresses Dr. Jenkins gave us and composed a series of messages that would pass the spam filters. Once these e-mails were opened, a spybot was planted, which gave us the particular computer. Then we planted a keystroke program, and from that, we were able to decipher the passwords and phrases. It took us some effort to get into the cloud, but we were lucky and quickly figured that one out."

"Forgive me, but I've never proclaimed to be a technical genius even though our company makes this stuff," Middleton said. "What do mean cloud?"

"It's a form of remote storage," interjected Ken Middleton.

"That's right," Mykro said. "Many small businesses use it. Some of these remote storage facilities are called farms. The people we're dealing with have their own server farm somewhere because of the sheer volume of the material to be accessed. They probably did that to maintain portability as well as security."

"You have these things here on the table. They're small enough, and they're portable. You just put one in your bag with your laptop," Middleton said.

"That can certainly be done, sir," replied Mykro. "While the capacity of these external drives is three terabytes, which is a gigantic amount of storage, they weigh only about two pounds and are only about seven by five inches by an inch and a half. Perhaps if it were only me, I might do just that. Of course, I'd have a backup in the office. However, if more than one person needs to access all the material in the drive, there would be a need for as many drives as people in need, and of course, security is then compromised."

Mykro scanned the table for questions. "These two drives on the table, which are almost full by the way, have backups at our office in Tel Aviv. One of our biggest problems and one of our biggest concerns has to do with the sheer magnitude of the data stored. Once we got into the cloud and checked out the size of all the files, we knew that with our present capability, we were looking at three to four days of download time if not longer. That was too long a time to risk downloading and hoping no one noticed. So we hacked their server and temporarily changed the destination address of their backup program."

"I'm impressed," said Middleton.

"Thank you," said Mykro with a smile. "First, we'll show you the file structure. Once we downloaded everything, we reorganized the files based on the programs that run them. We ran across plenty of graphics that require different applications, spreadsheet files, and text files. Everyone with me so far?"

Everyone nodded.

"All right, Taff, let's go," Mykro said.

Taffy started tapping her keyboard, and a picture appeared on a monitor.

"You're looking at the main file structure," Mykro said. "Notice the filenames—Elections, Entertainment, Judiciary, Media, Military, Science, and so on. All these files are then broken down into subfiles. Taff, would you expand the Military file? As you can see, Military expands to 01 Air Force, 02 Army, 03 Marines, 04 Navy, and 05 Other. These subfiles are further expanded, and the expanded files are further expanded on and on. You get the drift. Let's start with the Elections file and show you what we've discovered about voting. That's where everything started."

"Why's that?" Middleton asked.

"Just that, Mr. Middleton. One has to be in office in order to wreak havoc. You'll see what I mean after David and Sharon do a little spreadsheet surfing. I think you'll find it rather interesting. Also, what they're about to show you is the only thing we've been able to spend a little time on. After we go through the voting, we'll move on to other categories that are many and extensive. Each contains a synopsis followed by plans of action, lists of people complete with dossiers, and so on."

"Okay," said David after Mykro passed the ball to him. He tapped away, and a graphic of the United States appeared on a monitor. "Here's a map of the country with a number in each of the states. The number represents the electoral votes, but that's not what we've found interesting. The map is interactive. When I click on Florida, for example, note how the state is divided by county. The map can be blown up so certain parts of the state are easily visible. Because of the size and configuration of the state, it's necessary to manipulate the scale to get a clearer picture.

"Sharon will give you a side-by-side comparison. She'll display the same map, but the county boundaries will turn to blue, and the congressional legislative districts will be defined by red lines. To save you the time counting, let it suffice to say that Florida has twenty-five congressional legislative districts. There are similar maps for the Florida senate and house. Now I'll bring up the same map as Sharon and then click on a legislative district. Watch what happens. It won't make any difference which districts because the same thing will happen unless I right-click.

"Now you see a spreadsheet with twenty-six-plus columns with the name of the first column being polling stations. The other columns represent the election districts and are numbered one through twenty-five. Everyone with me? I'll right-click on a district. Watch what happens."

An Internet address appeared.

"Anyone willing to hazard a guess what this means?" David asked. "I can also right-click on the same district and get the same result."

"It's an address with a set of instructions attached," answered Ken Middleton.

"Go to the head of the class," David said with a chuckle. "That's exactly what it is. A set of instructions for another computer. Note the capital letter V with the subscripts and superscripts. They're the instruction subvariants. All one has to do is substitute the value."

"Hold the tape!" yelled Wharton. "Are you telling us this is all about election fraud?"

"Exactly."

Middleton started to say, "How the fuck …" but quickly corrected himself in deference to the women. "How the hell do—"

"Do you mean how do they do it?" asked David. "It's easy, sir, particularly now that all voting is electromechanical or electronic and the whole process has become computers talking with computers."

"If this is all about voter fraud," said Jenkins, "I'm assuming the values in the instructions you mentioned are designed to change the results. Would you mind elaborating? You say it's very simple, but nothing's ever simple. I'd appreciate an explanation in layman's language."

"No problem. I've just used the word *simple* advisedly. While there may be technical differences depending on what state we're talking about, the systems are comparable. Let's go through a typical process and assume a given electoral district has twenty polling places, and each has a dozen voting booths. Each voting booth will have some sort of apparatus voters will use. This apparatus works similarly to a computer keyboard and mouse that send instructions to your computer. Only in the voting booth, you might have a touch screen or cards where you darken in a circle by your choice, and then the card or cards are scanned. With the touch screen, you will have the equivalent of the keyboard Enter key to touch when you've made your choices. With the cards, once they're scanned, it's the same.

"So once you've made your choice, this tabulation is electronically sent to a computer that transmits the results to the precinct computer, which transmits to the state computer and on to national, the media, and so forth. This is why these days we get instantaneous results."

"It's that easy?" asked Middleton.

"For us it is," David said. "But there's a little more to it."

The room became quiet as everything David said began to register. It was Mike Middleton who broke the silence. "Mr. Perlinger, I think I understand what you've said, and if what you've been explaining is in fact happening, if they can affect the outcome of an election, why did the president win reelection and not John Kerrigan? And why did we lose only the House and not the Senate? Something doesn't compute. Also, if this is in fact happening, do you have any idea when it started?"

"Jesus fucking Christ," muttered Evans as he slowly shook his head. "It was there all the time and I missed it."

"What did you say, Larry?" asked Mike Middleton.

"It started in 2006," answered Evans looking like a deer caught in the headlights. "Shit! It was there the whole damned time! I just never saw it just like I never saw the real picture regarding the usage of associations. It was all done on purpose. It was in the transcripts, but I missed it. She was going to be president. He wanted to know how they could keep fucking when she was in the White House!"

"Larry, you all right?" asked Ken Middleton because Larry had started to repeat himself.

"It was planned that way," said Larry instead of answering the question.

"Why don't we call a halt for some lunch?" asked Ken addressing his father.

"I think that's a good idea."

Brad and Jack quickly agreed.

"Stan," asked Brad, "why don't you take the troops out for lunch?"

CHAPTER 63

Terrace Restaurant
610 New Hampshire Avenue NW
Washington, DC
Tuesday, February 19, 2013

"You sure you're all right, Larry?" Mike Middleton asked after their drink orders were taken. "You started to get us concerned."

"I'm all right, Mike. There's nothing wrong with me a drink won't put right."

"I sure as hell hope so," said Ken Middleton. "I'm damned glad Nancy wasn't in the room to see you."

"What happened up there?" Jenkins asked. "What was all this about 2006 and Lowen wanting to know how they could keep screwing around?"

"Yeah?" Wharton asked. "What plan were you referring to? And what the devil were you misinterpreting?"

"They were crafty as hell," Larry said shaking his head. "We bugged the daylights out of them for four years but misunderstood everything. We were almost ready to throw up our hands and cut our losses. Then this morning, as David was explaining things, I suddenly saw the whole picture. I think that's what got to me."

"Well, if you saw the whole picture," said Mike Middleton, "I wish you'd give us all a copy. I don't think any of us has a clue what the hell you're talking about."

"It was a very well-thought-out plan, Mike."

"Yeah, you've said that twice already. So what the fuck was the plan?"

"For Pellegrino to become the first female president."

Jenkins, Wharton, and Ken Middleton looked at each other in disbelief. Then, Wharton said, "Oh shit!"

Evans, sensing that Wharton had twigged the plan, continued. "Tracy Clayton has been the one all the pundits and the chattering class thought would be anointed, but it won't happen because whoever is behind Lowen and Pellegrino have no intention of letting it happen."

"Larry," said Mike Middleton, "start at the beginning, or the beginning as you see it."

"It's all there in the transcripts. They made their first test run during the 2006 elections. Then in 2008, they made sure George Branch won the primaries to become the presidential candidate. Remember how George came out of nowhere? No one gave him a ghost of a chance. It was the same story for the main event. Garson was the odds-on favorite, and all the polls had him winning, but George squeaked through because they saw to it that he came out of nowhere to win the presidency. To them, he was the weakest candidate."

"Shit!" said Wharton. "Now I know how Pellegrino became Speaker of the House last month and why they got rid of Nate Grishom in 2010."

"Exactly," Evans said with a nod. "Then they saw to it that George won again last year. It was right in the November transcripts, which I got around to downloading only last month. They were drinking champagne and celebrating George's victory while lamenting about doing a lot of work to throw Kerrigan under the bus when they didn't have to all because of Goody Two-shoes and Lover Boy."

"Should I assume the Goody Two-shoes reference was to Candy and me?" Jenkins asked.

"Yes, it was."

"They plan on taking the Senate two years from now, don't they?" asked Wharton.

"Yes, and then they'll impeach the president and vice president and see that the Speaker of the House, Barbara Pellegrino, becomes the first female president. It's that simple."

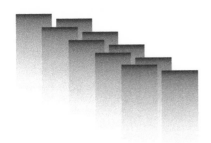

CHAPTER 64
Association Research
600 New Hampshire Avenue NW
Washington, DC
Tuesday, February 19, 2013

"There was only a half-bottle in the cabinet," said Wharton as he held a bottle and three glasses while taking a seat where Jenkins and Ken Middleton were sitting like deer caught in headlights. "I hope you all like bourbon."

"Any port in a storm," said Middleton shaking his head.

"Amen," said Jenkins. "Today was quite a day."

"I may have more than one to calm me down," said Wharton as he poured two fingers of bourbon into each glass.

"I'm in shock after hearing what Larry said this afternoon," said Jenkins.

"Maybe we should try to get some of the registration books," said Middleton. "That might be possible through a Freedom of Information request. They should show who actually voted, by name, and their parties. That way, we could verify some of what we learned today."

"For Christ's sakes, Ken," Wharton said, "do you really need proof that the Democrats cheat? Hell, it's in their DNA. They believe their ends justify any means. Pellegrino and Lowen are probably cheering right now, and if that isn't bad enough, we have a lot of wimpy squishes on our side of the aisle who are scared to take them on."

"All right, Jack," said Jenkins. "It's been a bad day at Black Rock, but we merely confirmed what we already knew."

"I guess you're right, Brad," Wharton said. "I was in a state of shock when Nate Grishom lost. Then one day, I listened to an expert on cyber intelligence tell a group of us how easy it would be to hack into voting machines, and I was convinced that Nate had lost due to fraud. Now, David and Sharon come along and confirm everything I've felt in my heart of hearts."

"Changing the subject," Middleton said, "where do we go from here?"

"For starters," answered Jenkins, "I'd keep our powder dry. We're not trying to prove anything at the moment, so I'd forget any Freedom of Information requests. Not only would such an attempt to be a waste of time; it would also surely result in blowing our cover, so to speak."

"Do you plan on sitting in on another chapter of *The Road to Liberaldom*"? Wharton asked.

"I think I'll give it another try," answered Jenkins. "But after tomorrow, if I can last all day, I'll give it a pass and have the kids make some copies for me to look through on my computer."

"What about your father-in-law? Do you think he might be coming tomorrow?"

"I'd bet money on it, Jack. That's one of the reasons I'll be here tomorrow. After what we've learned about voter fraud today, I'm sure after Mike tells him what we've learned, nothing could keep him away."

CHAPTER 65

Association Research
600 New Hampshire Avenue NW
Washington, DC
Friday, February 22, 2013

"Thanks for coming in early," said Brad Jenkins to Mykro Lehner. "There are a few things I want to discuss with you before I head off to that other office in the Executive Office Building. I didn't want to wait until later in the day and run the risk of you and Taffy taking off for the weekend."

After the second day of watching the monitors while Mykro, Taffy, David, and Sharon attempted to explain the data being displayed, Jenkins had suggested that perhaps they were going about everything the wrong way. There was just too much to see and digest, and at the rate they were going, they would still be staring glassy-eyed at the monitors for another month. He suggested that copies be made and distributed to everyone to be read at their convenience, an idea everyone agreed to.

The next day, Jack Wharton drove Mykro and David to a computer store to buy external hard drives. Four pairs would be assigned to Paul Bernstein, Jack Wharton, Ken Middleton, and Jenkins. Mike Middleton, Larry Evans, Royce Bartlett, and Harry Reason, and his two associates, Ralph Peterson and Douglas Northridge, would be assigned six pairs. One pair would go to Alberto Garcia, President Branch's chief of staff, and one pair would be stored in the safe at Association Research. Each of the drives would be loaded with the applications necessary to access and view the data files that would be copied. In addition to this chore, a special presentation, not to exceed an hour's length, would be created for the president to view.

Mykro had estimated that it would be the first of March before all this work would be finished.

"What I wanted to discuss with you, Myk," said Jenkins, "is where we go after you copy all the material for everyone and finish with the presentation."

"I was wondering that myself. What did you have in mind?"

"A couple of things. Ever since Tuesday, I've been thinking about the scope of all the data you've downloaded. One or two people could come up with the plan for the left to take over the country, but it would take more than one or two people to dig up all the dirt on all the people mentioned. The amount of data is so great that it obviously took many people a lot of time to collect. Also, a hell of a lot of money would have been required. I think with a conjunction of a lot of money, people, and time, there would be weak links somewhere. If we could find them, perhaps we could find out who all were involved in all this."

"And you want us to start the search?"

"Correct. Actually, in a way, you've already started when you were trying to find a way into Lowen's computer. I'd like you to return to Tel Aviv after you finish the president's presentation. This brings me to item number two, Stan and Carol. We could use their help. I think Stan's very interested in the financial aspect of our discoveries. Back in Tel Aviv, we're protected, but here, our necks would be on the chopping block. That's why I was hoping you could talk them into periodically returning to Israel. They could work there a while and then here for a while."

"I'll see what I can do, Dr. Jenkins."

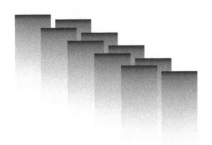

CHAPTER 66

The White House
1600 Pennsylvania Avenue NW
Washington, DC
Monday, March 11, 2013

President Branch had had another restless night. Every night since his meeting with Harry Reason and Brad Jenkins on the fourth had been restless. Half of him was in a state of shock, and the other half was fatigued because his brain had been working overtime.

This morning, the president had gotten up earlier than usual and had gone to the Oval Office before any coffee or breakfast. The way he felt made the thought of drinking or eating abhorrent. As he gazed out on the South Lawn and beyond into a darkness broken only by the glow of a few monuments in the distance, he heard a door opening and closing.

"Good morning, Al," said President Branch to his chief of staff and friend of many years. "You decided to come to work extra early?"

Garcia was a Mexican American and the son of an illegal from south of the border who had found himself in the American army during the Korean War. As his father had in Korea, Alberto had been awarded the Congressional Medal of Honor, but unlike his father, his performance in the line of duty without regard to his own life had caused his military career to come to an end via a medical discharge.

"I had this premonition that you might be here earlier than usual today," said Garcia. "I thought this might be a good time for a tête-à-tête, particularly after seeing you walk around like a zombie after Jenkins's presentation."

"There was a lot to absorb, Al. I'm still struggling with it. Have you managed to make it through everything Brad and Harry left for you?"

"As best I could. After trying to absorb it, I'm scared they might succeed. All she needs to do is become president, and Katy bar the door. She'll do anything she wants, and no one will try to stop her. It's bad enough she's a woman, but she's also a protected species."

"I know she's supposed to be black," said the president with a chuckle. "But she's almost as white as us. Actually, she looks more Italian than white."

"That may count in Realville where Rush Limbaugh is the mayor, but in the court of liberaldom, she's black because her father is black and so are her grandparents."

"So we just roll over and play dead?"

"I'm not saying that, but they've worked out an almost perfect plan that destroys our party and corrupts and captures all the major business interests. Destroy the country by overwhelming the system with spending, taxes, and regulations. Overwhelm it till it collapses, and every middle-class person is dependent upon government and voting for Democrats to keep their checks coming so their families survive. Pass all kinds of social legislation such as health care under the guise of fairness, and exempt the Congress so there's no pushback. Co-opt big business in a way that they support you and you them with all the small businesses getting screwed. Throw in a disregard of our immigration laws and solicit all those undocumented Democrats from south of the border. Hell, by the time she's finished pulling all this off, it'll be the end of the country. I don't know what kind of country we'll have, but it won't be a capitalist, socialist, or a fascist one either."

"You sound like you're ready to surrender."

"No, not at all, because I think they have made a big miscalculation. George, it's obvious after watching the tapes that they selected you because they thought you were the weakest link. Shit, George, you're just a fucking Texas cowboy to them, someone who lives on a ranch in flyover country. They don't know or understand the world beyond their own prisms. They selected you and made sure you won the primaries and the general election because they figured getting rid of you would be easier than getting rid of anyone else. They never knew you as a person, and they never knew the kind of people you would select to work with you. And they sure as hell never knew that Mike had learned of Lowen and Pellegrino or that Brad Jenkins would enter your life."

"What are you trying to tell me, Al?"

"We have their invasion plan. I don't know how we can stop them or if it's even possible, but with all we know in conjunction with our meager resources, I can't see us not trying."

"It sounds like in spite of all this you might have an idea."

"I wish I did, George. I'm not worried about any ideas of what to do or how to handle this. I figure we have two years to think of something, work out some sort of plan."

"Al, we don't have two years. That's what's been bothering me. Time is not on our side. Perhaps you should go back to the drawing board."

"George, I wasn't worried about a plan because I was seeing one problem after another. And these problems need to be taken into consideration before developing any plans."

"All right. Tell me about your problems."

"First, everything we have, from Mike's bugging of Pellegrino to Dr. Jenkins's people hacking into accounts, was illegal."

"I'm sure there's a way to get around the legal niceties. The NSA and the FBI do it all the time. No one needs to know how we came by the data."

"I wouldn't be too sure of that, but that's another story. A second big problem would be our government agencies. If they're all as infiltrated as the downloaded data suggests, we couldn't trust them to do diddly-squat. We're a prisoner of our own resourcefulness. And if the media ever found out what we have, they'd be yelling and screaming and would ridicule you worse than they did Reagan over Star Wars, and of course the people involved in all this would fade into the woodwork. George, we're temporarily fucked, and that's worse than being between a rock and a hard place."

For several moments, President Branch sat with his eyes closed and slowly shook his head. "Al, there's more than one way to skin the cat. We have to find that way."

"I do have a fallback position," Garcia said, chuckling.

"Do I dare ask?"

"Dr. Jenkins has teams of assassins working in the Middle East. He calls them surgeons, but they're really assassins. Perhaps some of them are working in the wrong country."

The president chuckled. "Al, believe it or not, I've had similar thoughts. But I think this whole affair is bigger than a few people."

"I will record for the record, George, that you didn't say, 'No way, Jose' or even 'No way, Alberto.'"

"Nor did I say, 'Do it,' my friend."

"Then it sounds like we're back to square one."

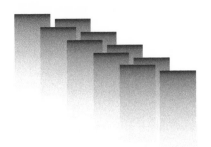

CHAPTER 67

Middleton Estate
Big Basin Way
Boulder Creek, California
Friday, March 22, 2013

It was before-dinner attitude adjustment time when Mike Middleton and Harry Reason were having their conversation in Middleton's large paneled study about the events of the past several weeks.

"Hasn't George said anything?" asked a frustrated Mike Middleton.

"Only that he needed some time to think things over," Reason answered.

"Damn it, Harry, I feel like we just learned the Japanese fleet is nearing Pearl Harbor and we're not doing the first fucking thing about it. We uncover what's probably the biggest fucking scandal in our history, and all we're doing is sitting around with our fingers up our asses."

"The only thing George has said to me was that he wanted me to save the military," said Reason with an air of resignation.

"Nothing else?"

"Just that he didn't give two hoots and a shit how I did it just as long as I did it."

"What about Brad? Hasn't George said anything to him either? Christ, he sees George at times just like you."

"George hasn't said anything to him yet either."

"Incredible. Fucking A, incredible. I would have thought that after learning how the Democrats handed him two elections in a row, how they just took the House and the plans for him and Chandler after they steal another election in twenty fourteen, he'd be a little concerned. Shit, that bitch Pellegrino is to the left of Lenin. If she becomes president, you can kiss the country good-bye."

"Tell me about it, my friend," said Reason as he shook his head in disgust.

"George wants to pontificate. Brad knows nothing. We know nothing. We can't just sit around and fiddle while Rome is burning."

"Actually, Brad has taken it upon himself to do something. He has the kids working. He feels that the scope of everything is so great that many people with a lot of time and money are involved."

"I guess that in addition to George wanting the military saved, that's a step in the right direction. But these people just might be too smart to send e-mails back and forth. Look at this character from New York who kept traveling to Washington to meet with Pellegrino's chief of staff. It's obvious he was just a courier."

"That's not how it works, Mike. Brad's people weren't successful because they were reading e-mails. They were successful because someone opened one. According to him, all they need are some names and some e-mail addresses. Once anyone opens an e-mail, they'll own that computer and no one will be the wiser."

"I hope the hell you're right, Harry, but I still feel we have to do something instead of just sitting around while someone is out there attempting to fundamentally transform the country by turning it into a one-party pseudo democracy."

"You're the idea man, boss."

"Yeah, I know. My brain has been working overtime, but I keep drilling dry holes. I'm either getting too old or the massive scale of what we've uncovered has gotten to me. The closest thing to an idea I've been able to come up with is thinking we may have to fight fire with fire, but don't ask me how."

CHAPTER 68

Evans Residence
Foster City, California
Saturday, April 6, 2013

"Sometimes, I wonder where the hell you get your ideas, Larry," said Royce Bartlett while they chewed the fat on Evans's deck overlooking the waterway. "If I didn't know any better, I'd think Mike was whispering in your ear."

"Believe it or not," said Evans, "I got the idea from Babbsy baby. Ever since the election, she and Lowen have been quite vocal."

"Quite vocal? Or are you just now getting used to the lingo?"

"Probably a little of everything. Now that we can see the trees in the forest, understanding what they're saying is a lot easier."

"Yeah, the video cameras, which I assume you were referring to metaphorically, have been a great help. We've also got some great pornographic material we can use just in case."

"You know, Royce, I want to kick myself in the tush every time I think how wrong I was with so many of my assumptions. Because of them, we've dicked around for four years."

"I wouldn't sweat it, Larry. It may have been a circuitous row to hoe for a few years, but all those assumptions led us to the mother lode. It's time to look ahead and forget what was. Besides, some good has come of things. Hell, Ben's daughter got herself a husband because of your assumptions."

"And her friend Carol come to think of it. Speaking of husbands, it appears my two granddaughters may be taking the plunge."

"With whom?"

"The sons of the colonel, the friend of Ken and Brad. You met him in Hawaii, remember?"

"There you go, my friend. Two more good things happening all because of your assumptions. But we're digressing. Have you mentioned your militia idea to Mike, or is this something you're winging?"

"I drove to Boulder Creek about ten days ago. We had a little confab during lunch."

"I guess he liked the idea or we wouldn't be here talking."

"Actually, he had mixed emotions, much like the good news bad news routine."

"That doesn't sound encouraging. Give me the good news first."

"With or without the expletives?"

"Either way."

"He said, 'Finally someone has come up with a fucking idea'."

"And the bad?"

"That we'd be venturing into uncharted territory and if we pursued this we should be extremely cautious. I told him we've always made sure to cover all bases."

"His advice is on the mark."

"Can we count on everyone if we pursue this?"

"According to Will and Ben, the men of Charlie Communications would follow the captain and major through hell if they were asked to. So I guess it's a go in that regard."

"Then we have some work to do."

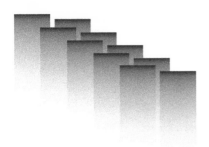

CHAPTER 69
Office of the Secretary of Defense
The Pentagon
Arlington, Virginia
Monday, April 8, 2013

"I gather by the way each of you looks this morning that you've finished your homework," said Defense Secretary Harry Reason with a fiendish grin.

"I don't know about Doug," answered Colonel Ralph Peterson, "but I think you were trying to get even with me for giving you that flash drive a while back and telling you it was required reading."

"Oh," replied Secretary Reason with a smile as he remembered something about a badass Colonel. "That was a while back."

"Whatever that was about," Colonel Northridge said, "it had to have been pretty tame stuff compared to what you gave us. Where the hell did you get all this?"

"Why don't the two of you get yourselves another cup of coffee and come back? While you're at it, you might want to add a little something adult if you can find any around here. I think it's time for me to tell a story or two."

"And that's pretty much the story of how we got here," said Harry Reason after forty-five minutes of storytelling. "Had my friend Michael not gotten the tip about Pellegrino and her chief of staff, we wouldn't be having this meeting."

"We also probably wouldn't be having it if you and your friend hadn't tried to be matchmakers," said Colonel Peterson. "We should thank our lucky stars that your son-in-law put together his little organization."

"I'll drink to that," said Secretary Reason. "When it comes down to it, we've been lucky as hell at so many steps along the way."

"Well," said Colonel Northridge. "It's nice to be lucky once in a while, but that's not a winning strategy."

"I couldn't agree more," added Colonel Peterson. "But where are we going from here?"

"The only thing I can tell you is that the president has given me marching orders to save our military," said Reason. "And he doesn't give a rat's ass how I do it. So the old ball is now in our court."

"For God's sakes, Harry!" said Colonel Peterson. "While I sympathize, what the president wants is easier said than done. Half the damned officers we've selected for advancement, according to our original plans, have made their debut in all those files we've spent months looking at."

"I'm with Ralph on that one," said Colonel Northridge. "We've worked our rear ends off for four years trying to weed out the incompetents and develop a cadre of senior officers with professional competence. Now this comes along and we learn that some damned good senior officers like Mark Sutton, one of our task force commanders in Afghanistan, and Vince Farrell, our deputy commander of CENTCOM, have been compromised."

"Yeah," added Colonel Peterson. "I'm still amazed at how many of those damn generals are or were involved in extramarital affairs. What was not clear to me though was if these guys have been blackmailed."

"If they aren't currently blackmailed," Colonel Northridge said, "they're certainly blackmailable and so are their paramours. Some of those women involved are pretty well-known socialites, and one of the women mentioned is of Arab descent."

"Whatever," said Reason. "We have a manpower problem. Whatever plan we come up with, we need more bodies, and that presents a problem because we need bodies we can trust implicitly. People who believe in things like sacred honor and our constitution. At this point, I can think of only one way to assure that. Do you remember me once telling you about the time I was a guest speaker at the Command and General Staff School and how I wished I could have been a bug on the wall?"

"Oh my God!" Colonel Peterson chuckled. "You want to bug some of these officers?"

"More than some, Ralph," said Secretary Reason. "We'll bug the whole fucking senior officer corps to the best of our ability. We'll bug every place they sleep, sit, eat, and pee. We'll bug their golf carts and maybe their clubs while we're at it. And that's just for starters. Blackmail can work both ways. These officers can be given a choice—duty, honor, and country—or we'll ruin their lives.

"Now, in keeping with the president's instructions, there are a few military facilities in California I think might need a bit of my time and attention. Might be a good idea if the two of you tagged along. It's time for you meet a few people."

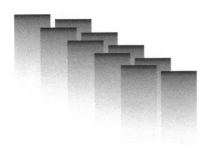

CHAPTER 70

The White House
1600 Pennsylvania Avenue NW
Washington, DC
Friday, April 19, 2013

While his restless nights had subsided somewhat since his conversation with Al Garcia a month ago, the president still found himself experiencing the occasional restless night followed by rising earlier mornings than usual. The pressure of the office was usually enough to make anyone have the occasional restless night, but the revelations of a vast left-wing conspiracy more than a month ago had finally forced him to make a few decisions.

His first decision had been to keep quiet until he knew who all the conspirators were. His second had been his marching orders for Harry Reason to save the military by any means. Now, he was about to issue a presidential directive that would require an act of God to be fulfilled.

"Good morning, Brad," said the president. "I was about to ring for coffee. Care to join me?"

"Thank you, sir," said Jenkins.

"Ever since that meeting with you and Harry, I've felt like adding brandy to my coffee."

"After reviewing all that information, I understand. Is that why you wished to see me this morning?"

"Yes. Brad, when I came to Washington, I had deep misgivings about our government agencies. Now, thanks to Mike Middleton's little bugging operation and your Abraham team members, these misgivings have been validated. I think I owe Mike, Harry, and their partners in crime an apology for thinking that nothing good would ever be achieved. But being doubtful wasn't the only mistake I've made. One was thinking I could work with the Congress as I worked with the legislature back home. There, the people I had to deal with cared about the state, and our main differences were more about how to get there rather than worry about being there.

"There are only about thirty or forty members of Congress who really care about the country, and I may be being generous with that figure. Most of those on the Hill think only of themselves and their massive egos. Heaven help getting between some of them and a TV camera.

"From the beginning of my business career, I've always made it a practice to surround myself with competent people who would tell it to me the way it was and not what they thought I wanted to hear. I've done my best to do the same thing when I came to this town, but there must be something in the water here. Some very talented and capable people in my administration have found it difficult to be completely honest in their assessments. I've learned there are only a handful of people I can depend on to tell it to me the way it is. You're one of them."

"Thank you, sir."

"Brad, the person behind this desk is supposedly the most powerful man in the world. He can swivel this chair around and reach for one of these phones and almost instantly can get in touch with other powerful people anywhere. He could even start a war if he chose. Please note that the operative word is *supposedly*. Since the revelations, I've felt like a prisoner. While I can still call powerful people and perhaps make war, I can't risk contacting a few damn government agencies to deal with the problem we now have to confront. That's why I wanted to speak with you this morning.

"I once facetiously asked you to play God, and you didn't let me down. For the sake of our country, I'm asking you again. We must win the struggle against the Islamic forces preaching jihad regardless of which party is in power. That's a struggle we can't afford to lose. I realize it's a lot to ask of any man, and I'm also probably being unfair, but our world today is not about fairness, it's about survival. As long as I'm president, I'll do my best to provide you with whatever you need."

"Thank you, sir. I guess I have some work to do."

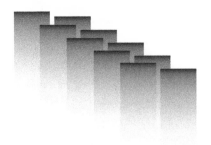

CHAPTER 71
Frank Rawlings Residence
Fort Collins, Colorado
Thursday, May 19, 2013

It had been a long afternoon, and Frank Rawlings had been tasting a cold can of Coors ever since he had gotten on Interstate 25 and began driving north. He and his wife had left home shortly before twelve to make the sixty-four-mile drive to Denver International Airport where they had planned on having a leisurely lunch before her three fifty-seven flight to Seattle, but airport construction activity had created a series of navigational and parking problems that had translated into a lousy McDonald's hamburger and a lot of hurry up and wait.

As Rawlings turned into his driveway and pressed the button on the garage door remote, his thirst had grown by another can. A cold six-pack was only moments away.

After entering his mud room and turning off the security system, Rawlings hung his car keys on the rack above the keypad and headed to the kitchen fridge and extracted a cold one from the six-pack on the bottom shelf, popped the top, and took a long, pleasurable swig. He was about to take another swig when he felt the hairs on the back of his neck stand to attention. Immediately his built-in antenna told him he was not alone. Slowly, he walked toward a cabinet to the left of the sink and opened the top drawer. As he reached under the folded towels for his SIG Sauer P227, he heard a man's voice.

"It's not there, Frank."

Rawlings froze.

"Turn around, Frank. It's all right. No one is going to hurt you. Just come on into the living room and have a seat. Don't turn the light on."

As Rawlings entered his living room, he saw a figure seated in a chair by a window with its blinds angled in a way that kept any facial features hidden.

"Have a seat," said the man. "It's easier to talk when one is comfortable."

As instructed, Rawlings sat down, but he said nothing. *Who is this man?* he wondered, but the late-afternoon shadows were preventing him from seeing the man's features clearly.

"I'm surprised you haven't asked the obvious questions."

"Who are you?" Rawlings finally said. "What do you want? How did you get in?"

"I'm someone who believes in the same things you do, Frank. My name is unimportant. What do I want? My associates and I wish to explore the possibility of collaboration. How did we get in? We unlocked the door. Security systems present no problem for us."

"Trespassing is no problem either?"

"We thought this was the best way to have a private discussion particularly as your whereabouts are closely monitored."

"Who are you, the feds?"

"No. We are not from the government, but we are here to help."

Whoever this guy is, he has a sense of humor, Rawlings thought as he stifled a grin.

"By breaking into—check that—by walking into someone's home uninvited?"

"Frank, we don't have a lot of time. You have something we feel would be very useful though not in its current form."

"I don't need a landscape partner."

"Come on, Frank, cut the dance. We know all about you from the day you were born until the present. Your complete history is on this little thing I have here in my hand. You know we're talking about all those friends of yours running around, playing soldier, and making a lot of people in Washington very nervous."

"Whatever some people think, I haven't done anything illegal, so whoever is nervous can whistle Dixie."

"That's not the way it works in the real world, Frank. There's a lot of information on this little device that can result in all the wrong conclusions being drawn. I'm afraid informants don't always tell the whole truth and nothing but the truth. I'll trade this little device for your cell phone."

"Why do you want my cell?"

"For protection." The shadowy figure turned to someone who now stood in the entrance to the living room. "Get his phone and give him this."

"What are you going to do with my phone?" Rawlings asked as he exchanged the phone for a flash drive.

"He's going to remove the battery and then put the phone and the battery along with your landline phones in your car and lock it. When we leave, we'll put your car keys in your mailbox. By the time you get the key, unlock the car, and make a call, we'll be long gone."

"What's on this flash drive, if I may ask?"

"Your life's history. FBI and BTAF reports. A list of the informants who have infiltrated your organization. An outline of what we wish to achieve and how we would like to work with you. And how you can securely get in touch with us whenever you wish to meet again."

"You seem to be rather well organized."

"We try."

"The car's here," said a third man.

"We'll be in touch. By the way, your security system is in proper working order again."

CHAPTER 72
En Route to the Fort Collins Marriott
Fort Collins, Colorado
Thursday, May 19, 2013

"How did it go?" asked Will Rikker after Larry Evans, Royce Bartlett, and Ben Sorenson got into the minivan.

"Like clockwork," Sorenson said.

"Forget the damn clock," said Royce Bartlett. "Let's get the hell out of here."

"I second the motion," said Evans. "But I suggest you stop for a moment after we make our first turn so we can get the tape off the plate. We don't want to get caught with our plates covered."

"What do you think Rawlings is doing now?" Bartlett asked after the plates were uncovered and when they had turned off Rookery Road onto County Route 9 and were heading north.

"Unless he's still in the process of retrieving his cell phone," said Evans, "he's probably heading for his computer to see what's on the flash drive."

"Suppose he's too smart or too suspicious to stick that thing into his computer?"

"I think he'll stick it into his wife's computer, but it won't make any difference. I'm sure his wife will send or forward something to him at some point, and we'll end up owning his machine."

"You don't think he'll call the police?" asked Sorenson.

"Ben," said Bartlett, "the police will be the last people he'd think of calling."

"So where to now?" asked Rikker.

"Back to the Marriott," answered Evans. "We can give the wives a call and let them know we're still alive and then head for the bar for some refreshment before dinner. Then a good night's sleep. We'll be wheels up sometime after breakfast tomorrow unless the bottom falls out of the world."

"How long do you think we should wait before we do a number two?" asked Bartlett.

"I think we should give it a couple of weeks," answered Evans. "You know, allow enough time for seeing what happens regarding Rawlings. You know there's always the possibility we may need to make some revisions to our approach."

"You guys made it all look so easy," said Sorenson. "I haven't had this much fun and excitement since I retired."

"We've watched a lot of movies and read a lot of books, haven't we, Larry?" Bartlett asked with a chuckle.

"That's what Mike keeps reminding us. Plus, we also have a lot of experience."

"Whatever," Sorenson said, "you made it look easy, and I enjoyed myself. I'm looking forward to the next one."

Yes, thought Evans as Rikker made a left turn onto East Harmony Road. *It's always easy when you're lucky and other people are stupid. People should never divulge their travel plans on Facebook.*

While they had been lucky, they had also made their own luck. It all started with some computer research that had led to their discovery that Rawlings's wife used Facebook. Using a trick or two he had learned from Mykro Lehner, he had simply hacked the account and learned of Virginia Rawlings's travel plans. With knowledge of date and time, the four of them had come to Fort Collins several days earlier and had played detective.

They surreptitiously watched the house. By using scanners, they were able to steal the garage door code and learned how to access Rawlings's smartphone. Their plans to access the house by posing as ADT security were not necessary; Rawlings's security system was wireless, so they could access it via his phone. Once they learned the code, everything else was a piece of cake.

As he and Royce had done with love nests east and west, they had bugged the house and had hidden a transmitter in the attic. They had also bugged his smartphone while it was in their possession. While Royce and Ben were attending to the house bugging, he had accessed Mrs. Rawlings's computer, which was not password protected, and installed a spy program. They had all the bases covered. It was only a matter of time.

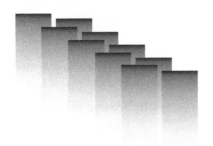

CHAPTER 73

Wharton Residence
McLean, Virginia
Thursday, July 4, 2013

It's been a long but successful and interesting day, Jack Wharton thought during those magical forty-five seconds between when his head touched the pillow and he went to sleep. Wharton had called it a coming-out party because it was one of the few times Candy Reason and Brad Jenkins had shown their faces in public since election time the previous year.

When he had thought about having the boat party, Wharton had wondered if it had been because Dave Hawkins had asked too many questions or if it had been something Jenkins had said that morning at the Holiday Inn the day after the wedding of Colonel Golden's sons and Ken Middleton's daughters. Whatever the reason, Wharton knew deep down it was the right thing to do.

After leaving the Pentagon marina, they had headed south on the Potomac to Mount Vernon and had turned and headed back upriver with brief pauses near Fort Washington and the Gaylord Convention Center complex before anchoring near Memorial Bridge where they would be in an ideal position to watch the annual fireworks.

During the whole afternoon and early evening of cruising as they sipped and nibbled, there had been many conversations of a political nature that considering the people involved he had known would happen, but it had evolved slowly after everyone had felt his or her way.

Of his Abraham friends, only Brad Jenkins had met Nate Grishom and David Hawkins and their wives before, and that had been three years earlier. Since then, much had changed in their lives.

When Candy Reason had become secretary of state, Wharton told Nate Grishom and David Hawkins and by extension their wives that his wife, Susan, had been asked to become Candy's chief of staff. Though the names of Nancy Middleton and Michele Golden to become respectively deputy secretary of state and deputy chief of staff had become public knowledge, Grishom and Hawkins had not realized the connections to Jenkins and himself until he had introduced everyone.

"Jack," said Nate Grishom as they were sailing and enjoying a cold brew, "what a tangled web of relationships you weave. Why haven't you ever mentioned any of Brad's other friends?"

"Just one of those things, Nate. I'd met Colonel Golden once or twice in passing when Brad was helping me on my treks, but the others and the relationships I never knew about until after he had met Candy, and then, because they wished not to make their marriage public, I said nothing. Consider this afternoon's coming-out party a substitute for not saying anything to you two earlier."

"If I were a conspiracy theorist," Grishom said with a chuckle, "I'd think this marriage business was a setup to sucker in the libs."

"You can think whatever you wish, Nate. The records were there for all to see, but as we all know with the media, it's always the allegation. I suspect even if someone in the media did some detective work and actually learned the truth, the storm would still have happened."

"They made a big mistake, though," Hawkins said as he appeared holding three bottles of beer. "A line was crossed, and that's what did them in. Because of that, the Boy Scouts and a lot of wounded service members' organizations will benefit. I'm sure as hell glad I listened to you."

"Whatever," said Wharton. "I'm sure they're glad it's all behind them now."

"It will never be over for them," said Grishom. "I think they will have bull's-eyes on their backs the rest of their lives. Remember, they fought the media elites, won, and made them pay a tremendous price."

It was probably the women who really engaged in exploring each other. They were all attractive, well-educated, competent, and self-assured women who could rival the famed women of Fox News. Gerri Grishom had been her husband's chief of staff for Nate's whole political career. Evelyn Hawkins was also a journalist like her husband; she wrote a metro column for the *Times* three times a week. Gerri and Evelyn naturally took an interest in Candy, Nancy, and Michele.

"I'm surprised to be partying with the State Department this afternoon," Gerri said to Candy. "I was surprised when I learned Susan had been asked to be your chief of staff, but I had no idea of the other interlocking relationships."

"Nor did I in the beginning," Candy said. "When I presented Brad at that Friends of Israel dinner, I had no idea any relationship between us would develop let alone that he knew the Whartons, the Middletons, or the Goldens. Small world."

"I was also quite surprised when I learned Susan was going with you to State," Evelyn Hawkins said. "Knowing how Jack always liked to get on his soapbox and rail about the Arabists in the State Department, there were several times I felt tempted to call her and ask if you were following any of his advice."

"We're trying," said Nancy Middleton. "Now only half of State is pro-Arab. Unfortunately, the other half is anti-Israel."

"I can hardly be accused of being a feminist," said Gerri Grishom, "but I'm glad to see the four of you at State. I was surprised when the announcements were made, but I knew of Susan's qualifications because she ran Jack's business. And your credentials, Candy, are impressive. However, being the curious creature I am, I did a little research on you, Nancy, and was impressed, but I struck out on you, Michele."

"I guess that was because most of her life she's been busy being the wife of an army officer and the mother of two," said Susan Wharton sensing Gerri had crossed a line.

Gerri Grishom was apologetic.

"I've noticed that Candy's husband always calls your husband Mustafa," said Gerri, attempting to move on from an awkward moment. "That seems a rather unusual nickname. You don't call him that, do you?"

"Heavens no," Michele said. "I call him Marshall or Marsh. Only Brad and sometimes Ken call him Mustafa."

"How on earth did he ever get such a nickname?"

"They grew up together in Lebanon. Their parents were friends, and the story is that it was easier for Brad to say Mustafa than Marshall at the time, and it stuck. It took some getting used to for me in the early years, but I'm used to it now."

"Might I ask how you met your husband?" Evelyn asked.

"We were seatmates on a hijacked plane that was made to land in the deserts of northern Iraq," Michele said.

"My heavens!" said Gerri. "That had to have been a horrible experience."

"It was. When we were told to get off the plane, he told me to stay close to him."

As the day went on, the subject of politics, especially Middle East politics, came up.

"I'm not asking you to talk out of school, Brad," said Nate, "but after seeing you on Greta one night a few weeks ago and the president's latest news conference, was it you who had advised him to avoid any entanglements in those countries, or had he made up his mind and told you what to say?"

"Off the record, I advised him."

"Would I be out of order asking why?"

"Nate, before I answer your question, I would like to say that personally, I'd have no problem interceding in that part of the world if we could do it the right way. Unfortunately, the right way would cause a lot of people to either wet their pants or get apoplectic."

"What would you do that would make people over here wet their pants?" asked Grishom as he laughed and displayed his boyish smile.

"For instance, I once read something on the net about what General Pershing did in the Philippines after we defeated Spain. I don't know whether it's true considering the source, but the story was that after capturing a bunch of Muslim rebels, he had his men slaughter a pig and dip their bullets in the blood. They executed all the rebels except one, who was allowed to go back and tell his fellow terrorists what they could expect if they were captured."

"My God," said Gerri. "Surely you're not suggesting we execute everyone."

"See what I mean, Nate?" said Jenkins laughing. "No, I'm not suggesting anything like that, Gerri. But what could be done is get the message out that any suicide bomber, for instance, would have their body parts scraped up and buried with pig parts."

"You're right, Brad," said Nate Grishom laughing even more. "It's not in our mental framework to think like that."

"Nate, we're not good at getting involved in societies we don't understand. As a country, we don't understand that part of the world, nor do we understand what pretends to be a religion but in actuality is a dictatorial way of life. The real reason I advised the president to not get involved was because both sides in what is shaping up to be a civil war are our enemies. When you find yourself in a hole, you're supposed to stop digging. When your enemies start killing each other, stand aside and let them get on with it."

"Brad's right," said Colonel Golden. "The West doesn't understand anything about that part of the world. Most of what we as a country get pumped at us is rubbish."

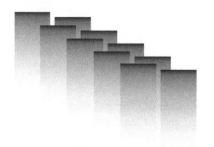

CHAPTER 74
Thelma's Restaurant
51 Main Street
Saranac Lake, New York
Friday, July 19, 2013

Lester Pearson's morning had started as every other morning had since he had moved to Saranac Lake—breakfast at Thelma's Restaurant before going fishing or pursuing other enjoyments. Usually, Pearson would find a booth where he could sit alone and enjoy coffee while meditating or monitoring his iPad.

There were exceptions, however, when a local would join him and they would engage in an animated discussion on how to set the world right. This morning, the three men who slid into the booth were not local.

"Do I know you?" asked Pearson trying to act unsurprised.

"No, Les, you don't," said one, "but we know you. That's why we invited ourselves for breakfast."

Pearson tried to be nonchalant. "In these parts, when people invite themselves to breakfast unannounced, they pick up the tab."

"No problem, Les. Have you ordered?"

"Just about to."

"What do you recommend?"

"The blueberry pancakes are something to write home about."

"I will assume that was meant to be a compliment as well as a recommendation."

"I don't think you'll be disappointed," said Pearson as he motioned to the waitress. "Margi, my friends and I would like to experience the pleasure of Thelma's famous blueberry pancakes."

"Would you gentlemen also like coffee?" she asked.

"Coffee and some orange juice for me," said Larry Evans.

"Ditto," said Ross Bartlett and Ben Sorenson.

"Now that we've dispensed with the important things," said Les after Margi had poured coffee, "what do my newfound friends who suddenly appear at my breakfast table want?"

""We would like to explore the possibility of collaboration," said Larry Evans.

"Gentlemen, I'm flattered, but I don't think I have anything anyone would like to collaborate with."

"On the contrary, Les," said Evans. "You have a very interesting organization. In fact, we're not the only ones who are interested in your organization, but we think given your druthers, you'd rather do business with us than the other interested parties."

"Even if I had an organization, why would I want to do business with you?"

"Because we believe in the same things, Les. Things like duty, honor, and country."

Instantly, Pearson realized the three men were also ex-military. He glanced at the two across the table from him. They appeared to him to be in their late sixties or early seventies. *Too old to be federales acting like this. If they're ex-military, their war had to have been Vietnam.*

When breakfast was over, Pearson said he would give due consideration to a proposed collaboration. He said that it had been nice meeting everyone but that he had things to do. Ben Sorenson then stood to let Pearson slide out of the booth and sat down after Pearson had left.

"What do you think he'll do now?" asked Bartlett.

"I'd bet the farm his curiosity will get the best of him and he'll head for home to see what's on the flash drive."

"You want I should give Rikker a call?" Sorenson asked.

"Okay," Evans said. "Find out if he was successful with the homing device, and find out where he is now. Ross, why don't you activate the tracking program on your phone. I want to leave mine free for when he inserts the drive. That's assuming of course he's heading home to satisfy his curiosity."

"Will says Pearson is headed north on Broadway and everything is kosher," said Sorenson a minute later.

"Let's enjoy another cup of the black stuff while we wait," said Evans. "If Pearson sticks the drive in his machine, it will show up here, and we'll have him by the you-know-what. Then we can head back to Placid and finish out the weekend."

"That'll chalk up number three," said Bartlett. "We're making it look easy."

Yes, thought Evans, *we made it look easy, but that was because we had expended the time and effort.*

They had flown into the Adirondack Regional Airport at Saranac Lake on a company plane earlier in the week with their wives. After picking up two rental cars from Hertz, they had driven to Lake Placid, where they and their wives were staying at the Crowne Plaza Resort Golf Club. By coming as a group of eight people, they had thought they would blend in with the myriad of other tourists who came to Lake Placid in the summer. Like this morning, they had driven to Saranac Lake each day to do their detective work while the wives enjoyed their creature comforts. And, like the previous two militia leaders, Lester Pearson had also made a simple mistake. May their good luck continue.

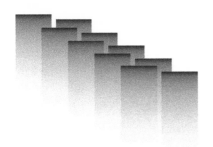

CHAPTER 75

Hay Adams Hotel
800 Sixteenth Street, NW
Washington, DC
Tuesday, August 6, 2013

It was eleven fifty when Brad Jenkins stood in front of the hotel and looked at his watch. He had timed his arrival perfectly. As he entered the hotel, he wondered why a possible incoming prime minister of Israel would want to have lunch with him. *Probably something to do with Abe. Yet Natansky had said nothing about Abe Saturday evening when Candy and I met the man even after a long conversation. Why's he in the States to begin with, and why's he staying at the Hay Adams and not at the embassy?*

After announcing himself, Jenkins was greeted by two tall, well-dressed men, wearing suits expertly tailored to conceal the weapons he knew they were carrying. "Good afternoon," said one of the men in Hebrew, alerting Jenkins to the fact they knew he spoke the language. "This way please."

With a man on each side, he was escorted to the elevator. When the elevator stopped at the penthouse level and the door opened, Jenkins was greeted by two additional security personnel, each like the two who had accompanied him up. "This way, please," said one of the men as the elevator doors closed, returning his two original escorts to the lobby.

After a few steps along the corridor followed by a crisp knock on a door, Jenkins was greeted by a fifth security type who beckoned him to enter.

I must say I'm impressed with the choreography, thought Jenkins as he entered the suite. *Obviously everyone has a radio but I didn't notice any. I wonder why so much security. It's obvious they know I speak Hebrew. I guess anyone connected with Benjamin Natansky is well briefed.*

"Ah, good afternoon, Dr. Jenkins," said Benjamin Natansky, a tall man in his midfifties with a round face and thinning black hair with streaks of gray, in perfect English, as he strode across the room hand outstretched. "So good to see you again. You are very punctual."

Then, with an almost imperceptible nod, he dismissed his security and gestured with a sweep of his hand toward a pair of French doors. "Please. The view is exquisite."

As Natansky suggested, Jenkins walked across the room to the French doors and stood for a moment gazing at the view. Directly below was Lafayette Park teeming with people enjoying lunch. Beyond the park was the White House, and beyond that a picture-perfect view of the Washington Monument. "Fantastic view," said Jenkins as he sat in one of the two armchair chairs.

"Some champagne to start with?" asked Natansky as he took a seat in the opposite chair and reached for a bottle of champagne in a bucket. "The French may disagree as it comes from Israel, but it is very good Israeli champagne."

Effortlessly, Natansky eased the cork from the bottle and poured two glasses. "Shall we drink to friendship? Ours and our respective countries?"

Jenkins raised his glass. "To friendship."

"Before we get engaged in conversation, might I ask a favor?"

"By all means."

"I have read your books and I have read the dossier on you as I assume you have of me. Therefore, might we dispense with formalities and call each other by our given names?"

"I have no problem with that," said Jenkins.

"Good. From now on, I am Ben, not Benjamin, and you shall be Brad, not Bradford. You are no doubt wondering why I wished to have lunch with you so I will get to the point. There will be another war in my part of the world and probably sooner than later. When it happens, it might be the West's last chance. But for the West to prevail, America's full participation will be required."

"I must admit you are right," said Jenkins as he slowly nodded his head in the affirmative. "But to get engaged in such a war and prevail, my country would be required to fight two wars: a cultural war at home, which must be won before it can successfully fight an international war against the Arab jihadists, and that would practically be a revolution.

"We would also have to be willing to face a series of realities we haven't shown a willingness to do before. We must be willing to admit to ourselves who our enemies really are as well as deal with them accordingly. This is something that we, in the United States, have not quite come to grips with since World War II."

"Very interesting." Natansky nodded and smiled. "And who might our enemies be?"

"It's a long list," said Jenkins with a chuckle. "Very long. We have the usual surrogates such as Hezbollah, Hamas, Syria, Al Qaeda, the Taliban, and various sympathizing groups and countries, but the three main ones are Iran, Saudi Arabia, and the Western media."

"How interesting you consider the media one of our enemies."

"It's something that's rather hard to ignore with anyone who takes the time to observe. Just look at how Israel is always treated each time it tries to defend itself. All you have to do is look at how the media reported the Vietnam War and the American involvement in Afghanistan and Iraq. The problem with most of our Western media is their practice of selecting news stories and then shaping them to advance an agenda. They always have a narrative, and their reporting is always from that perspective."

"Brad, my friend, you've said that for your country to get engaged in a war, we each believe to be on a not-too-distant horizon, it would require fighting two wars and one would be tantamount to a revolution. If that is the case, would it not mean some sort of coup? If so, how easy would it be to effectuate such a coup?"

Jenkins was dumbfounded. *Did I hear him correctly?* "If you mean the typical coup where the presidential palace is surrounded and the local radio station is taken over, it would be an impossibility."

"Philosophically speaking," said Natansky with a grin. "Could it be done another way? You Americans have an expression about there always being a way to skin a cat."

"I suppose there is something that might be possible, but if something like that were to ever happen in the United States, it would have to happen in such a way that the American people would never know what had happened."

CHAPTER 76

Candice Reason's Condominium
Watergate South
700 New Hampshire Avenue NW
Washington, DC
Tuesday, August 6, 2013

"And that's the size of it," said Brad Jenkins to Ken Middleton. "Almost word for word as best I can remember. What say you?"

After Jenkins had left the Hay Adams after an almost three-hour lunch, he had walked across Lafayette Park in a daze as he attempted to replay the afternoon's conversation between him and Benjamin Natansky. After crossing what used to be Pennsylvania Avenue but was now only an extension of the park, Jenkins headed to his office in the Old Executive Office Building where he attempted to concentrate on his job but found it difficult to think of anything other than the luncheon. After thirty minutes, he gave up and decided to go home.

Instead of taking a taxi to the Watergate, he walked west on Pennsylvania Avenue to Washington Circle, then headed south on New Hampshire to the Watergate.

In the condo he shared with his wife, Candy, he made himself a drink and stepped out onto the balcony and watched the Potomac flow as he replayed his conversation with Natansky. *If only Candy were here*, he thought. He wanted to tell her about the luncheon, but she was in the Philippines with the president.

After finishing his drink, he went back inside and started to make himself another drink, but feeling desperately in need of someone to talk to, he called his friend Ken Middleton and invited him for a drink.

After Middleton arrived, he and Jenkins made drinks and took them into the living room, where Jenkins told Middleton about his luncheon with Natansky.

"Amazing," said Middleton. "I can see why you could think he wants you to stop one coup and start another, but it still doesn't make sense. Why the hell would someone like Natansky, who's only another politician, not the prime minister, ask such a question? And what the hell coup is he talking about?"

"Maybe he meant this damned left-wing conspiracy we've uncovered."

"If he knows about that, who the hell told him?"

"Maybe Sharon. Maybe she's still part of Israeli intelligence and is working for General Gul."

"I suppose anything's possible, but I don't believe it, and I don't think you do either. You said that you had had a talk with her and that she had said she wouldn't say anything about what we discovered. She's never given me a hint that she'd go back on her word."

"Okay, we can always revisit that one. What else do you think?"

"Well, I agree with you that the term National Velvet he wrote on that piece of paper he gave you has nothing to do with that old Elizabeth Taylor movie. It could mean something else entirely."

"Possibly, but I think the term was used in the context of a coup."

"That's something else we'll have to explore."

"All right. What do you think about this circle-of-three business he mentioned?"

"It might make sense to someone but not to me. How the fuck could there ever be a circle of three? That's an impossibility."

"That's the way I see it at the moment, but my reading of Natansky is that everything he says he says for a reason. If he uses a metaphor, it's for a reason."

"Brad, if Natansky has a good reason for saying whatever, he's also someone who carefully selects his audience. Why were you chosen for such a weird conversation?"

"There may be other reasons he's selected me, Ken, but me being the president's NSA is no doubt one. I also think he knows all about Abe. He never said anything about it when Candy and I met him at the embassy, but during lunch, he did say he and Paul were childhood friends."

"You think Paul might have told him? I would be very surprised if he had."

"I don't think for a moment Paul said anything. There are other possibilities such as Gul or even the prime minister. Hell, even someone in our alternative to Al Jazeera production crew could have said something."

"Possibly."

"All right," said Jenkins as he opened the envelope Natansky had given him from his jacket pocket. "Give this a once-over. It's the list of names I told you he gave me."

"Surprise surprise," said Middleton after perusing the list. "Dear old Dad and Uncle Harry leading the list. I wonder what the hell else they're involved in."

"I found that rather curious myself. What about the other names?"

"A lot of the names are military types as evidenced by their titles, and I think most of the rest are politicians. I recognize only three or four of those names. What I do find curious, though, are four names of people I know of, four scientists who work in our aerospace division."

"Oh? I didn't know Globaltronix had such a division."

"It's been around for quite a while. It's the prime contractor for an ABM system, a system that really works. I don't know that much about it other than it's a laser-based system mounted on a UAV and not a rocket-launched system. The four people whose names I recognized are programmers who are involved with the program."

"How come I don't know anything about this?" asked Jenkins momentarily forgetting his conversation with Natansky. "Why haven't you said anything to me about this before? I have a feeling even the president doesn't know."

"Why don't we go on up to our place. You can have dinner with Nancy and me, and I'll clue you in on things. But bear in mind that much of what I'll say will be supposition."

CHAPTER 77

Middleton Family Condominium
Watergate West
2700 Virginia Avenue NW
Washington, DC
Friday, August 9, 2013

After having dinner with Nancy and Ken Middleton Tuesday evening, Jenkins had taken a rest from the Natansky business for a day. Then Jack Wharton, who had just returned from Tel Aviv, had joined them for dinner the previous night, and the Natansky business was revived.

As Jenkins and Wharton stood on the periphery of the small crowd of White House staff and journalists watching as Marine One landed on the South Lawn, Jenkins was looking forward to seeing his wife, who had been away for almost a week. He also wanted to tell her about his meeting with Natansky.

President Branch, his wife, Candy Reason, Susan Wharton, and the rest of the presidential entourage deplaned. After the photo ops and a short speech by the president with TV cameras rolling, the wives were free to leave. After the hugs and kisses welcoming them home, they all headed for the limousine that would take them to the Watergate.

"We're glad to see you all back in one piece," Jenkins said.

"I'll second that," said Wharton.

"How are you two dealing with the jet lag?" Jenkins asked.

"Tired," said Candy, "but I'm not sleepy."

"How about you, Susan?" asked Wharton.

"Pretty much like Candy. Why do you ask? I sense the two of you have something in mind."

"If you're up to it," said Jenkins, "Ken and Nancy had the cook prepare some snacks. We're all invited up to their place. The two of you can unwind and tell us about your Manila adventure."

When Jenkins, Wharton, and the wives arrived at Nancy and Ken Middleton's condo, they all poured themselves glasses of wine. Then the husbands first listened to their wives' stories, but Candy, who had known about Brad's luncheon date with Natansky, had been more interested about that, and the Pacific Summit meeting in Manila was forgotten.

After Brad told his story, Candy and Susan were quiet for what seemed an eternity. Candy was the first to speak.

"As you said, it was an interesting lunch. I understand why you talked about it all week."

"You must have had some interesting dinners," said Susan Wharton to Nancy Middleton with a chuckle.

"Did we ever," said Ken Middleton. "We were really racking our brains, but we managed to come to a few conclusions."

"I agree that our marriage and positions as secretary of state and national security adviser are reasons why Natansky met with you," said Candy. "He also probably does know about Abraham."

"I agree that your and Ken's fathers are related to all this," added Nancy referring to the list of names Natansky had given Jenkins. "They seem to have their fingers in everything."

"I couldn't agree more," answered Candy. "Obviously, some research is required."

"I was going to do that," said Jenkins, "but I didn't have the time. But at least by talking about it every night, certain things began to make sense. For instance, that circle-of-three metaphor. For a while, we were hung up on such a thing being an impossibility, but I finally figured it out. The circle part represents a circle of friends or family. The number three represents India, Israel, and the States. More specifically, Raj Kumar, Natansky, and me."

"Who's Raj Kumar?" asked Susan Wharton.

"An old friend of Brad's," Candy said. "He was the person I had the most dealings with in 2009 when I was negotiating the rapprochement with India the president hoped to achieve."

"My, the two of you do get around, don't you," said Susan Wharton. "I understand two-thirds of the connections, but how does Natansky fit in?"

"When President Branch asked me to work on the rapprochement, he also asked me to involve the Israelis," said Candy.

"So it's your connection with Natansky that's the third part," said Susan.

"I don't see how. I knew of him at the time, but I never met him until last Saturday when Brad and I were at an embassy function."

"I've figured out that one also," Jenkins said. "I did some research and discovered something very important. In fact, it might be the real key."

"What?" the five others asked in unison.

"All three of us—Kumar, Natansky, and I—have had parents killed by Islamic terrorists."

CHAPTER 78
Double R Bar Ranch
Kendall County, Texas
Monday, September 2, 2013

Today is the day, Jenkins thought as he and Harry Reason started down the woodland path. Because of Harry Reason's travel schedule and various other things, the desired conversation with Jenkins's father-in-law had kept getting postponed. Ultimately, Jenkins and Candy realized the ideal time to talk would be during the Labor Day holiday when they were all at the ranch in Texas.

"Why the devil do you always want to go for a walk, son, whenever you want to talk about something?"

"Why are you always so suspicious?"

"Because you're just like Candy."

"Exercise is what helps you live longer."

"And so does a nice nap after lunch."

"You're a tough old buzzard, Harry."

"That's what else has helped me live longer."

"I'll never win with you, will I?" said Jenkins chuckling.

"Let's quit the skirmishing and get on with it. What's on your mind? What's so important we need to take a walk to discuss it?"

"How about National Velvet for starters? And I don't mean the Liz Taylor movie."

"Do you want to tell me, or should I tell you?" continued Jenkins after waiting several moments for Harry Reason to speak.

"You sure know how to go for the jugular."

"You're the one who said we should get on with it."

"It's just a name given to some contingent planning studies," said Reason, who was visibly shaken. "You know how they conduct all kinds of studies at the Pentagon for all kinds of what-ifs. There's a whole section that does nothing but what-if planning."

"Yeah, like a plan to take over the government," said Jenkins. "You have any idea how the media would react if they got a whiff of your contingency planning?"

"My God, son, it's only a contingency plan in case of an emergency."

"Christ, Harry, it doesn't make a damned bit of difference how contingent or how much a national emergency, if the media were to learn of National Velvet, it would be worse than the shit hitting the fan. If I can find out about it, the media sure as hell can. You know damned well they can do their job when they want to."

"Might I ask where you got your information?"

"From an unimpeachable source."

"That's impossible. Only a handful of people knew about the study, and I'd trust those people with my life."

"Harry, you and your staff have made more changes in the officer corps than George Marshall on the eve of World War II. Everyone you work with may be good, but that doesn't mean absolute secrecy."

"Son, you can believe what you want to believe, but I'm positive."

"Then pray tell how have the Israelis found out?"

CHAPTER 79

Association Research
600 New Hampshire Avenue NW
Washington, DC
Sunday, December 8, 2013

As Brad Jenkins made his way from his condo to the Association Research office next door, he regretted not wearing his topcoat on the cold morning in spite of his short walk. *I sure as hell hope Ken's father-in-law is all right, but something important has happened or Ken wouldn't have gotten me out of bed on a Sunday.*

"Is Larry okay now?" Jenkins asked Ken Middleton, assuming the reason Middleton wanted to meet with him had had to do with his father-in-law.

"Larry's all right. It was a false alarm. Something stress related, I think. He's out of the woods and back home acting as ornery as ever."

"That's good news. When you said you had something important to discuss, I'd assumed he was the reason you wanted to get together so early."

"Actually, he's the subject this morning but not in a medical sense."

"Now that I've thawed out after stupidly deciding to not wear a coat, I'm all ears."

"It all started about seven thirty in the evening the day after Thanksgiving when Nancy's mother screamed and Nance and I came running. Everything happened quickly. I attended to Larry as Nance was dialing 911. In what seemed like moments, the ambulance arrived, and Larry was off to the hospital. Sylvia, Nancy, and I followed in the car.

"It was shortly after eleven when Nance and I got back home. The crisis had passed. Seems Larry hadn't had a heart attack after all, but they were going to keep him in the hospital for a couple of days for observation. Sylvia stayed the night at the hospital. Nance was wiped out and hit the sack as quickly as she could. I think it was one of those times she wished she were a man and could just strip off her clothes and hop into bed without having to remove makeup and so forth.

"Anyway, even though I was also dog-tired, I was geed up after having to look after two distraught women, so I decided to have a couple slugs of brandy while sitting in Larry's recliner. It was when I turned out the light that I noticed a glow coming from his study and went to investigate.

"When I walked into the study, I noticed the screen savers of his laptop and desktop working and assumed that Larry was like me and had disabled the hibernation features. That's one of Windows' features I'm not enamored with because you always have to retype the password after the computer hibernates. I was about to shut down his computers when it all happened."

"Now what happened?"

"As soon as I moved the mouse to shut down his desktop, a document appeared on the screen. I have no idea what caught my eye or if it was just simple curiosity, but I ended up reading it, and that led me to spend the next couple of hours surfing both his computers.

"When I finished, I knew there was no way I'd close down either machine until I had a copy of everything. I spent the rest of the night ghosting everything from both his computers onto the spare external drive I always have with me."

"My God. It was that bad?"

"Wait till you see the copy I have for you. You remember Ross Bartlett and Ben Sorenson?"

"Sort of. Wasn't Bartlett the golfing buddy of your father-in-law last year in Hawaii when your father and Harry asked for our help? And Sorenson is Taffy's father, correct?"

"Right. Larry, Ross, Ben, and another person by the name of Will Rikker have been recruiting militias."

"Militias?"

"Yeah, those people who run around playing soldier."

"You serious?"

"I couldn't be more serious. It's all there on the drive. I guess someone is planning on countering the national police force Pellegrino and company have been talking about creating."

"You said militias. For Christ's sakes how many?"

"Five. One each in Colorado, Missouri, California, New York, and Idaho."

"Jesus fucking Christ. Incredible."

"That's just for starters. There's more. Remember National Velvet?"

"The National Velvet Harry said was a contingency plan?"

"That's the one, but it's not a contingency plan. It's an operational plan for bugging the whole senior officer corps."

"The what? How the fuck could they possibly hope to pull that off? Christ, there have to be thousands of officers in the military."

"They're doing it. There's a no-bid contract that has been awarded to GT Communications to survey all electrical and communications systems for all military housing."

"Who the hell is GT Communications?"

"The GT probably comes from Globaltronix, but the company itself is actually Charlie Communications, Dad's and Uncle Harry's old outfit in Vietnam and the founders of the company or what's left of them. Including Dad and Uncle Harry, there are about thirty-two of them left."

"Fucking incredible. Have you mentioned any of this to Nancy?"

"Not yet. With her worries about her father, I thought I'd wait. I wanted to talk with you first because it's obvious that my and Candy's father are up to their eyeballs in all this crap."

"You know you'll have to tell her, and obviously, Candy has to be told."

"I know, I know. But before we do that, though, there's something else I wanted to run by you. Before I shut down Larry's computers, I loaded one of Mykro's programs on each machine. Now, every time he sends or receives an e-mail, a copy will be forwarded to me."

"I have no problem with that. You know that old saying about what's good for the goose is good for the gander. About time someone spied on the eavesdroppers."

"That's not what I wanted to run by you. You know how Candy's mom and dad and mine alternately visit each other for Christmas?"

Jenkins nodded.

"This year it's Mom and Dad's turn to visit Aunt Kym and Uncle Harry. I was thinking we could pull a Pellegrino on them."

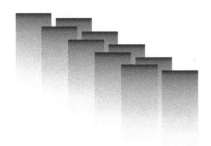

CHAPTER 80
Double R Bar Ranch
Kendall County, Texas
Saturday, December 21, 2013

"It was a hard day's work," said Harry Reason, facetiously referring to the trimming of the Christmas tree that afternoon, "but somebody had to do it."

"Spoken just like a man," said Kym Reason.

"Well, Brad and I did help a bit."

"If you want to call sitting and watching Candy and I help."

"No, that was called controlled supervision. Don't you agree, Brad?"

"I think I'll sidestep that one," Jenkins replied as he held up his glass, "and just say, Happy Saturday before Christmas."

"Happy Saturday before Christmas," said Harry, Kym, and Candy as they raised their glasses.

Candy's and Brad's smiles had nothing to do with looking forward to dinner moments away or Christmas; their smiles were a silent communication of hope that everything they had planned would go off without a hitch. It was a plan they had devised after Ken Middleton's revelations of two weeks earlier, but it had required an awful lot to be done in little time.

"I was thinking we could pull a Pellegrino on them," Ken Middleton had said. "I think the last thing they would ever dream of would be our doing to them what they've done to others."

"Can you get all the components?" Jenkins had asked Middleton.

"I think so."

"Do you know how to install this stuff?"

"I think so."

"That's hardly a vote of confidence, Ken. You're talking about some pretty sophisticated equipment, and electronic eavesdropping has never been part of my job description."

"Brad, hear me out. The fact that my father-in-law is involved recruiting militias means that Dad and Uncle Harry are involved. Nancy, Candy, and I told you how our fathers operate. If one has his hands in the cookie jar, it means they all do. What Uncle Harry told you Labor Day weekend was either a lie or he was playing games with the truth. They're all doing something they've been hiding from us for some reason.

"Back that morning when we all had breakfast at the Holiday Inn the day after my daughters got married, you expressed fears about Abraham. When we asked you what the president was going to do, you said you didn't know. You knew only that he had asked Uncle Harry to save the military and you to find a way to win the war on terror—his words, not ours. I don't think the folks are waiting for the president to make up his mind about our revelations and are getting antsy. Mom and Dad will be going to the Double R for Christmas and New Year's. This might be the only opportunity to find out exactly what Dad and Uncle Harry are up to."

"Ken, I'll buy into the fact that Harry was being disingenuous. What's the game plan?"

"Simple. I order the material, and we fly to Houston to pick it up and go to the ranch."

"I hope the hell you're not planning on calling Candy's brother."

"For God's sakes no. We can't take any chances. I'll place a will-call order."

"You know the ranch is northwest of San Antonio. How do we get from A to B?"

"We rent a car in Houston and drive to our distribution facility and then to San Antonio. That's about a four, four-and-a-half-hour drive. I haven't checked any schedules, and I hate the thought of the long drive, but I think if we tried to fly commercial, we might have a problem with all the boxes unless we unpacked everything, but that would create other problems. I thought of using a company plane, but that would create a record of us going and coming."

"All right, Ken. You've obviously been thinking about this since your discovery, but there are three things that concern me."

"Shoot."

"The equipment. Do you know what all we need?"

"I spent some time on the net going through our catalogs. I think I have that one all figured out. What else?"

"The two most important things, like two wives and the staff at the ranch. I can appreciate you not wanting to say anything to Nancy while she was thinking her father was dying, but there's no way you and I can just take off without telling her and Candy. We've never kept anything from them before. I don't want to start now. We have to tell them."

"I suppose you're right, Brad. Why don't we take the girls to the Four Seasons for Sunday brunch and bite the bullet? You and Candy can wear your disguises."

"Sounds like a plan."

The possibly of going to the Four Seasons for Sunday brunch became a reality. Ken Middleton told the women the story as they were drinking mimosas. As it had turned out, it was the thought of having to tell Nancy about her father that was the most difficult part because when Ken had finished, Nancy said, "Actually, I'm not the least bit surprised, and I don't think Candy is either."

"While I'm at it," said Jenkins after everyone had said Happy Saturday before Christmas, "how about a lovely and successful holiday season?"

"You know something I don't," Harry said.

"Not that I'm aware of," Jenkins said. "Why?"

"Just my innate curiosity I guess. I thought you might have figured out some way to save the world as George had asked you to do."

"If winning the war against terror is what you're referring to, that's a work in progress. I did have what I thought was a good idea, but I couldn't figure out how to implement it."

"Sounds like we may each be having similar problems. What was the idea?"

"I thought we'd just round them all up and then sink them somewhere. Trouble is, I could never figure out how to get all the manpower needed."

Everyone laughed. The conversation changed as thoughts of Christmas began to supersede all else. Brad Jenkins glanced at his wife and knew her thoughts mirrored his. Marianne and Mike Middleton would be arriving the next day, and if all went well, Harry and Mike would probably engage in a lot of private conversation that if they were lucky would be recorded.

The only concern was the time he and Ken had been at the ranch. This was something that had always worried them because they could hardly ask any staff to not tell anyone that they were there. That was why they had concocted a story about him and Ken attending a seminar in San Antonio and hooking up with some friends who were passing through. It was a pretty flimsy story, but they thought they just might be lucky.

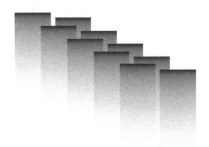

CHAPTER 81

Clyde's of Georgetown Restaurant
3236 M Street NW
Washington, DC
Sunday, January 5, 2014

"You're planning on having just snacks when Candy and Brad come, aren't you?" Ken Middleton asked as he sipped a martini while studying the menu.

"Yes," answered Nancy Middleton as she carefully removed the olive from her martini. "I think after the long travel day, they'll both be pretty tired and won't want a big meal."

"Well, I'm hungry, so I think I'll indulge myself and have the good old-fashioned meat loaf with the hearts of romaine Caesar salad. How about you?"

"I think I'll just have the grilled Atlantic salmon salad," she said. "I'm not that hungry. I think what we've been doing all morning has gotten to me."

Ken Middleton knew his wife wasn't hungry because the whole affair regarding Candy's father and their respective fathers had been bothering her ever since she was told about what he had discovered on his father-in-law's computer as well as the plans for eavesdropping on his and Candy's fathers during Christmas.

Nancy and Ken Middleton had returned to Washington with Michel and Colonel Golden after spending the holiday season at their home in Silicon Valley the previous evening. Because Michele hadn't been feeling well, the couples hadn't gone out to dinner together. Instead of going out to dinner themselves, Nancy and Ken had decided to stay home and have only sandwiches and soup. As Nancy was making the sandwiches,

Ken fired up his desktop. After loading the eavesdropping program, the downloading of the audio files from the time his parents had arrived at the Reason ranch until the day they left had begun. He knew the computer would be working all night.

In the morning, after they had their breakfast, Nancy and Ken had gone to work organizing the files. Ken hadn't used the merge feature of the program, so each of the bugs at the Reason ranch had been transcribed into six different files, which meant a lot of reading and then organizing into something comprehensible. It had been a lot of work and they needed a break, so they decided to go to lunch.

"I wonder if Brad was able to listen in on any of their conversations," Ken said after they had ordered.

"I'm surprised you didn't try while we were in California," Nancy said.

"Believe me, I wanted to, but with Michele and Mustafa as guests and the time difference, it wasn't possible. But if Candy or Brad managed to do any listening, they probably got an earful."

"They sure did if they listened to the first couple of conversations we transcribed today. I thought they were quite revealing."

> "All right, now that the gals have gone to bed, perhaps you can tell me what's been bothering you all evening."

> "Shit, you too, Harry."

> "So Marianne did notice."

> "Of course she noticed for Christ's sakes. She's a wife. They notice everything."

> "What did you say when she asked you what was wrong?"

> "I told her nothing was wrong."

> "If she believed that, I have a bridge to sell her."

> "Well, before you dust that bridge off, she didn't believe me."

"So you told her."

"Hell no. I didn't tell her because I didn't want a two-hour inquisition."

"She'll be back asking. You know wives are like terriers with a bone when they want to know something."

"Yeah, I know."

Pause

"Look, Harry, I'm just frustrated, that's all. I feel like we've dicked around all year and haven't done a damned thing. Sometimes, I wonder why the fuck we ever got involved in that damned bugging operation. There were so many times when I almost pulled the plug and said screw it. Perhaps if I did, we could have marched on in blissful ignorance, letting the country go down the tubes."

"But we didn't, Mike."

"No, we sure as hell didn't, and as I said, there were so many times the plug almost got pulled. As a matter of fact, if it hadn't been because Larry and Royce were bored, we might well be sitting here having a different conversation."

Laughter

"There was no way, Harry, that Josh Morton could have known that Lowen was screwing the shit out of Pellegrino. That had to have been just some stupid, facetious remark he made to his father, but it got Tyler's attention, and he mentioned it to Larry, and soon, he and Royce were playing detective. They did that only because they wanted something else to do besides golf and sailing. The next thing I knew, our great detectives confirmed that

Pellegrino and Lowen were indeed shacking up, and we began down the slippery slope."

"I don't know if I'd call it a slippery slope."

"For Christ's sakes, Harry, what else would you call it? We no sooner got involved in our little bugging operation than our great detective number one starts reaching all the wrong conclusions, and I think what's gotten to me is that I bought into everything. First, it was the associations. He made a very good case, and I went running to George, and George, because he didn't trust his own damned government, handed the ball back to me. The next thing I know I'm hiring two young women."

"In view of all that's happened this year, I think George has been proven right when it comes to trusting our government."

"But that's a different story, Harry. I think if Ben Sorenson's daughter hadn't written that damned book for her doctoral thesis, Larry never would have gotten a case of associations on the brain. In retrospect, I'm surprised I bought into it all, but that's now water over the dam."

Laughter

"I still remember how pissed you were when George wanted those young women to work for Brad and in Israel no less."

"Yeah, I remember. The things our kids do that we don't know about. Who the hell would've thought they were running some sort of antiterrorist operation in Israel?"

"I'm with you, boss. Like you, I thought that Brad was only doing some special consulting work for George and

Ken was helping. I wonder what might have happened if you hadn't asked Ken to give the girls a hand when they inadvertently found themselves in some Arab websites. I think that's what really concerned George."

"Who knows, Harry? Maybe they'd still be in Washington researching associations."

"If they were, I don't think the revelations of earlier this year would have happened."

"Perhaps, but that leads to something else our number-one detective screwed up on. Thank God they're at least super cautious or they'd have found themselves on *Candid Camera*."

"Amen. I wonder why Lowen never turned those cameras off particularly when he was screwing her from just about every position imaginable."

"Who knows? Maybe he wanted to look at the reruns. All I know is that we have so many pictures of them performing that we could make a good porno flick."

Laughter

"If it hadn't been for the cameras, we might also be having a different conversation tonight. We'd never have found those flash drives."

"That's another area where our esteemed detectives rose to the level of their incompetence, and because of that, we needed to go to Ken and Brad hat in hand and ask for their help, help they weren't willing to give unless we told them everything."

"Yeah, I remember. You weren't a very happy camper. But at least his people broke the code and we finally got the holy grail of espionage."

"Big fucking deal, Harry. We got the total set of blueprints for how the left plans on transforming the country by making it a one-party state, and nothing's being done excepting your trying to find a way to save the military and Larry and Royce screwing around with some of these militias."

"You forgot Brad. He's got his people trying to find out who all is involved in this attempt to take over the government."

"Big deal. Nine months later and what have we to show for it? That's why I'm so frustrated. We need to be doing something now. If we don't, we may as well kiss it all good-bye."

"Let's worry about what to do tomorrow. My glass is empty. The fire in the fireplace is almost out, and I'm tired."

"What do you think they're trying to achieve by this feeling they need to do something now?" Nancy asked.

"I don't know. If anything, I think they're frustrated just as we are. We have this vast conspiracy unfolding before our eyes, and all the president has said is that he wants Brad to find a way to win the war on terror. Even if he doesn't care about what extreme Brad goes to, that's hardly any clear direction.

"Even telling Candy's father to save the military at any cost is not really direction. So I can to a point understand where Dad and Uncle Harry are coming from, but what they're doing is far more dangerous than anything we're involved in."

"I hope they've been careful. We may not have anything to do with what they're doing, but you know how things will work out. We'll all get tarred with the same brush. Then everything will be over."

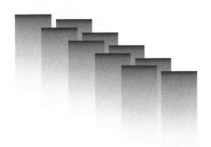

CHAPTER 82

Middleton Family Condominium
Watergate West
2700 Virginia Avenue NW
Washington, DC
Sunday, January 5, 2014

"So boss, what do we do? You're the idea man."

"I wish the hell I knew, Harry. My brain has been running in overdrive all year, and I keep arriving at the same conclusions. It's been a pretty shitty year, and no matter how hard I've tried, I've never been able to come up with the first fucking thing we could legally do to change anything."

"Welcome to the club, boss, or should I have said ditto?"

Laughter

"You know, we've been between rocks and hard places before, but never anything like this, Mike. After all these years, imagine someone outmaneuvering us. We can't tell a fucking soul diddly-squat about what we know, and even if we could, who the fuck could we tell? Shit, I doubt half the people who are supposed to be on our side would believe us, and even if someone did, what would be done? Nothing."

"That's what's so fucking frustrating, Harry, and to top it off, as I said last night, George doesn't appear to be doing the first damn thing about it other than telling you to save the military and Brad to save the world."

"You know George. Shit, he didn't trust his own Justice Department back when you approached him about the associations."

"And he still doesn't. He keeps saying we'll work something out, but if he doesn't get off the stick, next year's going to be over and he'll be out of a fucking job and in no position to work anything out for anyone. Hey, I'm beginning to run dry. I think I'm going to pour myself another couple of fingers. You want yours topped up?"

"Hell, why not."

Lull in conversation

"So what do we do? Where do we go from here beside me saving the military and Brad saving the world?"

"Let's keep Brad and the kids out of it, Harry."

"That might be easier said than done."

"I know, but I think it's best for all, particularly with what Larry and Royce are up to."

"All right, no kids, but we still have to do a lot more than we've been doing, and there's no guarantee at the moment that anything we do will work out."

"How about we put a bullet between her fucking eyeballs?"

"I thought about that one once. In fact, I had a couple of colonels volunteering to pull the trigger, but we decided even if we could get away with it, it wouldn't change anything."

"How have your two colonels taken this so far?"

"They were shell-shocked at first. Now they're royally pissed. They know a lot of people on the list. That's why they're shell-shocked."

"So we're back to square one. Right now, I feel royally you-know-what. We have no friends."

"Whatever we do, assuming we do something and not just roll over and play dead, it will have to be done soon, and that's not much time considering the magnitude."

Laughter

"You're probably right, Harry. I think we have to adopt a long game if we hope to recapture the country. We're not only going to have to figure out a way to do that; we're probably also going to have to do a hell of a lot of things we never dreamed of."

"We better cool it. Here come the girls."

"I know I shouldn't be surprised, but when I read something like this, I'm still surprised," said Candy after reading the transcripts given her by Nancy and Ken Middleton.

"I know how you feel, Candy," said Ken Middleton. "I feel the same way."

"What are they trying to do, start World War III?" asked Candy.

"I think they're frustrated."

"And their frustration will get us all into trouble and bring down the administration," added Nancy Middleton. "Have they any idea what the consequences of their actions would be if anyone found out?"

"They probably think they won't get caught," said Candy. "Actually, I think what bothers me the most is how they apparently look at us like little children while also insulting our intelligence."

"They certainly have done that," added Nancy Middleton.

"What do you think, Brad?" asked Ken. "Brad?"

"Oh, I'm sorry," responded Brad Jenkins. "I was lost in my thoughts."

"About what?"

"You said they're frustrated. And you're concerned about being treated like little children and having your intelligence insulted."

"Yes, but," said Ken.

"But I haven't heard you disagree with your father-in-law recruiting militias. I've only heard you complain about being tarred with the same brush if they get caught."

"Brad," Candy said, "where are you going with this?"

"Just that we have our surgeons and they have their militias."

"That's not the same thing."

"It isn't?" asked Jenkins. "I would say in a way, Harry, Mike, and company are attempting to do what we've been doing here in the States. Don't get me wrong," Jenkins continued as his wife looked at him in disbelief. "I'm not for a moment attempting to justify their actions. Like you, I thought we were all a team, and I'm not pleased to learn we aren't. It's time to make a decision as to what we really want and then maybe how to do it. We're already in 2014, and as far as I'm concerned, we wasted a lot of time last year.

"Back then, we seemed to be on a roll. But then after the weddings, everything seemed to change. We lost our momentum, and we got blown slightly off course. I was going to approach Harry but had to wait until Labor Day weekend. You girls and I had to go to work for the government five days a week, which I think in a way crimped our style, and Ken and Jack were off to Tel Aviv several times. Then we got preoccupied with the Thanksgiving weekend discovery and bingo, here we are."

"Brad has a point," Nancy said after a moment of silence.

"So where do we go from here?" asked Candy.

"Nance and I were talking about that this afternoon," said Ken. "We think the next step should be to bring the rest of the gang up to speed. We've not kept any secrets from them before, and I don't think we should now. We also think my father and Uncle Harry need to be confronted. The question is do Candy and I do it together or separately. Remember, Uncle Harry lied to Brad."

"I don't think separately would get us anywhere," said Candy with a sigh.

"I agree," said Nancy. "Separately is not a good idea. Besides, my father is also involved."

"Perhaps our getting together with the Goldens and the Whartons should include a little more than just how to approach our parents," said Candy.

CHAPTER 83

Middleton Family Condominium
Watergate West
2700 Virginia Avenue NW
Washington, DC
Saturday, February 1, 2014

"I think our guests are beginning to get a little restless," said Ken to Brad.

Brad surveyed the situation and came to the same conclusion. The confrontation they had discussed several times since the beginning of the year that had been put off until this evening would begin momentarily. He hoped everything would go the way he had been assured it would. He had not been completely sold on the great confrontation as they had called it. To him, it seemed like something that would happen only in a novel, but Ken, Candy, and Nancy had assured everyone that it was the way to go and that the confrontation had to include the wives.

"You don't know our fathers like we do," Ken, Candy, and Nancy had said. "And you most assuredly don't know our mothers like we do."

So after several meetings between Jenkins, Candy, Jack and Sue Wharton, Colonel and Michele Golden, and Nancy and Ken Middleton, they had decided that a show of force that also included Miriam and Paul Bernstein would be better than confronting Mike and Harry individually. It had also been determined that Larry Evans and Royce Bartlett should be at any meeting with Mike and Harry and that their wives should also be included. Perhaps with the wives present, Jenkins hoped, the four men would be embarrassed.

The game plan had been to announce that they had made a significant discovery and would like Mike, Larry, and Royce to come to Washington.

Of course, there had been pushback; Mike Middleton had suggested they just tell Harry, but they had refused. The dickering went on for a couple of weeks before Mike had agreed.

As part of the plan, Ken had told his father that he and Nancy, considering everything, had decided to combine business with pleasure and would have a dinner party at which time Jenkins would advise everyone about the latest developments.

The first hour of the dinner party, which was a buffet dinner and a self-service bar, had gone smoothly, but crunch time was just moments away.

"All right," said Mike Middleton, who had risen from his chair and walked over to his son, Ken, and Brad Jenkins. "I think we're all ready for this big announcement. That's the real reason we're here, right?"

"I guess this is the moment everyone has been waiting for," said Jenkins once everyone had quieted down. "I apologize for possibly having misled all of you when we said there is something significant to tell everyone because I think it was a poor choice of words. A series of developments would be a better choice."

"Let's disregard the semantics," said Mike Middleton. "We're still talking about the same thing, aren't we? You wouldn't have asked six of us to fly east unless something important has developed."

"Uncle Mike," answered Jenkins with a smile, "you're correct. Something very important has developed and all because of a series of mistakes just a year ago."

"I thought so," said Mike.

His wife, Marianne, put her hand on his arm and told him to be quiet.

"What we've discovered is quite significant and impacts us all," continued Jenkins. "I'll let Ken continue because he's the one who should be given credit."

Ken looked at his father and mother. "If it hadn't been for a series of mistakes, we might not be here this evening."

"I'm sure," Mike Middleton said, but his wife stopped him from saying anything else.

Ken noticed his mother silencing his father and glanced at Brad, who had also noticed and was smiling. "Just indulge me, Dad, and I'll get to the point. We're living in two Americas. If any of you are in doubt, just visit some of the left-wing websites. There's no way you could conclude otherwise. But I don't think anyone here is in doubt. We've seen evidence far more compelling than some Looney Tunes could convey on a website. But that's just one side of the coin.

"The other America we're living in supposedly consists of people like us. Unfortunately, the political establishment, particularly the Washington elite, wants nothing to do with anything that involves any disturbance of their arrangements. I guess we could call that approach business as usual or going along to get along.

"I'm sure there are ten people in this room who are wondering why I seem to be beating around the bush and not getting to the point."

"Speaking of points," said Mike Middleton and Larry Evans almost in unison, but before they could say anything else, Marianne Middleton told her husband to shut up and Sylvia Evans squeezed her husband's arm and whispered to him to be quiet.

"The point I was attempting to make," continued Ken Middleton, "is that we are opposed by an array of forces against us far greater than those we discovered a year ago. To have even a ghost of a chance of combating these forces will require an unimaginable and well-coordinated effort, and that's why a series of mistakes led us here tonight.

"The first mistake was that Larry and Royce couldn't access three flash drives. While I can't fault them, it was the beginning of what I'll call a little adventure. The second mistake was Brad and I being asked for help by some people in this room who had no intention of asking if they could have avoided it. The third mistake was that Uncle Harry purposely attempted to mislead Brad last Labor Day weekend. Brad let it go, but none of us ever bought the idea of a contingency plan."

Ken had hardly finished mentioning the third mistake when Harry was attempting to stand and say something, but his wife had hold of his arm. "No," she said.

"The fourth mistake," said Ken, "was Larry's developing a lot of bad computer habits. Your loss, our gain. The fifth mistake was Larry having an attack of indigestion. Because of his bad habits, I was able to read and copy everything on his desktop and laptop. Surprise surprise."

Jenkins saw four very unhappy men being restrained by their wives.

"The sixth mistake," Ken said, "was Dad and Uncle Harry never thinking anyone would ever do to them what they've been doing to others. Amazing what one discovers when the tables are turned. Might I have the envelope please, Nancy?

"Mom, you, Kym, Sylvia, and Joan might find the contents in this envelope very interesting. It contains the transcripts of several conversations between Dad and Uncle Harry, conversations in which they insult our intelligence and agree to keep us uninvolved in any attempt to combat powerful forces attempting to destroy our country, attempts they learned about through us. There are copies for each of you. When you're finished reading, I think you might become as disappointed in the men in your lives as we are.

"There are ten of us here who once thought we were part of a team, but obviously, we weren't, in spite of our best efforts. If treating us like children and insulting our intelligence isn't bad enough, think of the repercussions if anyone other than Brad and I had discovered what we did. That's all I have to say. I'm sorry that this night had to happen."

"So am I, Ken," said his mother as she turned to her husband. "Mr. Middleton, I think it's time we all said good night."

"So what do you think will happen?" asked Jack Wharton ten minutes after Harry, Mike, Larry, and Royce had left with their wives.

"If I know my mother, I wouldn't want to be in Dad's shoes tonight particularly after she reviews the material I gave her."

"What about the other men?"

"I think they'd prefer to be anywhere than where they're going," said Nancy.

"While I think we may have had a successful evening, I think we need to be prepared for the worst," Paul Bernstein said. "In case we're left to our own devices, I think we need to do some serious thinking about what the future holds for us."

Ten people glanced at each other and nodded.

CHAPTER 84
Association Research
600 New Hampshire Avenue NW
Washington, DC
Sunday, February 2, 2014

Brad Jenkins looked around the conference room and at his watch. His father-in-law and his three friends and associates were due to arrive any moment. He had received a call from Harry about everyone getting together after lunch.

Jenkins had told Harry he would call back after speaking with his people. Then he had called Ken and learned that Ken's father had also called him. After a few moments of conversation, it was agreed they would meet with Mike and Harry if they could get hold of Colonel Golden and Jack Wharton. Inasmuch as Paul Bernstein was a houseguest, he was not a problem.

Consequently, a meeting time of one thirty was arranged, and Jenkins, Bernstein, Wharton, Middleton, and Golden had arranged to meet at one to discuss how to handle things before the face-off.

"I guess I don't have to tell you your mother read me the riot act last night," said Middleton addressing his son to begin the meeting.

Ken smiled and nodded.

"Ditto," said Harry and Larry.

"We wanted to meet with all of you this afternoon to see if we can forget what happened and go on from here," Mike said.

"It's not that easy, Dad," said Ken. "I thought last year when we were all involved in uncovering what I will refer to as the Pellegrino conspiracy that we had become a team. But almost immediately, you and Uncle Harry decided to go it alone for our supposed good without the first thought of how we'd all be affected if your little schemes were ever found out. What I don't think the two of you and Larry have understood is how hurtful this has been to Nancy and Candy. Also, you've insulted our competence and intelligence."

Larry Evans took up the slack. "What I think your father would like to say is that we're sorry we let our frustrations take over. We'd like to work with all of you if that's still a possibility."

Ken did not immediately answer his father-in-law's question. As planned, his pause was the passing of the baton to Brad.

"Only if certain conditions are met," said Jenkins.

"Such as?" asked Harry.

"There are no secrets, and we function as a real team with a purpose. You agree, Paul?"

"If I understand my American history correctly," said Bernstein, "Benjamin Franklin once said something about hanging together or separately. While I don't think we're about to be hung, I think we need to work together to achieve whatever we're trying to achieve. While there's no guarantee that collectively we can be successful, most assuredly, separately, we will fail."

"Rightly or wrongly," said Mike, "I'm assuming a decision to work together has been made, but I'd like to explain why we let our frustrations get out of hand. Other than to tell Harry he had to save the military and you, Brad, to win the war on terror, George hasn't really said a damn thing.

"Personally, I see a storm coming if Pellegrino and her ilk get a chance to take over the country, and it won't be pretty. George hasn't wanted to talk about it, but we've discussed it, and we see the possibility of a civil war. We've already learned how the election process has been subverted. Throw into the mix how our morals and religion are already being destroyed by all manner of perversions and horrors."

"You forgot that little ditty about the homegrown terror attacks," Royce said.

"Yeah," said Mike. "That one really frosted me. One thing we picked up via our eavesdropping was a conversation between Lowen and this— shit—what's his name, Larry?"

"Atherton, Charles Atherton. He's an associate of Paul Thoros."

"Yeah, Atherton. He and Lowen had this conversation about committing a series of terror attacks that could be blamed on right-wing extremists. What got to me was how they were laughing and saying how they could say anything they wanted about Republicans and people would believe them. What pissed me off in particular was that they were right."

"We all understand," said Jenkins. "So, let's put aside our emotions and move on."

"Thank you, Brad," said Mike. "Considering everything, I think Washington should be the focal point for any further discussions from now on. While this may pose some inconvenience to those of us on this side of the table, Harry excepted of course, I suggest we all think about everything for a few weeks and get together again. While I think we've made good progress here, Rome wasn't built in a day."

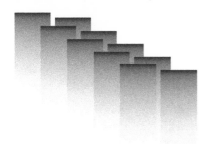

CHAPTER 85

Candice Reason's Condominium
Watergate South
700 New Hampshire Avenue NW
Washington, DC
Sunday, February 2, 2014

To a woman, the wives asked the obvious question—"How did everything go?"

After the momentous meeting, Jenkins, Middleton, Golden, Wharton, and Bernstein had returned to Jenkins's and Candy's condo. While the men were gone, the wives had been anxiously wondering how things would develop.

"I think we had a very productive meeting," said Jenkins. "They were all quite contrite."

"Of course it helped that Mom had read Dad the riot act," said Ken facetiously. He turned to Nancy. "I think Sylvia did the same to your father."

"So all you little boys kissed and made up until the next time," quipped Miriam Bernstein.

"Well," said Paul Bernstein jokily, "they didn't see their shadows, so I think it was a rather successful Groundhog Day."

"Instead of going on about it being a successful day," said Miriam. "how about telling us what happened. We've been sitting here on pins and needles all afternoon waiting to see if the world was going to end."

"Well, for starters," said Brad, "most of our time was spent asking questions. That is, after they all promised to be good boys and team members. Ken's dad was the one who encouraged the Q&A. He said that we'd been pretty successful in learning all about them, so rather than just tell us anything, he wanted us to ask questions."

"So you all just asked questions and they dutifully answered like good little boys."

"Only after we said we had no problem asking questions as long as we knew we would be getting truthful answers. Of course, we already knew the answers for some of the questions. We knew Royce and Larry had been recruiting the militias because the left was planning on creating a civilian national security force that would actually be an internal paramilitary force.

"We also knew that National Velvet was not a code name for the takeover of the government in an emergency and that it was in reality the code name for the bugging of the senior officer corps. Uncle Harry explained that while he would have liked to have bugged the whole officer corps of all the service branches, it just wasn't realistic and they had no choice but to accept what the left had obtained. That's pretty much it except for some interesting tidbits."

"Might I ask what kind of tidbits?" asked Candy.

"Just things like you apparently were always a political animal and that you were the reason your father and Uncle Mike got into politics to begin with."

"Oh!" exclaimed Susan and Michele.

"How interesting," said Susan.

"Seems Harry and Uncle Mike would always be bitching about something of a political nature whenever the families got together. One day, she told them that if they felt so strongly about things, they should do something instead of complaining."

Everyone laughed, and Candy's face started to redden.

"So they got involved in politics," Jenkins said with a smile. Candy stuck out her tongue at him.

Mike Middleton had gotten involved in California, and Harry Reason in Texas, and one thing led to another. Harry bought the ranch in Texas and met George Branch and Alberto Garcia, and they all became friends. Harry talked George into running for governor, and he and Mike talked him into running for president. By that time, Candy had climbed the academic ladder, and George took a liking to her and often used her as a sounding board.

As the game plan developed, they had wondered who they could find to succeed George after eight years as president and an idea was born. Four years as NSA, two years as secretary of state, and then Bob Chandler, the vice president, would step down for health reasons, and she would be appointed to fill the remaining two years.

"And all this was without her knowledge," continued Jenkins as he remembered how surprised Candy had been on election night when the president had told her that Gene Powers was resigning and he would nominate her for secretary of state. Harry said they had never said anything because circumstances could change quicker than the blink of an eye."

"So your father and godfather had plans for you to become the first female president. I find that rather interesting," said Miriam.

"You may find it interesting," said Candy, "but it will never happen because someone else had a similar idea involving a different woman."

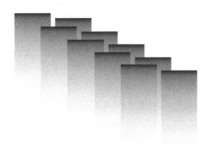

CHAPTER 86
Association Research
600 New Hampshire Avenue NW
Washington, DC
Sunday, February 16, 2014

"I still don't like the idea of George Washington's Birthday being called Presidents' Day," groused Mike Middleton as everyone sat at the conference table. "It's another step in losing our culture."

Because Friday had been Valentine's Day, Mike Middleton, Larry Evans, Royce Bartlett, and their wives had flown to Washington on Saturday to meet with Brad and company on Sunday and Monday. Presidents' Day, a federal holiday, was Monday.

"I'm assuming all of you have done some serious thinking since our last meeting," said Mike.

"We've done that in spades," said Ken Middleton.

"Good. So have I, particularly about how we proceed. Nine of us meeting like this and discussing the things we're interested in could be called a conspiracy, but our discussing the same things in an academic environment would just be scholarly discussion. That's why I have taken it upon myself to do something I hope you'll approve of."

"You're not trying to wing it alone again, are you?" asked Ken. "You agreed to no more secrets and that we'd function as a real team."

"I don't think you'll have a problem with this. I was thinking about bringing it up during our last meeting, but nothing had been cast in concrete at that time. Now, to bring you all up to date, I've signed a letter of intent with the Mulholland Group to purchase the two Watergate Office buildings and the retail space. It'll take about a month for all the i's to be dotted and the t's crossed. I decided to do it because the money involved was like stealing.

"I've also instructed our attorneys to draw up the necessary papers for what I will call for the moment the Middleton Institute for Domestic and International Studies. As a think tank, this framework should allow us to reasonably and practically discuss with each other any number of what-ifs and do any theoretical planning without the risk of being accused of conspiracy."

Silence reigned for several moments.

"Don't everyone talk at once," said Mike with just enough of a chuckle to conceal his concern.

"I like the idea," said Paul Bernstein breaking the silence.

"So do I," said Jack Wharton.

"I guess it would work," said Jenkins as he leaned back in his chair. "We can have our own contingent planning section just like they do at the Pentagon to study all kinds of what-if scenarios."

Bernstein, Wharton, and Golden burst out laughing.

"Am I missing something?" asked Mike.

"I think they're trying to take the Mickey out of me," said Harry with a chuckle.

"What's this think tank business all about?" asked Ken once the laughter had ceased.

"The thought started out originally based on something Candy once said."

"Oh!" exclaimed Jenkins. "Now what?"

"She once said one of the problems with our political system was that those running for president would have to expend an enormous amount of time and money to get elected, and if they were successful, they had only a couple of months to cobble together a government that often included people they didn't want. So I thought if our plans worked out and she became a candidate, she'd need a vehicle. The Mulholland Foundation in Los Angeles had approached our real estate department about purchasing the foundation's assets just before Christmas, and it's been percolating in my mind ever since."

"So you're talking about a Candy Reason campaign committee tucked away in the bowels of a nonprofit whose real purpose would be to figure out some way to prevent the left from taking over the country," said Jenkins.

"That's pretty much the size of things," said Mike.

"While I like the idea," Wharton said, "if we want to stop Pellegrino from becoming president, we have to decide when to do it and how to do it, but there's no chance in hell of stopping her plans for next year. If we tried, regardless of the best of plans, I think all we'd do is expose ourselves, and then all would indeed be lost. The only thing we've got going for us at the moment is that we have a copy of the invasion plan.

"Whatever we end up doing, I think we have to look at things from two points of view. I think we need a short-range plan that for want of something better I'll call planning the plan. At the same time, we need to look down the road and recognize some facts of life because there is more involved than the wicked witch of the west becoming president."

"As an army officer with considerable knowledge of strategy and tactics," said Golden, "if you want to win a war, you first must win battles, and to win battles, you must pick them and the battlefield carefully. We must distinguish between strategy and tactics."

Harry nodded and smiled. "As an old warhorse myself, I quite agree with you. I'd be surprised if anyone on this side of the table would disagree."

"Gentlemen," said Mike, "we've just determined our agenda for tomorrow."

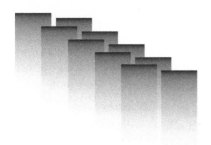

CHAPTER 87

Clyde's Restaurant
8332 Leesburg Pike
Vienna, Virginia
Monday, March 10, 2014

Nate Grishom studied the greenery of the live palm trees in the Palm Terrace of the restaurant. "Very nice," he said to Jack Wharton. "Gerri and I used to come here occasionally once upon a time, but it's been a while. I guess that's something else we've gotten away from."

"Sue and I used to come here also," said Wharton. "Like you and Gigi, that was also in another life."

"Is that why you chose this place? So we could reminisce?"

"The thought never crossed my mind. I was thinking of more practical reasons such as this place is sort of midway between our homes and neither of us has to worry about driving too far if we have too much to drink."

"Sounds like you plan on us doing some serious drinking."

"It's after the main lunch crunch and before happy hour, and you know how we get when we try to solve the problems of the world."

"But usually then, we've always had a third party present, so something tells me you're not thinking about solving world problems this afternoon."

"Not this afternoon, Nate. What I want to talk about is not for those who always have digital recorders or pens and paper with them."

"What do you want to talk about, Jack? Whatever it is, it must be of particular importance to you."

"I want to make you an offer you can't refuse."

"I must admit that whenever I hear those words, my antenna stands to attention. Go ahead."

"How would you like to become vice president?"

"Well," answered Grishom after a momentary silence, "there's a short answer and a long answer to that question. The short answer is who wouldn't, given the opportunity. The long answer is history is against me and I wouldn't have any more chance than a snowball in hell, so I think you're just trying to jerk my chain a bit for some reason."

"Suppose I wasn't jerking your chain, Nate. Suppose there really was the possibility?"

"Under those circumstances, I guess it would depend on who'd be the president."

"Suppose it was Candy Reason?"

Grishom's jaw dropped and he was speechless for a moment. "Jack, you can't be serious!"

"On the contrary, Nate. I'm dead serious but there's a catch."

"You mean catch like in there's a catch to everything?"

"That's usually the way the world works, Nate, but the catch this time is something I don't think you'll mind."

"Perhaps then you won't mind telling me the rest of the story and stop playing games."

"Nate," said Wharton after a long pause, "I'm going to become the director of the international studies division for a new think tank. I've recommended you as the director of the Domestic Studies Division. Brad Jenkins will be the executive secretary and run the show."

"Brad! He's going to leave his position as NSA?"

"Not immediately, but he will come January or February."

"Does this new think tank have a name and where will it be located?"

"The name at the moment is the Middleton Institute for Domestic and International Studies. It'll be in one of the Watergate office buildings."

"I assume the name Middleton is for your friend Ken."

"Close but no cigar. Ken's father and three of his associates are the founders. Along with their wives of course."

During the momentary pause that followed, Wharton could picture the wheels in Grishom's head crunching the ones and zeros as he tried to analyze their conversation. Then suddenly, he could picture the lightbulb in Nate's head turn on as he connected all the dots.

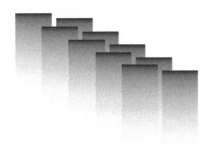

CHAPTER 88

Association Research
600 New Hampshire Avenue NW
Washington, DC
Tuesday, March 11, 2014

"So," said Ken Middleton as he sipped coffee while leaning back in his chair with his feet on the desk, "how did everything go yesterday? I thought that perhaps you'd stop by the office on your way to get Susan."

"Ken," said Jack Wharton, "after two martinis and two bottles of wine, I wasn't in any shape to drive anywhere. It was a good thing my car knew the way home."

"That bad, huh? I hope it was worth it."

"It was. Everything went according to plan for the most part. All we need to do now to clinch the deal is to bring Gigi into the fold, and we'll do that at a dinner party at our place this coming Saturday."

"How much did you have to divulge, or shouldn't I ask?"

"A lot less than I thought. I pretty much told him everything about Abe except for Golden's surgical strike force because Nate's pretty good at reading between the lines. We've known each other for too long for me to have tried to beat around the bush."

"I just hope you know what you're doing, Jack. Remember, he's a politician. He may be a conservative, but once a politician always a politician."

"You won't have anything to worry about, Ken. I've known Nate and Gigi for several years. She can't stand Pellegrino, and when she learns how and why Nate lost the election in 2010, she'll probably volunteer to shoot the bitch."

"She'll have to get in line. We seem to have lots of people who'd love to pull the trigger if it would solve our problems and if they could get away with it. How did he like the idea of becoming vice president?"

"That got his attention. We'd barely started our martinis when I asked him if he'd like the position. After he was convinced I was serious, it was only a matter of telling him about the institute and how your father was funding it but that we were the ones who would design the curriculum and do the recruiting. That led me to tell him about Abe, and after he got over his surprise, we got into one of our philosophical conversations. You know, things like the political and ideological divide in this country that's so wide that most people don't have a clue about what's going on.

"That led to a discussion about the left and how it would do anything it could to achieve its objectives. Somewhere during this discussion, it was as if we were already designing the curriculum for the institute. So all we gotta do is hit them both between the eyeballs Saturday night with a few pictures of the wicked witch of the west in her birthday suit and the presentation Myk made for the president."

"Sounds like you didn't tell Nate about the eavesdropping of Pellegrino."

"Nope. I danced around that one. I believe one should always leave something in reserve for the coup de grâce."

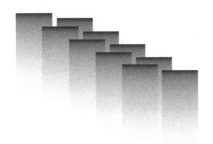

CHAPTER 89

Wharton Residence
Chain Bridge Road
McLean, Virginia
Saturday, March 15, 2014

"I think tonight turned out to be one of our more successful dinner parties," said Jack Wharton as he loaded the dishwasher while his wife was putting the leftover food in the refrigerator.

"We may have them onboard," said Susan Wharton. "But I wish we didn't have to tell them everything."

"You know how Nate's mind works. Even if I didn't tell him about Abe Monday and Pellegrino tonight, there would have been a time when we would have had to tell him, and it probably would have been sooner rather than later."

"I hope it all doesn't come back to haunt us," said Susan Wharton hopefully as she closed the refrigerator door and gathered up the napkins and placemats on the counter to take into the laundry room.

"It won't. You saw how they reacted to what we showed them, particularly the stuff about the voter fraud. You know as well as I do that they connected the dots when I said we could *make* Candy the next president. We're off and running. They have no choice but to go with the flow."

No, Jack thought. *Just like lunch with Nate Monday, everything had gone according to plan this evening.*

"I gather some congratulations are in order," said Gerri Grishom starting the commentary of the evening.

"Congratulations for what?" asked Colonel Golden.

"For keeping what you all have been doing a secret," Gerri said with a chuckle. "Particularly in this town."

"Gee, and I thought you were going to congratulate us on our ability to take it to the enemy," said Jack Wharton in mock disappointment.

"Well, that also," Gerri said. "How were you all able to resurrect an idea Nate and I thought was dead five years ago?"

"Back in 2010 when I first met President Branch," said Jenkins, "in one of those moments of complete candor and in response to some of his questions, I remembered the alternative to Al Jazeera Jack and I had talked about many times. It had been one of the reasons we'd gone to Mogadishu the year before.

"Seems our president had little faith in some of our agencies at the time and thought if he attempted to do what I was proposing, he'd read about it in the *Washington Post* and the *New York Times* the next day. To my surprise, the next day, he contacted me and asked if I was willing to quietly work with the Israelis in pursuit of some of my ideas."

"The Israelis!" exclaimed Gerri.

"Yes. Our original funding was via a foreign aid grant to Israel. Of course, as time passed, we relieved a lot of the terror organizations of their ill-gotten gains and became self-sufficient. That's the real reason Candy and I never made our marriage public."

"Amazing," said Nate. "I thought at the time that when VOA got involved, all hope for any public-private alternative to Al Jazeera was gone forever."

"Well, now you know who's behind all the griping in the Arab world. How about we move onward? We have a lot of ground to cover this evening. We have a one-minute presentation before the main event, which will take an hour, so we'll have to top off our drinks and help ourselves to some food before that. I'll dim the lights. Ken will start it. You can all enjoy wide-screen, high definition TV."

"I guess you all know this woman," said Ken Middleton a few moments later as a video clip of Barbara Pellegrino in the nude sipping a glass of wine with Rob Lowen appeared on the screen.

"Oh my God," gasped Gerri.

"Here they are again," said Ken as another video clip of Lowen between Pellegrino's legs played.

"Notice how she wraps her legs around him so he can't get away," said Jack. "They exercise like this every Monday, Wednesday, and Friday."

"I can't believe what I'm seeing," said Gerri.

"Amazing," uttered Nate.

"Typical liberals," said Jack, "trying hard to earn merit badges."

"How on earth did you get these videos?" Gerri asked.

"It's a long story," said Ken. "So I'll just give you the short version. Seems that one of Senator Feldon's staffers made a facetious remark to his father about Pellegrino having an affair with her chief of staff. The father told a couple of his associates, and they decided to play detective. As you just saw, the facetious remark turned out to be true.

"Originally, the game plan had just been to do some electronic eavesdropping of the love nest in San Francisco and the one on Capitol Hill, but soon afterward, it was discovered that each of the love nests was being protected by a couple of Internet security cameras. Fortunately, the cameras were manufactured by one of our subsidiaries. This stroke of luck made it relatively easy for two people I'll refer to as Larry and Royce to access them."

"I can't believe they didn't turn them off when they were playing romper room," said Nate.

"I don't think they were worried," Jack said. "After all, it was probably only Lowen who was ever going to access the cameras."

"The love nest on Capitol Hill was used for more than athletic pursuits," Ken said. "Lowen also met there evenings twice a month with someone else, and on one occasion, Larry and Royce observed a man by the name of Charles giving Lowen some computer instructions that led to the discovery of some flash drives they copied. Those drives led to our being here and the presentation you're about to see."

By the time they had finished showing Gerri and Nate the one-hour presentation Mykro had given Jenkins to give President Branch the previous year, he knew they were hooked. They had been successful without having to mention Ken's or Candy's fathers' involvement. But they decided to play one more card: a well-chosen graphic of a conversation Pellegrino and Lowen had soon after Nate had been defeated.

"You know, Babbs, the beauty of it all is that asshole Grishom probably still doesn't have a fucking clue."

By the time the evening was over, he knew it was payback time for Nate and Gigi. Revenge sometimes was a wonderful tool.

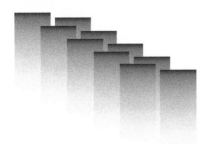

CHAPTER 90

Candice Reason's Condominium
Watergate South
700 New Hampshire Avenue NW
Washington, DC
Sunday, March 16, 2014

Candy and Brad usually slept in Sunday mornings. This morning as usual, Brad retrieved the paper outside their condo door, took it to the breakfast area, and made them each a cup of coffee.

"Would you like some scrambled eggs, sausage, and toast?" he asked Candy after he had finished his first cup of coffee.

Instead of verbally answering, Candy just nodded her head.

"Is something wrong? You look like you're preoccupied with something other than reading."

"Nothing's wrong, dear. I was only thinking about a few things."

"They must be pretty heavy because you look like you've got the weight of the world on your shoulders."

"I was just thinking about last night. I do hope we're doing the right thing."

"Why now, almost a year later, are you having second thoughts?"

"I'm not having second thoughts. I'm just thinking that getting there would be easier than being there or staying there."

"Isn't that why the Institute was created? So we can think these things out?"

"Brad, dear, that's an understatement. We'll have the media to contend with. They make believe they're a news media, but you know their agenda. Remember the 2012 election and how they crucified us?"

"And we beat them and made them pay."

"Oh they paid all right. Have you ever thought about revenge? But forget about them for a moment. There's also the entertainment industry, Hollywood and the music world. We also have a corrupt judiciary and a failing educational system. I could go on, but—"

"It sounds like you're getting cold feet."

"No, not for a moment. Remember, I saw the tapes just like you. We have no choice because the alternative is worse."

"Have you discussed all this with the girls?"

"Only to a point."

"What do they think?"

"They're not happy with what we'll be doing, but they know there's no alternative. If we don't do something, who will? They're all thinking of their children and grandchildren and what kind of world they would inherit. We've all seen the tapes, so we all know what the future will bring if no one stops them."

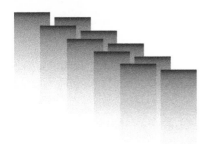

CHAPTER 91

Beit Aghion
9 Smolenskin
Jerusalem, Israel
Monday, July 28, 2014

It was about fifty-five minutes from the time Brad Jenkins had left the Bernsteins' condominium in Tel Aviv until he was driven to the front of Beit Aghion, the Israeli prime minister's residence in Jerusalem's Rehavia district. After a glance at his watch and a look around, he walked up the steps to the arched entry. A well-dressed security man accompanied him. They were joined by another security man at the top of the steps who ushered him in.

"Ah, Brad, my friend," said Benjamin Natansky as he extended his hand. "Or should I say Solomon?" he added with a laugh. "So nice to see you again. You are very punctual as usual."

"I'll stay with Brad," said Jenkins, who had traveled to Israel under an assumed name. "I won't become Solomon again until I'm near Ben Gurion."

"Come in. As it is such a lovely day, we will be lunching on the patio. I think you will be pleased with the serenity and conduciveness to conversation."

As Jenkins took a seat in one of the wrought iron patio chairs with deep cushioned seats and backs, he noted a smaller table on which sat an ice bucket containing a bottle of champagne. A slight smile crossed his lips because he knew, from previous experience, how luncheon would be conducted this afternoon.

"Some champagne to start with," said Natansky as he eased the cork from the bottle and poured two glasses. "Did I not say we would meet again and it would be in Jerusalem?"

"Yes, I believe you did."

"When I was advised that you wished to meet with me, I wondered if it would be in connection with our discussion of last year. But inasmuch as you have traveled here as Solomon Wachstein, I assume your request has to do with something else of great importance."

"What I wish to discuss with you is something very important, but as you've made reference to our lunch last year, I do have a few questions before I get to that."

"By all means proceed as you wish."

"Ben, we have only met twice before; but, I think you are a person who always has a good reason for saying whatever you say. I also believe you are a person who carefully chooses words and the words you choose always have meaning. During our last luncheon, we did a lot of dancing."

"Dancing?"

"I use the term metaphorically. During that luncheon, you used many metaphors, and there was much innuendo all of which I think I later figured out, but why couldn't you have been direct?"

"Brad, my friend, I have always believed it to be much more productive to let people reach their own conclusions rather than spell things out or attempt to tell them what to do."

"Why couldn't you have just let me know that you were aware of the conspiracy? Did Sharon Perlinger tell General Gul?"

Natansky smiled.

"Yes. Something else I figured out."

"No, Mrs. Perlinger has never broken a confidence. I would like to say that our discovery of the election fraud was due to superior intelligence, but actually, it was really a case of luck."

Jenkins was stunned. *Did I hear that correctly? Does Natansky misunderstand me?* It was almost unbelievable—Natansky thinking the great, left-wing conspiracy had to do only with election fraud.

"How did you learn about it?" asked Jenkins after recovering his composure and thinking that Natansky knew of the whole conspiracy.

"For some time, we were monitoring the movements of a Chechen organization. It was when we made a move against two organization members in Mombasa that we ultimately learned of the attempt to influence American elections."

Jenkins shook his head in disbelief. *Only the elections.* "When did you learn of this?"

"July of last year."

"Why didn't you mention this when we had lunch in August?"

"Brad, former Prime Minister Sharon and I may disagree on a lot of things, but two things on which we have never been in disagreement have been the love we have for our country and the value we place on our relationship with America. At the time, the decision was made to advise your authorities, the election dice here had already been thrown, and it was a foregone conclusion I would become the next prime minister. That is why Prime Minister Sharon asked me to personally advise your president."

"You spoke only to President Branch and about the elections?"

"Yes, only the plans for manipulating the American elections."

It was the way Natansky looked as he answered the question that caused Jenkins to ask the question, "You're not aware of the rest of the story?"

"The rest of the story?"

"I'm afraid there is a lot more to the election fraud than you are apparently aware of, and it's not a very pretty story."

"Brad," said Natansky almost an hour later, after Jenkins had told him about the discovery of the vast left-wing conspiracy. "Last year, I told you I would do anything to ensure the safety and survival of my country. I meant it then and have not changed my mind even if it means doing the unthinkable. Thus I am willing to help you any way I can with whatever you find necessary to do as long as there will never be any Israeli fingerprints."

CHAPTER 92

Bernstein Condominium
102 Sderot Rothschild
Tel Aviv, Israel
Monday, July 28, 2014

"It was unbelievable," said Brad as they sat enjoying their martinis. "I don't think we talked about our alternative to Al Jazeera for fifteen minutes."

"You came all this way after not being in Israel for more than a year and you talked about it for only fifteen minutes?" asked an incredulous Miriam Bernstein.

"We got sidetracked right at the start. Before I had a chance to make my pitch, he made a reference to our lunch last year, which led me to ask him why he hadn't told me about the conspiracy at the time. But he thought I was talking about the election fraud. To say I was stunned when I realized he knew nothing about the conspiracy would be an understatement. Seems the Israelis were monitoring the movements of a Chechen organization, and when they made a move against it, they learned of the attempt to influence our elections."

Paul Bernstein glanced at his wife as the calendar in his head began a quick data scan. "Brad, if my memory's right, you met with Natansky in August. It was March when you and your father-in-law briefed the president. Something isn't computing."

"I thought about that on the way back from Jerusalem, Paul, but I'll ponder that one later because all hell is probably going to break out here. Last year, Natansky told me he'd do anything to ensure the safety and survival of Israel. He reiterated that this afternoon and told me he'd help me any way he could as long as there were never any Israeli fingerprints."

"Amazing," said Paul.

"Yes. I think for starters, Myk, Taffy, David, and Sharon are going to have a hell of a lot of help."

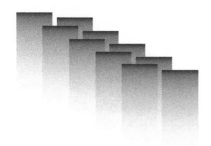

CHAPTER 93

InterContinental David Tel Aviv
12 Kaufmann Street
Tel Aviv, Israel
Thursday, October 23, 2014

Because the desert winds from the east had not met with the Mediterranean winds blowing east, which usually brought light rain this time of year, it was an unusually warm and comfortable afternoon as Ken Middleton and Paul Bernstein lunched at the terrace restaurant of the hotel overlooking the Mediterranean.

"Yes," said Ken in answer to Paul's question, "Jack will bring another group over here for the Christmas holidays, and Brad's agreed to help him this time and bring Candy if she can shake her State Department bodyguards, but that's another story."

"And I suppose the people he'll be bringing will as usual be asking the what-if questions about peace in this part of the world."

"I'd bet the farm on that one," said Ken with a chuckle.

"When will they ever learn that there will never be peace in this part of the world unless we find a way to drive a stake into the heart of Islam?"

"I couldn't agree more," said Middleton. "But driving that stake would require doing things that would make most people in our part of the world wet their pants. You know how people are, particularly if they're media types."

"Perhaps that's what we have to do considering what we've learned yet have really done nothing about. Something that would make most people cringe."

"Why do I suddenly have this feeling you're trying to tell me something in my old age?"

"I have something for you to take back for Brad," Bernstein said. "Miriam prepared it. It's called thinking outside the box or at least how to think about how to do something particularly inasmuch as we've not really done anything since learning about that left-wing conspiracy even though our Israeli friends have offered their help."

"Whatever it is, I get the impression the two of you have been giving this a lot of thought."

"It's part of our nature," said Bernstein. "Particularly mine. I grew up here. Looking for ways other than the conventional is how this tiny country has survived and become successful in the face of overwhelming odds and world opinion. We've been successful with Abe because we've always been adapting and have gone against the conventional wisdom. Why not use the same approach to take back the country we will surely lose if Pellegrino and her backers succeed?"

Thoughts raced through Middleton's mind particularly about what would happen the first Tuesday of November when the Republicans were programmed to lose the Senate by a huge majority. Yes, perhaps it is time to do something that would make most people cringe.

CHAPTER 94
Candice Reason's Condominium
Watergate South
700 New Hampshire Avenue NW
Washington, DC
Wednesday, November 5, 2014

After a quick check of the previous day's election results, Jenkins went into the kitchen and made himself a cup of coffee and then sat in the breakfast area and began to meditate. Miriam Bernstein had given him what she had said was an outline for a novel she hadn't gotten around to writing because of her involvement in their alternative to Al Jazeera. He had meant to read it seven days ago but had placed it on the desk in his study and then placed something else on top, inadvertently causing it to be lost for a week. He had just gotten around to reading it last night. As a result, he'd had a restless night. Several times during the night, he had lay in bed wide awake with his mind running in overdrive as his thoughts ran wild. Just before six this morning, he had made his way to his study and started working.

Jenkins went through the synopsis page by page highlighting the pertinent parts. Then, he booted up his computer and typed, retyped, and moved things around in a logical order for two hours. When he was finished, he called Ken Middleton and told him he had something interesting to show him and suggested Ken join him for a cup of coffee.

"Before I show you what I have," he said shortly after Ken's arrival, "I have a philosophical question."

"Will it be necessary to add something to my coffee before answering?" asked Ken with a chuckle.

Jenkins smiled. Instead of answering the question, he said, "when was the last time we ever talked about overthrowing the Pellegrino government? Actually, when have we ever talked about overthrowing anything? When have we ever talked about effecting a coup?"

For a moment, Middleton was speechless and had to gather his wits. "We've talked several times about getting rid of Pellegrino."

"That's not the same, Ken. I'm not trying to get into a game of semantics, but there's a big difference between *getting rid of* and *coup* and *overthrow*. Think about what we've said and done from the beginning. Uncle Harry is told to save the military. I'm told we need to win the war on terror at any cost. Larry and his buddy Royce are recruiting militias. The institute has been created. We say we want to defeat the left. I could go on and on, but I think you get my drift.

"Back in February when we were meeting with Uncle Harry and your father, Jack said we needed a long-range plan and a short-range plan. At the same time, Colonel Golden said something about the difference between strategy and tactics. I think all we've done from the very beginning is a form of tactics.

"Back in July when I went to Israel, I wondered when we were getting close to being thrown out of office why making changes to our alternative to Al Jazeera was such a priority. But that's a different story. The real story is that Natansky and I barely discussed that little ditty. The rest of the time, we talked about the left-wing conspiracy and how it would affect Israel. Remember what I told you when I returned about how the Israelis discovered the election fraud business and how Natansky was sent here to speak to the president?"

Ken nodded.

"When Natansky came and spoke to the president, George already knew about the voting fraud business. We'd already made a presentation about that for him. Then hot on the heels of Natansky meeting with the president, he and I were having lunch and I was asked how easy would it be to effectuate a coup in this country. While he said that in the context of something else, there was no mistaking what he meant. That was the only time since we made our discovery that any mention of a coup was ever made until this." Jenkins handed Middleton four pages.

"What's this?"

"It's an outline I prepared based on Miriam's synopsis for a story she never wrote. I'd like you to also read her synopsis, which is almost fifty pages long, and give me your two cents. I have a copy of each in another envelope for you to give Jack. I'll give Colonel Golden a copy when he gets back from the Pentagon."

"Mind if I take a quick peek at the outline?"

"Not at all."

"My God," said Middleton after he finished reading the outline. "What the hell is this? What the hell was Miriam's synopsis all about?"

"It was for a story about how to overthrow the government of the United States without the American public ever knowing."

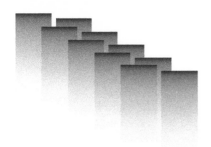

CHAPTER 95
Coffee Shop, Pro Center,
Kaanapali North Course
Sheraton Maui Resort and Spa
Lahaina, Maui, Hawaii
Wednesday, November 26, 2014

"I guess we'll have two foursomes this morning instead of two threesomes," said Brad Jenkins to Ken Middleton as they made their way toward the table where Michael Middleton and Harry Reason sat with Larry Evans, Royce Bartlett, and two others.

"Certainly looks that way," said Ken, "especially at six in the morning."

"I wonder who those two are."

"Guess we'll find out."

"Good morning," said Ken as he and Jenkins approached the table. "Who's playing with whom?"

"Before we get to the fun and games," said Mike, "if the two of you will sit, we have a little business to conclude before breakfast."

"Hopefully it's about that material you and Harry were given at the beginning of the month," said Jenkins. "I was beginning to wonder if you would ever get back to us."

"There was a lot to read and think about," Middleton said.

"Yeah," said Harry Reason. "That author friend of yours has a vivid imagination."

"When I told you about Miriam," said Jenkins with a chuckle, "I told you that's why she's always had a number of best sellers in the thriller and suspense genres."

"You really took her ideas and ran with them," said Mike. "That's why it's taken so long. Especially because you ventured into an area where we hadn't thought to go."

"Sounds like you're telling Brad you all approve," said Ken.

"That's about the size of things," Mike said. "Particularly once we got our minds wrapped around it all."

"Before we get involved in details," said Harry, addressing Ken and Brad, "I'd like you to meet Colonels Ralph Peterson and Douglas Northridge."

"Good morning," said Colonel Peterson as he reached across the table to shake hands with Brad and Ken. Northridge followed suit.

"Before we continue," said Harry Reason, "I want you to hear what Colonel Peterson has to say. He has an interesting theory that might explain why so much time has passed without our achieving much."

Brad and Ken gave Colonel Peterson a quizzical look.

"Dr. Jenkins," said Peterson, "as I understand it, your people cracked a code and discovered a left-wing plot by five very wealthy men to finance a Barbara Pellegrino presidency and a takeover of our government."

"That's correct," said Jenkins.

"And ever since that discovery, there has been what I will call a lot of wheel spinning for lack of a better choice of words."

"True," said Jenkins with a chuckle.

"I think, with the benefit of hindsight, I know why so much time has been wasted," said Peterson. "We have never had an overthrow of a government, and to my knowledge, there has never been an attempt or even a plan for one. That is until you came along with your outline based on a synopsis prepared by your author friend.

"The takeover plans your people discovered were so vast and far advanced that there was no practical way to prevent the people involved from achieving their goals. That meant the only way of thwarting them was a countercoup once they were in power. I believe if our country had ever experienced at least one overthrow, the wheel spinning since last year might not have occurred because there would have been no problem wrapping one's arms around the idea."

Everyone but Brad and Ken nodded.

"All right," said Jenkins. "Apparently, everyone here has his mind wrapped around the material we gave Mike and Harry and is in agreement that there is only one course of action. So where do we go from here? Anything we discuss from this point on becomes a conspiracy. Even if we discuss it just in the institute, there's no way it can be considered scholarly discussion in an academic environment."

"Brad, I agree with you," said Mike. "What we do from now on is too dangerous to include in the institute's framework. Back in February, using the institute as a vehicle to hide our conspiratorial thinking was a good idea, but I think we now require our own special setup."

"You mean like our own private war room?" asked Ken.

"Exactly. I suggest not merging the Association Research offices into the institute as planned, but we all work there together with no one being the wiser."

"If you all don't mind," said Larry Evans, "I'm hungry. They've almost finished setting up the buffet."

"All right," said Mike Middleton to Evans and Bartlett. "Why don't the two of you go help yourselves and we'll try to wrap everything up quickly."

"Brad," Middleton said once Evans and Bartlett left the table, "we like your ideas about stealing from the left's playbook. You know, making Candy the Republican candidate for president in 2016 and seeing she loses to Pellegrino, who then gets done to her the following year what she plans on doing to George next year."

"Will it be possible for her to assume the seat of that congressman friend of yours? That's a huge hurdle."

"I wouldn't sweat that one, Brad," said Harry. "Tom Sanford will love becoming the executive secretary of the institute and then becoming attorney general in Candy's administration. He also has a long memory and he would eagerly look forward to payback time. Also, Governor Pearson owes us a lot of favors, so there shouldn't be any problem calling in the chits at the appropriate time."

"What about the military?"

"That shouldn't be a problem," said Colonel Northridge. "We started solving that problem back when President Branch asked Harry to save the military."

"All right, Dad," said Jenkins to Harry in disgust. "What the hell have you been doing without telling us?"

"No need to get upset, Brad," said Harry. "All we've been doing was what George told me to do—save the fucking military."

"Dr. Jenkins," interjected Colonel Peterson, "as I think you know, Harry would have liked to have bugged the whole officer corps of all the service branches, but that idea had never gone beyond an emotional outburst because the electronic eavesdropping of thousands of officers was totally impractical. What we ended up doing was co-opting the left's game plan that was based on the theory that everyone had something to hide. Realizing that blackmail and coercion was a double-edged sword, we gave every officer of the senior officer corps the left had a dossier on a choice. Officers could have their lives destroyed by Pellegrino or they could have their lives destroyed by us.

"But we had a benefit the left didn't have. All the officers involved were actually good men in spite of their indiscretions. Duty, honor, and country still meant something to them."

"One of the things we liked in particular," said Colonel Northridge, "was how no one but us would ever know what happened. Once we really started analyzing things, we were surprised at how so much force could be available with so few people in the know. One of the things that had always bothered us was the possible corruption of the military. Then your outline and footnotes gave us further insight into how to work with the officer corps. While we won't be having a military coup, we'll have all that manpower at our disposal."

"What about inauguration night?" Ken asked. "That's a key element. Everyone involved would know exactly what was going on."

"The military wouldn't be involved in that part of the plan," said Colonel Peterson. "We think there are enough disgruntled ex-military out there who can be recruited. Hell, look what Larry and Royce were able to accomplish. We'll just steal a page from their playbook."

"What about our controlling the Congress?" asked Jenkins. "That's the key to the kingdom."

"We don't think that will be a problem," said Harry. "At least in the beginning. We think they'll all be clamoring for protection and won't mind the bodyguards."

"They might not object to bodyguards protecting them from the public, but all the people wanting access to the gravy train will. Plus, we need a way to control the staffers."

"I wouldn't sweat that, Brad," said Reason. "We have a couple of years to work out all the details. Once we can control Congress, we'll control everything. Who'd stop us? It certainly won't be the military, and once we put some power back into the hands of the people, I don't think we'll have to worry about any popular uprising."

"I think it's time to wind up, gentlemen," said Mike. "Our chowhounds are returning."

"One last question," Jenkins said to the colonels. "You really think we can pull this off?"

"Dr. Jenkins," said Colonel Peterson, "I think we have better than a fifty-fifty chance. We have the left's playbook and invasion plan. We have the monetary resources. We have conscripted the military. Our chowhounds, as Mike called them, have organized five militia groups. We have the remnants of Mike's and Harry's old Charlie Company. We have your surgeons, as you call them. And I think you have special friends we haven't yet discussed."

CHAPTER 96

InterContinental David Tel Aviv
12 Kaufmann Street
Tel Aviv, Israel
Wednesday, December 31, 2014

It was an unusually warm night, almost seventy degrees, when Candy and Brad slipped away from the New Year's Eve party and made their way to the terrace for a breath of fresh air. Only the muffled sound of the music from the small band that had been performing broke the quiet. For a while, they stood in silence looking up at the stars, each in deep thought, as they each reflected on the present year, which would be ending in a matter of minutes and the new year to come.

They had come to Israel for the holiday season with Susan and Jack Wharton. Jack had organized another trek to the Holy Land, and thanks to Miriam's brother, Sol Cooperman, who was now the ambassador to Israel, they had been able to enjoy a modicum of freedom from the State Department security. That had allowed them to secretly meet with Benjamin Natansky.

"When I look up at the heavens and just see the mass of twinkling stars like now, I can almost forget about the real world we live in," said Candy. "Even when I just look at the city lights fanning out into the distance, I can almost forget."

"That's because night shields us all from the real world," said Brad solemnly as he thought how Candy had been rather pensive all evening. In fact, she had been rather preoccupied for the past several weeks. He knew the ramifications of the decisions made five weeks earlier during the Globaltronix Thanksgiving week, and how those decisions could affect everyone's lives was still vividly etched in her memory. All he could do was comfort her.

Jenkins put his arm around Candy's waist and began walking with her from the terrace to the rooftop garden. In the garden, they stood and looked toward the black Mediterranean. To the west, the only lights they could see were the stars above and the glow of the moonlight on the water.

"I wonder how much time we have," said Candy.

"A few days. Possibly a few weeks, but I doubt it. Congress goes back to work on the fifth, and I don't think they want to waste time. I bet all the paperwork has already been done."

"But how can they do it?" asked Candy. "How can they impeach the president and the vice president at the same time? Why do they think they can get away it?"

"Sweetie, they'll get away with it because no one will stop them. And you know they won't want to go through the motions of impeaching George first and then have to wait a reasonable time before impeaching Chandler. Even if a judge somewhere were to rule against them, it wouldn't matter."

Candy was silent. She knew her husband was correct. That was why they were going to attempt to do what at one time would have been unthinkable.

"I wonder," said Candy, "what the president is thinking. It has to be a terrible feeling knowing you will be the first president in our history to be removed from office. If he had done something after learning of the conspiracy, maybe we wouldn't be here talking like this. But he didn't other than to tell Dad to save the military and you to win the war on terror."

"I'm not too sure I agree," said Jenkins. "I think Branch did a lot more than what we've been thinking."

"You don't!" exclaimed Candy. "What are you trying to tell me?"

"I think we've all underestimated the president, sweetie, even Miriam, which I find quite surprising considering how her mind works. I think George has read us all like a book and acted accordingly."

"Brad, are you telling me the president has been manipulating us?"

"That's exactly what I'm saying."

"If you think that, why haven't you said something before?"

"Because I came to the party late, sweetie. It was only after the meeting Ken and I had with Harry and his buddies during the Globaltronix Thanksgiving week that I got to thinking. Then I started remembering some things from when I met with Natansky back in July, and bit by bit, I started connecting the dots.

"It was March of last year when Branch was briefed about the conspiracy. It was five months later when I met Natansky at the Hay Adams, and he for all practical purposes asked me about effecting a coup. Then this past July, I learned that Natansky had already briefed him about the election rigging before our first meeting.

"I also remembered something Natansky told me during our second meeting. When I asked him why he chose to often use metaphors, he told me he found their usage to be more effective in getting people to reach the conclusions he wanted rather than attempting to spell things out and telling them what to do. I think the president did something similar. He was a crafty puppeteer who knew the right strings to pull, the right buttons to push, and all the right levers to pull, and he's done it without any one of us realizing what was happening."

"Why would the president want to go to such lengths when he didn't have to? Why didn't he just develop a plan of his own or at least work with us? Wouldn't that have been a lot easier than a lot of devious planning?"

"Perhaps, but remember what I said about reading us all like a book. Perhaps I should have said children's books. Whatever, he had his reasons."

"I think it's time for us to go back in," said Candy after several moments of reflection. "They'll soon be singing *Auld Lang Syne*."

"All right," said Jenkins as the lyrics of the song flashed through his mind, and he wondered what the morrow might bring.

Amazing, thought Jenkins as they walked back to the party. *Five very wealthy men have carefully financed and saw to the execution of a well-crafted plan to assume control of the government without the American people ever knowing what was happening.*

But the man whom they had made sure won the 2008 election, because they had perceived him to be the weakest candidate, had his own group of very wealthy men that was now plotting a countercoup to be executed in 2017.

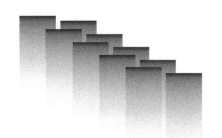

PART 2
2017

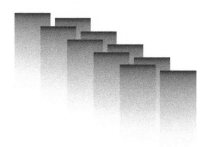

CHAPTER 1

Starbucks
1501 Connecticut Avenue NW
Washington, DC
Friday, January 20, 2017

It was a cool and windy morning just above fifty when Jenkins exited the taxi and made his way into the Starbucks between Connecticut Avenue and Nineteenth Street just north of Dupont Circle. When he left their condo, he had asked Candy if she wanted to go with him, but she had declined, saying she thought it best to stay put and work with the cook getting ready for the dinner party her parents were hosting that evening.

After ordering a latte and selecting a pastry, he made his way to a table in a corner where he thought he might enjoy some privacy. For a while, he sat enjoying his latte and pastry. Then, he retrieved a throwaway cell phone from his pocket and speed-dialed a programmed number, noting the time as he did so—10:16. The Azores were four hours ahead of Washington—2:16 in Terceira. Within moments, he was speaking with Ken Middleton, and for the next ten minutes, he told Middleton that everything in Washington was going according to plan, but their conversation was in Arabic as planned.

After Jenkins concluded his conversation, he finished his coffee and left the coffee shop on the Connecticut Avenue side and headed north to Q Street, where he intended to hail a taxi. As he walked, he said a silent prayer. The telephone call he had just made was one he hoped the National Security Agency had recorded.

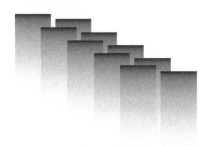

CHAPTER 2
Arab-American Imports and Exports
1050 Twenty-First Street NW, Suite 560
Washington, DC
Friday, January 20, 2017

It was nine thirty in the morning. Joseph Golan watched the last of the furniture leave the office. So far, everything had gone according to plan. His orders had been to do anything Dr. Jenkins requested as long as no fingerprints were left, but during the last two years, Jenkins had actually asked very little.

Aside from working first with Colonel Golden and later with Mr. Middleton, Jenkins had requested his help only in a scam involving the inaugural balls. Whatever the scam was had never been revealed, nor had he asked any questions. All he knew was that Arab-American Imports and Exports would furnish 286 limousines with chauffeurs to transport all the House and Senate Democrats to the inaugural balls. The scam had been easy to perpetuate because, as Jenkins had said, the people they would be doing business with might be liberals, but they loved money, particularly other people's money.

It all started two years earlier when Dr. Bernstein had created Arab-American Imports and Exports for the purpose of renting a small suite consisting of a reception area and two private offices. The offices were used by Ken Middleton, who had succeeded Colonel Golden, Mario, Ahmed, and himself as the base of their surgical operations.

After the 2016 elections, they put their plan in motion. Golden had called Haynes Jefferson, the chairman of the presidential inaugural committee, posing as the representative of Ahmed Shah, a wealthy Jordanian, to arrange a meeting with the representative of Mr. Shah.

A short time later, a meeting was held between himself playing the part of Ibrahim Hassan, the managing director of Arab-American Imports and Exports, owned by Ahmed Shah, and his surgical team member Ahmad Rashid using his own Arabic name and posing as the personal representative of the wealthy Jordanian. By the conclusion of the meeting, it was agreed that Ahmed Shah and his associates would provide the transportation for all House and Senate Democrats to the inaugural balls.

After the furniture was removed, Golan carefully scrutinized the office and with a towel and alcohol wiped every surface that might contain fingerprints. Then, he made a call on a throwaway cell.

At the conclusion of his conversation in Arabic with Paul Bernstein in Amman, he gave one more look around and left the suite of offices. He knew for sure as he closed the door behind him that he would watch the inaugural festivities that evening.

CHAPTER 3
Association Research
600 New Hampshire Avenue NW
Washington, DC
Friday, January 20, 2017

"The hard part," said Michael Middleton to Harry Reason, "is the waiting."

Reason laughed. "You had to be doing more than just waiting for Marianne to have kicked you out of the house this morning and asking me to tag along. What else were you up to?"

"Nothing really other than trying to play some FreeCell, but after about ten games, I found it difficult to concentrate, so I paced a bit. That's when she told me I was beginning to get on her nerves. Nothing more than that."

"Sitting here won't be any easier. Everything has long since been beyond our control. All we can do is wait and hope everything goes according to plan."

"That's what's so frustrating, Harry. You and I have always been hands-on, but ever since we passed the baton to the kids, I've felt marginalized even though we've always retained the advice-and-consent factor."

"Yeah, I know," said Reason with a chuckle. He knew his friend was only blowing smoke. They might have passed the baton to the kids in many ways, but they had still been hands-on in many other ways. Although he had come to Washington once or twice a month during the past two years, Mike had been very hands-on back in California working with Larry Evans, Royce Bartlett, Will Rikker, Ben Sorenson, and the militias on what became known as Operation Payback or Payback for short. What was really bothering his friend was similar to stage fright—hoping everything would go according to plan while worrying about everything that could go wrong. There was always the chance something could go wrong, but he doubted anything would because everyone had worked overtime to nail down all the details.

"I wouldn't sweat it too much," Reason said. "The kids and I spent a lot of time analyzing everything to death. That's why we've ended up with the intricate plan we have."

"We certainly have that," said Middleton chuckling for the first time that morning. "Miriam has one hell of an imagination."

"I think I'll give Tom Sanford a call," said Reason as he thought of Middleton's comment about the wife of Brad's friend Paul, who was working out of Tel Aviv. He wondered what they would have done without her. She certainly did have imagination, and their plan, Operation Restoration, was so intricate that he felt no one would be able to unravel it. "Maybe Tom's also driving his wife batty. We can order in a pizza for lunch to go with the beer in the fridge and watch Babbs lie with her hand on the Bible."

"Christ, Harry," said Middleton shaking his head. "You're having a dinner party this evening. I don't want to get sick before the fact."

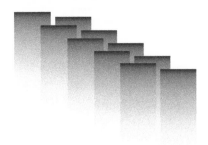

CHAPTER 4
Middleton Institute for Domestic and International Studies
600 New Hampshire Avenue NW
Washington, DC
Friday, January 20, 2017

It was not supposed to be a workday at the institute this morning, but Tom Sanford had decided it would be easier to sit in his office and gaze out the window rather than stay home and feel like a caged animal.

He had come late to the party, but once he had arrived, he had been salivating over the opportunity for revenge if everything worked out according to plan and he became the new attorney general. As he stared out the window, he could see the long list of people and organizations that would have done to them what they had attempted to do to others once payback time arrived.

First on the list would be the people in Texas, particularly a certain liberal district attorney who had worked overtime to criminalize political thought and had managed to get him indicted and convicted. Fortunately, the Texas Third Circuit Court of Appeals had overturned his conviction. Now it would be payback time in spades.

There would also be a number of people in President Pellegrino's Justice Department who would suffer the fury of the federal government, particularly that disgraceful attorney general Erik Hanson. Nothing short of seeing him behind bars for years to come would suffice.

Also on the list were a number of Pellegrino's cabinet appointees, all of whom had violated their oaths of office and had broken one law after another as well as a number of media outlets and professional organizations.

As he drained his second cup of coffee, he suddenly suffered a touch of nostalgia as thoughts of his twenty-one years in Congress brought back great memories of when he represented the people of the 21st Congressional District of Texas. *But that was another era*, he said to himself as his cell phone rang.

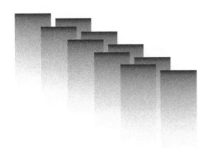

CHAPTER 5
Ralph Peterson's Condominium
1001 North Randolph Street
Arlington, Virginia
Friday, January 20, 2017

Ralph Peterson was pooped. He had gotten up very early this morning to make the last inspection visit of the secondary industrial site in Beltsville, Maryland, and the main industrial site on Hassett Street south of Lorton, Virginia. By the time he returned home and popped the top of a cold Bud Light and had sat down, he was surprised to find that his minute checks on things had turned into an eight-hour day, and it was early afternoon.

"Would you like me to make you a sandwich, dear?" asked his wife, Cheryl.

"I'd love one," he replied. "It's been one of those mornings."

As Cheryl Peterson stood in the kitchen making her husband's sandwich, she could not help thinking of her husband's involvement in an effort to restore what once used to be in another life.

Everybody knows the real threats to the country are returning vets, Christians, antiabortionists, and other right-wing extremists. That was all the talking heads on television ever seemed to say and all that ever seemed to be written in the liberal rags that posed as newspapers. She also knew that the Pellegrino Department of Homeland Security had more than fifty thousand agents trained in this way of thinking and were liable to shoot first and ask questions later if they felt like asking any questions at all.

As Peterson drank his beer, he attempted to review this evening's plan and some of its details for the umpteenth time. Harry Reason always referred to it as a very intricate plan and Operation Restoration contained many elements; all based on a synopsis prepared by the wife of a friend of Dr. Jenkins, a woman who wrote novels of international intrigue under a pseudonym.

Jenkins had prepared an outline with many questions based on Miriam Bernstein's synopsis, and during the past two years, every one of Harry Reason and Bradford Jenkins's associates had worked their tushes off developing and refining all the elements and the fallback positions if any were needed. But the execution of any plan, whether simple or intricate, required a starting point. Tonight would be that starting point, and the limousines were the key component.

It was doubtful any law enforcement personnel would be able to connect the 286 used limos purchased surreptitiously from around the country by several people and driven to the main industrial site at Lorton, where they had been serviced to make them look like they had just been driven from the showroom for the evening's festivities. The limos had special features installed to make it possible for the passengers to be put to sleep without affecting the driver. That had concerned him, and that's why they had practiced and practiced during the week.

They had also begun, earlier this week, to start moving the specially built trailers from site to site, particularly at night because this evening, when push came to shove, everything had to look as normal as possible.

"Thank you very much," he said to Cheryl when she handed him his sandwich and another beer.

"Would you like to watch the parade?" she asked.

"I don't have any particular desire to watch the parade. I think I'll take a nap after I finish my sandwich. I'd like to feel human again for this evening."

"What time would you like to leave for Kym and Harry's?"

"Five forty-five. Six is our projected start time."

Instead of saying anything further, Cheryl nodded and started to walk back to the kitchen.

"Cheryl," said Peterson sensing something was wrong.

"What?"

"Everything is going to be all right."

"I hope so."

"Remember—we're the good guys with the white hats and the guys with the white hats always win."

With that remark, a slight smile appeared on Cheryl Peterson's face. It was the first time today she had felt anything other than anxiety.

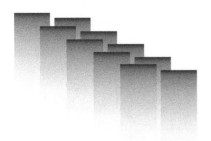

CHAPTER 6
1525 Thirty-Fifth Street NW
Washington, DC
Friday, January 20, 2017

His real name was John, but he had been called Mutt since he had been a sophomore in high school. Mutt Ammerman was similar to all the militiamen who went to work this evening. His father had fought in Vietnam. He had fought in the Iraq War, and his son had become a soldier, but his son had recently chosen not to reenlist because the Pellegrino regime had cut military spending to the bone and he could no longer support his family on his military pay.

Ammerman could also vividly remember the time that if anyone had suggested he'd be doing what he would be doing this evening, he would have said, "No way, Jose." But times had changed. First, it had been the politically correct military, then the mantra of the day throughout the country became political correctness on steroids. Society broke down; all the values he had been taught were under fire.

It was approaching seven in the evening when Ammerman pulled the 2016 Cadillac de Ville to the curb and stopped in front of the Georgetown residence of California Senator Dianne Feldon and her husband on Thirty-Fifth Street NW. Mutt knew there were 285 drivers like himself who were thoroughly disgusted with what had happened to the country and were particularly disgusted with the liberal politicians who had feathered their nests while screwing everyone else.

A shame, he thought as he pressed a button on his cell, got out of the car, and held the door open for the senator and her husband, who were making their way down the steps of a porch with a New Orleans–style railing and roof supports. It was a shame that what he and the others like him were about to do this evening had to be done, but as Colonel Peterson had said, "This is why a lot of South and Central American countries have death squads."

"Good evening, Senator Feldon," said Ammerman as the senator got in. "Good evening, Mr. Feldon." *Bitch*, thought Ammerman as he pressed a button on his cell again and slid behind the wheel. Melvin Feldon had been somewhat pleasant, but his overweight, dark-haired wife had spoken as if she were about to be poisoned.

By the time he had driven the three blocks to Reservoir Road NW, Senator Feldon and her husband were sound asleep because Ammerman had pressed the time-delay button on the canister of the fast-acting, odorless, colorless CCG under his seat and had donned the gas mask stowed in the side pocket.

A little more than three-quarters of a mile from Thirty-Fifth Street, Ammerman pressed the button of a small transmitter that looked like an overhead door operator clipped to the sun visor. He saw the rear portion of a specially built plywood trailer that resembled those used for landscaping services, drop down to form a ramp. Within thirty seconds, the de Ville was up the ramp and into the trailer, the ramp had come up to its closed position, and a black pickup was heading west with the trailer in tow.

All Ammerman had to do now was wait for the truck to make its way to River Road, then the Capital Beltway, and then head south to Lorton. Unfortunately for Ammerman, he would spend the hour-long journey thinking about Dianne Feldon, known as the Democrat constitution hater and the chairwoman of the Senate Armed Services Committee. In her senatorial position, she had steered so much work to her contractor husband that she was the richest and bitchiest member of Congress.

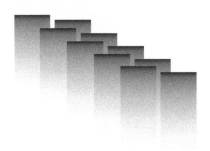

CHAPTER 7
Garfield Street NW
Washington, DC
Friday, January 20, 2017

There wasn't enough money in the world to keep Matt Flynn from doing what he would be doing this evening. Billy Bob Clayton and his bitch of a wife, Tracy, who hated the military, deserved everything that was coming to them that evening.

He couldn't prove it, but he knew that Billy Bob, while he was the governor of Tennessee, had been responsible for his father's death, a death that had been ruled a suicide. A former state policeman who had returned home after his National Guard unit served in the first Gulf war, he had risen through the ranks, ultimately becoming part of Billy Bob's security detail. But Billy Bob wanted to run for president, and his father, along with several others whose deaths had also been ruled suicides, had known too much, particularly about the affair Tracy Clayton had been having with another woman.

Thanks to his acquaintanceship with Doug Northridge, which went back to their Naval Academy days, and an economy that had gone from bad to worse under Pellegrino, he was involved in a conspiracy that not that many years ago would have been unimaginable.

After picking up Billy Bob and his wife at their residence on Whitehaven Street NW, he had driven to Massachusetts Avenue NW, made a left, and headed to Thirty-Fourth Street NW. At Thirty-Fourth, he made a right and drove north to Garfield Street, where he made another right. That was when he pressed the button of a small transmitter that looked like an overhead door operator clipped to the sun visor.

It was at Garfield Terrace where the police cruiser that had received the signal blocked further travel. "I'm sorry, sir," said the policeman who had walked up to his open window. "There's been an accident. I'm afraid you'll have to turn around."

"No problem, officer," said Flynn with a smile. He knew what would happen. He turned. "Looks like we have a slight change of plans, Mr. President. I'll turn around and take Thirty-Second Street to Cathedral Avenue. It's really not that much out of our way."

"No problem," said former President Clayton in his usual affable manner. "Go for it."

"Yes, sir." Flynn glanced at his side-view mirror and noticed the police officer standing by the black Chevy Suburban chase car giving him a thumbs-up, the signal that the two Secret Service agents in the SUV were sound asleep after receiving a good dose of the CCG from the small canister the policeman was holding.

As he turned the Lincoln Town Car around, Flynn flashed his lights to tell the person in the police cruiser that his passengers were also sound asleep; immediately after answering Clayton, he had pressed the time-delay button of the CCG canister under his seat and donned the gas mask in the side pocket.

As he made his way back along Garfield Street toward Massachusetts Avenue and the trailer on Pilgrim Road NW that awaited him, he knew it would only be moments before the police cruiser, which really wasn't one at all, would also be making its way to a trailer on Thirty-Fifth Place. Then there would be a thirty-seven-mile drive to the industrial site in Virginia. It would be the last trip the Claytons would ever be on.

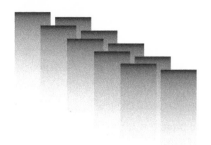

CHAPTER 8

Harry Reason's Condominium
Watergate West
2700 Virginia Avenue NW
Washington, DC
Friday, January 20, 2017

"I hate to be a party pooper," said Colonel Peterson, "but I don't think FBI director Mueller will tell us anything this evening we don't already know. Besides, I want to be at our Lorton location before six."

As usually happens at dinner parties, once someone makes an announcement that it's time for them to go, the other guests tend to follow suit. Soon, the Sanfords, the Grishoms, and the Whartons were also saying they should leave.

"I'll see you both in the office early morn," said Jack Wharton to Nate Grishom and Brad Jenkins.

"We'll be there," said Grishom.

"And have the coffee ready," said Jenkins.

The dinner party had been fairly somber because everyone knew that death was in the air and that their hands weren't clean.

One by one, the couples had arrived and headed for the self-service bar in the kitchen. Candy and Brad were the first to arrive because Candy wished to help her mother with any last-minute details. They had been followed by Cheryl and Colonel Ralph Peterson, who, after pouring a glass of wine for his wife and himself, had fired up his laptop and connected it to a TV behind two panels in wall-to-wall shelving.

By the time Marianne and Mike Middleton, the Whartons, the Grishoms, and Peg and Tom Sanford had arrived, the television screen was showing a spreadsheet with 286 lines and eight columns with headings titled Number—Name—In Motion—Arrival—Departure—Trailer—Departure 2—Home.

Colonel Peterson explained that the columns stood for a limo number, the name of the congressional member to be picked up, that the limo driver was commencing his assignment, that the limo had arrived at the member's place of residence, that the limo had left the member's place of residence, that the limo had arrived at its assigned trailer, that the trailer was on the road, and that the trailer had arrived at base one or two.

He also explained that the limo drivers would press a button on throwaway cells that would send a signal to a modem in Harry Reason's study, which sent a signal to Colonel Peterson's laptop. Cells that turned green represented completed tasks. Their intention had been to alternate between watching the spreadsheet and the three inaugural balls, but that was a difficult task because everyone was more focused on the evening's game plan.

"God, I hope nothing goes wrong," said Marianne Middleton to her husband shortly after Colonel Peterson had completed his explanations.

"Keep the faith," said her husband. "We've taken just about every precaution imaginable."

"I hope so," said Marianne despite her husband's reassurance.

For the first two hours of the evening, hardly anyone spoke. When there was a conversation, it tended to be the men in the kitchen getting refills for their wives and themselves and the wives while they were waiting for their husbands to return.

"How did your day go, Nate?" asked Jack Wharton.

"God, you should ask?"

"Sounds like yours was a wipeout like mine."

"I had planned on working on that manuscript Miriam and I are collaborating on, but I kept drawing blanks. I couldn't even play a game of FreeCell. How about you?"

"Thank God for Stan Portman in my life. I wasn't worth a damn today."

"Do you think he's figured out what's going on?"

"If he has, he's never said anything to me, and I'd bet my life he'd never say anything to anyone else."

"I gather Michael was driving you batty this morning," said Kym Reason to Marianne Middleton.

"Yes. I told him if he didn't stop pacing around I'd scream."

"I was glad that Tom went to the office," said Peg Sanford. "That helped a bit because I was like a zombie most of the day."

"How were things in your household, Gerri?" Susan Wharton asked.

"If I said quiet, that would be an understatement. I think we were each afraid to say anything to each other."

"That's what it was like with Jack and me," Susan said.

"I think Candy and I had the easiest time," said Kym Reason. "It helped to be busy getting ready for this evening."

It was 8:35 p.m. when the last spreadsheet cell turned green and everyone let out a sigh of relief.

"We should be home free now," said Colonel Peterson. "All the trailers are home, and the only activity on the road now will be the container trucks heading to Norfolk. There should be no problem there because they all have military markings and the police don't usually stop military vehicles."

"Usually doesn't sound like a vote of confidence," said Marianne Middleton.

"If that should happen," said her husband, "all the drivers have fake orders."

For the next one and three quarter hours, they watched the inaugural balls with particular interest because as the hour hand moved closer to nine, the network talking heads had stopped chatting about evening attire and hairdos and had started focusing on the members of Congress who had not yet made their appearances. Finally, at ten thirty, the networks started saying that the director of the FBI would address the nation at eleven.

"How about a brandy to celebrate a successful evening?" asked Harry after everyone had left except Candy, Brad, and the Middletons. "We can sip while we watch what the FBI has to say."

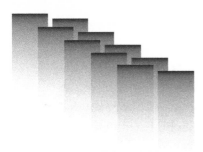

CHAPTER 9

J. Edgar Hoover Building
935 Pennsylvania Avenue NW
Washington, DC
2300 hrs, Friday, January 20, 2017

It was exactly 11:00 p.m. when FBI director Mueller stepped before the cameras and microphones and made a short announcement to the country. He didn't want to do it, but the media had been supposing, commenting, and speculating for over an hour and a half, and it had been time to set the record straight even though the investigation had barely begun and there were so many unknowns.

> This evening at approximately 8:15 p.m., inquiries began to be made to the bureau and the Secret Service regarding certain members of Congress who had not yet made their appearances at the inaugural balls they were scheduled to attend.

> These initial inquiries were made because members of their staffs had telephoned their places of residence and were told that the members had all left in the vicinity of seven this evening.

> At approximately 9:21 p.m., one of the Secret Service members assigned to former President Billy Bob Clayton and his wife, Senator Tracy Clayton, made an emergency telephone call to his superiors at headquarters. The agent said that the limousine carrying President Clayton and his

wife had supposedly been stopped by the Metropolitan Police because of a traffic accident. I say supposedly because one of the policemen who had spoken to the driver had also spoken to the agents just before he sprayed something into their vehicle that put him and his partner immediately to sleep.

When he and his partner woke up, their vehicle had been moved to a different location and they had been relieved of all communication devices. An immediate inspection of the surrounding areas in question proved fruitless.

At this moment, the whereabouts of former President Clayton and his wife are unknown. Also, the whereabouts of two hundred members of Congress and their spouses are unknown.

We are conducting a check of every limousine rental agency in the metropolitan area that may have provided the chauffeurs and limos that took the members and their spouses to the various balls.

President Pellegrino has not been nor is in any danger. At the time the initial inquiries were being made, the presidential motorcade was en route to the Wardman Park hotel. To assure the president's safety, after the initial calls to the Secret Service, the motorcade was instructed to return to the White House.

Therefore, in view of what we know at the moment, we must conclude that the missing members of Congress and their spouses have been kidnapped. That is all I am prepared to say this evening because this is an ongoing investigation.

CHAPTER 10

Harry Reason's Condominium
Watergate West
2700 Virginia Avenue NW
Washington, DC
Friday, January 20, 2017

"That certainly wasn't much of a speech," said Harry Reason with a chuckle as he sipped his brandy.

"That's because he didn't have anything to say," said Mike Middleton. "My guess is that Mueller didn't want to say anything but was forced to because of all the media blathering."

"I wonder what they really do know," said Candy Reason with a sigh.

"I suppose you could always speak to Len Roman's son Greg at the bureau," said Marianne Middleton to her husband.

"Yeah, and I could also talk to Rob Morrison's son Steve at Secret Service headquarters, but I'm not going to," Mike Middleton said as he shook his head in disbelief. They had spent the past two years planning something that had required more secrecy than the Manhattan Project. He was surprised that his wife had even mentioned such a stupid thing.

"I do hope nothing comes back to us," said Kym Reason. As was the case with the other wives present, she had been content to know about Operation Restoration only in general; the nuts and bolts of the numerous details had been left to their husbands.

"There's not a ghost of a chance," said her husband. "We spent hours in the war room covering all bases."

"Brad," said Candy to her husband as her father was answering her mother, "what do you think the FBI and the Secret Service will do?"

"Exactly what we thought they would do way back when we were doing the planning. If they did their due diligence, they would have gotten the name of the person who would be driving the limo Clayton was in and run a background check, and the check would have been on a real person who worked for one of the rental companies. We don't know if they did because we've heard nothing. But assuming they did, the driver also had a fake Virginia license in that person's name."

"How about the license plate?"

"Stolen from a preselected car complete with fake registration."

"Amazing," said Kym, who had tuned into her daughter's conversation with her son-in-law after her husband's comment.

"The director said they were calling the rental companies. I wonder when they started."

"My guess is right after they got enough calls to make someone suspicious," Jenkins said.

"We know they got nowhere doing that," added Harry Reason.

"Right," said Jenkins. "And because there are so many limo rental companies in the metro area, I don't think anyone began tying things together until the agents assigned to Clayton called in."

"They're probably calling every limo company between Baltimore and Richmond," Middleton said.

"They'll draw blanks on that too," said Harry. "The limos came from all over the country."

"I think it's time for us to call it a night," Brad told Candy. "I told Jack and Nate I'd meet them at Nate's office early tomorrow to go to our next step."

Moments later, everyone was giving good-night hugs and shaking hands.

"In case I don't see you tomorrow," said Harry as he shook Brad's hand, "have a safe and successful trip."

"I'll second that," added Mike. "Let's hope the media calls you and Candy tomorrow."

"I think that's pretty much a given," said Jenkins with a chuckle, "particularly in this era of the 24-7 news cycle. Forgetting Candy's other credentials, just being former national security advisers will be enough for the media to call us, and we won't be the only ones. They're probably working on their who-to-call lists now, and with so much time to fill, they may even call Mickey Mouse."

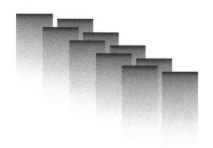

CHAPTER 11

Beit Aghion
9 Smolenskin
Jerusalem, Israel
Saturday, January 21, 2017

Prime Minister Benjamin Natansky was usually an early riser. Most mornings, he would slip out of bed and into his robe and then make his way downstairs to the breakfast area, where a servant would supply him with a cup of coffee. Coffee in hand, he would go to his study and peruse the morning papers until his wife joined him for breakfast.

This morning, however, because of the telephone call he had received from General Ari Ben Gul, immediately after entering the breakfast area, he had picked up the remote control and turned on the wall-mounted flat-screen television. In ten minutes, he had the answer to a question that had befuddled everyone since early November. *Why had the people working with Dr. Jenkins wanted to furnish limousines for the opposition to use?* He also understood the e-mail Joseph had sent to Ari the previous morning.

"I had to clean out my desk today because the company I worked for has gone out of business." Translated, the e-mail had said Arab-American Imports and Exports, the company that Dr. Bernstein had established two years ago, had now disappeared from the face of the earth.

Then Natansky remembered the answer to a question he had asked Dr. Jenkins when they had first met: "If something like that were to ever happen in the United States, it would have to happen in such a way that the American people would never know what had happened."

Interesting, he thought. He was sure what he had just learned was the tip of a very big iceberg.

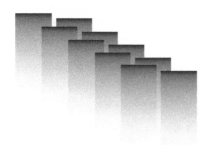

CHAPTER 12

Middleton Institute for Domestic and International Studies
600 New Hampshire Avenue NW
Washington, DC
Saturday, January 21, 2017

"Good morning," said Jack Wharton to Nate Grishom, who was gazing out the window of his office. "I thought I'd be the early bird this morning."

"Good morning, Jack," said Grishom. "I guess you didn't get much sleep either."

"I tried. When Susan and I got home, I had a nip of brandy thinking it might help me get to sleep, but no dice. After tossing and turning, I tried to read, but that was also a losing cause. So I showered and dressed, and you know the rest of the story. What did you see while you were gazing into space, or shouldn't I ask?"

"I didn't see anything. I had my eyes closed. I was running figures through my head. If you're a conspiracy buff, there are a couple of ways you could look at last night."

"I heard the word *conspiracy*," said Tom Sanford entering the office. "Am I interrupting something clandestine?"

"Surprise, surprise," said Grishom. "I thought that after last night, you'd spend some serious sack time this morning."

"That was the plan, but you know the story about the best of intentions. So what conspiracy are you talking about, ours or someone else's?"

"Nate was just about to explain how last night could be a couple of conspiracies."

"Two? Isn't one enough?"

"There are two ways of looking at the result of the numbers," said Grishom. "With the exception of those who came from New York and California, everyone who disappeared came from a state with Republican governors."

"What's that got to do with the price of eggs in China?" Sanford asked.

"If you were a typical liberal used to blaming Republicans for everything, it wouldn't be too much of a stretch to blame them for the disappearance of two hundred Democrats, would it?"

"Wouldn't that be taking the blame game too far?" asked Sanford. "Besides, didn't we take that into consideration?"

"They've already gone beyond belief many other times, so anything's possible. You can also look at the situation as whoever is responsible succeeding with a double whammy. First succeeding in the disappearance and second, letting the liberal mind-set go to work."

"Well, well," said Jenkins as he walked into Grishom's office. "Maybe you all should have stayed over last night instead of leaving before our esteemed FBI director spoke."

"It might have been easier," said Jack Wharton, "considering."

"Have any of you heard anything about the governor of New York dying of a heart attack last night?" Jenkins asked.

"I've heard nothing," said Sanford.

"Nor have I," said Wharton.

"Same here," said Grishom. "How did you hear about it?"

"I saw it on a TV news scroll just before I left to come here. You know how news scrolls across the bottom of the TV picture a lot of the time? That's where I saw it."

"Do you think anyone connected with us is involved?" asked Grishom.

"Good question," said Jenkins. "I don't know for sure, but the timing is rather coincidental. Maybe when Ken's father-in-law gets back stateside, I'll learn something one way or another."

For a few moments, the men looked at each other as what Jenkins had said registered.

"New York, you say," said Grishom. "The one state involved that had a Democrat governor. If I remember correctly, the lieutenant governor is a Republican. Very interesting."

"You're forgetting California," said Jenkins. "Last I heard, it also had a Democrat governor."

"I guess Nate was trying to forget California and all its problems," said Wharton. "I sure am glad I left the state and headed east after college."

"Are you sure it was only the governor of New York who had a heart attack last night?" asked Grishom with a chuckle.

"It wouldn't have helped in California," said Wharton. "The lieutenant governor is a Democrat."

"Damn it," continued Wharton. He felt his cell vibrate. "Let me see who the hell is calling me so early." He looked at the number. "It's our friend Dave. I'll take the call. This may be the beginning of what we're after."

"David, don't you believe in sleeping in on a Saturday morning? … Yeah, I'm awake thanks to you … Yeah, I watched TV last evening, but watching the Pellegrino special was the last thing I wanted to do. But Susan wanted to see what the women were wearing to the balls. She saw the beginning of what happened and dragged me to the TV … My take on what happened last night? I think the Republicans planned and executed the whole damned thing. They finally had it with the Democrats and got pissed enough to … You don't believe me? Yeah, yeah, I know. I have an irreverent sense of humor … All right, seriously, it was obviously a terrorist attack. Probably Al Qaeda or one of the spin-offs. Whoever did it, though, obviously spent a lot of time planning and probably a lot of money. Other than that, I don't know any more than you do. One thing I do know, however, is that if I were the president, I'd have the army here on the double. It's always possible another shoe will drop, and the Secret Service and the metro police just don't have the manpower … You couldn't reach Nate? Well, it's Saturday, and some people like to sleep in on occasion. I'd give him another jingle. He probably had his phone turned off … Talk to you later."

He turned to Nate Grishom. "Time to turn your phone on, my friend."

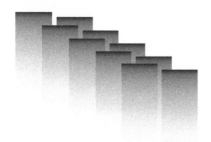

CHAPTER 13

Restaurante Beira Mar
Angra do Heroismo
Island of Terceira, Azores
Saturday, January 21, 2017

"According to local TV," said Mario Barrera after he and his wife, Anita, and Nancy and Ken Middleton had ordered before-lunch glasses of wine, "the Arabs did us a favor. We should probably send them a thank-you note."

"I think we'll give the thank-you notes a pass," said Middleton with a chuckle.

Mario Barrera had become part of the plan because for the previous six years, he had been working with Joseph Golan and Ahmad Rashid under the direction of Colonel Golden. After becoming part of the plan, Mario and his wife had been sent to Terceira to live and become their local eyes and ears.

"We have a lot to do, and there are only ten days left. The rest of the troops are arriving in three days. If I know Nancy's father, he'll ask me a million questions on the drive from Lajes to our hotel. It's question-and-answer time."

"I always thought it was called attitude adjustment time when we are partaking of the grape," said Mario with a chuckle. "Fire away."

"Mario," said Middleton as he smiled, "you remind me of someone I know, right, Nancy?"

Nancy nodded as she thought of Jack Wharton and his irreverent sense of humor.

Anita Barrera smiled. "He's been like that ever since he discovered Portuguese wines."

While he was amused with the conversation, Middleton knew he had to get the show on the road or they would end up spending the afternoon at Beira Mar drinking more than their share of the very good tasting Donatario white Mario had ordered.

"We have eighteen men to bring ashore in ten days," said Ken, "and the first question Nancy's father and his buddy will ask me is which one of the four places we looked at in October will be the location."

"I think the place to bring them in is that place where we saw the steps go into the water," said Mario. "We spent a lot of very early morning hours checking out everything between four and six o'clock. We also walked the areas day and night and took a lot of photos. And between the cliffs, the rocks, the streetlights, and the buildings, each one of the locations was a damned if we do and damned if we don't. As you know from when you were here in October, there's not an ideal location anywhere."

"What about privacy?" asked Ken. "By that, I mean no lights."

"Because there are a couple of bends in the road at that point, there is only one streetlight that is of concern. The steps go up to a parking area overlook, and immediately across the street, there is nothing but rubble stone walls. Our only problem is there is one house across the street, but it's at least a hundred yards away. We could probably shoot out that one streetlight for insurance. This would create a much greater dark spot to work with. What I would do is bring everyone ashore first and then call for the vans."

"Without lights of course."

"Not only no headlights; we'll also have all the bulbs for the interior lights removed. If everyone gets off the stick, we can be loaded and gone in sixty seconds."

"I hope so," said Ken with a sigh. "Let's hope no one wants to stop and see the submarine races at four o'clock."

CHAPTER 14
Dundalk Marine Terminal
Baltimore, Maryland
Sunday, January 22, 2017

The ghostly silhouettes of the high-rise buildings in downtown Baltimore were beginning to disappear as the dark of night began to give way to a new day when Brad Jenkins made his way to the navigation deck of the *Abu Maru* with a cup of coffee.

The time since yesterday morning has passed quickly, he thought as he stood and stared through the window as the ship began to move away from the pier.

Soon after Jack Wharton had spoken with David Hawkins, Nate Gresham had received a call from Hawkins. A short time later, Grishom and Jenkins had each received calls from the producers at the local Fox affiliate. After a ten o'clock interview with Fox, Jenkins had left for the Rayburn House Office Building to hook up with Candy so they could have lunch at a popular Republican watering hole before he caught a train to Baltimore. Like many other members of Congress, she had gone to her office because of what was perceived to be a national emergency.

When the train arrived at Baltimore's Penn Station on 1500 North Charles Street, Captain Mark Mason, the skipper of the *Abu Maru*, was there to greet him and drive him to the ship so he could stow his gear. It had been the first time Jenkins had ever seen the *Abu Maru*.

After a cook's tour of the ship, Jenkins, Mason, and the first officer headed back into town for an Italian dinner at Amici's in Little Italy. Upon returning to the ship after dinner, Jenkins made scripted calls to Ken Middleton, who was on the island of Terceira in the Azores, Colonel

Marshall Golden in Beirut, and Paul Bernstein in Amman. As was the case with his previous calls, he hoped the NSA had taken notice because the conversations had all been in Arabic.

"We're on our way," said the skipper to Jenkins.

Jenkins nodded as he watched the freighter continue to move away from the pier.

"Let's hope everything goes according to plan," the skipper said.

Everything will go according to plan, Jenkins thought. *It's a good plan. We've left nothing to chance. We've sautéed and frappéed it and then researched and rehearsed it for two years.*

Their departure on the *Abu Maru* was the second step of a multistep plan. As a freighter or container ship, it had been purchased for a song because it could carry only 250 containers, a small number compared to other ships. They had bought it for less than a million and had installed an autopilot system. It flew the Panamanian flag, but its registry would never reveal its true ownership. Paul Bernstein, the master of the International Business Corporation, had used the same processes he had used for Project Abraham and Arab-American Imports and Exports when he created the layering of many corporations and the use of straws.

To prevent even a hint of unusual activity, the *Abu Maru* had sailed from Baltimore with a cargo destined for Colon, Panama, three times before and had returned to Baltimore the same number of times with cargo. All the trips had been legitimate and profitable though only marginally.

This time, however, would be the last time the ship sailed anywhere. Instead of shipments of industrial parts, the cargo was automobiles of a similar size and shape as those that had gone missing Friday evening. Not included on the cargo list, however, was a lot of C-4, wiring, detonators, and a few other electronic devices hidden about the ship.

Unlike the previous times when the ship had turned to a southerly course after entering the Atlantic, this time, it would set a course for the Strait of Gibraltar, and seven days and eleven and one-half hours later, it would be about 130 miles north of Terceira, one of the islands of the Azores. There, he and the seventeen-man crew would depart in a modified blue-water boat and head south to rendezvous with a yacht that would take them to a cove on the north side of Terceira. Everything had been thought of. The only thing they had no control of was the weather, and February was only nine days away.

CHAPTER 15
N 39°3'55.17" W 27°9'48.24"
Seventeen Miles North of Terceira, Azores
Wednesday, February 1, 2017

Blowing up a ship in the middle of the ocean in such a way that people will jump to all the wrong conclusions is a simple idea, thought Ken Middleton as he glanced at his watch and noted they were almost at rendezvous time. But like all ideas, the devil was in the details. If the ocean was to be the Atlantic and Arab terrorists were to be blamed, having the ship sail from the mouth of the Chesapeake Bay to the Strait of Gibraltar would seem logical.

When the plan had originally been conceived, they had done a lot of Internet searching and had extensively used Google Earth. That was how they had come to decide on using the island of Terceira. Though the small island of Graciosa, thirty-one miles northwest of Terceira, was closer to the *Abu Maru*'s route, Terceira was larger and thus had more coastline. It also had a combination military-civilian airport with the US Air Force Sixty-Fifth Air Base Wing constituting the greatest portion of a joint Portuguese-US military presence.

But in spite of all the research, computers could accomplish only so much; it had become evident that boots on the ground were needed. That was why he and Jenkins had gone to Terceira almost two years earlier.

Soon after their arrival, their worst fears were confirmed. Everything they would be doing had to be in the realm of absolutes. They needed secrecy and guarantees that each part of the plan would work exactly as it was supposed to at the exact time it was supposed to.

Because they did not expect the crew to go down with the ship or float around the Atlantic on life rafts, they had originally planned on renting a boat that could meet the *Abu Maru* and bring its crew to shore somewhere. Unfortunately, the plan to rent a boat had proven not to be viable because anything large enough to hold eighteen people could be rented only with a crew, and that was unthinkable.

There was also a problem with the coastline. Because they had to arrive on the island in secrecy, that meant arriving at night. Terceira's coast was rocky. The west coast had been unthinkable, and the south and east coasts were too built up. That had left them only a small area from Vila Nova to Biscoitos on the north coast, and the main road along the coast was well lit at night. That was why the crew of the *Abu Maru* had been sailing toward the rendezvous point for the past five hours in a modified blue-water fishing boat and why Middleton was in a fifty-six-foot Challenge 67 yacht.

There also had been the problem with where to hide eighteen people until they could leave the island, but in that regard, they had gotten lucky and had discovered a house for sale that according to the estate agent could sleep ten. It was only two miles east of where the men would come ashore. *If you can't be good, be lucky*, he thought as his phone rang and he felt Larry Evans throttle back the engine.

After fifteen-plus hours at sea this time of year, Doug Northridge was bored. After the rendezvous with the crew from the *Abu Maru*, there would still be another two hours under engine power to the cove off Quatro Ribeiras, where they were scheduled to be no later than four that morning. There would probably be another ten to twelve hours back to the harbor at Heroismo.

But perhaps it wasn't boredom he was feeling. Perhaps it was anxiety because they were in a part of the world at a particular point in time doing something they shouldn't have been doing. *Only God knows what will happen if we're discovered.* He hoped that all the extra precautions they had built into their plan would make their current venture successful. That's why he had resisted shifting the route of the *Abu Maru* farther south toward Terceira. Fifty or even sixty miles might not seem like much of a deviation, but one never knew what the eyes in the sky were recording these days, and it just wasn't worth the risk considering the great lengths they had gone to in their planning.

After the decision had been made for the *Abu Maru* to carry a modified blue-water fishing boat and for the crew to sail it to the rendezvous point, the next decision had been about how to get the crew from there to shore. They had decided on another boat. It wasn't often one could steal a boat and get away with it, but their acquisition of the *Liberté* had been tantamount to stealing. The *Liberté*, a specially built ten-year-old Challenge-series yacht designed to sail around the world against the wind—worth almost half a million—had been part of an estate sale in England; they had bought it for just over $400,000.

After having berthed the yacht until October, Northridge, Ken Middleton, Larry Evans, and their wives had sailed the yacht the 1,300-plus nautical miles to Heroismo on Terceira. It had been an enjoyable ten-day journey; the weather had been good except for a few squalls and several periods of fog where the warmer air from the South Atlantic collided with the cold winds of the North. Usually, they experienced only low cloud cover where the billowy white clouds with their bottoms blackened by the rain they held floated along against a backdrop of gray skies that only occasionally gave way to small patches of blue much as they had experienced earlier today.

Larry Evans, the pilot, wasn't the least bit concerned about the weather. He'd sailed from Vancouver to San Diego many times, and the Pacific weather off the West Coast had been far worse in July or August than anything they had experienced since they first took the *Liberté* out of the harbor for a trial spin seven days earlier.

After leaving the marina at Heroismo at ten that morning, they had maintained a course toward São Miguel that they had maintained for fifteen hours before they had turned and sailed on a course of 30.90 degrees, which would take them to a point thirty miles east of the island. After three hours of sailing and two more under power, they had reached the turning point at latitude N 38°44' 36.29" and set a course of 298.03°, which five hours later had brought them to the rendezvous point at latitude N 39°3'55.17" and longitude W 27°9'48.24". All they had to do was wait for the Bayliner to appear on their radar.

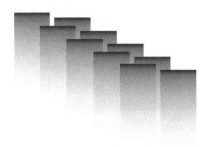

CHAPTER 16

The White House
1600 Pennsylvania Avenue NW
Washington, DC
Tuesday, January 24, 2017

President Barbara Pellegrino was not in a very good mood this morning as she stared across her desk at Rob Lowen, who was standing.

"I don't like it any more than you do, Babbs," he said, "but we had no choice particularly after all those dickheads on the damned Sunday talk shows."

Pellegrino knew that, but she was still pissed. Friday night was to have been a formal crowning, a coming out of sorts that had not happened because a bunch of goddamned members of Congress had disappeared.

Lowen knew Pellegrino was pissed and why, but he felt there was no time to lament the whys and wherefores. They had had more-immediate problems to resolve; they had to get ahead of the curve.

He had been at the Marriott Wardman Park Friday night waiting for Pellegrino and her husband when he had received word that something had gone horribly wrong. Within minutes of the news, he and his wife were in the limo and speeding toward the White House.

Minutes after arriving, while his wife sat on the loveseat in his office, he was on the telephone attempting to touch every base he could to be brought up to speed. With the exception of one call, he ended up knowing nothing more than he knew before he had left the Marriott. The only positive thing he had learned, according to Pellegrino's husband Norman, was that Babbs, after throwing a vase across the living room because the

Secret Service had ordered her motorcade to return to the White House, had been given a sedative and had been put to bed.

Lowen had remained in his office until after one that morning before deciding he was wasting his time and there was nothing else he could do, so he had awakened his wife, who had fallen asleep, and they headed home.

On Saturday, after a very short night, Lowen was back in his office early and on the phone again, and like earlier, he had learned nothing. Everyone he had spoken to had assured him that everything possible was being done and that if there was any breaking news, he would be notified immediately. Of course, that hadn't helped his disposition, and he had felt like throwing the fucking telephone against his office wall, but at the last moment, he was able to control his rage and save a piece of government property.

After calming down a bit, he had quickly checked Babb's appointment schedule for the next couple of days and left instructions for his secretary to reschedule or cancel all appointments for the next three or four days. Then, he called Stenny Hoover, one of Babb's speechwriters, to get him cracking on a short press conference speech. That's when Babbs had appeared on the scene or rather she had buzzed him from the Oval Office.

When Lowen walked into the Oval Office and closed the door, he noticed the other door was closed and she was staring at him like a deer caught in the headlights. "Do I dare give you a hug?" he asked in an attempt at being pleasant.

"I don't think this is the time," she responded with an air of resignation. "I gather you were here last night for quite a while. How long have you been here this morning?"

"I came in about seven and started checking everything out, but I still don't know any more than you probably know. Have you gotten over the shock and disappointment?"

"Why? Why the hell last night of all the effin' nights?"

"I suppose that was the plan regardless of who won the election. It was nothing personal. That was the plan of whoever did it. We just happened to be the targets of opportunity."

"Now what do we do?"

"I think you have no choice but to hold a press conference."

The look on her face told Lowen she wasn't very pleased with the suggestion.

"Look, Babbs, anyone with an ounce of common sense doesn't expect you to go around like Sherlock Holmes personally investigating everything with a magnifying glass, but the low-information people out there, the great unwashed, have been conditioned otherwise. Perception is everything. That's why you have to call a news conference. Remember what the fuck happened to Carter way back when. There's no way we dare getting tarred with that brush. We have no choice but to get ahead of the curve. That's why I have Stenny working on something for you to say to our media friends.

"You simply stand and read the script on the teleprompter, and when you're finished, that's it. If someone asks a question, you say, 'No comment' or 'I can't answer the question because of an ongoing investigation.'"

"Then what do we do?"

"There's nothing we can do but wait and see what happens."

And that's what happened. All day Saturday after Pellegrino's press conference and all day Sunday, they watched the TV screens in the Situation Room. On Saturday afternoon, they had been exposed to former national security adviser Bradford Jenkins, former speaker of the house Nate Grishom, and former secretary of state Candy Reason pontificate about how the metro police and the Secret Service did not have the manpower so it was necessary to bring army units into the city in case a second shoe dropped.

After the Sunday television talk shows with one member of Congress after another bloviating about how it was necessary for the president to order the army into the city to protect all the government monuments and buildings, Pellegrino had no choice but tell the secretary of defense to order in the troops.

As was the case with almost everything else, it had been easier said than done because Secretary Dirksen didn't have a clue and needed to do some consultation regarding what forces were available and that would take some time because it was Sunday evening.

"Just call the fucking joint chiefs," Lowen had screamed into the phone only to learn that Dirksen didn't have the phone number. *Heaven help us all*, he thought. "Get your ass in gear and find the fucking number!

Do whatever you have to do, but the president wants bodies in uniform walking around the Capitol Building and the House and Senate office buildings yesterday. I don't give a rat's ass if they're Boy Scouts as long as they're in uniform."

The first boots on the ground had come from Fort Myer across the river, but that wasn't enough to do diddly-squat. There had been only three active and under-strength battalions at Fort Myer, but bodies were bodies. The rest of the bodies came from Bragg, over 320 miles away, and all day Monday, units of the Eighty-Second Airborne had been entering the city.

"It may have had to have been done," answered President Pellegrino, "but that doesn't mean I have to like it. Those dickheads, as you called them, don't give a horse's ass about the damned buildings and monuments. All they really care about are their own asses."

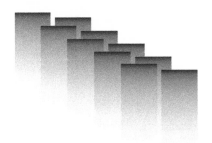

CHAPTER 17

Jaffa Court Restaurant
InterContinental David Tel Aviv
12 Kaufmann Street, Tel Aviv, Israel
Sunday, January 29, 2017

Sunday was just another workday on which to have a nice lunch at someone else's expense Lieutenant Commander Jason Greinwald had thought when David Perlinger called to invite him. Greinwald had met Perlinger a little over a year ago at an embassy function, and a week later, Ambassador Cooperman had given him a heads-up that had spelled Israeli intelligence. Thus, he had made a concerted effort to befriend Perlinger, and while so far his efforts had not borne any fruit, there was always a first time. *Today could even be that day*, thought Greinwald as he hung up the phone after the invite.

What Greinwald did not know and would never know was that he had been very carefully selected for his job as naval attaché and that his meeting Perlinger had been purposely orchestrated.

Something appears to be bothering David today, thought Greinwald. He studied Perlinger carefully as they made small talk while waiting for their drinks.

"Jason," said Perlinger once their wine had been served and he had taken a sip, "I'll get to the reason I invited you to lunch. I think you know a bit more about me than you've ever let on."

"And I suppose you think I'm more than just a naval attaché," said Greinwald smiling.

"Touché." Perlinger raised his glass in a mock toast. "Now that we understand each other, I'll get right to it. I'm sure you're well aware how closely we keep an eye on our enemies."

Greinwald smiled and nodded.

"For the past year or so, we've been monitoring a Hezbollah spin-off that seemed to have a particular interest in your country. I say a particular interest because three men we are aware of traveled to America and made contact with others in the Washington, DC, area."

Greinwald's antenna stood at attention. After what had happened there nine days earlier, the mention of the city's name would be enough to get any American's attention.

"Washington?"

"Yes. They made contact with at least two people we are aware of, and one of those two often made contact with others in Beirut and Amman."

"By contact I assume you mean by phone, or were there other means?"

"Phones. The ones to Beirut were probably to superiors, but the ones in Amman were in a place of business that, by the way, no longer exists. I have the names of all these people and can give them to you, but I doubt they will do you any good because they are probably aliases.

"Anyway, we're getting far afield because while I've told you something, I've actually told you nothing and that's because until this year, we were having problems assembling all the pieces. Though we monitored their cell phones, they always spoke cryptically. We didn't have a clue when they spoke about a political event and some automobiles."

"Oh my God! You're not—"

"I'm afraid so, Jason. That's what enabled us to put it all together. That's the reason I invited you to lunch. You know these guys are clever and dedicated, and some are even smart, but they're not professionals. The mistakes they made due to their euphoria resulted in our learning that your people who were kidnapped nine days ago, or at least some of them, are on the *Abu Maru*, a ship en route to the Mediterranean."

"Are you certain?" Greinwald's head was spinning.

"As certain as one can be in this business."

Commander Greinwald couldn't wait to get back to the embassy and transmit this information to Naval Operations, but his impulse was tempered by common sense and the realization that the United States and

Israel had not exactly been on the best of terms since Barbara Pellegrino had become president.

"David, why are you giving me this information? Our countries aren't exactly kosher at the moment."

"It's not our countries, Jason, it's our governments. We have nothing against the American people, and while some of those who were kidnapped were politicians who might not like Israel, terrorism cannot be tolerated under any circumstance. At the direction of my superiors, I have told you what we know. It's up to you people to make whatever decisions you wish. There's nothing we can do."

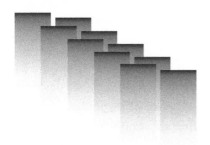

CHAPTER 18
N 19°35' W 66°30'—Milwaukee Deep
Eighty-Four Miles North of Puerto Rico
Sunday, January 29, 2017

"Shall we call this a successful mission, Dr. Richmond?" Royce Bartlett asked Will Rikker as the last container was lowered into the ocean under the glare of floodlights penetrating the night. "Or shall we call this a successful mission?"

"How about we call it a very successful mission, Dr. Barkman," Rikker said as he watched the last container disappear from sight and begin its five-mile journey down.

"I think some champagne would be in order, don't you?"

"You mean from that warm bottle in our cabin we don't have?" asked Rikker as he closed his laptop.

Bartlett laughed. "I guess we'll have to prevail on Captain Lambert again. He's been pretty agreeable when it's come to bending the regs for our benefit. Remember, we are civilian VIPs involved in high-tempo, arduous operations."

There certainly had been no disagreement between the two men on that aspect during the last three days. There had always been complete agreement between them ever since their mission had started. It was only because they had insisted on pushing the envelope once they had reached their destination that Bartlett had facetiously made reference to high-tempo, arduous operations.

They had left Naval Station Norfolk at 1330 hours the previous Sunday, and after a bit more than a four-and-a-half-day sail, they had reached the Milwaukee Trench, the deepest part of the Atlantic—28,231 feet down.

Ideal conditions would have allowed them to work only the daylight hours, but they were not attempting to dispose of normal hazardous materials, so they had insisted on stretching the workdays. If they had worked only from sunrise at 6:59 a.m. to sunset at 6:15 p.m. each day, it would have required an extra day, and they were worried about the bodies in the limos decomposing though the containers had been sealed. So Friday at 0700 hours, under the glare of floodlights an hour and a half after their arrival, they had started work and had continued until eight in the evening.

Saturday had been another grueling day starting at seven and working until eight, perhaps not for the crew of the *Jackson W. Ross* but for themselves because they were worried that the smell of death could escape.

That day had been a little better because they had only thirteen containers to worry about, and they sat atop the rest. The other fifty-seven containers simply contained inert metal objects to pad out the number to aid in the deception. They did not have to worry about their computers reading RFID codes and their transmitters sending signals to the trailers and the containers that would unlock spring-loaded hatches to allow flooding.

In addition to odor, they had been worried about buoyancy. The last thing they needed was for a container to refuse to sink. Even though tests had been performed over a year earlier and everything had been designed and built based on the test results, there was always still the possibility of Murphy's Law. The signals they had been sending were to open special trapdoors that would allow almost two thousand gallons of water to flood the plywood containers that housed the limousines.

"Gentlemen," said Captain Lambert, "you will of course join me again for dinner. I'm sure you must be greatly relieved now that we have rid the world of some very dangerous cargo."

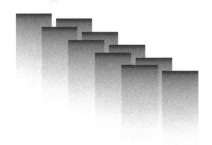

CHAPTER 19

The White House
1600 Pennsylvania Avenue NW
Washington, DC
Monday, January 30, 2017

"How come you know so fucking much?" asked Rob Lowen displaying his usual disrespect. If it had been for anything else, he wouldn't have given the admiral the time of day, but the information that had been passed from Tel Aviv had been the first breakthrough since inauguration night.

"I'm not implying I know so much," answered Chief of Naval Operations Admiral Kevin Moore. "I'm simply advising you about what our attaché in Tel Aviv has passed along. We think time is not on our side, and the information, which comes from a credible source, should be acted on immediately."

"If this information is credible, Admiral, why was it passed only to your people and not to the CIA station chief there?"

Perhaps the Israelis don't trust the CIA now that your people are in charge, thought the admiral. "I'm sure the information has been passed along. Perhaps our chain of command is shorter. Anyway, I've taken the liberty of already prepositioning a SEAL team nearby that can be ready to go once the president gives the go-ahead."

"You've what?" screamed Lowen. "What the fuck are you trying to do, start World War Four?"

"Mr. Lowen," said the admiral, "I've simply given the order to deploy, nothing else. No further orders will be given without the president's express authorization."

"Very well. Against my better judgment, Admiral, I'll let you speak with the president."

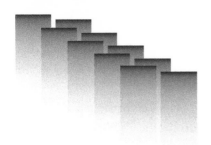

CHAPTER 20
N 40°56'49.62" W 26°35'57.78"
132 Miles North of the Island of Terceira, Azores
Tuesday, January 31, 2017

Brad Jenkins felt like an alien from outer space. He'd been exposed to many things in life, but this was the first time he had ever worn an insulated wetsuit and night-vision goggles. He was also nervous as shit. Sailing across the Atlantic on the *Abu Maru* was one thing, but sailing a hundred miles plus on the thirty-two-foot Bayliner at night without radar was another story.

The sleek cabin cruiser, built in 1979, was a blue-water boat that could be used for cruising and sports fishing. They had purchased it in Panama for less than $10,000. Of course, the modifications they had made added a considerable amount to the purchase price.

In addition to accommodating eighteen people, the Bayliner had to be capable of traveling a hundred and fifty miles at a high rate of speed at night, be undetectable from satellite observation, and be able to be at a rendezvous point in the middle of the ocean at a specific time.

To achieve this, the L-shaped dinette, over-and-under berths forward, the galley, and appliances had all been removed, and the rest of the interior had been stripped. The only thing retained in the interior had been the marine head for calls of nature. The only comfort features added were some bench seats and a table.

Because of the time of year, the average night temperatures, and the attempt to make the boat as invisible as possible, the steering system had been modified and the huge open cockpit superstructure above the hull had been lowered. The interior was enclosed. The Bayliner was as low to the water and as sleek as possible. In addition to the 150-gallon tank that had come with the boat, another tank was added as a precaution, and the T-350 HP 454 engines had been overhauled.

Completing the modifications to the Bayliner had been the latest navigation and communication equipment: a Leica Magnavox MX100 GPS system, a Thrane & Thrane Inmarsat Satellite Communications Terminal, and Raytheon R40XX twenty-four-mile radar. While everything but the GPS system would hardly be used, it had still been deemed a necessity in case of emergency.

"We're off," said one of the crew. Jenkins could feel the forward motion begin instead of feeling only the up-and-down bobbing of the boat.

"Has anyone brought my friend Jack?" asked one of the crew facetiously referring to a bottle of Jack Daniels.

"Oh shit," said another crew. "I forgot."

"Damn," said another crew. "And I was thirsty."

Jenkins knew they were only jesting. There was no way any one of them would risk drinking on the journey they were starting in the middle of the ocean; it was just to relieve the tension.

"Can you plug me in?" Jenkins asked Captain Mason. "Time to let them know we've left."

"No problem," said the skipper as he connected a cable to Jenkins's throwaway phone.

In moments, Jenkins was having a very brief conversation in Arabic with Ken, who was on the *Liberté*, telling him that they had left the *Abu Maru*. The message had been their only flirting with security, but as with their previous conversations, it had been for the benefit of the NSA while at the same time advising Middleton in a way that only each of them could understand.

For the next hour or two, they would be sailing blind under the power of the specially mounted eighty-six-pound thrust electric trolling motors powered by two twelve-volt deep-cycle marine batteries. By then, they hoped to be about ten nautical miles from the position where they had left the *Abu Maru* and twenty-six miles from where it should be before they fired up the 454s.

Then the real fun would begin—a hundred-and-fifteen-mile trip on a plotted course to latitude N 39°3'55.17" and longitude W 27°9'48.24" at twenty-three knots with no radar, only their night-vision equipment to help them avoid disaster. They didn't expect the eyes in the sky to start concentrating on the route of the *Abu Maru* for about six more hours, and by that time, they hoped to be separated by a distance of at least 150 miles. It would be an hour before the rendezvous time when they would briefly break radio silence, and probably thirty minutes after that, they would fire up the radar in search of the *Liberté*, which would be sailing north to greet them.

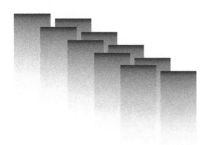

CHAPTER 21
666 Miles West of Lisbon
Approaching N 40°32'3.05" W 23°18'57.60"
Wednesday, February 1, 2017

As per the latest available information, the existence of only eight Navy SEAL teams had ever been confirmed, and SEAL Team Nine was not one of them. SEAL Team Nine was not only a special creation known by only a handful of people in high places; it was a black operation formed six months earlier for special ops that the team members thought would be occurring against the bad boys in the Middle East and run from their base in Rota, Spain.

Lieutenant Commander Derrick Olsen felt sorry for the other fifteen men of SEAL Team Nine. They were the best of the best, but despite that, these elite warriors were disposable pawns involved in an intricate game that if lost could result in the end of the country they had sworn to defend with their lives.

At age forty and with the rank of lieutenant commander, it was unusual for Olsen to be in command of a team on a mission like this, but he was a friend of Doug Northridge, and Northridge had friends in very high places.

Olsen knew the men were gung ho this evening because on four separate occasions during the past six months, they had been disappointed by being told to stand down at the last moment after days filled with physical training and mission preparation. What they didn't know was that those trials and tribulations had been purposefully scripted.

Tonight, though, had been different, and he knew they would give their all to assure success. Unfortunately, tonight's mission would not be a success in the way the men sitting stoically with their oxygen masks breathing from the aircraft's supplemental system were envisioning. It would be a demanding experience because anything involving water could be unforgiving. It would also be demanding because the mission would start with a HALO jump from 25,000 feet, and everyone would be free-falling at a terminal velocity of 126 miles per hour to 3,500 feet, where they would deploy their parachutes. At such a low altitude, extreme accuracy would be needed, which was why he had been particularly pleased that the aircraft they were using was a Hercules C-130J.

They could have used an older C-130C for the mission because payload and range were not major factors, nor was its maximum ceiling of 25,000 feet, but the new C-130J had fully integrated digital avionics and state-of-the-art navigation that included a dual inertial navigation system and GPS.

Commander Olsen could tell by the way the plane had suddenly started to bank that jump time was nearing. Sure enough, moments after the thought, the pilot came on the horn and announced they had located the target and it would be approximately fifteen minutes before the warning light came on.

At the two-minute warning, the team members quickly began switching over to their oxygen bottles and double-and-triple-checking equipment, connections, and bottle pressure while the jump master and physiology technician were watching for symptoms and signs of hypoxia.

After completing the same routine as the others, Olsen said a silent prayer as the rear cargo ramp of the plane started lowering. *All we have to do tonight*, he thought, *is intercept a moving container ship, surreptitiously board it, and find out if two hundred members of Congress and their spouses were anywhere onboard and if so effect a rescue.* If no members of Congress were found, they were to leave the ship just as secretly as they had boarded it, get in their boats, and wait for a submarine.

"Go," yelled the jump master as the green light came on. At the sound of his voice, men, two by two, were down the ramp and into space.

The first exclamation came two and a half minutes after the first two had leaped into space.

"What the fuck," came the voice through the personal communication systems of all the men as a flash of light appeared three miles to the west followed a few moments later by another accompanied by the loud boom of the first.

"What the hell is that light?" someone asked.

"It's a fucking explosion, you idiot," came a response.

"Jesus fuckin' Christ," said another of the men as a third flash appeared.

"Christ! It looks like the fuckin' Fourth of July," said Petty Officer Heller.

"Shit! Look at that!"

"So much for getting in and out," said Heller to Commander Olsen fifteen minutes later when everyone was in boats and the light to the west was diminishing.

"Yeah," said Petty Officer Farnsworth from the second boat. "Unless you feel like going for a long underwater swim."

"I don't understand it," said Heller. "It's like the bastards knew we were coming. But how? Shit, the time we jumped to the time our chutes deployed was less than three minutes."

"Dean," said Olsen, "I know where you're coming from. That's not enough time to do diddly-squat unless they had a lock on the bird from the get-go, which I doubt."

"What do we do now? We've been told to avoid any possibility of an international incident."

"I guess we just sit tight and wait for the sub," sighed Commander Olsen as he secretly let each of the two transmitters that were part of his gear fall into the ocean.

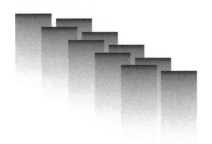

CHAPTER 22

Situation Room
The White House
1600 Pennsylvania Avenue NW
Washington, DC
Tuesday, January 31, 2017

It was 10:25 p.m. when Admiral Kevin Moore entered the Situation Room in the White House. *If I were a betting man*, he thought as he entered the room, *I'd bet all hell is about to break loose.*

"You son of a bitch," Lowen screamed at Admiral Moore. "Your men were supposed to be on a reconnaissance mission, not blow up a whole fuckin' ship!"

"I'm sure our men didn't blow up a whole ship or even part of one, Mr. Lowen," replied Admiral Moore angrily.

"Then what the hell happened? Those ragheads just decide to commit hara-kiri all by themselves so they could take a quick trip to paradise to start virgin selection? You said this would be a simple operation—in and out with no one being the wiser unless they discovered hostages."

"Mr. Lowen, please," said Admiral Moore in an attempt to calm down the chief of staff.

"Admiral Moore," said President Pellegrino, "I think it best for you to go. We can discuss what happened later."

"Yes, ma'am," said the admiral while attempting to retain his composure.

"All right, Rob," said President Pellegrino after the admiral had left. "Your yelling and screaming aren't going to help me or you, particularly if you get a heart attack. I think we have some serious thinking to do."

"You're right," said Lowen after taking a couple of deep breaths and reflecting on the president's advice. "It's obvious we can't let the public know anything about what we've seen and heard on the monitors tonight."

"What about the SEALs?"

"We can probably send them to Timbuktu."

"And the sub?"

"Send it to tundra land. I don't know. Look, Babbs, they're all military. Just give them an order. Tell them all to shut up."

"Excuse me, Admiral," said the Secret Service agent escorting the admiral to his staff car. "I need to take this." He extracted his cell and answered a call. "It's for you, Admiral. The president."

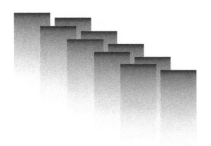

CHAPTER 23

Civilian Terminal
Lajes Field, Azores
Friday, February 3, 2017

"Have a good flight," said Nancy Middleton to Brad Jenkins and her parents, Larry and Silvia Evans, as she gave them hugs. "Watch out for the fools."

"I'll second that," said Ken Middleton as he gave his mother-in-law a hug and shook his father-in-law's hand and that of Jenkins.

"The ball's in your court again," said Jenkins with a chuckle before turning and heading for the security checkpoint.

"No problem," answered Middleton. "I have a good helpmate."

"You might not have that helpmate much longer," said Nancy as she and her husband headed to the exit.

Instead of thinking about Mario Barrera's desire to retire on the island, Ken thought of how smoothly everything had gone the past few days, all according to plan. The *Liberté* had met up with the Bayliner at the magical hour of 1:00 a.m. as planned. After everyone on the Bayliner had been transferred to the *Liberté*, the Bayliner was scuttled and the *Liberté* proceeded, under the power of its 130 HP Perkins Saber M130C six-cylinder diesel engine seventeen miles to the drop-off point where Jenkins and the seventeen *Abu Maru* crew members swam ashore.

Because of the rocky coastline, during the initial planning it had been contemplated that everyone would be brought ashore in a fourteen-foot inflatable boat powered by a forty-four-pound thrust twelve-volt trolling motor. However, that proved to be another seemingly good idea that was shot down because the usage of such created other problems to be resolved.

While it was assumed an inflatable boat and a trolling motor could be purchased in England and brought to Terceira on the *Liberté*, the four ex–Navy SEALs who were part of the *Abu Maru's* crew thought it would be a lot easier and faster to swim ashore rather than wasting time attempting to make five trips to shore and back. As they had pointed out, all that was needed was for the *Liberté* to get within three hundred yards of where everyone was to go ashore.

Two hours after arriving at the location where Jenkins and the crew of the *Abu Maru* would disembark, he had made a cryptic phone call to Mario, who was waiting ashore. "Liberté listo."

A few moments later, Jenkins saw the red-light signal from shore and heard the reply, "Bienvenue."

Quickly, three teams of six, each team led by a former SEAL with each team member linked together with lightweight nylon rope so no one could possibly become lost at sea, were swimming to shore. All they needed to do was to follow the leader while holding onto the inflated plastic bags that contained their personal gear and kick with their swim fins. According to Jenkins, everyone had quickly and safely made it ashore, and by 3:45 a.m., Mario Barrera was signaling for the vans that would take them to the house in Quatro Ribeiras.

Mario had been right about taking out the one street light to create a larger dark area to work in, but the only way to dismantle the bulb without being seen would have been to climb up the embankment part way and use a handgun or rifle with a silencer. After considering all the pros and cons, they had decided to leave well enough alone.

Fortunately, it was easy for the vans driven by Anita Barrera, Lynne Northridge, and Nancy Middleton to approach with the passenger sides facing the ocean so each group of six could quickly jump in from their hiding places. It had taken less than two minutes for the three vans to arrive, load, and leave with their cargo. It had taken that long only because they had allowed brief intervals between the vans just in case someone drove by.

Because the house in Quatro Ribeiras was only two miles away, everyone had arrived there by 4:00 a.m. The arrival of three vans at the house in a relatively short time had given pause for concern, but there were only two buildings directly across from the house, and only one was a house. The other was a milk collection facility that didn't open until five. Of course, there was another house immediately east of the milk collection building and one to the immediate west of the house directly across the street, but they were gambling that at 4:00 a.m., no one would be looking out their windows to see who was going up the driveway of the house across the street.

The safe house, as they called it, was set high off the road, high enough that the ground floor was actually a story and a half above the main road. This assured the utmost in privacy as it was impossible to see through any windows from the street. The only way anyone could be able to see into the house was to walk up stone steps or open the motor-controlled entrance gate to the driveway.

Upon arrival, the women made breakfast while the men removed their wetsuits, showered, and changed into the casual clothing they had brought with them in the specially made watertight ziplock plastic bags no larger than pillowcases that held their personal effects including passports. Upon their arrival, they were given coats, small pieces of luggage, and fake military passports.

The first group of six left later that morning in two vans for a ten thirty SATA flight to Lisbon with one of the vans returned to the rental agency. As they were supposedly airmen based on Lajes Field, their fake military passports were in case they were needed to be shown in Lisbon, but all flights from the Azores to Lisbon were considered domestic flights, so no problems were anticipated. The second group of three left the safe house in the afternoon for a four-thirty flight.

The previous day had been a repetition of the day before, except there was a group of five in the morning and a group of four in the afternoon, and another rental van had been returned. The third van in use had of course been purchased the previous year for Anita and Mario to use.

Today, Nancy Middleton's parents and Brad Jenkins were leaving. Lynne and Doug Northridge would stay until the four couples that would sail the *Liberté* to Jacksonville had arrived. Nancy and Ken Middleton would leave with the Northridges. Mario and Anita, who were seriously thinking about retirement on the island, were another story.

CHAPTER 24

Garden Restaurant
King David Hotel
23 King David Street
Jerusalem, Israel
Sunday, February 5, 2017

Daniel Appleton worked for the *London Daily Telegraph* as a stringer. He had come to Israel at an early age, at a time when large newspaper organizations had bureaus or offices in many cities around the world. But times had changed, and new technology in conjunction with necessary cost cutting saw the cutting back and eventually the eliminating of the offices and thus the reliance on stringers.

"So what's new, Ari?" he said to his longtime acquaintance General Ari Ben Gul as they sat down to lunch.

"Don't ask," said the general with a chuckle.

"Sounds like you might be having problems with the Americans again."

"We're always having problems with the Americans. At least for the past couple of years."

"What is it this time?"

"It appears the Americans can't do anything right."

"Now what did they do?"

"They botched a rescue mission and got a lot of their people killed in the process."

"So what? That's not Israel's problem unless somehow we're involved."

"That's the problem, Daniel. We're involved. We gave them the damn intelligence. I'm surprised the prime minister decided to help them."

"I thought we were at odds with the Americans these days."

"Not the Americans, Daniel, just their government."

"Perhaps you should do a little storytelling. I have a feeling you have an ulterior motive for our having lunch together today."

"Unbelievable," Daniel said thirty minutes later after the general had finished telling the story about the failed rescue attempt of the Americans' members of Congress. "Four days and no mention of what happened anywhere. I find that rather interesting, but then, governments don't like to advertise their failures."

"Particularly this government, Daniel. If they've kept things quiet this long, they obviously plan on continuing to do so."

"And now you would like me to write a story to out the Americans."

General Gul simply shrugged.

"You know if I write this story, Ari, there will be a tremendous pushback. As you have surmised, they have no plans on letting their failure seeing the light of day. They will lie, Ari, and they will have their media to help. It will be us against the world unless what you have told me can be proven."

"It can be proven, Daniel, trust me."

"I trust you, Ari, but my people in London will be reluctant to publish my story unless I can convince them what you say can be backed up."

"All right," said the general with a faked air of resignation. "I suspected something like this would happen, so I brought along a little present for you. This little thumb drive is a complete recording of the conversation between our intelligence officer and the American naval attaché he met with. I suggest, however, that when you write your story, you don't mention their names."

"The conversation you say is on this drive would prove only that we gave some intelligence. It wouldn't prove the Americans acted on it. Don't you have anything else?"

"There is something else, but I am not at liberty to tell you what at the moment. Nonetheless, rest assured that if your people publish your story and there is American pushback, we'll make that information available to the world."

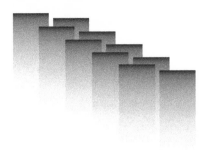

CHAPTER 25

Winfield House
Regent's Park
London
Monday, February 6, 2017

J. Malcolm Burridge loved to start the day early. Usually, he was up by six and would make his way to the solarium, where he would enjoy his first two cups of morning coffee while perusing the *London Times* and *Telegraph*. This morning had started no differently than other mornings since he had arrived in London to assume his duties as the US ambassador to the Court of St. James.

Around six, he had awakened and had made his way to the solarium where he was served his first cup of coffee and handed the two London dailies by a servant. After thanking the domestic, he had taken a sip of the hot coffee and had glanced at the headlines of each paper, a prelude to making the decision about which journal to peruse first. It was the two-inch headline of the *Daily Telegraph* that had caught his eye: "Rescue Attempt Ends in Tragedy."

He wondered what the Brits had been up to, but by the second sentence, he learned the story had nothing to do with any rescue attempt by any United Kingdom forces. As he read the story, he became horrified because he found himself reading about a rescue attempt somewhere between Gibraltar and the Azores that had resulted in the deaths of over two hundred members of the US Congress. It was a failure that had been withheld from the American public for four days and an operation of which he had had no knowledge. If the story were true, it was probably a rescue attempt that only a very select few in Washington knew about. He was sure there would be hell to pay when the story reached the other side of the pond.

After finishing the story, he quickly made his way to his study, forgetting all about the coffee that had gotten cold. There was no time to shave, shower, dress, and go to his office in the Chancery. Time was of the essence. He needed to satisfy his curiosity.

He booted up his computer and logged on to the website of the *London Daily Telegraph* looking for the electronic version of the same story, but it wasn't there. He dialed the White House.

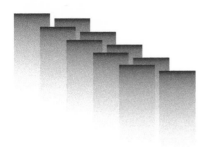

CHAPTER 26
St Clair Residence
South Kensington
London
Monday, February 6, 2017

Don Carter was another of the provisions of a multifaceted plan that left nothing to chance. After leaving Terceira the previous Wednesday, he had flown to Lisbon and on to London, where he had joined his English wife. After linking up at Heathrow, they had taken an Uber taxi to her parents' home in South Kensington. Though it was a miserable time of year to be visiting London, it was a family visit. However, his real presence in London was to monitor the tabloids and the dailies. It was true that Dr. Jenkins could monitor the London papers electronically every morning, but the five-hour time difference allowed too much to chance.

This morning, he had woken at six, and after slipping into his robe and slippers, he made coffee in the kitchen, something he preferred doing whenever he and his wife visited because his mother-in-law insisted on using one of those Cafetieres rather than the coffeemaker he had bought her and consequently, she couldn't make coffee worth a damn.

While the coffee was brewing, he made his way to the front door and retrieved the *London Daily Telegraph*. Immediately, he noticed the headline and said, "Bingo."

CHAPTER 27

Lowen Residence
Yuma Street NW
Washington, DC
Monday, February 6, 2017

It didn't happen like it was always shown in the movies. There was no light turned on before the telephone was answered. On the second ring, at a quarter to two in the morning, Rob Lowen awoke from a deep sleep and reached for the phone on the nightstand. "Hello?"

"Get your ass here immediately," someone said. The line went dead.

Lowen sprung out of bed as if he had been shot from a cannon. To the bathroom. To his dresser for some undershorts. To the dressing closet where he quickly dressed while thinking how fortunate he was to have shaving gear in his office. He was about to leave the bedroom when his wife asked him where he was sneaking off to in the middle of the night.

"To the office," he responded. "The call was about a national emergency."

To the foyer closet for his coat and then to his car in the garage, where he hit the button of the garage door opener as he turned the key in the ignition. In less than ten minutes, he was on Massachusetts Avenue heading east.

It was between Westmoreland Circle and Wisconsin Avenue when he saw the red light in his rearview mirror. "Shit," he said as he pulled over to the side of the road and stopped. A police car pulled in behind him. He rolled down his window.

Before the police officer had the chance to ask for his driver's license and registration, he showed the cop his license and White House identification.

"This is probably the first time," he said to the policeman, "that I've ever been glad I've been stopped for speeding. My name is Lowen. I'm the president's chief of staff. I just got a call about some sort of national emergency." He could see the policeman was not amused. "I'm not shitting—, I mean not kidding you. Check with your dispatcher. He or she will know what to do."

Thank God, he said to himself when the policeman turned and walked back to his car.

In a couple of minutes, the cop was back. "Follow me."

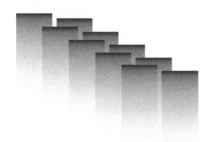

CHAPTER 28

The White House
1600 Pennsylvania Avenue
NW, Washington, DC
Monday, February 6, 2017

It was two thirty in the morning when Lowen, almost out of breath, charged into the Oval Office. "Babbs," he gasped, "what happened?"

Barbara Pellegrino handed him a piece of paper. "Ambassador Burridge called me at two this morning. That's a scan of a story that appeared in the *London Daily Telegraph*."

"Jesus fucking Christ," muttered Lowen as he speed-read the article.

"I don't think our media friends can duck this one."

He nodded. Pictures of every damned Fox affiliate in the country, the Drudge Report, the *Washington Times*, and God only knew how many more outlets running with the story galloped through his mind.

"Ever since Burridge called me," said Pellegrino, "my mind has been working overtime. It's your turn."

"Moore," he said. "That son of a bitch. We have to get him before this thing spreads."

"There's the telephone, Mr. Idea man. Go to it."

He didn't have a clue how to contact Admiral Moore, but thankfully, it was something he didn't have to worry about. The switchboard operators had a database of just about anyone who would need to be contacted. "Get me Admiral Moore," he said to the operator. "He's probably at home sound asleep, considering the time."

"One moment, sir."

"I'll hold."

It seemed like a lifetime before the operator came back. "I'm sorry, sir. All I could get was his voice mail."

"That son of a bitch," said Lowen as he hung up. "Fuckin' voice mail."

"Then call the damned Pentagon," Pellegrino screamed.

Lowen picked up the handset again. *Call the fucking Pentagon,* he thought. *Whoever you speak to, tell him to get that son of a bitch and bring him to the White House yesterday.* But instead of the expletives, in a stern yet pleasant voice, he just asked the operator to call the Pentagon and have someone get the admiral.

"Now!" said the president as he hung up. "What was it you said about Carter not too long ago? Something about not getting tarred with the same brush and having to get ahead of the curve?"

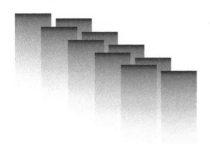

CHAPTER 29

Main Conference Room
Middleton Institute for Domestic and International Studies
600 New Hampshire Avenue NW
Washington, DC
Monday, February 6, 2017

It was ten in the morning. The six men watching the TV monitors knew they were about to see the Pellegrino administration implode and take several well-known news anchors down with the sinking ship.

The beginning of the final phase of their very intricate plan had started at one in the morning, when Don Carter had called Brad Jenkins from London.

"The excrement is about to hit the oscillating device," Carter had said, referring to the front-page story in the morning *London Daily Telegraph*. "It hasn't gone electronic yet, but it will soon."

After listening to Carter for a few minutes and getting a phone number, Brad phoned Jack Wharton. After a brief conversation, Wharton placed a call to David Hawkins giving him a heads-up and the number to call to get the details. By one thirty in the morning Washington time, Hawkins had telephoned Carter in London and had his digital recorder running while Carter read him the *Telegraph* story.

When the call to Carter had concluded, using a voice-to-text program, Hawkins quickly had a digital text copy of the *Telegraph* article and was beginning to manipulate the words into his own story. By two thirty, his story had been sent to the *Times* night editor, who quickly approved the story and sent it on to the composing department beating the three o'clock printing deadline by twenty-eight minutes. Thanks to the computer and electronic computerized printing, the *Washington Times* had been able to completely change the front page before the early-morning press run.

After calling Wharton, Jenkins had called his father-in-law and suggested that they all meet in the conference room at the institute by six that morning.

Harry called Mike Middleton and Tom Sanford, and Jack Wharton called Nate Grishom. Because of where they lived, Grishom and Sanford had arrived with a selection of donuts and Danish pastries as well as copies of the *Washington Times* with its bold headline on the front page, "Massive Cover-Up by White House." The *Washington Times* usually hit the streets by five o'clock, and by the time home delivery had started, the Fox affiliates had started their early-morning news broadcasts and had created a solid, one-two punch, and for the next four hours, the men watched each of the TV networks on the monitors.

By eight, CBS, ABC, NBC, and CNN had tepidly begun to run with the story though the operative word was the word *allegedly*. It had not been until moments earlier that the White House had issued a response that had been a firm denial.

"It couldn't happen to a nicer bitch," said Wharton as he poured Jack Daniels into his coffee in celebration of the White House denial. "She's walked right into the trap."

"Amen," said Nate Grishom. "The cover-up has begun, and as we all know, the cover-up is always worse than the crime."

"I wonder if they've gotten to the Israeli ambassador yet," said Tom Sanford.

"I'd bet he's on his way to the White House as we speak," Harry Reason said.

"Unless he's been told to make himself unavailable," said Brad, "which I fervently hope has happened."

"What about Admiral Moore?" asked Mike. "They've probably put all kinds of pressure on him since that ship sunk."

"No problem there," Harry said. "I told him to just do whatever Pellegrino told him to do, that there would soon be another administration in power and nothing would happen to him."

"I'm hoping nothing happens to him or the men involved."

"I'm sure they just ordered Moore to say nothing, and they've probably had the SEAL team sent to Ice Station Zebra."

"Take a look at the screens," said Jenkins. "It looks like circle-the-wagon time has begun."

"It took them all of fifteen minutes," said Wharton. "But then I guess they hadn't received their talking points yet."

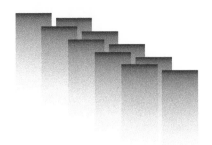

CHAPTER 30
Main Conference Room
Middleton Institute for Domestic and International Studies
600 New Hampshire Avenue NW
Washington, DC
Monday, February 6, 2017

"Gentlemen," said Mike Middleton at the 11:05 commercial break, "perhaps they should have changed their playbook. They're obviously going to double down and with the help of their media accomplices attempt to ride out the storm just as we thought they'd do when we were planning."

"Amazing," said Nate Grishom. "No wonder what poses as a media is getting beat in the ratings wars by Fox."

"What did I say before those twits started their blathering?" asked Jack Wharton. "I mean, could you believe that Amanda Mitchum at NBC?"

"What about that airhead on ABC?"

"I'm not sure who was worse, her or Judith Morrison at CNN."

"Is she the fat one or the skinny one?"

"How about Melanie Crawford at CBS? She brings new definition to the word clueless."

"Wait. Hold it everyone. There's a breaking news announcement coming."

Lovely, thought Brad Jenkins a few minutes after the breaking news that the prime minister of Israel would be addressing the Knesset regarding the failed American rescue attempt and Israel's role at seven o'clock that evening, noon eastern time, and nine in the morning on the West Coast. *No matter what Pellegrino does now, she'll soon be history. We couldn't have planned it any better.*

CHAPTER 31
The Knesset
Jerusalem, Israel
Tuesday, February 7, 2017

A trap is about to be sprung, thought Benjamin Natansky as he stood at the lectern waiting for the green camera lights to turn on. Sixteen days earlier, he had sensed what he had learned that morning was just the tip of a huge iceberg. He had to give Jenkins and his people credit for some very intricate planning that, while it involved Israel, had left no Israeli fingerprints.

"Mr. President," he said right as the light came on, "and distinguished members. This morning, the *London Daily Telegraph* published a story about a failed American rescue attempt that had been kept from the public for four days.

"The *Telegraph* story stated that the American attempt was to rescue members of the US Congress who had been kidnapped on the twentieth of January. The story also stated that information given to them by Israeli authorities led to this rescue that met a tragic end. At 10:00 a.m. Washington time, the American government issued a denial that such attempt had occurred.

"Not only was a denial issued; the denial insinuated that the story had been a fabrication based on incorrect information furnished the writer by elements of the government of Israel. To those of you watching and listening, I say to you I find the language of the American government denial not only offensive but also deceitful.

"On the afternoon of Sunday, the twenty-ninth of January, a member of one of our intelligence services furnished information to a member of the American intelligence services regarding a ship called the *Abu Maru*, which we believed to be heading for Tripoli in Lebanon. The conversation that ensued between the two parties was electronically monitored.

"At the time our representative passed the information to the US representative, though the American was told there was nothing further we could do, we still kept monitoring the people involved in the kidnapping. As I am sure most of the world knows by now, the US National Security Agency can listen to or read any electronic communication transmitted in the world. We too have our equivalent. It may not be as huge as that of the Americans, but it has served us well, and I can assure you that it is extremely efficient. To show you just how efficient, I will now play for you some audio communications.

"The first is part of a transmission between the terrorists on the *Abu Maru* and their compatriots in Beirut. It is in Arabic, but the English translation is 'We will keep looking to the heavens for the infidels.'

"Now," the prime minister said after a brief pause while thinking, *If the following doesn't sink the ship of fools, nothing ever will.* "The following I believe is self-explanatory. It is a communication between those attempting to effect the rescue."

"What the fuck?"

"What the hell is that light?"

"It's a fucking explosion, you idiot."

"Jesus fuckin' Christ."

"Christ! It looks like the fuckin' Fourth of July."

"Shit! Look at that!"

"I apologize for the language," said Prime Minister Natansky. "There is more, much more, and if the Americans would be kind enough to let us interview the SEAL team members whose voices you have just heard, voice-print technology could identify each person you have heard.

"I thank all of you for listening. I am sure that the Americans are now pleased to have learned that we have the capability to electronically eavesdrop on them as they have on everyone else. Thank you again."

CHAPTER 32
White House Living Quarters
1600 Pennsylvania Avenue NW
Washington, DC
Wednesday, February 22, 2017

Winds of Change
by David Hawkins

A strong wind blew through Washington yesterday, a gale-force wind that struck with the vengeance of a tornado that finally swept away the power and trappings of the Pellegrino administration.

Two years ago, after President Branch and Vice President Chandler were removed from office and Barbara Pellegrino and Charles Atherton were sworn in as president and vice president, the left was in a state of euphoria.

As all Liberaldom gleefully looked forward to the hope and change promised by the newly sworn in president, many of us on the right had our own hopes. We hoped she would fail.

It was with interest that Brad Jenkins read the article by David Hawkins, whom Jenkins had met on a few occasions. Hawkins had mentioned how the new administration swiftly replaced the Pellegrino administration with military precision. Jenkins also knew that everything that had happened had been very well choreographed. They hadn't stolen a page from the left's playbook and organized their forces for nothing.

The day after the former Pellegrino administration imploded, Congress, or what was left of it, quietly returned to town from Amelia Island, where they had agreed to be interred under guard for safety's sake, for a short stay on Capitol Hill.

In record-breaking time, the House and Senate elected new leadership. Candy Reason became Speaker of the House, and the House passed articles of impeachment against President Pellegrino and Vice President Atherton.

Two weeks later, on the twenty-first, the trial was held in the Senate. Neither President Pellegrino nor Vice President Atherton attended. Only their attorneys were present.

The trial lasted only as long as it took to read the charges and adhere to certain required formalities. It was immediately followed by a unanimous vote to remove Pellegrino and Atherton from office. Thirty-two days after their inauguration, almost to the hour, Pellegrino, Atherton, and their administration were history.

After the trial verdict, the defense attorneys had been detained for most of the rest of the day to allow certain incoming administration members to conduct their duties before any announcements were made.

Candy Reason and Nate Grishom quickly took their oaths of office, and the country had a new president and vice president. The new president put her signature and the date on her first executive order—the paperwork had already been prepared several weeks in advance—which called for the immediate dismissal of every Pellegrino political appointee. Then she presented paperwork naming her cabinet members.

Jenkins read the article with a hint of disquiet because of the long road that lay ahead. Seven years earlier, he had begun a book tour that had led to his meeting President George Branch. That meeting had led the president to ask him to play God. But some things in life never seem to go the way one thinks they should or will, and, by the grace of God, a vast left-wing conspiracy had been discovered. They had succeeded in doing something that had never been done before because they had the left's playbook and the monetary resources to thwart its invasion plan.

The path to power had been via a carefully crafted crisis—two hundred Congress critters disappearing on election night—leading to the military being called to protect Capitol Hill and all the national monuments. With the military being called into action, it had been easy to suggest that all congressional dependents be moved to the safety of Amelia Island in Georgia. That was when they had been able to seize control of the Congress, and with that in their hands, it had been easy to see that Candy had become the new Speaker of the House. After Pellegrino and Atherton were found guilty of the articles of impeachment, Candy and Nate Grishom had succeeded them. *Where do we go from here?* Brad wondered. *Will there be time?*

Candy's administration did not have the luxury of fifty or one hundred years to transform the culture. While it would be possible to make structural changes via the repeal of existing laws and the promulgation of new ones, to effect attitudinal change—if it could be done at all—would require drastic measures. That was why the left needed to be totally destroyed. There was no way it could be accommodated because any compromise or accommodation with evil would assure that evil would always win.

With the levers of government now in their hands, aided and abetted by the organized militia groups and the remnants of Mike and Harry's old Charlie Company, they would continue to soldier on until their mission was finished.

After Jenkins finished his coffee, he reread the final two sentences of the Hawkins article, nodding his head as he did so.

> Let us hope the administration that swiftly replaced the Pellegrino regime yesterday with military precision will quickly resurrect the American Dream that ended the day Pellegrino and Atherton were sworn into office.

> From this day forward, let us hope the pendulum that had swung so far to the left will swing back to the right and we can once again reclaim the country we once called America.

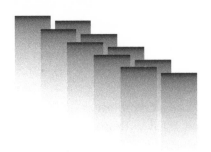

EPILOGUE

Authorities at Loss to Explain Disappearance of Billionaires

Associated Press

Monday, March 27, 2017

Confidential FBI sources have said they expect no further developments in the case of the five missing billionaires. It is believed that Paul Thoros, Murray Rosenberg, Michael Enright, Barton Wheeler, and Richard Gateson disappeared sometime between the evening of Friday, March 10 and the evening of March 12.

Rosenberg, Enright, Wheeler, and Gateson and their wives were guests of Thoros at his Ox Pasture Road Estate in South Hampton, New York.

Each of the billionaires was well known for contributions to various left-wing causes. Thoros made his fortune on Wall Street speculating in foreign currencies. Rosenberg, a former mayor of New York City, owned the largest financial publishing service in the world. Enright inherited his fortune from his father, who had in the early days of the Internet, developed a means for packet switching. Gateson made his fortune in the development of computer operating systems. It was common knowledge that each of the five was a big contributor to the presidential campaign of former president Barbara Pellegrino.

The inability of relatives of Thoros's employees to communicate with their loved ones led authorities to investigate. Police were reluctant at first to follow up on the several missing person complaints, but after an abundance of complaints, an investigation was conducted.

After discovering no security at the gated entrance, several telephone calls were attempted, but all calls made went to voice mail. It was then, with the help of the local fire department, that investigators managed to scale the high wall surrounding the immense estate and began their investigations. After a thorough search of the vast estate, no one was found. Subsequent investigations were unsuccessful.

Justice Department sources have said that Thoros was about to be investigated for voter fraud.

According to FBI director Kenneth Middleton, it was like one day everyone was there and then—poof—they were gone. Authorities are doubtful about any further positive progress.